By John Myers Myers

THE HARP AND THE BLADE

OUT ON ANY LIMB

THE WILD YAZOO

THE
WILD
YAZOO

JOHN MYERS MYERS

THE

WILD

YAZOO

E. P. DUTTON & COMPANY, INC.

NEW YORK · 1947

To SHY

a wife who knows her alligator horses

THE
WILD
YAZOO

CHAPTER I

I DIDN'T want to give up the house against which I was leaning. I had no idea where I was going when I perforce did so. That was a matter to which I wished to give all my attention, but the man in the chair next to mine on the white pillared porch was talking at me.

"You may shoot a man or take your pleasure with his wife as the situation indicates, but to do both is crowding the mourners."

I winced. "I hadn't meant to do either." This wasn't by way of defense. It was a statement of fact delivered by a brain too heavy to be capable of anything else. "In the case of Harriet it proved enough that she meant to."

"An insatiable bitch; why the devil did you have to get caught?" My cousin Edward—my late father's second cousin but near enough for Virginia purposes—removed his cigar and blew a clot of ashes from his shirt front. "And Cartwright?"

I started to pick up the stub of my own cigar; but it had gone dead and looked as bleakly repulsive as my immediate horizon. "After he'd nearly blown his own foot off he avoided my shot." I made a brief, inadequate gesture. "I aimed wide of him, and my bullets go where I want them to, but he side-stepped into it."

"H-m-m. Even his seconds admitted he stumbled, which is fortunate. Did he die right away?"

"Without a hiccough."

He looked at me with dispassionate interest. We both had the pale blue, Godolphin eye, bright and small in a deep socket, but his massive face contrasted with the angular wedge that had been passed on to me. "There's been much adverse comment."

"There should be," I conceded. It was a vile mess, and the fact that none of my part in it had been deliberate only made me feel the meaner. To be guilty of adultery and manslaughter without the driving force of intention was to fetch bottom in folly.

"Harriet is denouncing you as the ruthless and insidious destroyer of her Eden." My cousin tasted these words as they passed his lips and chuckled for the first time. "She ought to be really good at the funeral tomorrow. She's giving to flamboyant self-abasement all the implacable energy she usually reserves for other pursuits, and everybody is pleased with her. The county likes its melodrama thick, noisy, and saccharine. As for you——"

"I know. If I could not be killed in the interest of poetic justice, I could at least have proclaimed I was maddened by an unendurable passion."

"It's a good thing the Cartwrights want to bury the scandal. She's as casual as a hen sparrow, but I needn't tell you that a beautiful woman can be extremely influential. Already some are talking darkly of female frailty and man's duty to protect rather than prey upon them. With luck she might get you or somebody else shot, too."

This was an obscurely worded question; but I kept silent, and he tried again. "Perhaps Joe Cartwright's bony and colorless spectre intruded itself into your personal affairs as you in the flesh did into his."

"If you're referring to Delia, the note from the Rankins came this morning. It was formally worded but explicit." That, at least, had left few marks, and my pride wanted him to know it. "Except for the unpleasantness she won't be distressed. As for the Rankins, they'd been looking for a chance to break it off for months."

"You were thorough in furnishing one."

I grew irritated, then laughed. Throughout the interview I had been waiting for him to become admonitory or censorious. His consistent detachment was putting me more at ease. "As you're the sole person who's taken the trouble to call, I'm sorry the hospitality of the house isn't mine to offer any more."

He waved my apology away, still intent on his probing. "Another man might have shot Cartwright on purpose and incurred less ill will than you have for doing so unintentionally."

I knew what he meant. Even before this last incident my neighbors had marked me as probably deficient in character. At twenty-seven I had made no advance toward anything discernible, and the county was getting understandably bored.

When I quit William and Mary to accept my inheritance the newly deserted mansion was too much for my gregarious youth. When not visiting someone else I filled it with a constantly rotating series of young bachelors on the loose.

It took me a couple of years to discover that a plantation does not produce capital as naturally as a grazing cow produces milk. By the time I'd grasped that disturbing economic fact the bills were too many for me. Although I retained nominal ownership Spring Hill only remained in the family because my astute brother-in-law took over the property in consideration for paying my debts.

Disgruntled when the cockpit was abandoned, the racers sold, and the hounds given away, I mistook a passing interest in science for a call to the profession of medicine. Baltimore was my first taste of urban life, and I found it stimulating. To this day I think the director acted out of passion rather than judgment when he expelled me, but I cannot honestly say he weakened the ranks of Aesculapius.

Unabashed, I obtained a commission in the Army under the impression that here at last was a life of dramatic intensity. The impression didn't survive a tour at a small post in South Carolina. The commanding officer was not only a drunkard, to which I didn't particularly object, but a bad-mannered oaf, to which I definitely did. Then just before a steeplechase I caught his orderly giving my horse buckets of water. After the quarrel I was allowed to resign my commission.

But although I'd twice tried afield for a career the notion of giving up Spring Hill had never entered my head. As a prosperous doctor—naturally I hadn't thought of being any other kind—I had planned to pay off my brother-in-law and live on my estate in the only fashion I understood. Again when I had looked forward to being a distinguished soldier, I was to be that and the owner of Spring Hill. After winning honors in wars conveniently declared for the purpose General Godolphin would retire to the life of a well-to-do planter amidst his life-long friends and kinsmen.

It was after my one and only promotion, home in the splendor of my dress uniform, that I had courted Delia. By the time I had returned in mufti we'd both forgotten why we'd thought of marrying, but nobody knew how to make the first move. Formally announced engagements are not lightly broken in the county.

Yet by that time I and all who had an interest in me were becoming uncomfortably aware of my position. I was reaching toward thirty and had no record of either achievement or dependability. Virginia was rich in ability, and a man had to come to scratch early or be ignored as younger men pushed by him. The youths I had gamed and caroused with might still like their pleasure, but they were men of affairs and heads of families. They might like to talk of the high old times, but their attention was given to a less hilarious present.

As a last desperate expedient my friends tried to launch me into politics. The facts that I had influential connections and an education of sorts were urged to enlist me in the tail of the local political chief, Richard Cartwright. I was at his house in the capacity of secretary when his brother had chosen to come on a prolonged visit, bringing the restless Harriet.

I let out my breath quietly. Footsteps on the stairs told me that my sister and brother-in-law were at last departing for some county festivity. As Cousin Edward had not been announced they didn't join us to pay their respects. I heard them walking toward the carriage door on the side.

They would not, to my immeasurable satisfaction, be back until some time the following day. Vivien was ten years older, half of another generation, and we had never been close. Still I liked this only surviving member of my immediate family, which is more than I could say for her consort. He had done me no more injury than my own foolishness had invited, but his were alien lights.

In my relief at their going, I settled myself more comfortably, crossing my outstretched feet. Now that they weren't there to breathe down the back of my neck, I set out to conclude the interview with my companion. "Sir, you know I'm bankrupt of money, reputation and prospects."

He tossed the well-chewed butt of his cigar out on the grass. "That's right," he said with sudden briskness.

THE WILD YAZOO

"I haven't told Vivien, and I wouldn't burden you with the information, but you're a lawyer. I might as well deal with you as with
any other. I'm leaving Virginia tomorrow, and I'm leaving my
sister whatever title to Spring Hill I still possess."

A sigh told me that this was indeed what he had been waiting
for. "I came to tell you you had to go if you didn't see it yourself.
I'm glad you're not hanging on to any strings." He smiled fleetingly
to acknowledge my surprise at his sudden warmth. "I spend most
of my time at Richmond—I was there when this happened or I
would have been to see you earlier—but well—" He shrugged. "Well,
you're not old enough to understand the sentimental interest of a
man in a dead friend's children."

I felt I ought to say something. "It was nice of you to come."

"There was also," he said more crisply, "the matter of keeping a
Godolphin from being a lingering local buckshow. But you've made
your own decision."

"I hate to retreat under fire," I said, perversely doubtful now that
I was being encouraged.

"Can you tell me any other reason for retreating?" he demanded.
"All right, you're going. Where?"

"Oh, I don't know. New York or Boston first perhaps; then I'll
see."

"In other words you have no plans beyond vague adventurous
expeditions to places where they won't understand a word you're
saying." He sniffed. "I'll sell my sword in foreign lands."

That blow landed. I flushed. "A man's got to have some idea."

"I can give you a better." He rose, offered me another cigar, and
when I refused it stuck it into his own mouth. "We in America
haven't men to waste on other countries. Though you make this
locality seem overcrowded there are plenty of places where additional ciitzens are hailed and prized." He rolled the cold smoke in
his lips and stook looking down at me. "America Transmontana's
the place—Mississippi for choice."

This, as he had been acute enough to guess, was not the exotic
foreign pageantry I had envisioned. Nevertheless, I politely pretended to give the matter thought. "I'm no pioneer," I said finally.

He snorted at this weak offering. "Pioneers aren't a species;

they're an accident. Adam might not have been a pioneer if Eve had had any field of choice. Whatever you are, you're a Virginian and an aggravated case at that. You could no more turn yourself into an Italian or an Austrian than you could into a Yankee."

My plans, if anything so nebulous could be so styled, hadn't called for me in the role of citizen of any other nation. I hadn't really faced any of the implications; but a mind that flees from the present and does not dote on the past must still have a place to go. In the light of his realism, however, the course of my imagining became too indefinable for even the mind to tread.

"What would I do in Mississippi?" I asked.

"What you want to and can." He sat down again and turned toward me. "It's all open. There's a state to be made, and there's a free hand for the fashioner. Half the available land hasn't been claimed now, and there's a new treaty afoot that'll send the Choctaws west of the river to give the state a vast new territory." He clenched a hand. "That country must and will be settled, and it's better that it be done by Southerners."

Knowing what he was talking about, I nodded noncommittally. If I hadn't been the best informed secretary a rising politician could have, I yet knew of the national struggle that was going on between the rural wealth of the South and the industrial wealth of the North. At times I'd given it considerable thought myself, but I couldn't get excited about it now. As I couldn't seem to handle my own problems it seemed the least I could do to spare the nation my bungling.

Cousin Edward, evidently a partisan, didn't notice my lack of response. "We've got to build up power in the new territories," he insisted. Then he descended from his rostrum and smiled. "Fortunately the state is rich in Godolphins and can well spare Mississippi one from her bounty."

His attitude made the project seem feasible, and because of my need for a definite course I was beginning to consider it. "The state seems almost too eager in its generosity. Would you care to suggest a field of activity?"

"I don't know enough about the country to advise you."

"Oh." Going to a wilderness with no means of livelihood seemed even sillier than going to countries where it had already been proven that people could prosper.

Not heeding the flatness of my rejoinder, he reached into a saddlebag he'd brought along when dismounting. "I have, however, some land interests out there myself and an attorney as representative on the spot. This evening in fact, I dispatched a letter to him authorizing a draft on me in your favor should you care to collect."

This was too much like throwing a dog's bone through the door so the animal would go outside to eat. The assumption that he could buy my future, however vague a one it was, was an affront.

"That was kind of you," I said out of my throat. "I don't need your money."

"Perhaps not," he agreed, "but you need somebody's. Your stipend from Dick Cartwright couldn't have been any fortune." His voice softened soothingly. "You may well argue that an honest gift should have no strings, but this one has. Yet it is not forced on you willy-nilly as most gifts are. You will only get it if you really want it."

He was fumbling among papers in his saddlebag as he spoke, while I fidgeted, waiting for him to finish and leave. Eventually he looked to see what he was doing and fished out a bulky package. I tried to ignore the fact he was intending to give it to me, but he rose once more to stand directly in front of my chair.

"No matter what you decide about the other this is yours in freehold. Wherever you go I want you to have a little more to remember your kind by than the shape of your hide and what's beneath it. These were our grandfather's, your dad's and mine, and good things to have on any road."

His ideas on that subject might not coincide with my own, but the thoughtfulness brought me to my feet. Before I could think of anything to say he had shoved the bundle into my hands, clapped me on the arm and started to go. "If you want to give Spring Hill to Vivien send me a declaration of intent properly witnessed and notarized," he said over his shoulder.

"All right. Thanks for this, but wait!" I did not want to accept his treasured heirlooms, whatever they were, only to leave them behind; but he mounted his waiting horse without again speaking, his back turned now like that of everybody else in the county. Shrugging, I carried the package moodily indoors to a drawing-room table. I was nervously weary and sick with self-disgust, not so much for any specific acts as at the pass to which I had brought myself. To travel as a decision to go is one thing, but my going was an admission that I could not stay. To have to leave the accrued associations of my twenty-seven years was an intolerable defeat.

Or to say it wasn't was to confess that I had built nothing worth while for myself, which looked near enough to the truth. Shaking my head, I walked slowly through the hall to the broad stairs. There was a little packing to be done now that I was at last free to move unobserved and unquestioned.

When I was through I did not dare try to sleep and so descended to potter about in the library, now and then fingering a book I had no heart to more than glance at. While so doing I had the luck to run across a cigar I'd left in one as a place mark a few months earlier. It was stale as dust, but as I was out of smokes and would not use my brother-in-law's, it was a treasure. I lighted it at a candle and took comfort from its dry bite.

So armed, I re-entered the drawing room and stretched out on a divan. Early in the morning when no one would be likely to mark me, I would leave the county on the Norfolk stage. There I'd take ship—for the North, I supposed. As I reconsidered the tenuous details of my original plan the alternative suggested by Cousin Edward came to mind. Turning my head, I peered at the package he had oddly taken the trouble to bring me. In a little while I meant to get up and see what it contained, but I had lost tenseness and felt dopily comfortable. Before the cigar was fully smoked I was asleep.

CHAPTER II

I WAKED just after dawn, chilled and with a tingling malaise in my body and brain. Never did man feel less of an adventurer than I did when I rose to pull up what roots didn't break off and stay in Virginia.

Noticing where my cigar had left a burnt mark on the floor, I rubbed my foot in that last memento of my residence and hitched my clothes into some sort of shape. As I looked up my eyes fell on the unopened package, and I slumped toward it. There was no reason why I should not have waited until I was wider awake, but with the aimless determination that often attends soggy discomfort I started unwrapping it.

The first thing the enfolding paper disclosed was a slip bearing a name and address

> Henry Artenay, Esq.
> Natchez, Miss.

I took this to be my cousin's legal representative and, as there was no fireplace handy, shoved the paper into a coat pocket. Under it were a knife, a book and a leather case. Taking them over to a window seat, I examined them in order.

The knife was a long, heavy weapon. As I took it from its rotting sheath I remembered that my great-grandfather had served against the Indians. The blade was discolored but not rusted and looked as if it would take a good edge. The hilt was ivory, with a yellow patina from age and use, grooved for the fingers. I was not interested enough to do more than turn it over and heft it before I resheathed it.

The cover of the book was not in as bad repair as that of the knife, but it was worn and cracked with broken gold tracings on the leather. The title page discovered to me a volume I had often heard of but never seen before. It was a collection of old John Smith's writings about Virginia. After my heavy eyes had strained irritably at the first black-letter page I turned to the box.

This, too, was leather, scuffed but not yet seamed. There was a catch at the side which permitted the lifting of the lid. It came hard and I had to pick the box up in order to force the retaining peg from its corroded metal loop. It was heavy for its size, and for a moment I feared Edward had had the dubious taste to present me with a set of duelling pistols.

What I beheld, however, was a far more useful invention, though also designed for two. It was a traveler's decanter, a fine, commodious one, with a small noggin nestled at each shoulder. The tarnished silver of which it was fashioned was dented here and there, and intricate chasing framed an inscription. Because here was a useful gift that filled a gap in my equipment I held it to the light to examine it. The words formed a sort of rhymed directive as follows:

What I have I must not hold,
Don't spare me;
I must be given, never sold,
So share me.

Picking the flask out of its container to see what might be on the other side, I almost dropped it in my excitement. It was full!

Breathing a prayer that the contents was not also an heirloom, as liquor so kept for so long would have turned to a sort of distilled whey, I unscrewed the cap with trembling fingers. One ecstatic whiff cured me of fear. Here was the essence of good whiskey, warm with dynamic sweetness and controlled power.

Fervently I blessed my cousin Edward for his kindly act. Since Cartwright's death I had been in drinkless isolation. Of the food grown by Spring Hill, still my own in title, I did not scruple to partake, but I would receive no other hospitality from my aloofly disapproving brother-in-law. There was a lovely keening as the liquor ran out.

I filled one noggin then, after an instant's reflection, the other.

There were, after all, rites to be performed now that I had the wherewithal. The first I took in three parts dedicated to the past as represented by Spring Hill, my great-grandfather and Edward Godolphin, prince of men. It drove the bleak chill from my body and spirit alike, and I took up the other to return the toast with a better heart.

"From the Godolphins of Virginia," I spoke boldly for the past, "to the Mississippi outpost." The fact that I had decided that I would probably go elsewhere carried no weight at the moment. In my bitter need my cousin had come, unsought, to do me this kindness. To refuse him such a thing as my destiny seemed churlish.

Exhaling gustily, I returned the flask to its box. Things had to be done, and now that I was no longer completely in the horse latitudes I proceeded to move with dispatch. Ascending, I changed my clothes, shaved, nibbled the breakfast of cold biscuits and ham I'd set aside the night before, and picked up my valise. That was all there was to it except for stowing away Edward's gifts.

Without looking back at Spring Hill, hushed as only a house can be in the dim of the morning, I strode away, my heavy bag grinding my shoulder. It was overcast and cool that early fall day, but I know little more of the scene than that it must have been as always. Now that I was on my way it was not my intention to gaze wistfully at the landmarks of memory.

Where the Spring Hill road joined the highway I plumped my luggage down behind a bush. Then seating myself on a stump, I wrapped myself in my cloak.

If I had any train of thought, which I doubt, it left no mark on my consciousness. I was emotionally suspended to such an extent that I was not even impatient during the hour or thereabouts I waited. There had been a past and presumably there would be some sort of future, but that would only commence when, as and if the stage arrived.

A cart creaked by, but there was no other traffic until I heard the cadential clopping of four in hand. At that sound I roused myself from my almost insensate lethargy for preconceived action.

A stage does not by ordinary take on passengers except at inns and other specified stations of call. Moreover, a man asking it to halt at a lonesome place and hour might be regarded with suspicion. There had been for some time, however, piles of brush near the gateway, left there to dry for the fall burning. Grasping the key branch from one of these, I tugged it into the middle of the road. I repeated the process with another pile or so and thus established an annoying hazard. This done, I retreated up the Spring Hill road once more.

The driver was evidently dozing when the coach drew near, but the horses were more alert. They did not want to step into a tangled mass of branches and finding they were not being coerced they stopped. In a few moments the lack of movement roused their director. He straightened, reached for his whip and then saw why they had refused to go on.

As the brush was indifferent to his loudly voiced indignation, he at length descended to move stiffly about the business of clearing the road. This was my cue, and, whistling loudly, I tramped down to the highway.

"Good morning!" I called out cheerfully.

He was removing the branches one at a time, clearly disheartened by having to make such efforts after a chill night's run.

"Mornin'," he growled, not conceding the good.

"This stage going to Norfolk?" As I asked this I peered within. There were only two passengers, both collapsed in sleep.

The driver threw a branch from him and kicked a couple of others out of the way. "It's goin' there if damn fools keep from choppin' the damn forest down all over the damn road."

Ignoring this exaggeration, I opened the door and tossed in my valise. "Well, anyway," I comforted him, "you've got another passenger."

I was already seating myself before he got around to making a protest. "See here, we don't take on folks only at regular stops."

Settling back, I answered his stubble-darkened frown with a smile. "You've already done it. Don't worry; I'll pay you from your last point of call on."

My fellow passengers had not been awakened by our conversation. They were both on the rear seat, so I had the front one, which faced them, all to myself. By the time the stage lurched forward I, too, was huddled in a corner, cloaked to the ears, with my beaver hat down over my eyes. It was in this way, seeing nothing and feeling not much more, that I rode backward out of the county.

My rest the night before had still left me short on sleep, so for the first few hours I dozed fitfully. When I finally sat up my lethargy had gone and no defense stood between me and my damnable situation.

That I could not have adjusted myself to the part of the world where I'd been born was a theory to which I didn't pamper myself by subscribing. Yet I had notably failed either in doing so or, for all I could see, in fitting myself to live anywhere else.

Rub my problems around my mind as I would, I could find only questions; no answers. I could go North or I could go West, and I would still be no farther than at another starting point, with nothing important solved.

As for capital, I had been fortunate at a horse race two days before the Cartwright duel, and that night I had profitably invested my take in a game of brag. These I knew to be unreliable sources of income.

Yet I had no other, nor any prospects unless I wished to count the draft Edward had authorized in the event I chose to follow his advice. To doing so, notwithstanding my whimsical inclination when I opened his gift, I was still opposed. As I had told him, I could not visualize myself in the role of pioneer. Much more to the point, I couldn't imagine how I'd survive in the West.

My musings went on while we stopped at The Three Turks Inn and continued through dinner, a clause to the bite. It would be so much easier if I had friends in Europe to start me off right. Of course, I had relatives in England and Ireland; but then I had them in Virginia, too, and sorry most of them were for it.

A darky announced the stage was ready, so I took my cigar and my troubles outside. All I had accomplished so far was to decide that no matter what I did I would probably regret it.

The dourness of my reflections must have shone through my face. Dinner had brought quiescence to the occupants of the rear seat, but a new passenger who shared the front one with me remained restlessly alert. I had been made aware of him from time to time as he leaned out the window to spit. Now he spoke.

"Mister, if you want to cut your throat, don't stand on ceremony. These gentlemen are just about asleep, and I'm sort of used to it."

Amazed at this effrontery, I simply stared at him. He was big, lean of face save where it was swollen by his quid. Beneath his beaver hat there were lank, dark bangs, and grey eyes. He was unperturbed by my iciness, though he at length turned away to suck noisily and let fly.

"Did I ever tell you," he said conversationally, "about the greatest disappointment of my life?"

"No," I breathed.

"Well, sir, I love bobcat tails, and every now and then nothin' else will quite suit. My belly sets up a holler and demands 'em, and not even hoop snake and sugar-cane greens can quite take the place. Usually in the spring it is, when a man's stomach is most pernickety for pamperin' anyhow."

This time when he turned back from expectorating his face had a sentimentally soft expression. "Agrippina and I hadn't been married very long, and—you married?"

"No."

"Then there ain't no use tryin' to tell you of our tender farewells, for a bachelor ain't got soul enough to understand." He sighed reminiscently. "Well, I knew I wouldn't be fit to live with till my hankerin' was satiated, so I called Rumple and Moonsong and Witch and Piddler. Did you ever hunt bobcat, stranger?"

"No," I said again.

"I like your frankness," he decided. "A lot of folks would've put on that they was experts, and I wouldn't explain nothin', thinkin' it wasn't necessary. Have a chaw?"

"No—thanks."

"I was runnin' kind of short anyhow. Well, the main thing about bobcat huntin' is to have dogs that's trained. A bobcat don't run on the ground if there's trees around, don't you see."

"Yes," I conceded helplessly.

"And a dog don't run anywhere *but* the ground. That means you got to have dogs that's trained to follow the scent reflected on the ground from the branches the bobcat's runnin' on. I couldn't do it," he admitted, "and likely you couldn't either."

"No," I returned to my original refrain.

"Rumple wasn't much good and Witch was a pup just learnin', but Moonsong and Piddler was two of the best reflected-scent dogs I ever hunted with. We got a mess of cats that day. Piddler and Moonsong would tail 'em to where they was at and then stand bayin' with their backs to the sun. That way the light'd be in the bobcat's eyes and he couldn't see me when I sneaked up for a shot. I didn't want 'em turnin' to run right when I got set. Did you ever sink your teeth in a bobcat's tail and strike a lead pellet?"

He was spitting again as he concluded this question, and I merely grunted.

"It goes straight through you," he assured me. "Well, I didn't want to risk that or shootin' off the tail neither, so I was careful they was all facin' me when I pulled trigger. Of course, once in a while a cat will jump you, but only a couple did that day." He pulled up the sleeves of both his coat and the shirt underneath it to expose what did indeed look like the scars of a vicious clawing. "One got me on the leg, too, but I didn't mind much. I had a couple of pecks of tails, all prime. What's your favorite food?"

Had it been my intention to reply he would have saved me the trouble. "It don't matter what it is exactly. Suppose you'd had a special cravin' for it for days and finally you was sittin' waitin' for it to cook, the smell of it all around you like a breeze loaded with honeysuckle. I was droolin' like a hound dog when finally Lobelia——"

"Agrippina," I reminded him.

He looked at me reproachfully. "You don't reckon I'd have let Agrippina lift a finger of one of her magnolia-bud hands, do you? It was Lobelia brought them in, steamin' hot and smothered in gravy. Well, sir, I jabbed a fork in, speared a big, fat one, shoved it in my mouth, and—stranger, I hate to have to tell you this——"

He stopped and having been his companion, however reluctantly, so far, I could not leave him. "What?" I enquired.

"That fool nigger had taken the hair off, spoilin' 'em completely!" His gaze was serene for one who had so much sorrow to impart. "And so when my choppers, after all my hopes and all my work, met on that ruined bobcat tail, I just sat there with the thing in my mouth lookin' about the way you looked when I first spoke to you."

CHAPTER III

HE SAID the last words so gently I could hear them hardly better than I could believe them. There was a long pause, then I threw back my head and laughed. Once I'd started—it was the first honest mirth I'd enjoyed since Cartwright dropped— I let it roll. It felt good.

The two across the stage opened their eyes, then seeing nothing in particular going on, closed them again. The bobcat tail fancier had twisted to spit after observing my reaction. Now he turned back to me, a crooked grin on the free side of his face.

"The name's Harry Pace."

In the county I was accustomed to use my full name to distinguish myself from an uncle. "Mordaunt Fitzmaurice Godolphin," I introduced myself automatically.

He stared at me thoughtfully. "You sure you ain't holdin' back nothin'?"

Having resented the name myself until maturity brought stoicism I smiled wryly. "That's all of it I was told about."

"'T aint as bad as havin' a wart on your nose. Where are you goin'?"

"Norfolk," I temporized.

"Well, I'm goin' there directly, and a slough of other places, too. Where'd you come from?"

"I just got on a stop or so before you did."

"Live in these sticks, do you? Then you can tell I don't. I just spent the night at The Three Turkeys——"

Captain John Smith, one of whose favorite exploits was thus commemorated, probably wouldn't have liked this. "Three Turks," I corrected.

"Never heard 'em called that. The signmaker must've run out

[27]

of paint. Anyhow I'm a ways from home. Come from Mississippi."

He was peering to see how I would take that announcement, and he must have been gratified.

"Mississippi!" I echoed, amazed and delighted at the chance to obtain information about a place so newly in my mind. "Why that's remarkable!"

"'T is," he agreed complacently. "Most of us can't be bribed to leave there, but I'm sort of a missionary."

"Ah?" I wouldn't have suspected any such proclivities.

"Sure. I'm a kind of finger pointin' out to sufferin' humanity the way to the promised land."

I still wasn't certain enough to comment, but he went on without prompting. "That's a great state, mister. The rivers, the trees, and what counts more, the cotton bolls are bigger'n anywheres in the world."

As this statement confirmed what little I knew about Mississippi I nodded sagely. "I've heard it's quite a place."

He scorned the quality of my compliment. "Anybody who told you it was quite a place has got the soul of a water puppy. You might as well say a b'ar is quite a varmint. Stranger, a b'ar is the war chief, pope, and president of varmints, and Mississippi's the cape jessamine, smoked ham, and old Monongahela of states.

"When it shines there deserts sidle up to see how it's done, and when it's dark there lightnin' bugs hold hands so they won't lose each other. When you plant corn there you got to step lively or the shoots will tear your pants, and the swamps there are so deep you can get boilin' water just by lettin' down a jug in a bog hole. We wouldn't bother with a possum there that wasn't big enough to feed the whole family and two preachers who'd dropped in for dinner, nor we don't call it a real snake if he couldn't kill you just by thinkin' about it."

"What are the people like?" I ventured.

"Just plain mortals no better than you or anybody else till they get there." He smirked modestly. "'T aint for me to say, mister."

Following this comment he drew from somewhere about his person a tremendous, bone-handled knife. With it he slapped at and split a fly hitching a ride on the stage's paneless window and commenced paring his nails. I looked for him to amputate a finger, but the jolting and rolling didn't seem to bother him in the least.

Either because mention of the earthly paradise he had left had made him homesick or because he had already used up his small interest in me, he fell silent. I on my part found myself very curious about him. His clothes were well made but lively, what with his cream-colored beaver, bright green jacket, flowered waistcoat, and checkered trousers. When I thought of Westerners at all I thought of them as wearing homespun or buckskin. What was he? It was difficult to picture him as a reverently fatalistic soil-grubber; no more was he of the primitive hunter breed—slow spoken and abashed when translated from their beloved wilderness—of which I'd also heard talk. One of us, it was clear, didn't know how a pioneer should act.

He was as disturbing as a Dutchman who didn't wear more breeches than he needed, or as a Frenchman who didn't lust after the hind legs of a frog. My ignorance about a portion of my own country was brought home to me as so abysmal that I didn't even know enough to ask intelligent questions. I made one final effort, however. "What sort of a town is Natchez?"

He looked up thoughtfully. "Did you ever see a pretty girl sittin' on a rampagin' razorback boar?"

Despairingly I shook my head and gave up. As Pace sketched it, Mississippi was foreign beyond reach of my mind. And the inhabitants, if he was a sample, were so to almost the same degree. We were, with some reservations, verbally comprehensible to each other, but we seemed to share little else except nationality and the same seat of the stage coach.

When I had thought I had understood Mississippi in a general way I had not been much interested, but now that it was revealed to me as a mystery it became fascinating. It might be worth a visit; indeed, it must be. At the same time I bore in mind that I was in quest of a livelihood and had no funds to spare on sight-seeing. A country where the newly planted seed endangered one's trousers in its haste to sprout must have its share of prosperity. Nevertheless, I shook my head dubiously again. I had learned—just too late to save Spring Hill for me—how complex a business farming is.

THE WILD YAZOO

I was aware that it was possible to obtain land across the mountains for little money or even just by giving evidence of intent to exploit it. But land had to be cleared before even the most eager of seeds could send up shoots from the most potentially fertile of fields. That demanded labor and equipment, which is to say it demanded capital. Agrarian wealth was the essential root from which other businesses and professions could grow, but what were they? What did Pace do, for instance, when not engaged in the ambiguous missionary work he'd mentioned?

Unlike him I had been bred to respect the privacy of strangers, though at the moment this was an inconvenience. He had put his knife away and was leaning out the window, turning his head from side to side as if taking in everything. Now that he had drawn me from my pit of introspection he seemed determined to talk no more.

I shrugged, alert enough now to be bored with the journey. I envied the somnolence of the pair on the rear seat, and as I was in the process of doing so one bestirred himself and nudged the other.

"We're almost there," he said.

"There" didn't seem to be any place in particular. We merely arrived at a side road a few minutes later, and the driver pulled up. No houses were in sight, but our fellow travelers evidently had business thereabouts. Making quite a bustle, they unloaded a couple of bags and paid their fares while we watched with the vacant steadiness of idle minds. It wasn't until the coachman was climbing back to his high seat of power that either did anything worthy of the attention we were giving them.

"We might as well finish it," one said.

"All right," said his easily convinced associate. With the words he produced a bottle which may have accounted for their torpor all during the afternoon.

As we drove off a moment later we saw the presumably empty flask sail into the bordering woods. I had watched the proceedings with only mild interest, but my companion was stirred. Groaning aloud, he turned to me. "Mr. Godolphin, ain't there no end to this wilderness?"

Coming from such a source the question was startling. "What!" I exclaimed.

"Oh, I know. You think I'd ought to be used to it. Well, I am back home and act accordin', but here in the East I don't expect to ride for hours and hours without findin' a doggery."

I didn't understand, as he promptly perceived. "A grocery, a tavern. A man could catch an ague on a day like this, and the kind of constitution I got don't respond to camomile tea. In Mississippi, you see, I'd figure there wasn't more'n one or two bars per capita, and knowin' there wasn't so many capitas I'd tote a pocket pistol." He looked at me anxiously. "How far is it to the nearest liquor, do you know?"

Putting my feet up on the coach's middle bench, I smiled with sudden complacence. "Share me," the silver decanter had urged with all the force of ancestral wisdom behind it. Besides, his was a direct question and not to be evaded with courtesy.

"Oh," I said, my voice offhand, "about a yard away. From you, that is; from me it's not quite so far. Of course, it's only whiskey, so if you'd rather wait an hour till we get to Portsmouth, I'll understand."

He was ramrod straight by then, his eyes gleaming. "If you mean business, I don't mind your talkin'."

Pleased at being able to act the foresighted man of the moment I proudly unpacked the leather case and opened it. Never was heirloom displayed to more appreciative eyes. "That's somethin' to have," he said with the simplicity of positive conviction.

I watched with interest to see what he would do with his quid, but he didn't remove it, even momentarily. Instead he clamped it into the pouch of one cheek to form a bulge that wabbled as, making no use of the noggins, he gulped.

"What I can't figure out," he said as he wiped his mouth and passed the decanter back, "is why anyone with good whiskey like that should look as much like a mud turtle with the bellyache as you did awhile ago."

This was the opening I'd wanted. Smelling the good fumes, I drank in turn, though more sparingly than he.

"I was trying to figure out where I'm going."

"Don't you know?" He was trying to be polite to the owner of the whiskey, but I could see my statement didn't make much sense to him.

"Well, I decided to clear out and live somewhere else—on the spur of the moment, you see——"

He saw with considerable clarity. "Have they told the sheriff, or did you get a good start on him?"

Although that wasn't exactly the case, it might well have been. Yet I had no wish to pose as a fleeing desperado.

"I'm not being hounded by the law; I just decided to leave the state for personal reasons."

Once out, the statement sounded absurdly unconvincing, especially with such an audience. But if I was speaking to skeptical ears, they were also the ears of tolerance.

"You ain't in any trouble as long as nobody knows where you're at," he summed up his view. "I've met lots of people in your boots."

His cool acceptance made it ridiculous to protest that I was no fugitive. "Have you?"

"Why sure. Mississippi owes some of its most interestin' citizens to the fact they had too much character for other places."

I considered that remark while he drank again. Here was another aspect of pioneer culture alien again to the concepts of my ignorance. His words were elastic enough to reach around outlawry.

"Good enough to embalm an angel." He patted the decanter and looked at me benevolently. "Why don't you come to Mississippi?"

"And do what?"

"Oh, hunt b'ars, love girls, eat venison, drink whiskey, swap hosses, grow cotton, raise brats, buy niggers, get religion, pilot boats, start cities, get lost, cuss the heat, call turkeys, bank faro, build houses, swim swamps, get shot at, vote for Jackson, gouge eyes, and learn Choctaw—what would you want to do?"

"I'd thought of making a living, so I could afford at least a few of those pastimes."

"You can do that, too. We're just inventin' the place as we go along, so if there's nothin' there you want to work at all you got to do is start it up." Then he asked the question I'd been fearing. "Got any money?"

"No."

My answer didn't give him the expected pause. "Didn't reckon you had. A man travelin' with money generally knows where he wants to spend it, or where he wants to hide it." Patting the decanter again he surrendered it. "Most folks comin' our way could use one address just as well as another, though the kind I'm lookin' for have money to invest. You see, I'm a speculator."

"What do you speculate about?"

"Land claims—some that I've got and some that I hope to have. That's what I'm doing now: lookin' for purchasers and backers. But, hell, there's plenty of land left for those who got to go to the trouble of provin' on it themselves."

This was one of the things that sounded easy but probably wasn't. I weighed his words at some length until, noting his restlessness, I gulped hastily and passed the whiskey.

"Suppose I did take your advice and go out there, where would be the best place to start?"

"Mississippi's like a pie or a riot. It don't matter where you start in on it. But let's see. If you're goin' by way of Norfolk you'd most likely take the boat to Mobile and go up the Tombigbee, or to New Orleans and——"

"New Orleans," I said firmly. I knew or thought I knew about where that was.

"In that case you likely wouldn't stop at the first point you'd come to. You'd go a little farther and hit Natchez. That's where I live when I'm there."

I thought of Edward's letter and decided not to mention it. Still I eased down into my corner, pleased at this evidence of cosmic symmetry. For the first time in days I felt that the future was not merely time that hadn't arrived yet. Pace's words, aided by the liquor and relief from tension, now that I'd left the county, were temporarily freeing my will to believe. I had not yet made up my mind, but just to be able to talk of specific possibilities was heartening.

"Would you say Natchez was the best place to live?"

"Well," he said obliquely, "it's right lively in spots. I tell you what. When you get there you look up Tom McConnell and tell him you're a friend of mine. He knows more of what's goin' on there than anybody else."

"Tom McConnell," I nodded. "Where can I find him?"

"Wherever there's a girl, a bottle, a law suit, a fight, a card game, a horse race, a man he likes or a man he doesn't like. Anybody that hasn't kicked the bucket or skipped the state can tell you where he is." He sighed thoughtfully. "I'm sort of sorry I'm not goin' to be able to go back there with you."

I wasn't. Greenhorn though I undoubtedly would be, on the frontier—if I went there—I didn't want to be in anyone's leading strings.

CHAPTER IV

IT WAS TOWARD Mississippi, after all, that I sailed. Indeed, as I was compelled to admit, after pacing along the quays and streets of Norfolk for a couple of days, I was able to think of no other course with any elements of practicality.

Once aboard the Baltimore-New Orleans packet I experienced for the first time the feeling of achieved adventure that is the due of a man setting forth on a momentous voyage. Alas, the heroic mood died as speedily as most bright, fragile things. The coastal waters of America were, I vaguely knew, of ill repute among seamen. At first hand I now discovered the reason, learning at the same time I was not a good sailor.

The winds came out of the east to crumple the shallow ocean against an endless shore. From North Carolina down this went on, with no change save that at times the ship tossed more agonizingly than at others. Rounding between the Scylla of Cuba and the Charybdis of the Florida Keys we got tangled in the skirts of a hurricane. Then counter winds harried us across the Gulf while screeching gulls battened on my rejected and ejected provender.

There were other passengers aboard, but there is no enemy to social intercourse the equal of nausea. Like Niobe I had no friend but my grief, and others were but as phantasms of delirium until the night the vessel nosed into the mouth of the great river.

From that point on, crossing as it were the threshold of a new existence, I had a mind to wonder with. Even as I was approaching, not too happily, a new country, so also my ancestors had once drawn near Virginia. Conceding that they might have taken more kindly to the sea, how had it been with them? I had always looked upon them as foresighted opportunists, confident of abilities they were eager to exploit. Now I knew in my homesick bones it wasn't so. Who would leave his perch in elements known to him and among birds of his own plumage unless it had been kicked out from under him? Who'd willingly walk into nothing he could imagine? Whatever else was true of those early settlers, yes and most later ones, no doubt, they didn't come because they were happy or successful at home.

My stomach quivering at rest, I gained one night of healthful sleep before I waked to a new appetite, a new country, and New Orleans. This was a somewhat fabled city, even in the East, but at the time I saw no more of it than the dockside. I had been to enough cities to know that town life for a transient is expensive. There was no money to spare for pointless indulgence, and I was relieved when I found that a Natchez bound steamer would rescue me from temptation that afternoon.

Content to lounge and muse, I regarded the river boat as being in the same category as the stage and the coastwise vessel—a mere conveyance toward new prospects. My mind was thrown forward, impotently questioning the character of the destiny I was approaching; and I ignored the clues sauntering and regaling themselves all around me.

Instead I gazed at the moss-hung trees and the great plantation houses in their semi-tropical settings. But this was in long-settled Louisiana, and these things I had seen in South Carolina. The river had more to tell, and I watched broodingly when it swept an ark-like flat boat or a sprawling raft down toward us. The feral-looking water nomads at ease among the careless piles of cargo were a total surprise to me. Nobody had prepared me for aquatic pioneers.

It was difficult to gather much about them. Although some waved or shouted more or less friendly greetings, most just stared appraisingly. Among themselves they were a loud-voiced lot, much given to song. Once while we were taking on wood a singer drifted by on a barge close enough for me to catch the words. The initial stanza told me no more than I was ready to believe:

> "Oh, the river's wet, and the ground is dirt
> And a yam's a sweet pertater;
> And what ain't fleas beneath my shirt
> Is mostly human natur."

The succeeding strophes seemed to be a sort of catalogue of towns into which "human natur" led the songster. I noted one because it mentioned my destination:

> "Oh, I met a girl in Natchez town
> Like a picture in a locket;
> But before I got my breeches down
> She'd gone and picked my pocket."

That was interesting but didn't help me to picture my own fortunes when I disembarked. It wasn't until late morning of the day we were to land that I was roused from my mooning. I ceased wondering about when I was going to reach Mississippi when it detonated all around me.

Since leaving southern Louisiana there had been no mansions to break the pattern of cane and trees. The only residence of man or even sign of his being was the occasional hut of the woodseller. Wretched hovels askew in the rank bottom mire, they were each dwarfed by the piles of wood cut to size for the refueling of paddle boats.

It was just after we'd idled away from one such way stop and the paddles were beginning to dig in against the stream. I had been leaning over the rail watching the logs being stowed aboard and was lingering to ponder on the complete isolation of the wood vendor. Therefore, I was among those who saw the man break from the forest and dash to the bank. With his dirty red hunting shirt, coonskin cap and rifle he was an arresting sight to my Eastern eyes. Yet his actions were more entertaining than his costume.

"Stop!" he cried, throwing up one arm imperiously. "Come back here! I want on."

The engine made a long, powerful stroke, starting to gain headway, though the progress was still slow. "Chug!" it replied.

The woodsman was not at first ready to believe that his trade was being spurned. He trotted a few steps along the bank and shouted: "Back up! I want on! Hey! Hush that God damn raft up so you can hear what I'm sayin'!"

"Chug!" went the engine, more deeply than before.

If the pilot was aware of the would-be passenger, he was above giving a sign. A ship's officer, however, retained the human touch. "Swim up to the next landin'," he bellowed. "We'll be there in awhile."

The ship started moving faster, and so did the man ashore, now losing patience. "Lemme on that water box! An' lemme on quick or I'll whip everybody on it, an' you," he howled, jabbing a finger toward the mate, now that he could fix responsibility, "I'll whip you twice! I'm warnin' you, you bas——"

Whatever it may have been his intention to add to that syllable, it was never uttered. Loping heedlessly along, he tripped on a root and fell silent, face down in the mud.

Not so the delighted mate and several diverted passengers. As for me, I cut short my guffaw in hopes of hearing the woodsman's comments.

He made none at first. Scrambling to his feet, he snatched up his dropped weapon and made sure it wasn't clogged with dirt. "Stop that boat!" he roared for the last time, speaking to and aiming at the no longer amused ship's officer.

"Put that gun down!" the latter bawled just as futilely.

The bullet struck the railing where he had stood an instant before and zoomed off somewhere. I had been absolutely unready for so violent an end to mirth, but I was even more startled by the prompt response.

Of the half-dozen or so passenger spectators at least three produced pistols and joyously shot at the woodsman. Not that only, but the cabin erupted men with weapons drawn or drawing. Most didn't know what was going on, but all were alert to participate. After eager questioning some of them took pot shots for luck while others sought out eyewitnesses and demanded the story.

As the distance was far too great for pistol accuracy no harm accompanied the fun and excitement. The man who got left was now drawing what solace he could from their failure to hit him. He leaned his weapon against a tree to free both hands for nose thumbing while he yelled mocking obscenities.

Then in turn his glee was sobered as swiftly as the mate's. A latecomer sprang from the cabin, a huge, easy runner in a leather shirt and moccasins, long haired and bare headed, with a snarl of red beard. He had a great knife in the belt that snugged his shirt and an immense rifle at trail. Leaping to take his stance near me, he swung his sights in line and snap fired.

On the instant the nose thumbing stopped, and the insults finished in a shriek, as the other fell over and crawfished frantically behind a woodpile. The marksman gave a remarkable imitation of a crow convulsed with mirth, spat largely at the river, and turned away.

"Just nicked his ear," he remarked. "Hell! You can't really blame a hoss for gettin' mad about missin' a boat, but he shouldn't cuss a boat with women on it."

"Or shoot at it," I observed.

"Well, I dunno as I'd say that," he said. "A man can tell where he's shootin' but not where he's cussin'."

I was admiring this metaphysical nicety when a figure thrust furiously between us.

"Cain!" he shieked. "Ahab!" And with the words he snatched at the big fellow's rifle. He actually succeeded in whisking it from the other's unprepared grasp. But as he swept it up with the obvious intention of tossing it overboard there was a knife at his throat.

"Scat or die!" the bearded man thundered and regained his property with one big hand.

As a former soldier I recognized the lethal seriousness of tampering with another man's weapon, but the offender wasn't abashed. "Murderer!" he cried, backing away, allowing us all to take him in. A lank, blond man, he had a long arm behind his finger of indictment. "Blood-stained sinner!" he added, glaring around to gauge his growing audience.

One glance was sufficient to tell him all he wanted to know about us. "You're all alike!" he announced. "Black-hearted worms hatched out of evil to crawl through the filth of your lives till you reach your destined home in hell!"

The big rifleman had put away his knife and was chewing stolidly, watching the fanatic with unblinking attention. A couple of the rest started edging away, while others shifted their feet, their faces showing the uneasy conviction that it was the thing to do to stay and listen. As usual nobody seemed to know what to do about this sample of evangelical rudeness.

Meanwhile more people, women among them, drew near to investigate the cause of the gathering. The preacher greeted them with fierce joy.

"Yes, yes, sons and daughters of Belial, come here and let me tell you what's going to happen to you, the sinful. And you!" He sent a tongue of flame at the several trying to ease out of earshot. "It won't do you any good to try to run away. The devil will find you whether you listen to me or not."

"What's son of Belial mean?" came bluntly from the red beard. "I want to know what's bein' said when I'm bein' cussed at."

"*He* doesn't know what a son of Belial is!" The evangelist snapped at this cue like a starved hound at raw meat, and the long arm pointed again. "*He,* a man I caught drawing the red hand of murder from his brother's blood." He withered them all with a hot run of his eyes. "*You* all saw him, but *you* did nothing. *I* saw him, and *I* tried to save him; debased as he is he's still a creature of God. But he would not be saved! When I tried to take Cain's staff from him he drew his assassin's knife to slay me for my act of grace."

Having had enough of this rant I was about to leave in the wake of the others dedicated to Satan when a man across from me in the encircling group spoke up. "You got a license to preach, mister?"

The evangelist gasped and waited as if expecting prompt heavenly punishment to follow the presumptuous question. It wasn't forthcoming, and the arm reached skyward.

"My license," he thundered sternly, "comes from there!"

"Yes, but what ticket you votin'?" The catechizer was a firmly built, short man with a round face. The cigar he chewed seemed to punctuate his blandness. "There's lots of 'em, you know, and they all claim the same home stand. How do we know you ain't stumpin' for Mohammed or the Natchez Big Sun? It would be a hell of a note for a man to get saved and find he was squattin' on the wrong pre-emption claim. Let's see your license."

"This is a free country," the blond man declared, abandoning the support of Heaven for that of the Constitution. Then he attempted to rally. "Who are you to interrupt a son of God on a holy mission?"

The stocky little man took the cigar out of his mouth and spoke in the sober tones of a citizen who sees the course to be followed. "I think we ought to hold a court of triflin' equity and vain appeal."

Whatever that meant it was popular. The shuffling crowd became cheerfully animate.

"Bullen's got the idea!"

"Grab him!"

"Who'll preside?"

The change-over from uneasy defendants to eager prosecutors of justice was too rapid for the preacher to follow. As he stood nonplussed, four men seized and held him despite demonic struggles and threats effective both in this world and the next.

Aside from this phase of it the business was conducted with notable decorum. A slight, elderly man, richly dressed in black, was enthroned on a stowage locker. He selected a prosecutor and a defense counsel, appointed Bullen bailiff, and ordered each side to choose three jurors. Of these I chanced to be one, and somewhat dazedly I took a chair among those drawn up for the panel. I would have preferred the role of spectator, not being sure of what was going to happen, but I decided to accept without demur. After all, should it seem necessary for someone to intervene, a juror has a tribune's voice.

As soon as everyone had found a perch or something to lean against, the "magistrate" called for order and commanded Bullen to deliver the charges. The latter, who had sacrificed his cigar for the dignity of the court, complied in a rich, smooth drawl.

"The critter dragged before this court was apprehended open mouthed, preaching without a license, which means, ergo, to wit and damn his impudence, he was abusin' citizens of this commonwealth and threatenin' 'em with hell fire on his own hook. Moreover, without benefit of clergy he assaulted one Arkansas Dillon, a bear hunter, and tried to make away with his visible means of support in manifest alliance with a vicious character on shore."

The prisoner tried to shout a protest but quieted when threatened with the additional charge of contempt of court. He seemed no more sure than I how seriously to take the business, and for some time sat subdued.

Counsel for defense was a man, to my lay ears, of considerable legal knowledge. He started by admitting that his client didn't have a license, self-evident in as much as it could not be produced, but he denied any deliberate malfeasance or even lawlessness as far as the preaching was concerned. He dwelt on the constitutional rights of zealots to proclaim their notions about this or any other world and pointed out there was no corollary provision designed to spare the ears and feelings of reluctant auditors.

"The national fathers who designed the Constitution," he propounded, "relied on the size of this nation as being so large that everybody could talk at once and none need listen who hadn't a mind to. The envisioned method of being spared distasteful speeches was for the annoyed listener to avoid, give ground or leave town rather than to stand pat and ram a guyascutus down the throat of the contumelious speaker.

"It is unfortunate," he concluded, "that, wise as the founders of this nation were known to be, they had not foreseen the narrow physical limits of a Mississippi paddle boat. That is a misfortune on the part of his hearers rather than a fault of my client. However, pending the passage of an amendment, no likely event before the conclusion of this trial, the Constitution is crystal clear on this point. Anybody distressed by the rhetoric of my client is firmly advised by the great men who established these our United States to grab his nose and jump overboard."

This merciless logic seemed to carry the weight that was its due. I hugged my knee and waited for the rebuttal. Even the evangelist, though mystified at some of his counsel's conclusions, looked relieved at so strongly worded a defense.

The prosecuting attorney, like his opponent, commenced by making inevitable concessions. He would, he declared, argue neither with the Constitution as it stood nor with the lucid interpretation offered by his colleage. Rather he intended to base his case on the slanderous accusations made against and in point of fact directly to one Arkansas Dillon, a bear hunter. "These accusations," he declaimed, "are of a nature to lessen his credit and impair his pro-

THE WILD YAZOO

fessional reputation. In a word, he accused Mr. Dillon of shooting to kill a man whom many observers saw to remain very much alive."

A moment later Dillon was duly sworn and seated in the improvised witness box. He now held his rifle as if he had never seen one before and was somewhat afraid of it; his glance was demurely wondering, as if being the center of attention was more than he could stand; and his chew wabbled uneasily in a bulge of the red beard.

In the presence of such stage fright the prosecutor was kindly. "Now just take your time, Mr. Dillon, and give us the facts in your own words. Just what took place between you and the defendant?"

The bear hunter shuffled his feet. "Well, sir, I was out huntin' b'ars, about three days ago it was, an' I was havin' a pretty tight tussle with a b'ar on account of forgettin' to load m'gun an' on account of the b'ar takin' a mean advantage of it, when my leetlest boy caught up with me. Cute as a bug he is, and his maw says he's the spittin' image of me, but I wouldn't like to say."

"Of course." The prosecutor seemed to admire such modesty. "And then?"

"Well, sir, he said I was a great-grand-orphan on account of my great-grandmother havin' died; and I cried so all the way home I could hardly drag the b'ar, which had died of fright from findin' my knife in his gizzard, along with me."

"And so?"

"Well, sir, I talked it over with the squaw, an' she said it ain't every day a body gets to go to his great-grandmother's funeral, an' so I was standin' at the railin' thinkin', how sad everythin' is and watchin' a jigger like to bust a gut because he missed the boat. Cussed, he did, and I was just thinkin' how awful that was when along come this yaller-haired varmint an' said I tried to murder him."

"I see." The prosecutor clicked his tongue sympathetically. "And did you?"

"Well, sir, you likely never had a great-grandmother die or you wouldn't ask that. Like I told you, m'gun wasn't loaded when I caught up with the b'ar, an' I didn't get time to load up before the b'ar caught up with me, an' since my leetlest boy come along with

[43]

the awful news I never give it a thought. To prove what I say, it ain't loaded right this minute."

The defendant was trying to make himself heard, but his lawyer squelched him. "Your honor, the point is not whether the gun *is* loaded but whether it has been fired recently. Surely that can be readily ascertained."

"Quite right," nodded the judge. "Invoke competent testimony."

"Very well," the defense counsel agreed, taking the gun from the witness. "I need not inform anyone here," he remarked, holding it up, "that even the most untrained nose can detect a recently discharged rifle. I have been instructed to invoke competent testimony. Where can I look for more knowledge and less bias than in a juror?"

Nobody gainsaying him, he approached the panel and to my profound astonishment put the heavy weapon in my hand. "The court awaits your decision."

My confusion was but momentary. I knew now something of where I was and with whom I stood, and I was determined not to be found wanting. The warm fumes from the bore were so rank that it was all I could do to keep from sneezing. Yet I inhaled lustily without a change of expression and repeated the business after lifting the priming trap. When I had done so I looked around. Everybody's eyes were upon me, the judge's aloof, the defendant's confident, the lawyers' professionally alert, the hunter's interested, Bullen's snapping with curiosity. I let them wait for a moment.

"No more smell than a diamond," I finally announced.

I looked directly at the judge as I gave this evidence and only heard the sigh from the audience. Meanwhile there was a scuffling as the preacher once more sought to shake off his attendants.

"It's a lie!" he shouted. "I saw it fired! Heard it! You all did—a lot of you did! Where's somebody who saw him?"

"Silence!" the judge ordered sharply. "We have just heard uncoerced testimony that the weapon has not recently been fired from this," he nodded courteously in my direction, "indubitable citizen of Mississippi."

CHAPTER V

THERE WERE few other preliminaries after I had spoken. The jury then voted a verdict of guilty, and the confounded prisoner was hauled up to hear judgment.

"You've been accused," the judge stated solemnly, "of unlicensed contumely, assault, attempted destruction of property, and whang-doodleism. You have been convicted of flouting middle, high, and low justice by aspersing the integrity and good aim of Mr. Dillon. Doubting the marksmanship of an Arkansas bear hunter has in the past proved fatal to more than bears, so you will no doubt marvel at the clemency of this court when you're merely put ashore at the next landing." When the prisoner's yell of rage yielded to a hand held over his mouth the magistrate went on. "This sentence is suspended pending the giving of any other offense."

After the evangelist had flounced away, muttering malevolently, his honor rose, chuckling. "I now leave the bench for the bar."

I was well pleased with the whole business and not least with my small but crucial part in it. Several men nodded to me with friendly grins, as many of us followed the judge. Slight as the recognition was, it was comforting to my strangeness. A phrase can brace mightily, so cunningly can the spirit use what it must when lacking what it needs. A citizen of Mississippi, the judge had called me, and by that calling he had made it plausible. Some aspects of the people I'd come to join were novel, but the odd was no longer the alien. I was being accepted, and the notion of making my way there ceased to be fantastic.

Imitating my neighbor, I procured a rum punch with a strong core to its refreshing citrous depths. It was proper ballast for a heart newly unburdened and in little mood for other freight. As I sipped, I laughed frequently at the remarks of others, mostly dealing with the trial, though I took little part in the conversation myself. I was growing fat on that mirth, my first since setting sail.

It was Arkansas Dillon who asked the one question I badly wanted to, although I would never have dared so to imperil my new citizenship. "Say, Mr. Bullen," he roared from his place at the other end of the bar, "how did you happen to know that about licensing preachers?"

Bullen, stationed at one remove from me, took the glass out of his mouth and replaced it with a cigar. "The law," he said cryptically, "has got to be a flexible instrument."

It was late afternoon when we rounded into the southern end of the final straightaway. The west bank seemed hardly to rise high enough to contain the river, while on the east the bluffs piled up toward the clouds. High against the sky at the end of this stretch I could see steeples, a bubblelike white dome riding above the trees, and the roseate mellowness of brick construction. That city was the gateway to the new land of my harried choosing.

Below on a narrow spit between the bluff and a cluster of shipping was a community I learned to be Natchez-under-the-Hill. From salty remarks passed by a couple of men standing near me I gathered that it was in this suburb rather than in the town itself that lustful men had their pockets prematurely picked. At first view, however, it was deceptively drab. The place had rather the aspects of the important inland port it undoubtedly was. Its wharves, I observed as we approached, were loaded with cotton and the goods for which the wealth it bought were exchanged. That and a row of colorless commercial buildings were about all I could see as I waited my turn to step ashore.

There were not enough passenger vehicles to take care of all of us, but once I had entrusted my valise to the luggage cart of a hotel, I was glad enough to walk. I was in that pristine stage of reaction to a new country when all phases were stimulating.

Picking my way across the muddy street, I turned to get my bearings. Far up and down the river beyond the steamboats there was a jumbled mass of less formal shipping: flat boats, sailing scows, barges and rafts. Many of the flat boats were silted in, half deserting the river for the shore. Their cabins seemed to furnish permanent residences for the dockside rabble or housing for less domestic establishments. This was picturesque, but I was content to admire from afar.

As surely the first act of a right-minded newcomer should be to salute the land that is receiving him I rounded a corner searching for an agreeable tavern. The buildings on the next street behind were more presentable, as one might justly argue that a mud pie is more presentable than a horse apple. I looked appraisingly up the street. Save for the dock workers the denizens of this blowzy commune were hardly astir. There were a few people slouching along or lounging in doorways, but the only really active beings were some black pigs, businesslike and quarrelsome as they nosed for offal.

Turning to peer down the street, I inadvertently shouldered a man rounding the corner. I put out my hand to steady him and was framing a suitable apology when he forestalled me. It was, indeed, the first time I had been addressed since setting foot in Mississippi. "All right, stranger," he said, knocking my hand away. "What's it to be, drink or fight?"

He had already stowed his cargo of liquor, early as it was and much as his mighty frame promised he could hold. His broad, Indian-like features were slack with it. I guessed, too, that drinking with him would be no reliable appeasement, even if I had felt like humoring him. Giving him a curt nod, I started to leave.

"Look here," he said, catching me by the shoulder, "you ain't goin' off without speakin' to me. If you don't want to drink, just say so an' we'll fight."

The absurdity of the situation didn't conceal its danger. The fellow was powerful, ill-tempered, and probably vicious. Moreover, several people had popped out of buildings, drawn by the same instincts and sharing the same ominous hopes as buzzards. Self-consciousness added to my natural annoyance began to stir my anger. Yet I was aware any words I said would be used against me. I made one more effort to go my way.

He thwarted it as roughly as he had the first. "God damn it!" he roared. "I'm tryin' to treat you square an' not whip you when your back is turned. You had your chance to drink. Now we're goin' to fight."

He was backing away in preparation for a roaring charge. Action was inevitable, and I reached in the grab bag of my mind for something I could use. Looking at his snarling face and great hunched shoulders I was suddenly reminded of a certain payday in the Army. There had been a hulking drunken recruit intent on doing away with the tyranny of all sergeants as represented by one in particular. I had been favorably impressed by the sergeant's method of taking care of him.

I put one hand to my ear and leaned forward. "I'm sorry, but I'll have to ask you to repeat that. I don't hear very well."

The recruit, too, had wanted his victim to know about his punishment in advance. "I said I was goin' to—oh hell," the fellow broke off, dropping his arms disgustedly and moving nearer. "I said I was goin' to blast you open and salt you."

"You hope I what?" I kept my hand to my ear, and he swaggered up to stand beside me.

"By Jesus, I'll make you hear!"

He was shouting in my very ear by this time but stopped when my shoulder came up under his chin. I gave him an elbow in the solar plexus and a slashing hook behind his jaw, then paused for observation. His buckling was slow but complete.

After I'd watched him a moment, still hot and seething, I conceived the notion that allies of his might be among the spectators. Looking suddenly and warily up, I found my eyes engaged by those of a merry-faced man with a spike-tipped moustache. A florid, large-eyed fellow he was, standing tall in his boots, both hands on a cane resting in front of him.

My look of challenge seemed to amuse him. "When you've stamped on him," he suggested, "it'll be my pleasure to——"

"I'm not going to stamp on him," I growled. But my wrath was seeping away.

"Not one kick in the ribs to honor the customs of the country?" He smiled. "Very well, then. He took care of the fighting, so I'll handle the other end of his dual option. How about a drink?"

My anger had all but drained, leaving me a little shaky. I managed a grin. "Do you know where to go?"

He tapped my antagonist lightly with his cane as he stepped over him. "I always know where to go. It's my strength as well as my weakness. Have you met your opponent?"

"Not before."

By this time he had linked his arm in mine, and, a little surprised at the familiarity, I found myself borne along. "Well, next time you meet him ask him to show you his bottled collection of pickled eyes, ears, and nose ends. You're a newcomer, aren't you? Here, this dingy portal is ours."

The establishment behind the door, in so far as the dimness allowed me to judge, was much less dismal than its exterior. We passed through a gaudy dance hall, empty except for the tables and chairs along the walls, then down a hallway to a smaller room with a large gambling table in the center. At the rear was a little bar.

Mr. Philips, as my companion had introduced himself, put his hat and cane on a table in the corner and gestured toward a chair. "You know what to do, Caligula," he told the grey-whiskered darky who presided.

If Philips was somewhat foppish, what with his fawn-colored coat, plaid trousers and exceedingly high stock, he was also generous. He cried down my attempt to buy the next round. "I presumed to offer you this hospitality," he answered a question I hadn't felt like asking, "not only because of your distinguished appearance but because I was edified by the way you handled Rufus Doanes. He's one of the most perilous ruffians in Underhill, and when you've said that you've said all. He isn't often handled, and, no offense to your prowess, I think it was fortunate for you that he was more than usually drunk."

"I think so, too," I said sincerely.

My host put down his glass with a hand that I now noticed shook just a little. "If he remembers you next time he sees you and you can't keep out of his way, shoot him down," he said. "If you don't he'll kill or cripple you."

The coolness of his tone impressed me with the fact that I was receiving advice from a native; otherwise I might have laughed. "I don't make a habit of carrying weapons."

I might as well have told him I wasn't accustomed to wearing trousers. "And you're wandering around Natchez-under-the-Hill with night coming on!" His genuine amazement infected me with uneasiness, but in a second his face cleared. "Well, tonight you'll be with me."

A few more men came in while we were finishing the second glass, and I could hear women's voices from the dance hall. Natchez Underhill was finally astir, and Philips took due note of the fact.

"Now the moth of evil delights at the promise of darkness. Let's watch it delight."

The street was indeed alive as we stepped out into the mild if tainted dusk. By twos, fours and sixes a mixed throng was promenading in search of acquaintances, diversion, excitement, drink, women and the scatterings of fate. There were well-dressed youngsters, presumably down from the bluff to see the sights and get into trouble. There were backwoodsmen and deepwoodsmen, steamboaters, flatboaters, and the amphibious louts such as haunt every port—never seen on the water or away from it. The women varied only in the minor distinctions of size, feature and color. White, gingerbread, or blue gum they were whores; and the brutal fact obliterated their characteristics to make them one.

Here was a balanced market where the supply was neatly fitted to the demand. Besides taverns, dance halls, gambling establishments, whore houses, and various combinations of the four, there were peep shows ranging from the vile to the monstrous, wrestling and prize-ring displays, cock fighting, dog fighting and sundry exhibits of *léger de main* and *montrer de jambe*.

Such an assemblage in such a milieu held infinite possibilities, few of which were unfulfilled. I saw, for instance, one young girl whose face was sliced open plunging through the crowd with a maddened riverman in pursuit. No one tried to stop either.

The cock-fight crowd was remote from the gatherings of sportsmen to which I was accustomed. They took it as a personal insult when their judgment of form went awry and weren't above crowing like the triumphant roosters when they were vindicated.

No more grace was to be met with among the admirers of the dance. Their anatomical comments were loud, pithy and exact. They called for assignations from the back of the room and bragged openly of the satisfaction they were equipped to offer. Betimes, too, they railed broadly at each other's pretensions and a row resulted. One boaster was holding forth on his prowess when a bored listener cried: "All right, inchworm, sit down!" And such was inchworm's wrath that they mixed in an affray that cost his traducer the top of one ear.

I had wondered, notwithstanding his own explanation, just why Philips had taken such an interest in me. In the first place, he was of the sort that's miserable without companionship. In the second place, he had a citizen's natural pride in showing items of local interest to a satisfactorily astonished visitor.

He proved an entertaining if persistent conversationalist and an embarrassingly generous host. For Natchez Underhill he was a knowledgeable guide, zealous to explain and unfailing in his interest in my reactions. Without him it would have been a briefer as well as a duller trip; but eventually I began to grow a little tired of it and him.

As the evening wore on the number of nights he'd spent in acquiring his explicit knowledge began to show up on him. He was getting drunk and in a peculiar fashion whose symptoms were known to me. There is a great difference between the inebriety of the man on an occasional spree and that of the man whose constant high level of alcohol is raised to lap over the levees of his control by adding a given number of drinks. There was no health or spontaneity in Philips' way of getting drunk. It was just suddenly and quietly too much for him. If he'd been rowdy it would at least have seemed healthy. As it was, he was simply a man falling apart.

Unfortunately, I was by then bound to him. Having accepted so much hospitality I could not abruptly desert him: I had to tag along, feebly protesting every now and then that what we both needed was rest. He was an implacable devotee of hard living, however, and when I suggested leaving one place he merely led me to another.

It was while I was trailing balkily in this stage of our association that I saw an immense man in the gaudy trappings of a successful professional gambler bear down on us. What had chiefly drawn my amused attention was his lordly air. As he swept the two trollops that hung on his arms along with him he reminded me irresistibly of a bull guarding his prerogatives in two cows against all comers.

A half-breed snatchpurse took a more practical view of the man's situation. Evidently reasoning that a man with a woman on each arm is handicapped, he darted forward, even as I looked, and reached for the fellow's plainly exhibited watch chain. It was his last earthly act. With what seemed to be one motion the doxies were shucked off into the passing crowd, a cane the gambler carried turned into a sword, and the pickpocket was spitted through the heart. Picking up and replacing the end of his cane, the big fellow offered his arms to his consorts and sailed on.

Drunk though he was, Philips had more sense than I. I was looking at the dead man irresolutely, but he knew better.

"Come on!" he said sharply, then added as we hurried on: "Never show interest in a corpse here."

He was dealing in actualities, and I saw that my lingering was sham. I wasn't going to do anything. Nevertheless, I couldn't help looking behind me. There was no furor, although a little group had gathered to talk about it. In this they showed no more humanity and less wisdom than my companion. And only one considered the civic aspects of the situation.

"A man that kills a man," he was complaining, "ought to take him off the street. Somebody's going to stumble over him sure as hell."

CHAPTER VI

AT LENGTH I told my apparently tireless host that I was getting sleepy and intended to leave him. He had just finished dropping a hundred or so at faro, a loss that didn't seem to disturb him. Before he took back the cane he had entrusted to me he looked at a huge gold watch.

"It's just the right time, Godolphin," he announced thickly. "We'll eat where we're going now, then we'll go home."

To this I made no objection. In the course of the long evening I'd had all the liquor I could manage myself. Putting some food on top of it was only good sense. The establishment to which he led me was on the second floor of a building standing well back from the street and so not the object of every man's curiosity. We reached it by an outside stairway and were admitted only after Philips had identified himself.

The place was noteworthy in Underhill both for cleanness and lack of pretension. It was a decently furnished coffee room of moderate size. From its wainscotting prints of the nation's great statesmen looked down with a sobriety not even the many candles could lighten.

Even more remarkable, considering where we were, was the homogeneity of the clientele. Everybody looked prosperous and everybody except me probably was. It was a well-behaved assembly, too, although quite a few others had had their spirituous quota.

The bird they served was delicious but new to me and Philips told me it gloried in the name of golden plover. He himself was past the stage of being able to handle food gracefully and soon pushed it from him to call for brandy. On the other hand I discovered that nourishment was exactly what I had needed. In conclusion I ordered coffee and thoroughly enjoyed the smoke I had over it.

In retrospect the evening seemed quite satisfactory. The paramount gift demanded of a new country is novelty of experience. Granted that the type supplied by Natchez Underhill was nothing on which to build, my arrival had not simply been marked by the sight of new surroundings. If it took violence to celebrate my advent, why violence unspeakable went into the welding of the world and green things grew thereafter. There is no philosophy so genially universal as that which is the effluvium of cigar smoke, coffee, good food and a judicious amount of liquor. Wisdom was in me, and I felt like sharing it, done up in well-phrased apothegms.

My companion, however, had lost his garrulity along with most of his *savoir-faire*. He gave little attention to my attempts at conversation and instead stared across the room. There was nothing in his line of vision but a door I had not yet seen opened. In time I became aware that in the room at large talk had withered to syllables. I looked around. Everybody had either one or both eyes on that door. I started to watch it myself.

Abruptly it opened far enough for a man with a peg leg to stump through. Asked to guess, I would have said he was a cross between an Indian and a Portuguese sailor. His clothes were a patchwork of bright colors, and a ring in one ear flapped and flashed as he vaulted up on the room's tiny bar. Almost before he was settled he had shoved a violin under his chin and commenced to play.

His music was of a type to which I was unaccustomed, but I found it pleasing. The chords didn't flow into each other but were saucily at odds or skipped off by themselves. Such contrariness led to petulance among them, then to anger waxing more bitter by the moment. At the height of this war of harmonies the door opened again.

The immense figure which strode in fulfilled my conception of a Turk, which required no exactitude of characterization in as much as I had never seen one. He wore a turban, drooping wisps of moustaches, a long, curved knife, voluminous trousers and shoes that seemed to be looking back over their shoulders. I looked at him with mellow satisfaction as he stepped aside and leaned against the wall with folded arms. There was always the chance that he was a Cherokee rather than a Mameluke, but I preferred to believe.

Yet it was obviously not for a sight of either of these, arresting as was their appearance, that such a gathering burnt its eyes. The music stopped, and there was one, sweet, aspiring chord that stopped in mid flight. At its whispered death the woman that had to follow it entered.

No more than anybody else there did she take the fact of her meerschaum loveliness calmly. It was a weapon of war, sharp and bright, a craftsman's product, neither dulled by disuse nor marred by misuse.

There was a sigh as everyone leaned a little toward her. I put my cigar in my mouth and leaned back to look around. For the time being women were not for me. I had muddied that source of man's delight for myself and would have to wait until it cleared. At the moment, however, I was feeling grateful to Harriet for the antidote of our curdled lust. I could take an impersonal satisfaction, watching the involvement of others, in the ravages of this conqueror.

So aware was she of the stunning impact of her beauty that as she yielded her cape to the expressionless Turk she smiled gently in sympathy. However, she was not there to be gentle but to have her way with men. She now went about it. Her gown, a filament of revelation, billowed as she sailed across the floor to where the fiddler dangled his violin along his timber leg. Her voice carried only enough to tell she was speaking, but she was presumably giving instructions to her accompanist. At one point she reached up and patted him on the cheek, and I heard someone groan. There wasn't a man of them that didn't feel the touch of those blossom-skinned fingers.

"I will sing," she stated after she had swept to the center of the floor and looked at us one by one. "You will not understand the words, perhaps—but you will understand."

Her voice had an accent which had the effect of furnishing each word with a grace note or so. I wasn't linguist enough to decide as to the derivation or indeed as to the genuineness of this foreign salt. As she sang I recognized several songs as French, while others were in some other language—Italian, perhaps.

Her prefatory statement was justified by the first stave of the first song. She had promised that alien words would be no obstacle to comprehension, and they were not. She didn't exactly dance as she sang but accompanied herself with a sort of flowing charade. A mincing glide, a closing of the eye, a yielding of the hip, a wince of the shoulder, a dip of the knee, a languorous flip of the hand; these things proved sufficient as she drifted idly here and there. Of a truth she need not have sung, though her sweet, throaty voice gave coherence to illusion.

I looked once at Philips and saw what she was doing to them all. Desire had captured more than his physical faculties. He was in a transport, seeing the erotic and the impossibly ideal in one obtainable bargain package. He had no doubt she was singing for him.

Her first sign of putting a period to this ecstasy was when she halted in mid floor and looked at us one by one again. "You like it?" she asked easily.

Clapping and cheering, each trying to prove by his delighted expression that he was the true appreciator, they rose. Then the money started to flutter and spin. How much of it there was I couldn't estimate, but Philips tossed a couple of large notes, and the hard cash was gold only. She looked down demurely as if the bills and coins at her feet were so many flowers. "You like it," she decided.

However, she did not gather it nor show any further interest. The Turk did the garnering while she floated over for another conference with the piratical-looking violinist.

"Who is she?" I asked, dubbing out my cigar.

Philips' eyes remained on her, but after a moment he spared me his voice. "Countess Eulalie Balaton."

Having feared as much, I sighed. Of course, she might have been a countess. Never having met one I was in as little position to pass judgment as I was concerning Turks.

"What's she doing here?"

Sensing my skepticism, he looked at me angrily. "What are you doing here?" he demanded, and I had no answer for him.

She had turned from the fiddler and was moving toward us again. Instantly all conversation ceased, and I reasoned that even a countess should be satisfied with such an intensity of attention.

"Three nights now I sing for you," she stated, "and three times you show me you like it."

There was confirming applause which she waited out. "Because you have been very nice and because I sing no more at Natchez now I have a special treat." She cut incipient cheers short with a lift of her hand. "I work all day to learn a song in English for you. You wait here?"

There being no hurricanes or earthquakes to move them, they did wait there. I searched my memory for an American or English song suitable for her profoundly intimate mannerisms but could think of none. However, the idea was immensely popular and hopes were high.

"At last," I heard one youth breathe gustily, "I'll know whether she's talking about what I think she's talking about."

He was not to have his doubts clarified through her agency. When she returned she remained swathed in her long midnight-blue cape. She had removed the dancer's fillet from her head, letting her hair narrow her face to a white streak of enchantment within its lustrous folds.

Her eyes looked enormous, and as she started to sing my own grew sufficiently big. The words were a poem by poor Fred Limberlock whom I'd known in Baltimore before he decided the Great Dismal Swamp was romantic and stepped in a nest of water moccasins. I wouldn't have thought her personality would have found a vehicle in his lush Byronics, but it did. She was desperation in pantomime and no less persuasive than before. The "Haunted House" was one of these symbolic affairs, and as near as I could follow Limberlock, which was never very close, it dealt with someone of indeterminate sex bracing his or her lover to a suicide pact. Comprehended or not, it had been a great thing to read to girls a few years earlier, and I could have almost said the last stanza word for word with the countess:

"You and I in a haunted house—
The years that led to this our meeting,
Peopled how somewhat we know:
Some ghosts linger, others, fleeting,
Seldom reach from the dim ago

To touch and tell us what we were
When there were clearer depths to stir.
Beneath implacable mortmain
Can we have met to wince in vain,
Or can we steal beyond its power
To find us;
Run, toss regret, the tainted flower,
Behind us?"

In the slight pause with which she tailed this line I heard the heavy breathing of more than one who seemed willing to make the spiritual experiment with such a partner. She had been staring at us haggardly, one hand stretched toward us beseechingly. Now she became animated. From out the folds of her cape she whirled a dagger and held it in one of the hands with which she reached tautly for the ceiling.

"Then outside in the limpid night,
Purged of memory's pale blight,
What should we see when the moon comes up?"

With the words the dirk darted down, plunged to her waist, cutting whatever flimsy ties she had improvised. The cape slipped floorward, and like the moon of which she had sung her naked symmetry rose above it. All in all it was the most calculated act of wantonness I had ever seen.

It temporarily unseated my celibate complacency, and its general effect was cataclysmic. One of the older men present jumped up, groaned, and, overcome alike by lust and liquor, pitched forward on his face. There were loud reports as several sent bullets through the ceiling as the only adequate expression of their feelings. Philips' hand shook so much he could not manage the glass he tried to lift to his lips, and he had to put it down.

Through the uproar and in response to the whoops and cheers she retained her gentle smile until a couple of overweening youngsters pushed forward for a closer appraisal. It was then that the true function of the giant Turk was apparent. He swept them back with a thrust of his body, then proffered the cape. Giving him her knife, she accepted the cloak with the graciousness of a woman about to leave a box at the theater.

Then, bequeathing a comprehensive kiss, she obtained instant silence by a wave of the hand that threw it. "That will be all until I come some day again. Now, wine for me: brandy for my friends."

Taking for granted that the last part of her imperial edict would be somehow obeyed she moved forward. She appeared to be heading for us, and Philips was convinced that she was.

"Ah," he said, clambering not too steadily to his feet and snatching back an empty chair, "this is an honor."

"Honors go to seekers only sometimes," she said coolly and walked past us.

I was trying to feign I hadn't heard, but others had a more robust reaction. White-faced, my companion caught up his hat and cane, tossed some money on the table and fled from their laughter.

I gazed after him, quizzically perplexed. He wouldn't want any company, least of all mine just then. That I regretted, for in addition to being a pleasant fellow when sober he was my first Mississippi associate. Now it seemed that the good-natured insolence with which he had entered my life was matched by an exodus no less abrupt.

The fact I had turned to watch him permitted me to observe without staring that the entertainer had seated herself at the table just behind me. Of the two men, her new companions, one was a sandy-haired, freckled-faced young fellow, squint-eyed with excited good humor. The other had a tomahawk face lifted from coldness by a humorous scroll of mouth.

At the moment the latter was in the act of sitting after acknowledging her arrival, the mixed look of courteous welcome and astonishment still on his face. She settled herself composedly.

"Only wine: nothing to eat," she said as matter-of-factly as if she had been invited. "I pick you two because I like your faces best."

Looking about me, I decided I did also. Then my interest in the matter lapsed as I caught the waiter's eye and magnanimously assured him that Philips' change was his alone. I didn't know how I was going to thread my way up the bluff, but the time had come to make the effort.

It was a close fit easing my way by the woman's chair. I had just accomplished the maneuver without jarring her when I heard her speak.

"I'm sorry I drive the hopeful man your friend away. You sit with us."

Nonplussed, I halted. She was looking at me with bright interest, and I was not so little of a man as to ignore the fact. The light-haired fellow was oozing mirth at the seams as before, seemingly overjoyed at my embarrassment. Yet it was at his companion that I looked most searchingly. He brushed aside a dark lock trailing athwart a tanned cliff of forehead.

"I've seen you in worse company," he offered tentatively.

"The lady excepted, I wouldn't be sure," I told him. In spite of the attraction I instinctively felt, it was no part of his business to criticize my associates.

"Well, the lady asked you to sit down, though I don't know why, so we'll have to put up with you." He grinned, and as I took the indicated chair I smiled guardedly back at him. I was still moving as carefully as circumstances would permit, and I was still so strange I didn't know the precise value of words.

The countess, however, was not passing over any reference to herself. "I ask him to sit," she said calmly, "because I like his face even though he look at me like through a window."

Startled at her observation, I flushed. "Even so, it was delightful," I managed.

"Of course." The wine was put before her, and her eyes looked at me over it as she sipped. "You do not know these men, Mr. Dudley and Mr. McConnell?"

"I don't know anyone here," I answered, but at the same time I put one hand flat on the table as if marking a place. Though she hadn't said which was which I thought I knew. There could be other McConnells in Natchez, but it seemed likely this was the man to whom Harry Pace had advised me to present myself. Not for an instant did I think he could be other than the saturnine, dark-haired man.

Before the introduction could become a fact there was an inter-lude. Some of the patrons had already left, but of those who remained at least one was still hopeful of sharing the singer's company. With a harvest moon flush to his fairness he lurched over and obtruded himself between her and the man I had decided must be Dudley. Putting a hand on the chair of each, he bowed his broad shoulders so that his face was almost at eye level with ours. He was the bearer of good tidings and forthwith delivered.

"I'm going to join you."

Of a sudden Dudley looked as if he had never been good-humored in his life. "Go where you're wanted, if there is such a place."

The mood of the intruder changed with equal speed, but his theme was a constant. "I'm going to join you," he reiterated, domineeringly this time. "Or—" he fumbled for a suitable threat and finally found it, "or if that isn't all right she and I won't stay with you."

His hand had closed over her wrist, preparatory to dragging her away when McConnell cuffed him. He staggered back, sputtering, dismayed but not for long. A second later he was struggling to produce a little snub-nosed pistol that wouldn't quite slide free of his sleeve.

McConnell watched his efforts over the much more businesslike weapon he himself had drawn. "Take it, Larry," he said finally.

With the swift, careful movements of experience his friend did so and drew the cap. "Go on home, Vickers," he ordered.

Vickers was furious, outraged at the turn of events, and largely unafraid. Uppermost in his mind was the drunkard's unilateral code of justice.

"I was being friendly and he hit me. I'm not going home before I challenge McConnell to a duel."

"You did, we had it, and you lost," the man behind the gun spoke up. "Do you want to get shot, too?"

"Well, I want a fair chance," said the one who previously hadn't thought the fact that he was going to draw a pistol worth mentioning. "You hit me, and I'm going to challenge you. If you don't accept," we could see him striving for an adequate punishment, "I'm going to put it in the *Natchez Gazette*. You'll be the laughingstock of Mississippi."

"The competition's pretty sharp," McConnell observed mildly, albeit keeping his gun leveled. "You go home, Vickers, and if your wife will let you challenge me after you've slept it off I'll put a bullet through you with all due formalities. But if you don't get the devil out of here now I'm going to ask the countess to look the other way and plug you where you stand."

Vickers shifted from one foot to the other uncertainly. "All right," he muttered at last, "If you haven't left town in the morning my seconds will call on you."

When he'd left, the woman set her glass down and watched McConnell put his pistol away. "I do not see you shoot an unarmed man," she observed.

He gulped his whiskey and winked at her. "And I do not see you turn your head while the shooting's going on."

They were intent on each other, and I had almost decided she was going to resent his directness when she smiled slightly. "No." She dipped a finger in her wine and popped it into her mouth. "I do not refuse to see what life has for me," she said when she'd removed it.

Dudley was turning from signalling the waiter, but this wasn't meant for his ears, or mine either. McConnell leaned forward slowly. His glance darted first at me, then at Dudley, who was now deliberately looking elsewhere. It was not only a certain amount of self-consciousness that reddened his face. Out of the one eye toward him I could see a temple vein swell. His voice was offhand enough, however.

"Perhaps I can see you to your door?"

She was wide-eyed with surprise. "Oh, but I couldn't take you away from your friends."

Dudley snickered, and I busied myself with a cigar I didn't want. "We'll send somebody to look after them," McConnell said tightly.

She rose and ran a hand caressingly through Dudley's hair. "Soon he have somebody to look after him. I know."

Whatever she guessed it made him squirm, and she turned for a shot at me. I had my own sufficiently costly armor, and as our eyes met she shook her head.

"No words for deaf men," she said without rancor. "Good-bye to

all but you," she concluded, looking at McConnell. "I walk past
when ready."

"Who do you think she is?" Dudley asked when she was gone.
"A real countess, do you reckon?"

"Well," McConnell answered, "Mississippi has everything else
from cholera to cape jessamine. There's no reason for leaving countesses off the list, and as a matter of fact we haven't. We get them
through here every now and then whenever there's trouble in some
foreign country. Of course, some of them wear more clothes."

"Yes, but I thought countesses were supposed to have wads of
money." Dudley's knowledge of the peerage was about as nebulous
as my own.

"Only the stay-at-homes. Those they export have to scratch.
Being a native son," McConnell went on, albeit keeping his eyes on
the door through which the singer had passed, "you don't understand that the exile's severest grief is that nobody will pay for his
meals. I was horrified by the discovery when I left my boyhood
paradise in Georgia and perhaps you could get verification from
our Virginia friend here."

He glanced at me inquiringly. "Godolphin," I said.

Having already mentally named them I was not surprised when
he waved a hand toward his companion with the words: "That's
Larry Dudley. I'm Tom McConnell."

I bowed acknowledgement with a ceremoniousness that was
partly of the Old Dominion and partly of old spiritus frumenti. I
was pleased at the revelation I was about to make, and perhaps
turned it into something of a pronouncement.

"It's a lucky coincidence that I should have met you thus unex-
pectedly and this soon after my arrival, Mr. McConnell. Just before
I left Virginia, I had the good fortune to meet a great admirer of
yours: Mr. Harry Pace."

To my chagrin he merely pursed his lips. "I never heard of him."

I looked at Dudley, but his face was equally blank. They all but
had me convinced when I suddenly took cognizance of my new en-
vironment. "Well, he knew about you," I struck out boldly.

"Has my fame reached so far?" he wondered.

"Yes," I nodded. "He said you were the ugliest reproduction of the image of God that ever played thimblerig with a blind man, stole a nigger's mule, fed shot to a bantam, took sugar from a baby, pinched a soldier's widow, or lied to a stranger."

I was half heated when I had finished. He'd brought it on himself, and he could fight or laugh; I didn't care which. McConnell, however, did neither.

"I remember him now," he said gravely. "How is Harry?"

Before I could answer, the countess, as she had promised, started walking past. He kicked back his chair.

"I'll meet you at the theater Saturday."

CHAPTER VII

NATCHEZ-ON-THE-BLUFF was as different from Natchez-under-the-Hill as Pace had indicated. It was a clean, energetic little city, the financial capital of a preposterously fertile new country. Yet it was not of itself a frontier town. There could be nothing smelling of raw stumps about a community where exiles from three great European countries had successively thriven for nearly a hundred years before Jefferson's purchase. France's ruined fort was there; so were the sweeping balustrades of colonial Spain and the red brick of manorial Britain.

Many of the new homes were similar fortresses of domesticity snugged away in the live oaks and chinaberry trees, which also stretched their long arms over the hustling business section. Countless fall blossoms were a pervasive charm, including orange blossoms like giant fireflies in the sombre foliage.

The air was at once douce and lively as only autumn air in the South can be; for the bottomland reek didn't rise to the bluffs. I walked gingerly in this freshness as a man will who has looked too long at the lights of the night before. Yet I enjoyed my rambling tour, viewed the city with possessive satisfaction and observed its inhabitants with a neophyte's interest. They were a mixed lot as to condition, dress and color, but a community takes its tone from the positive spirits regnant. Here aggressive cockiness was fostered by a quorum who felt that nothing was beyond their reach.

This was all very pleasant, but my vanishing resources insisted that I decide upon some line of action. For a starter I adopted the one requiring the least initiative. The paper on which my cousin Edward had written still reposed in a coat I'd left at Spring Hill, but I hadn't forgotten the name—Henry Artenay.

His residence was on the outskirts of town, a white, wooden

mansion of precise lines. The tree-shaded sward around it met the horizon at the bluff, though a summerhouse on the brink commanded a view of the great river and the Louisiana wilderness beyond. It was toward this lookout that I was directed by the door's black warden.

Mr. Artenay, I was glad to find, was the only occupant. A letter is flimsy human liaison, and the letter Edward said he had written him was the only pretext I had for presuming on this man's time. I didn't want his attention engrossed by people of more interest to him. However, when he closed the book on his finger and looked up at the sound of my footsteps I had a pleasant surprise. He was no less a person than the eminent river jurist, the presiding judge of the court of trifling equity and vain appeal.

He didn't recognize me, though he did recall that he had seen me before. As he put his volume down and rose I could see him trying to reach for my name. Just as I crossed the threshold he gave up with a disarming smile.

"I'm sorry, sir, but it's my cross to be able to recall the names of dull people only." In the act of extending a hand he drew it back and smote his brow. "It's my state's witness."

"Yes, sir," I said, relieved that he had finally placed me. "My excuse for intruding is a note, which I hope you've received from my cousin, Edward Godolphin."

"No friend of impartial justice is a trespasser on my time," he smilingly assured me. "Yes, I got it and I've been expecting you. Sit down, please. I don't think Persius will fail us."

Casting an eye at the tawny sweep of river and at the forest beyond, that ended only with the curve of the earth, I obeyed. "Your cousin and I have had some pleasant correspondence in the course of our business relations," my host was observing. "I'm sorry I don't know him."

I was wishing I knew Edward, too, for no better reason than that it would give me some insight as to what he might have written about me. It made me feel rather foolish to be weighed against a scrap of unknown message.

"Let me see, as a client he has empowered me to honor a draft upon him up to five hundred dollars," Artenay said. He looked at me to see if this was news.

He must have been aware, as I was, of the dubious implications. If a man really wanted another to have some money he wouldn't have to offer it at a thousand miles' remove. I flushed.

"I don't want it," I said stiffly. Then I threw my pride an extra sop. "After all I spent a good part of that sum en route. Didn't he mention that I was coming out here to make my way?"

"Yes," he agreed, looking at me with bright interest, "but he said nothing about your plans."

"I have no plans," I said, abruptly descending from my high horse. "I just came here because I wasn't getting along where I was." Yet in making my blunt admission I could not help but wax a little defiant.

Throughout my own changes of mood he had remained soothingly unmoved. "There's a local proverb to the effect that if you can't make a living in Mississippi you can always shoot yourself or go to Texas. However, neither desperate measure should be necessary."

"I'd greatly appreciate any advice you could give me, sir." I was anxious for the particulars of action. "Is Natchez the place?"

He naturally felt none of my urgency. "I can answer that better over Persius' oil of philosophy. I knew he wouldn't fail us."

Either I had arrived at the right hour or a guest was always his cupbearer's signal. In any case Persius Africanus was nearly upon us, soundly freighted with whiskey, cold water, and glasses. The liquor, I was grateful to discover, was grain's own holy ghost.

My host stretched out his legs after the salute and the first ceremonial swallow. "You or anybody who can keep one lesson ahead of an obstreperous brat or calculate the price of a bale of cotton can always find employment in Natchez," he told me by way of resuming our discussion. "What do you want?"

I shrugged and spread out my empty hand. "I want what there is."

He seemed to understand. "In general here there is room on top only for men in special categories or for men who bring success with them. As compared with the rest of the state this is a settled community with the cream allotted." He began to take on the warmth of excitement all Mississippians seemed to feel when contemplating the infinities of their state. "I've established my mode of living, and I like what I've established, but if I were younger than I am I'd leave because I couldn't bear not to. There's more than half of Mississippi open for man's creation, and I would have to make sure that some part of it quickened to my arrogance."

He chopped the air with the side of his free hand. "Where you bring down a bear you blaze to mark the spot. I'll build a town there, you will say. Then you will take the empty map, locate the spot and write: 'Godolphin's Kill.' Do you see?"

I saw as I had not when Edward had talked to me, or even Harry Pace. Artenay had momentarily succeeded in transferring his imagination, and I knew a nameless exaltation. "Just anywhere?" I demanded.

"Within limits, but almost everywhere north of the Big Black. Half of the territory that should be ours is in the hands of two sovereign nations and therefore not actually in the United States at all. It is Choctawland and Chicasawland. But this year—you've probably heard of it—there was the Treaty of Dancing Rabbit Creek."

My cousin had referred to some prospective treaty, but that name! "There couldn't be!" I breathed.

"But there was!" he insisted triumphantly, flourishing his glass. "Never since Runnymede have politics so served poetry. Of course, they also served the state."

"And what were the terms?"

"The Choctaws, who have the major holdings, were given the choice of leaving under the terms of the treaty—or leaving."

I examined this statement. "I take it that they didn't want to go, and yet it was intolerable that they stay."

"More than intolerable!" he cried. "A denial of reality. Are they going to be allowed to maintain an alien civilization, never advanced and now rotten, within the very bounds of the state? Not if we can help it, and we can help it. Those morally opposed to the treaty, and they are in some numbers, are either residents of another state or already well seized of land in this." He put down his glass. "The elect have not yet grown so coldly logical that

[68]

they're willing to shed the profits of ancestral thieving and return to Europe."

Up to that moment I had scarcely heard of the Choctaws, but John Barleycorn can expand the heart to embrace most of creation. "Of course, it's pretty hard on the Indians," I murmured.

"The question is not whether it's hard on them, but what's going to happen," he said briskly. "It's hard on a cow to be a beefsteak, and that it's not hard on a potato to be boiled is only our side of the story. It hurts my wife to bear the children I joyously engender. But will I stop? Not I! For all I know trees may flinch at the axe and iron weep at being burnt from the rock it nests in." He snapped his fingers. "If we followed some people's advice we wouldn't move our bowels for failure to produce roses."

Though I was interested in his philosophy I was still more interested in finding out what I wanted to know. "Did the Choctaws all agree to just pick up and go?" I asked after a suitable pause for reflection.

"They have till next year to move to their new lands out West. There are decencies even in implacability. And as a matter of fact no individual Indian will be required to leave; it is merely the sovereignty of the Choctaw Nation which has been abolished in Mississippi. Any who care to remain as American citizens can claim a section of land and take their chances of survival with the rest of us."

He grasped a lock of his grey hair and held it out disparagingly for my inspection. "It will be one of the mightiest wrestlings for land since Caesar opened Gaul, and if it weren't for this I'd be in it and come out with my share. But that's where you belong. Are you a bachelor?"

"Yes, sir," I nodded.

"Fine! It's a battle for prime stags, a thing like that, with their thwarted rutting lust to drive them."

Again I sucked in some of his excitement, but I had a monstrous fault to find. "But that won't be until next year!" I was at once concerned with the practical problem of survival and aghast at the inertness of time. "What could I do till then?"

He smiled as Chiron might have when his charges grew restive.

"Half of the men in Mississippi are marking time, waiting for the new country to open. Yes, and a good few of the women. Every other man is trying to meet someone who is useful or who knows somebody who might be useful in helping them to grab off the best lands. Step among them and claim you know a Choctaw mingo or that you once got drunk with an Indian agent and dozens will fawn upon you."

He turned and swung his hand with him to indicate north by east. "Jackson is crowded with those intent on suborning members of the government into recognizing premature claims to vague and unvisited tracts."

His tone told me that neither course had his approbation, so I refrained from comment. "If my sons weren't serving their country in the Army and at Washington," he said as his eyes fixed me, "I would urge them to go in there now, find what they want, and take hold, ready to fight it out with Coke, Littleton and pistol when the time comes to establish legal tenure. In their absence you're welcome to the advice."

Notwithstanding the manner in which I had let my own heritage slip from me, the lust to possess land was a basic Godolphin ingredient not omitted from my own make-up. The vision of myself cruising over a vast countryside appraising tracts and claiming at last the most desirable of all was overwhelming.

"There is still the matter of keeping alive," I murmured, staring into the future as if I was already confronting a wilderness. "What can I find to hold me together in—just where is this country anyhow, and what do they call it?"

"Choctawland—the New Purchase; up the wild Yazoo from the Old Purchase. You'll live on the standard woodsman's bill of fare: bear meat, whiskey and corn meal. You'll need a rifle, a knife, a blanket, and a frying pan. You won't need a razor, and you can get along without a horse; but a hunting dog is a key to survival—and I'll give you one." Pleased with this inspiration, Artenay rose. "He's only a year old, but if I'm any judge he has the right nose to go with prime teeth and wind. Let's take a look at him."

The animal he showed me when we strolled over to a little village of kennels behind the carriage house was obviously born to war with something bigger than foxes. There was hound in him, as testified by the lean waist and cabbage-leaf ears; but he had jaws and shoulders too heavy for that following breed. He was a gripper as well as a finder, and already had a battle seam or so on his tawny pelt. I admired him as he stretched his chain to meet Artenay's caresses, but I kept my hands in my pockets to avoid any show of possessiveness.

"His name's Talisman," my host said. "He'll stand up to a coon, and he hasn't grown up to his feet yet. Do you want him?"

I did, but I was still unwilling to be stampeded. After all, urgent though the necessity of making decisions was, I had been in Mississippi hardly more than twenty-four hours. "Sir, that's mighty fine of you," I assured him, "but my plans are still in the egg. Could I defer acceptance awhile?"

He gave the dog's extended throat a final rub. "Certainly. Although you can only have him if you're bound for the Yazoo. He's ripe for adventure, and has more weight than we need for our hunting here. Now let's have one more appetizer and see what's on the board."

Artenay's Ledge was the house of a man who could afford to indulge his wife's sound taste in luxurious living. Mrs. Artenay proved as pleasant as the house she had created, and the others there assembled completed an enjoyable gathering. In chief these included young Corinna Artenay and a couple of yearlings she was putting through their paces. It made for plenty of laughter to go with the wild turkey and wine.

After the youngsters had paid fidgeting respect to the port and had escaped to Corinna, Artenay and I retired to his study. The brandy encouraged the conversation and the conversation encouraged the brandy, so that I needed no encouraging at all to spend the night. After he'd gone to work a ride finished what was left of the next morning. Then following the nap brought on by dinner I sauntered back to town.

It was the hour for promenading in the little park that had once been the parade ground of the old French fort. Watching the damsels sweep by in their parasol-shaded elegance it was startling for me to remember that the moil of Natchez Underhill was only a few hundred feet away. An acoustical dispensation, however, kept all but occasional smothered sounds from ascending out of the pit. Nor, except by crossing the parapet and stepping to the brink, could anyone see what was going on in the lap of the river.

As a visitant of both communities, I was interested to see how many men I recognized from two nights before. Among them was Larry Dudley, mincing along with his neck at a fixed angle, gazing down at a dew blossom of a brunette. He looked up as I was passing them, his beseeching eyes paralyzing my hand as I was in the act of raising it to my hat.

"Go and transgress no more, sinner," I grinned to myself, though in truth, from what I had seen, Dudley's conduct had been innocent enough. Still it was undeniable that the best way to avoid being seen in a place is not to go there.

There was no danger of my forgetting my appointment, for promenade chatter was largely concerned with the troupe that had just arrived from New Orleans to inaugurate a week of dramatic variety. When McConnell had offhandedly volunteered to meet me at the theater I had been astonished, but conversation indicated that formal drama was here no novelty. For my purposes what was playing was not a decisive factor, in as much as I was committed to attend, but it seemed that *Lear* was scheduled for that night.

The theater, I found when I got there, was a neat, suitably designed edifice; but for reasons clear, perhaps, to its founders it roosted in an abandoned potter's field. By the time I'd walked around it and read all the bills concerning coming attractions others began to arrive. Leaning against a tree, I looked them over.

Some came afoot. The women entered the building; the men gathered in groups outside to whittle with long knives, argue, swap news, and spit sophisticatedly. More were riders either on horses or behind them. They dashed up, flung themselves off, tethered their mounts with a flourish, and slapped their boots with whips as they strode to hail each other. They rode in brightly painted coaches and were helped to alight by darky footmen or by the horsemen who ambled beside them. Corinna had two such servitors though I did not recognize in them either of my young acquaintances of the night before.

The announcement that the play was about to begin had long drawn everybody else inside when McConnell came briskly striding across fields through the gloom. As he drew near he kicked something out of the grass which skittered along and caromed off my foot. I saw it was a skull from some rain-discovered grave and booted it back to cover.

"Good evening," I said.

He snapped the broad brim of his hat with one forefinger. "My horse threw a shoe, and I had to walk him in," he explained. "Sorry I've made us late."

Within, the players had been involved with Lear's domestic troubles for more than one act. "Mean lot of kinfolks," I heard one man say as we shuffled out when the curtain again descended.

"Meaner'n an angel on his night off," his neighbor agreed. "But that Kent looks like the real grit to me. I don't think he'll sit still for it much longer."

We lit our cigars at a convenient candle and walked forth to stand in the sallow glow of the lanterns beside the door. "You met Pace in Virginia, and he asked you to look me up," my companion said by way of an opening. "Did he add why?"

"We had a whiskey introduction in a stage coach," I said diffidently. "Maybe he was just making conversation."

"Harry doesn't need to make conversation any more than grasshoppers have to practice hopping. He must have meant it."

Seeing no way to make what I had to say sound well, I just came out with it. "To cut it short, we discussed the fact that I was going to Mississippi without money, friends or prospects. I was grateful for his suggestion that I get in touch with you. If you in turn have any suggestions I'll be grateful for them."

He nodded, neither offering help nor disclaiming the possibility that he could give some. For the time being we left it at that and soon filed back into the theater. There, to the audience's great delight, it was proved that Kent was indeed of the real grit. The enthusiasm reached its climax when he made his stirring declaration of defiance. One long farmer whooped, sprang to his feet and looked around challengingly. "By God! I'm for him, and anybody who ain't for givin' him a fair chance has got me to whip!" The audience cheered his manly sentiments, he waved to them, sat down, and the play went on.

Coffee was served in the lounge by some of the ladies following the third act. As we mingled in the gathering we passed Corinna, who addressed us both by name. McConnell looked at me enquiringly. "For a man who knew nobody when he arrived you seem to be picking up quite an acquaintance."

"I had a letter of introduction to her father and called yesterday to ask him about the same thing I'm asking you."

"Old Artenay?" His look of interest was enough to establish that gentleman's local standing. "What did he have to say?"

We had edged away from the serving table and were working over to a relatively uncrowded spot by the door. Before I could answer him a young man, well turned out except for a puffed eye and a torn collar, sprang into the room. "Gentlemen," he announced with controlled excitement, "the river's rising!"

A couple of women shrieked, and as if by signal all the younger men put their cups down. It didn't make any sense to me. Even had it been the season for floods, no deluge since the one that made a seafaring man out of Noah could bring the Mississippi up to those heights. By the time I had got so far in my reasoning I was shoved out the door by the pressure of hurrying men. McConnell was strides ahead of me and gathering momentum.

Still ridiculously balancing my cup, I spurted to catch up with him. "What's happening?" I demanded. "What does he mean?"

Others were dashing for their horses or pounding pell-mell toward the center of town. If there were any sounds of disturbance from that direction, however, they were drowned out by the ominous pealing of church bells. McConnell was moving swiftly but not running, as if holding his strength for action upon arrival. "The scum's washing over the bluff and looting the town," he said curtly. "Happens every now and then. You coming?"

CHAPTER VIII

HOWEVER ONE MAY sit at ease with debauchery, it must be made to stay on its assigned reservations. Natchez Underhill should not rule the bluff, and being sure of so much I could not stay aloof while others acted. I tossed the cup somewhere to add its fragments to the potter's field bric-à-brac. "Yes," I said.

Under the chinaberry trees the night was almost opaque to hurrying men, though we could see glints of light from houses deep in the shrubbery. If McConnell hadn't touched my arm I might not have known just where he slipped between the hedges down a narrow path.

The church in front of us was in silhouette against the clear autumnal stars. A smaller building loomed above the pale cluster of gravestones. Here where it was possible to discern shape and size, I could see men moving about or waiting in groups beneath the belfry whence the tocsin still sounded.

My companion stopped a little before we reached them, and, although new arrivals passed us, there we remained. I didn't see how any counsel could be taken while those bells outraged the air above us, and after a little the same thought must have occurred to the ringer. The tolling slowed. Then the bell clanged once more and hushed.

"McConnell speaking; who's here?" the man beside me demanded.

"Ransom hasn't come yet," someone answered. "I reckon you're in charge."

"Dudley?"

"Here, Tom."

"Give me your horse. You wait here for late-comers and take them to the parade at the head of the Underhill road. You know what to do when we drive 'em toward you. They'll be down among the stores now. The rest of us will swing around to the other side of town and hit 'em from there." Just before he left he remembered me. "You're not mounted so you'd better stay with Dudley."

Notwithstanding its informality here was some sort of military organization. My soldier's training came back upon me as I recognized I'd been given an order. "Yes, sir," I said.

Excitement made Dudley forget how he had passed by unspeaking at our last encounter. "Glad to see you, Godolphin," he said when he and I were alone. "Go over to the sexton's shed there and pick yourself out a club."

After fumbling around in the shack I had noticed, I selected a well-balanced bludgeon and rejoined him. "That's better in a brawl than almost anything," he remarked, adding: "And don't be shy about using it. If you let one of them come to grips with you they'll put their thumbs where your eyes used to be and tooth-tear you like the wild dogs they are."

I had seen enough of Underhill to know he was speaking literally. "Right," I grunted.

On the whole I was startled as much by the matter-of-fact attitude toward the attempt to sack the town as by the eruption of brutality itself. For all its settled appearance and contrary to my first conception, Natchez was a frontier city and took frontier emergencies for granted.

"What gets them started?" I asked.

"Oh, Underhill's like a boil. It swells up and busts from its own poison every now and then: but from outside you can't tell just why or when it's likely to happen. Sometimes it's because a few of them are ordered off the bluff for misbehavior and preach a holy war. Sometimes a heavy faro loser starts it to get something he can sell for a quick stake. Or sometimes a mudcat Napoleon just thinks Natchez-on-the-Bluff is too rich and too handy to be overlooked. It takes a leader to whip 'em to it, but every now and then one happens along."

In the course of the next few minutes a half-dozen men joined us. "We could use more," Dudley said, "but it's time for us to be where we're needed. Let's move."

It was not far to the parade. The little park that had been filled with chattering promenaders during the early evening was now occupied only by vast trees. On the near side of it was a street lamp marking where the road dipped steeply down from the bluff. Crossing the pool of light it cast, we waited in the flood of shadow beyond. Anybody making a retreat down the road could thence be ambushed at the moment of their greatest vulnerability.

"I've helped drive 'em, but I've never been on this end before," a man whispered as we leaned against the parapet. "Just what do we do here?"

"We see that any small groups don't get past with their loot. When the main party comes we take 'em in the rear just when they get crowded to the edge of the bluff. If we can we'll take a prisoner or so for trial and example."

"Have you ever failed to smash them?" I enquired.

"No, and we won't this time," Dudley said with conviction. "If they tried to beat us first and then began their thieving they might get along better, but it's in their nature to do things the other way around. I remember once when we couldn't muster very many because it was summer and a lot were out of town——"

He stopped as angry shouting was borne to us. "It's started," someone remarked unnecessarily. "The first of them ought to be along shortly."

This turned out to be an accurate prediction. Staring fixedly, I thought I saw a mass detaching itself from the darkness. I wasn't sure enough to cry out, but Dudley had hunter's eyes for the night. "Four—six—maybe ten," he whispered. "Get ready to hit 'em!"

They were coming briskly but not pushing themselves, seeing that nobody was crowding them. We could hear them talking as we crouched to await them. "Let them damn fools do the fightin'," one chortled. "We got what we want."

"Sure, the hell with that business of throwing everything together and splittin' it even," another rejoined. "You can't tell what you'll get."

When they were under the street lamp, blinking, we took them on the flank out of the darkness. It is said of monkeys that if what they seize makes for a larger fist than the hole through which they thrust a paw they will let themselves be caught rather than surrender the prize. So it was with these astonished despoilers. Magpie greed had loaded them to the staggering point, and they could not immediately bring themselves to put their treasures down.

As I bore down on the man I'd picked out, I noted that his stance was a comic betrayal of indecision. Among other things he had in his arms a fair-sized statuette of Psyche. His was a perilous love of beauty. Still clasping Psyche, he was belatedly trying to flee when I pounced. My medical training guided me as to where and just how hard to hit him without fracturing his skull. With a groan he fell and Psyche dropped from his relaxed arms.

By that time I sensed somebody so close upon my back that I dared not turn promptly. Without stopping I leapt over my victim and took three great strides before I whirled. Even so, my pursuer was pressing me so hard that he brushed me as I side-stepped, knocking me off balance. The contact did the same to him, however, and by the time he'd recovered I, too, was on my guard.

He had disencumbered himself of his loot but not of the lengthy knife for which I found him chiefly remarkable. It dangled at the end of his arm, quietly ready as a poised snake.

I wanted to reach inside my coat for my pistol, which I'd carried ever since my night in Underhill, but I was afraid that it might be the signal for his spring. I backed slowly, holding my bludgeon poised while he crept after me. Handy as a club is in a melee, it is a clumsy duelling weapon, and we both knew it.

This stalemate was fortunately broken in my favor when Dudley came up behind my antagonist and felled him with a rap. The broil, as I then had leisure to see, was ended. Several of the thieves were dropping hastily down the Underhill road. Two or three others were fleeing back toward town. Peering around for Psyche's ravisher I saw him rise and stumble weakly into the clutches of two of our party. When our group recrystallized I found that we had four captives all told.

"The others won't have much but bruises to show for this raid," Dudley said with satisfaction. "Any of us hurt?"

"Ogilvie's got a slashed hand,"

"And the one who gave it to me has a broken arm," growled a

man with a handkerchief wrapped around one fist. "Who's got whiskey?"

That sounded to me like the voice of fatuous optimism, but three flasks were instantly proffered. Yet again I was wrong when I looked for him to use it as a disinfectant.

"Make the ones we've bagged lie down by the parapet and shoot 'em if they move," Dudley ordered. "You watch them, Ogilvie: you can do that without banging that wound around." He stood looking in the direction of town and listening. "They've quieted down, but somebody's coming. Duck back where we were until we see what's what."

In a minute a mounted man trotted up. "Larry?" It was McConnell's voice.

"What's happened, Tom? Did you eat 'em all up?"

"We didn't find enough to satisfy a medium-sized mouse." The light words notwithstanding, McConnell sounded puzzled and nettled. "How many came this way?"

"Nine or ten since we've been watching."

"Well, we only found about fifteen or twenty, but I'm told there were about a hundred to begin with. That's sixty or seventy unaccounted for."

"Where else could they go?" someone wondered.

"Well, they could duck down between or through the buildings and out into the country, then filter back when we went scouring for them. Ransom's in charge now and that's what he's done—broken us down into parties and scattered us down all roads."

"But suppose they did file back?"

"That's what I suggested," McConnell growled. "Ransom's a canny cotton broker—and a fidgeting, gnat-brained damned fool. The others didn't have sense enough to wait and do nothing either. It feels much more important to be riding fast. Anyhow I begged off on the pretext of seeing how you were making out."

"They're bound to be heading for this road sooner or later," Dudley declared.

"Isn't there any other road down?" I spoke up for the first time.

"Not to Underhill, and if they did get down to the bottoms up or down stream a ways there's no route along the river."

In addition to items that are remembered for a purpose or because of their intrinsic power there is a sort of turgid stew of memory into which most things are promptly absorbed. Sometimes, though, an identifiable object floats whole on the surface at the one instant of a man's life he can use it. I picked one out now, knowing I had something, but not sure of its worth.

There was no reason why I should have recalled a specific sentence from the conversation of the men we had ambushed. I had not been consciously listening to them, had only been interested in the fact they were coming. Yet this tag stayed with me.

"One of those we encountered said he didn't want to meet with the others to pool his loot."

"I'd forgotten that!" Dudley snapped his fingers. "A rendezvous! But how would they get back, especially loaded with junk?"

"If they don't plan to come through here they've got to use the river," McConnell said slowly. "Got any prisoners, Larry?"

"None we're very proud of, but a few."

"Ransom couldn't be bothered to hold his horses when I suggested it to him, but let's try a little duress on them. One at a time."

We selected the most unhappy looking and took him aside. "You'd better believe what I'm saying," McConnell told him coldly. "I'll have you hanged if you keep silent and let you go if you talk."

"I reckon you'd just as soon kill me," the fellow went halfway with him.

"You can believe the other, too, or keep your mouth closed until a rope on your windpipe pops it open for good. Tell us where the others went, how they're getting back to Underhill, and, if by river, where they're landing."

It was not to be expected that such men, especially in view of the fact they had refused to cooperate with their peers, would prefer a show of staunchness to life and well-being. Once he did begin to talk the rogue found he could derive some relish from what he had to say. "They got you beat this time. They're cuttin' across fields to some place a ways up river where they've got some rafts hid. Then they'll just load up and ride down till they see a couple of big fires at the lower end of Underhill spit."

I nodded at that last point. Even I knew that landing at night

THE WILD YAZOO

was something that couldn't be done on that river unless a craft was somehow guided into slack water.

"Whose idea was it?" the questioning went on.

"Well, I don't reckon he thought of it, because he ain't got no more brains than I have; but Rufe Doanes was the one that told us."

"Ransom and his damned midnight cavaliers! I hope they enjoy the ride!" McConnell cursed disgustedly. "All right, Larry, you can go back to your young lady now. Tell everybody at the theater that the streets and the roads are safe."

"What about the prisoners?"

"Have somebody lock 'em up along with the ones we caught in town. We'll boot this fellow off the bluff in the morning and hold the others for trial."

When the rest had gone he slouched over to the parapet and hoisted himself up. Somewhat uncomfortably I followed him. He didn't act as if he particularly wanted company, but I felt, in view of the fact we had had an appointment, I ought to take some sort of leave. Certainly it was no time to discuss my own affairs, but I hoped he would suggest another meeting.

"We didn't have much of an evening," he observed in a flat, weary voice.

"Is it too late to do anything?"

"Oh, hell—they've got our hides nailed to the door. We can't storm Underhill with the few men left, and by the time Ransom and the others get back they'll have split the swag and gone their ways rejoicing." He slapped the stone wall with his bare hand. "The worst of it is, not that we let them make fools of us, but that they'll be encouraged to try it soon again. They've never outsmarted us before."

In the silence that ensued it occurred to me that his words held the key to something that could be done. "A man or two can often go where a party in force cannot," I murmured tentatively. "If we could locate the beacons that riverman mentioned we could see who gets off the raft—and who meets it. Then we'd at least know whose doing this was."

"By God, you're right!" he acknowledged. He jumped to the

ground. "And once we know who the leaders are we can find some way of grabbing them."

I wasn't as sincere as he was, yet I was more purposeful. Within limits I was partisan to the cause of Natchez City, but I was also intent, now that I saw the chance, of enlisting this man's good will. "I think it might be wiser for me to go alone." And as a matter of fact I did think so. "You're well known to a lot of them there, whereas they don't know me from King Lear."

He chuckled delightedly. "I was thinking of trying my own hand at disguise, but you're the man with the idea. It's no time for amateurism; let's see what our theatrical friends can supply. As their patrons have just left they'll probably still be there."

We found the manager supervising the dismantling of the stage and McConnell made his request with the directness I had come to see was habitual. "If we don't bring your costumes back it'll be because we're being buried in them," he finished with a gustiness I found a little gruesome. "Have you got anything we can use?"

I had expected a reluctant, clausal acceptance if any at all; but McConnell expected hearty cooperation, and he got it. The manager, in fact, seemed delighted with this chance to put his professional knowledge to new and strange uses.

"I can make you look like anything you want." He was guiding us backstage as he made this boast, wagging his pointed beard first at one then the other, and patting his bald head. "For instance, I could make one of you resemble a tree in which lovers couldn't resist carving their names, or I could turn both of you into such a horse that sparrows would hop expectantly in your wake and passing mares would hope from you more than you might be prepared to give."

"We hadn't thought of troubling you for that much magic," I told him. "We'll be content to remain just men if we can be pretty sure of remaining live ones."

CHAPTER IX

WITH THE AID of costumes from *The Bold Frontiersman* the man did an artist's job. McConnell was dressed in a hunting shirt and homespun jeans, neither of which was quite big enough for him, and a limp, broad-brimmed hat. From crumpled beaver to torn boots I looked like an unsuccessful gambler of the lesser sort. The long-haired wig irritated me a little, and I was not used to grease paint, but our features were wonderfully changed.

"Stay outdoors, where you can't be examined too closely and you'll do fine," the manager said with satisfaction while we were admiring ourselves in the mirror. "Do you chew?"

Of course I did at times, like anybody else who has learned the dangers of smoking around stables, and McConnell nodded, too. Working on the tobacco with which he furnished us, we walked through the deserted town and down the Underhill road.

At its foot we found more company than we wanted. A dozen men, one of them holding a lantern that illuminated their rifles and pistols, blocked our way. I had reason to be glad I had not followed my original plan of trusting to the fact I wasn't known there. Doanes, who Philips had declared would try to kill me on sight, was at their head.

"Howdy," McConnell said easily, as we stopped short.

Doanes and the holder of the lantern advanced. In a place like Underhill, always half populated by drifters, there was no reason for him to suspect us just because he didn't know us. But he wasn't in a good humor.

"I bet you were picked up and had all your plunder snatched, too," he said with a mixture of contempt and indignation.

Evidently he was not merely guarding the road against a possible expeditionary force from the bluff. He or someone had been long headed enough to foresee that some of his associate thieves might try just what had been attempted by the party we'd attacked. The fact that he hadn't obtained anything from the others he'd searched had put him on edge.

Habit is as often a matter of blind stupidity as it is of discipline. For no better reason than that it was automatic procedure I had transferred my wallet to my borrowed garments. Now, though I glumly realized I was bound to lose it, I thought it might be possible to get a little good will in exchange.

"We wasn't damn fools like some of 'em, tryin' to grab enough stuff to stock a peddler," I said, attempting to flatten my Tidewater accent. "And as long as we was headed for here not carryin' anythin' they could see, nobody tried to stop us."

The innuendo was sufficient. "Well," he said in a tone of anger withheld, "what did you get then?"

"While he," I rambled, fumbling in my pocket with one hand and jerking the thumb of the other at McConnell, "was sort of attractin' the attention of one of 'em by pokin' him in the eye, I borrowed this."

With the words I handed over my entire worldly fortune. As such it was pitifully small but considered as a purse for the evening it was well enough filled to gladden a robber of reasonable expectations. It was still a possibility that Doanes might have us mauled because we didn't have more or because he felt like it. I waited uneasily while he examined the bills and coins.

"You wouldn't have told me about this if you hadn't had to." His tone was jeering but mollified.

I shrugged. "Would you?"

Meanwhile his companions had searched McConnell and myself also in hopes of further treasure. "They ain't got nothin' only pistols," one announced disappointedly, "except this other one has a black bottle."

Perhaps the fact that we had furnished Doanes with his first profit that night had operated in our favor. "Let 'em keep the whiskey." But before he let us go he disclosed one more reason why he was posted there. "Don't you hosses come around lookin' for your share when we start handin' the stuff out. I'm helpin' split it up, an' I'll know you both."

In my relief at squeezing past our primary hazard I felt at once lighthearted and weak. I gave a shaky chuckle which my companion echoed.

"You didn't throw him a bone any too soon," he said. "If they'd started getting rough they'd have pierced our sham, and once they'd found out who— Let's have a drink on it."

With that he drew forth the flask which Doanes had permitted him to keep. After partaking I sighed to feel my restive nerves join hands again. I drew a long breath. "Does everybody in Mississippi carry one of these?"

"Everybody but a preacher and after the sermon he just borrows one from whoever's handy." He was storing the flask away, still chuckling in a mood of high-spirited reaction. "It's a portable philosopher's stone. Suppose you get treed by a bear, say, or suppose your fiancée swoons. There's nothing you can do about either of those things, you see, but a man's got to have some course of action. So you take a drink. You'd better get one."

"Maybe I will. Do you reckon you can find those beacons?"

"We'll just ease down to the water front and slip south." He started walking toward the river again, and I fell into step beside him.

Underhill was not having a prosperous business evening. Lacking patronage from the bluff and from rivermen alike, most of the establishments were closed and the rest almost empty. Men were scarce, and the idle harlots, lounging in doorways and leaning out windows, speculated on our potentialities without reserve. Opinions ranged from the worshipful to the contemptuous, while one school of thought simply held that we should be returned to the womb for reprocessing.

From this venereal atmosphere we eventually passed, walking by grounded flat boats and squatters' lean-tos until we rounded a shoulder of the bluff. Hugged against it were the beacons, two huge driftwood fires about fifty yards apart. There were a few men idling in the vicinity, so we stopped well short to observe. There were large reserve stocks near each fire, and while we watched a man dragged a log up to one pile, dropped the end he held and joined his colleagues in loafing.

"Come on," McConnell said, turning on his heel. "We ought to be able to find some absent squatter's wood supply." We did after some searching and, loaded with a modest log apiece, plodded toward the beacons once more. Each in turn we tossed our burdens on the nearest stack, grunted dutifully, spat manfully, and shambled through the sand out of range of the heat.

It was somewhat chilly, but we couldn't afford to be conspicuous by remaining closer than the outer orbit. Nobody paid any attention to us as we stretched out, leaning on folded elbows. We could see everything lighted by the fire, but nobody was present save men from whom we were more or less indistinguishable in appearance and pose.

"How long do you think it will be before the raiders get here?" I wondered.

"It depends on where they started, naturally. Not too long, I should say, though rafts can't be hurried."

Unspeaking then we eyed the fires and their other watchers. It was an intimate silence, for we were two alone against whoever else was there or would arrive. The circumstance gave the illusion that we were already of primary importance to one another and made for confidential talk when we spoke again.

"What did old Artenay suggest for you to do?" he asked curiously.

"He wanted me to go into Choctawland, nail down a claim and worry about legal blessing later."

"Did the old brigand advise that?" He seemed interested rather than astonished. "You know, some such scheme is on my own books."

"It is!" For a moment I had hopes of planning a joint expedition. "When are you leaving?"

"Not for a while," he said regretfully. "I've got too many pressing commitments. Young Dudley and I had been counting on going next spring, but I'm just about to forget about that. Matrimony's snaring him, if I know the signs, and I don't think he'll get too far from Natchez."

"That's too bad," I murmured, although Dudley could take a

dozen wives without distressing me. "Where does Harry Pace come in?"

"Harry's a land speculator who controls the sale of God knows how many acres in the Old Choctaw Purchase which haven't been taken up yet. Clearing the Indians from the New Purchase will make his tracts in adjacent territory much more appealing than they have been. The nearness of blanket Indians has badly retarded settlement, partly because the idea is alarming. Then imaginary boundaries do not in the least impress a Choctaw; and he doesn't think a person has any more claim to an unshot cow than he does to an unshot deer. So there's some reason for the skittishness too. In any event Harry reasons his present holdings are sure of sale, but that the price will depend considerably on the development of the valley as a whole. Therefore, he's in the East trying to raise money for even more imperial projects farther up the Yazoo. He'll make a fortune."

This didn't entice me. With a planter's upbringing and instincts I saw land as something to acquire and hold. It seemed rather ridiculous to scheme up ways of getting rid of valuable properties. "Are you and Pace partners, then?"

"Not exactly. He's my client. You see, once when I had a sprained ankle the only book handy was Blackstone. I have dined on its pages, with some help from brag and euchre, ever since."

This surprised me more than it probably should have. After all he had to have some means of livelihood, and the errand on which we were then engaged testified to the need of lawyers.

"Of course, I'm not going into the territory just to look after my client's future interests," he went on a moment later, "for as yet he has none there. But when the scrambling begins it will be a lawyer's happy hunting ground such as never before was provided by the greed of man. Liberal and ill-defined grants were made by every government that pretended to ownership from France on down to my native Georgia. Claims appendix to them will be revived as soon as the country opens. Many of these claims overlap, and the resultant disputes will comprehend assault and murder. If I can survive the business of collecting fees in such a maelstrom I should do well."

THE WILD YAZOO

This that might have interested me at another time I heard forlornly. The more McConnell talked the more difficult it was to see how we could team to the profit of either. Yet my circumstances were such that nothing which might affect my condition could be left unsounded.

"If I go to the Yazoo country," I said doggedly, "I've got to go now. My total funds were in that purse I handed Doanes. I can't afford to mark time, even if I wanted to, which I don't."

In place of commenting he jerked his head to call my attention to a group of new arrivals. It comprised three men of a different stamp from the hangers-on of crime already lounging around the fires. They were gamblers of the lordly faro and blackjack caste, big takers and great spenders. They stood apart when they halted, and nobody saw fit to trespass on their society.

"They're the ones," McConnell whispered. "This raid was planned too well to be the ordinary mob eruption; but there's plenty of misused brains in the gamblers' association."

"Association?"

"They've started a sort of thieves' guild recently. Only the steamer operators and dealers for prosperous houses belong. I've heard of trouble they've caused in smaller towns up and down the river."

"Do you recognize any of them?"

"Two. That little, wizened fellow I never saw before. Man, we've got 'em though; they'll pay, they'll pay." He was grimly delighted and pounded the sand with his fist as he spoke. "They come up to the bluff, that kind. They fancy themselves gentlemen and like to be seen drinking and eating in fashionable taverns. They can't resist showing their fancy clothes on the parade at the promenade hour. We'll pick 'em off like cackling chickens from a hen roost."

The arrival of the gamblers was shortly followed by that of Doanes and the men who had helped him to rob us of our pistols and my money. "They must have some reason to believe the rafts are approaching," I suggested.

"Probably some torch signal," he agreed. "I think I can hear voices on the river now."

Listening carefully, I could, too; then I didn't have to listen carefully. The raiders were near enough to see the men around the

[88]

fire, and a triumphant exchange of shouts was inaugurated. As Mc-Connell had pointed out, rafts can't be hurried; but in a few minutes I heard a sweep churning. Then the first raft, loaded with men holding up the miscellaneous fruits of their thievery, drifted into the patch of water lighted by the beacons.

As the others rushed down to meet them we took advantage of the moment to retreat securely into shadow. We had no wish to watch them gloat over the spoils we so bitterly begrudged them, but with our retreat assured, we watched a moment more. Out of the crowd at that instant stormed a great figure I had last seen striding over the half-breed pickpocket he had stabbed. Now, however, he was in a genial mood.

He must have waded ashore from the raft, for we could see his boots glisten. He was hatless and neither of the arms he raised for attention held the sword cane with which I'd seen him accomplish murder. "Where's Jack Garland?" he yelled in a voice that obliterated all lesser noises. "Hand him out to me!"

When Jack Garland was identified and thrust forward, as directed, he proved to be the little, slim gambler whom McConnell had never seen before. Pouncing on him, the big man hoisted him bodily to perch him on one of his own wide shoulders. "This is the man who had the plan that worked!" the huge gambler roared. "Let's give him a cheer."

With the responding shout of praise ringing sourly in our ears we moved off. "Anyhow," McConnell said, "it won't be a complete defeat, thanks to you."

He was much more pleased with me than I was with myself. All the while we were puffing up the steep Underhill road I was wondering where I would go when my landlord discovered I was penniless.

Back on the bluff once more we paused to get our wind. "I'm sorry those two belts we took finished what little was in my flask," my companion said ruefully. "I didn't get a chance to fill it up tonight, and the taverns are shut."

In addition to being down in the mouth I found myself with that peculiar weariness that visits a man who's been too much on his legs too late at night. I could use a drink, also; and once again I was grateful for Cousin Edward's forethought. "There's some liquor in my room just over yonder in the hotel."

If he had been pleased with me before he was fulsomely admiring as I poured generously from my great-grandfather's decanter. "Godolphin," he assured me, "you're an adjunct to our society."

It seemed likely to me that an adjunct of society who couldn't pay his bills would soon lose his standing. Being thoroughly tired I looked as I felt, and McConnell was quick to notice.

"That's right; you've got pressing problems, and due to your devotion to our cause." Having gulped the first drink he seated himself to sip the second, leaning back and putting his feet on my table. "Let's see now," he said in a tone of mellow thoughtfulness.

By then I had no confidence in anything profitable to me being offered. I waited, looking at him with a sort of dreary patience while he apparently thought hard. Finally he brightened.

"Did you ever do any surveying?"

This was no better than I expected. "No," I admitted gloomily.

He wasn't the least discouraged. "Never mind. You'll learn by the time you reach the New Purchase. I've a book and some instruments—all I ever collected out of a combination fee and euchre debt before my client skipped to Texas. I'll hire you for Harry."

"Hire me for what?" I asked exasperatedly, unable to take him seriously and impatient of flights of fancy.

"A surveyor, damn it! It's just the thing. I was going to put it off till next spring, but it'll be much better to have somebody go up there now. It'll allow time for doing a thorough job."

I stared at him. I'd had a reasonable amount of mathematics, and surveying was no such abstruse science that many hadn't mastered it. But taking money for it, as if I was already an able practitioner, was something else again. "Has it occurred to you," I demanded, with a quietness more pointed than sarcasm, "that it may be some months before I'm qualified?"

He snorted. "Qualified, Hell! There's too much work to be done in a new country for people to waste time qualifying for things. In Mississippi you look around, and if there's nobody to show you how to do something you do it anyhow. I was going to pick up the

THE WILD YAZOO

surveying myself, but I've been pretty busy. You'll be just the one
for the job."

"Granting that, for the moment, what would I do?" I persisted.
"You've already told me that Pace didn't have any interests on the
upper Yazoo."

"But I also said he's going to have, and he wants to know what
in the way of prime land is there. So do I for that matter. You're
hired."

He meant it. Only when I grew convinced of this did I realize
how distrust of the future had shackled me. Nobody had ever
shown too much anxiety for my services, and now I had arrived in a
land where a stranger would pay me for a craft I hadn't learned
applied to a district neither of us had ever seen. I tossed my drink
down as a free man.

"Suppose I took you up," I said with far more nonchalance than I
felt, "how would I know when I got there? I'd hate to run some
lines for Mr. Pace and find out belatedly that I was in Alabama or
Tennessee."

"It's easy," he smiled. "Don't go west of the Mississippi or east of
the Pearl, and keep heading north. The first real river is the Big
Black and the next is the Yazoo. If you're in doubt as to whether a
stream's a river or just a bayou, measure the alligators. You won't
have any trouble."

"I can see that now," I murmured. "What would you recommend
as a means of locomotion?"

"You could go by boat part of the way, but traveling across country is more educational, and you won't be quite so surprised at the
Yazoo when you arrive. I can lend you a horse; and if you don't
lose it in a bog hole you'll have it to use when you get there.
Horses don't speak Choctaw either, so you'll have much in common."

Instead of taking these words for folly I winced. They suggested
as well as a long harangue on the subject would have, the lonely
self-dependence that would be asked of me venturing singly into
the Yazoo fastnesses. A man might well be glad of a horse's company after a few weeks spent in solitary woods running. And this

was but a single coin of the price asked. Seeing so much, I nodded at it and to myself.

McConnell noticed the unconscious gesture. He grinned at me challengingly. "Well?"

Accepting the fact that a man does what he can't avoid, I knew I was bound for the New Purchase. Employment as such was welcome, but I didn't feel called upon to act joyous about it.

"All right," I said soberly. "I'd like to sleep late tomorrow, but I'll leave the next day if that's satisfactory to you."

CHAPTER X

THE AFTERNOON of the next day I set forth to accept ownership of Talisman. Artenay had assured me that a dog was a necessity, and I was positive I wanted one. Dogs are usually more socially apt than horses.

Rested now, I was more cheerful rather than more hopeful. By taking the employment given by McConnell I would also be taking the advice given by Artenay. Once I'd finished my assigned task I would be in a position to exploit the unlimited possibilities of an undeveloped territory. Withal I could call up no roseate visions of accomplishment. Four times before—at Spring Hill, when I had commenced studying medicine, entered the Army, embraced politics—I had thought myself on the way to making my mark. Something of optimism had failed to survive those four disastrous campaigns of achievement. There had been great plans and no results. Now I was waiting to see.

Whether I would find the fact helpful or not, I recognized that this was unlike my other ventures in one important respect. Here I was not attempting a specific career; I was on the lookout for whatever I found I could do. The possibilities were unlimited, the factors were only two. There was the country and there was myself. In as much as the country had been getting along without me for a considerable stretch of time I was the one on whom the burden of proof rested.

All that would be asked of me was to produce something, and the only one that would care enough to do the asking would be myself. For the country would be seized and settled. Men would come among the hills, the bayous and the great forests to build after man's mighty fate and impulse. The one who could make nothing out of such clay and straw had no force of architecture at all. Here was a place, indeed, for ultimate answers.

I heard the horse running toward me, but introspection was leaving no time for matters not liable to affect me. It was only at the last moment, as a cursory precaution, that I looked up to observe that the approaching rider was Corinna Artenay. I had just time to raise my hat when she thrust her crop neatly up under it. As the beaver was thus snatched from my grasp she held it aloft with a gurgle of triumph and sped on. My astonishment was so complete that I merely gazed after her as she disappeared around a curve in the road.

I was vexed as well as perplexed. Had she stolen my trousers she couldn't have amazed me much more or confused me much less. A man, or at least on such faith I had been reared, didn't go calling hatless. Of course on the other hand, the young lady of the house I was visiting wasn't supposed to purloin my headgear before I got there.

Mooting these points, I eventually concluded that the best course would be to proceed. It would be silly to forego my visit because of a hat I would promptly remove upon my arrival. Also, if I was ever to see my beaver again Artenay's Ledge was the most likely place for it to turn up. It was unlikely that the girl would jettison it in the woods, though of this I could not be sure. Mississippi continued to surprise me.

Walking on, I soon heard her returning. Or at least I assumed it was she. I didn't turn my head, though I confess to flinching. It didn't seem beyond the realm of possibility that she would strike me.

Almost upon me, she reined up sharply, for I heard a slithering of hooves. I still didn't look around, and in a moment she was walking her horse beside me, rolling in the saddle with mirth.

"That was an awful thing to do," she chortled, "but you looked so dignified and formal when you raised your hat. And then you looked so astonished."

"I was astonished," I conceded. "Do I get it back now, or what's left of it?"

I hadn't known whether I was going to be curtly angry or just silently annoyed, but I found I would have felt ridiculous either way. The line between impertinence and pleasant familiarity is a matter of persons. Looking at her, I had to grant that lovely girls were among those from whom familiarity was permissible.

Therefore I laughed with her, albeit seeking for a way to pull level. "It was handily done. You have a nice seat—on the horse, too, I mean."

I was pleased to see that she flushed and started to get indignant before she continued with her merriment. "All right," she chuckled. "I'd never have guessed you were so observant from the way you ignored me the other night, though."

To say anything was to say the wrong thing. "That's the real reason I stole your hat," she went on when I was silent. "Those who can't attract attention have to win it."

"God help a liar," I said, glad to find some ground for my feet again. "I understand that because of you half the young men in Mississippi have fractured hearts and the other half have already bled to death."

She caught at the one word. "*Young* men! That's what I mean. You hid out in father's study as if you were nearer his age than mine, which you're not, relegating me to the children."

"Hat-stealing children," I pointed out. "Can I have mine now?"

She returned it to me as she'd taken it, holding it out at the end of her crop. With some effort I refrained from looking to see what damage it had incurred before I dropped it dutifully to my side.

"Are you going out to the Ledge?" she asked.

"Yes, ma'am, I was on my way—" I paused, trapped.

"To see my father," she finished for me. Without saying anything more she tapped her horse with her crop, and it leapt away with her.

At last free to examine my hat, I was reassured that it hadn't been punctured or sprung. Then I set it firmly on my head, as a man will in the trail of a gust of wind. Miss Artenay was out of sight by the time this was accomplished, but the impression she had made wasn't so readily dissipated. The thought crossed my mind that all the hazards of Mississippi didn't lie below the bluff or along the banks of the Yazoo.

Tranquillity had returned long before I reached Artenay's Ledge, although it was not and would not be henceforth the same building. To a young man the house once known to be the home of an attractive girl can never lose a certain erotic patina. I had previously been aware that she was resident, but, as she herself had complained, the fact hadn't been sufficiently impressed on me. She had remedied the situation. I did not especially want to see her again, but for the life of me I could not forbear to think that I momentarily might.

I had come to see Artenay and would not have proceeded had Corinna bothered to tell me he was not at home. She had not, and he was not. Persius, to make things worse, had a message which he did not deliver until he'd already trapped me by securing the fatal hat. Miss Corinna, in a word, would be down as soon as she had changed from riding habit into unspecified but other attire.

Annoyed but helpless, I waited in the drawing room where Persius stranded me. He had promised me that Miss Corinna would be down in a minute, craftily refraining from mentioning which. I grew tired going into the hall to consult the clock, and there were no almanacs handy, so I can't say how long I endured that awkward solitude. I couldn't smoke in the drawing room, and Persius, presumably because I was waiting for Miss Corinna instead of Mr. Artenay, didn't tender a drink. Nobody came near me, so I couldn't send a message of feigned regrets, and however aggravated I was with the daughter I could not so conduct myself in the house of her father as to stamp out wordless—and hatless.

When she did come I knew that I was so far out of poise that an attempt at suavity would only result in muffled pouting. I braced my legs and glared at her. "You look very sweet and beautiful," I said, speaking no more than the truth, "and that's a tribute from an angry man."

"I worked for it," she declared, turning her head to look behind her and in the act flicking a curl over a bare shoulder. "Persius should be here in a second, but I didn't order tea for you."

Almost on the last word Persius made good, and in spite of myself my eye softened at sight of the decanter. It was only sherry, but I wanted it for salve and fortification. Having determined to make the best of things, I found, as is so often the case, that it was the most soothing course. It would have been absurd to sulk in such company. She was not pressing her mockery but instead was being charmingly attentive to her obligations as a hostess. Having emptied my first glass more rapidly than its ceremonial nature called for, I replenished it, at her invitation, and sat back.

"I find this very pleasant," I remarked.

She smiled, looking genuinely gratified. "I hoped you would. I didn't want to have tea alone." That was as near as she came to making an explanation for conduct I could not but regard as highhanded. Evidently the women of this state as well as the men acted on the theory that the best way to get something done was to do it. Nor was my vanity ever persuaded that there was anything personal in her attitude. She wanted company, masculine company was the common preference of young ladies, and I had happened to be the only handy prospect.

Her tea was apparently not to her taste, for she ladled a little more sugar into it. "Father says you're planning to be a Mississippian."

It was flattering to find that I had been a topic of conversation, but I must have looked my surprise. "You see how much I know about you?" she chuckled. "We're near enough to the backwoods here that we have to know everybody's business."

"I don't even know my own business yet." Now that she wanted to be, she was an easy girl to talk to, interested in what I was saying in a cool, friendly way. "As for being a Mississippian, that's something the state and I will have to settle between us when we've looked each other over."

"They say it takes about a year." She examined me with eyes that didn't betray judgment. "By the end of that time if you haven't died, gone home, got shot, or been hanged you're naturalized. Father says being a Mississippian is a matter of quality. Hardly anyone was born here, you see."

That was natural in a place that had been a state hardly more than a dozen years. Yet the fact was one with which I hadn't before been adequately impressed. Even though McConnell, for instance, kept referring to his Georgia birth I had persisted in thinking him the epitome of native sons. Yet there must have been a time, not too far in the past, when he felt as foreign as I now did. The thought was heartening.

"Were you born here yourself?"

"Yes, but I'm the only one in the family. My brothers were born in South Carolina before my parents moved west. They made the trip overland, and I never have forgiven them for not waiting for me."

"It must have been quite an undertaking," I said, thinking of the two hundred roadless leagues.

"Oh, it must have been lots of fun. Father had to fight the Creeks a couple of times, and once when he was out hunting Mother shot an Indian that smelled the rum barrel."

I tried to picture the modish Mrs. Artenay in the wilderness, and could not. "Your father advocates pioneering as a career for me also."

She nodded. "He's very excited about the development of the New Purchase. He told me he's promised you Talisman if you go. Are you going to take him?"

Somehow, although what I did was none of her business any more than what she thought was a concern of mine, I was glad to be able to answer in the affirmative. The daughter of a lady that shot Indians was apt to have her own views on the worth of initiative.

"That's what I came out here for," I said, a shade more deeply than my normal voice.

"Would you like to see him?"

"If you please," I said, not rising so quickly that I didn't first drain my glass. "If I'm going to persuade him to follow me to the Yazoo tomorrow I've got to start making friends with him now."

After she had found a scarf to throw around her shoulders we walked around to the kennels. The dogs were as limp as only hounds can be as they drowsed in a sun that was dropping into Louisiana. Talisman was no more energetic than the others. He lay still at first, as if hoping we didn't mean it when we called his name. Finding we persisted, however, he yawned and got to his feet as if he was certain that the effort would be the death of him.

"I don't know him very well; we have so many dogs," Corinna said apologetically. "Father knows him a little, but he's nobody's dog really."

That was good news. I let him sniff me. World-weary though he was, he couldn't resist that. He indulged in it for a minute before he slumped to the ground as if all his bones had suddenly been removed. After patting him and scratching him a little I drew forth a piece of leather. I'd had to sacrifice a pair of boots when I carved it, but it had the smell of me ingrained.

When I handed it to Talisman he seized on it, and started worrying it. He was still puppy enough to chew anything his teeth could cope with. I watched him mouth and paw it, then stood up satisfied. For the immediate future he would know me night or day, which was the most I could hope to accomplish at this short notice.

"You'll get along with him," Corinna nodded approvingly. "When do you want to take him?"

"Tonight if your father permits it. I start tomorrow morning."

She put up a hand to fend the sun from her eyes. "Alone?"

"Well, there'll be Talisman and a horse. At least they tell me it's a horse. It looks part mule and part cow, though I'm informed it's just the animal for the swamps."

"Did you expect to pack bear meat on a Virginia Hunter?" She turned her back to the sun and looked me up and down with an amusement that was only tolerable because I felt she liked me. "And what will you yourself be like? Are you going to wear that costume into the woods?"

As a matter of fact my clothes were far from being an index of my finances. In spite of withering times and final bankruptcy I had always managed to dress well, fancying myself in a rich simplicity. As I'd left Spring Hill with light freight I'd filled such space as my luggage yielded with my best and newest apparel.

"I won't be dressed exactly like this," I grinned. "I have a shooting jacket."

She was delighted. "A shooting jacket on a Mississippi puddle nag! And the hat—the beautiful white beaver?"

At that I laughed outright. "It's the only one I have."

Again I looked at Talisman, still contentedly chewing the sliver of my boot. She endured my silence for a moment then quizzed me with the unfettered directness of a Westerner and a woman.

"What are you thinking about?"

I responded after my own kind, which is to say I answered whatever came into my head. "I was thinking that the country would no doubt mould both the hat and me to its uses. After this day neither of us will be the same again."

She giggled. "Will you come back and show me?"

"I can't speak for the hat, but nothing could keep me away."

"You lie like a Mississippian already," she said, taking my arm. "Shall we go over to the summerhouse while we wait for Mother and Father? They should be home pretty soon now."

Corinna was borne off to a ball soon after supper, but I spent a pleasant evening with the senior Artenays. I found my host and hostess more interesting than ever now that I knew they had reached their present luxurious estate by way of a forest trail. Mrs. Artenay in particular fascinated me on that occasion. Once when she was discussing Cooper in her gentle, cultured voice I marvelled to reflect that she, too, had looked down the sights of a rifle at a redskin.

My dog did not go with me when I left, though Artenay promised he would be brought to the hotel early in the morning. He was more faithful to his word than he needed to be, for his own conception of early was more literal than mine. Talisman was introduced to my room at sunrise and looked no happier about the reunion than I at the moment felt.

He was a little cured of his nervousness when he smelled me, though he was uneasy about the whole unexplained business of what was going on. He knew we'd met before, though he couldn't place me until I produced the mate to the piece of boot leather he'd chewed on the previous evening. As he sank his teeth into it his tail came out from between his legs, and a little later he commenced scurrying around the room to orient himself.

I wasn't concerned about the likelihood he'd never been indoors before until I returned from attending to the matters of eating breakfast, arranging for my horse to be brought forth, and settling my score. I had thought the management was badly overcharging me till I saw what the hound had accomplished in the brief hour at his disposal. The floor bore some resemblance to a cow pasture, a corner of the carpet was shredded, the leg of the table was ruinously gnawed, the wash basin lay shattered and scattered. Talisman was nowhere in sight, though I soon discovered him buried in the bed-clothes. He had done his work well and was resting.

After I had fed him, therefore, I delayed no longer but took him on short leash down stairs. Leading both a horse and a dog is even harder on the disposition than on the muscles; yet I managed it for a bitterly contested mile and a half. By then we were past the town with its recurrent, distracting sights, sounds and smells. Considered separately, the horse was never a problem, and once in open country I did not think the hound would be. Food, companionship and exploration are the three staples of canine luxury, and all these I could supply.

The horse had a shambling gait that was easy on the rider even if it failed of distilling pride of equipage. If unhurried, he was earnest and cheerful, and in time he schooled me in his philosophy. On a different mount it would have been a different journey, and I in a sense a different person. Carried on a likely horse, capable of swift coursing, I would have been above idle eavesdropping en route, for instance. It would have been more effort to stop and listen than it would to canter by.

On Goober the reverse was the case. He ambled so slowly that I became, as it were, an inmate of any bystander's sphere. He put me on eye level with the passing scene and perforce I became an interested observer of life along the Natchez Trace.

It was when we had left the Natchez district well behind that Goober took me into one of these encounters of the road. We had descended from the bluffs to the lower land eastwards, and the Trace seemed justly named. It was no more than a cut through the forest, here muddy and there muddier. It had no bed, though an aggravating substitute was sometimes offered in the form of corduroy. Open fields were by this time getting scarce, wayfarers scarcer, and the trees stood close about the road.

I had heard enough of predatory vagabonds on the Trace to be on

THE WILD YAZOO

the alert. When the shrill, angry voices sounded around a turn just
ahead I made sure of my pistol and speeded up. This lasted for
about fifty yards. By the time we'd reached the people we were
supposed to be speeding by Goober had slowed down to his normal shuffle. When I made the mistake of turning to look at them,
Goober stopped. Entertained, I let it go at that, and the horse
started nibbling leaves while I watched and listened.

There were two tow-headed boys, *aetat* eleven or thereabouts,
squared off at a safe distance from one another. Where they stood,
some twenty yards from the road, there was a floor of sward that
gave no impediment to their cavorting. In their absorption they
either did not see me or were passionate past concern for any
audience.

The crucial state at which their relations had arrived was proclaimed by the youngster on the right. "I was going to let you off
easy. I was only goin' to tear off your ears, wrap 'em up in your
lights, put in one of your eyeballs for flavorin' and make you eat it.
But now I'm mad."

"Who cares if you're mad?" the other wondered. "Who cares if a
toad has the ague, a mosquito has the bellyache, a snake has the
ground itch, or if you don't like anythin'?—Who're you anyways?"

"I'm a rantankerous Arkansas alligator hoss!" his rival took this
opportunity to declare. "When I get mad the moon takes in the stars
to keep 'em out of trouble."

"Well, I'm a Mississippi steamer with a bulgin' biler," he was answered. "When I get mad lightnin's scared to leave the clouds. The
thunderheads just make a lot of noise an' nothin' happens, just like
you."

I listened wide-eyed. Here was the tongue of paladins. Children
may ring strange changes on the conduct of their elders, but it isn't
their intention. When assured they are engaged in mature activities
their endeavor is not to interpret the acts of adults but to imitate
them exactly. Behind these Ossianic boasts I heard the deeper
voices of older backwoods combatants.

The moment was imminent, I think, when they would have generated enough frenzy for the assault each longed to make yet
dreaded. But just as I was anticipating the battle with gusto one of

the champions spoke to his foe as an ally. "Let's beat it! Here comes Mammy!"

That routed them, or to be exact it routed all three of us. I didn't want to have to explain to an indignant woman why I hadn't tried to separate the belligerents, and I prodded Goober on up the Trace.

CHAPTER XI

THERE WAS CANE around the bayous, slow creeks opaque as the earth that canalized them. Although they often carried some of the rankness of stagnation they betimes ran over their banks to create marginal swamps. Between cane brakes the forests were grand hard woods, oak, hickory and such, but a tangled rigging of vines gave a tropical cast to them. At certain seasons it would have been fine country to ride through, pacing a firm but never dusty thoroughfare past a clean, sweet-smelling woodland. This, however, was just after the fall rains in a district as deft to hold moisture as a tea saucer.

Fortunately Goober was used to the pudding roads of a wet, rockless land. He picked his way with skill, weaving without guidance to find the stablest footing. Sometimes he would leave the highway entirely for smoother faring through the woods. At other points this was not feasible. There was nothing for it but to slosh through a soupy pond that offered bottom only at depths of two or three feet.

The Mississippians themselves knew better than to travel at this season and didn't except under stress. I met a few horsemen, a few oxcarts, and a bedraggled stage coach or so whose storm-tossed inmates I pitied from my heart. Residences along the Trace were almost as scarce as wayfarers, but there were occasional towns. Fortunately, I had letters to prosperous residents and slept well the first few nights.

It was when I turned off north toward the Old Choctaw Purchase that my initiation began. I wouldn't have believed there could have been a more villainous road than the Natchez Trace, but I was on one. Talisman, the untrammelled and insatiable of movement, thoroughly enjoyed himself, but Goober and I, who had to put up with each other as well as travel conditions we didn't fancy, were more subdued.

As the day dragged on I began to long for its end, picturing the social pleasures and comforts of a wayside tavern. This I did because I had been assured there were places to stay all along the early part of my route. It was a statement I had not been on the frontier long enough to evaluate.

It was nearing dark when we reached the first hamlet. A passing boy assured me that it had a fine doggery and pointed it out to me with pride. I had only a premonitory twinge when I saw it. At that time I still believed in the validity of signs, and the one nailed beside the door plainly read "Tavern." It was otherwise a log cabin, distinguished from those strictly residential only by being a little larger; but I had too many fond associations with taverns to know fear.

I did think it ought to have more than the one window I could see, and I knew I was right as soon as I opened the door. The reek was no passive dweller, but a hostile, attacking force. I halted on the mud sill to peer within uncertainly.

"You ain't goin' to just stand there with the door open, are you, stranger?" a voice enquired. "Step inside and shut it."

This, I thought, was hoarding. Here was a man with smell enough in his house to taint the whole world, but far from being willing to share it he wanted to keep it all to himself. I obeyed his injunction but side-stepped swiftly to the window to get the benefit of the air that entered that sashless opening. The slanting sun that also entered enabled me to see my interlocutor.

He was leaning over a plank set on two whiskey barrels, staring at me from between dangling locks and a frowzy, full beard. Then he spat to add one more foul, little puddle to the dirt floor. "What're you doin' in these parts?"

"Traveling," I said, unhappily aware that I'd have to make some sort of decision soon. I hesitated to leave, for fear of finding no other hospitality, yet I was loth to admit to myself that I might remain. "Is yours the only tavern in town?"

"Depends on what town you're talkin' about," he said cautiously. "It's the only doggery in this one. You travelin' alone?"

I was tired and irritated at landing in this hole at the end of a hard day, and I had not yet grown used to this type of insistent catechizing. "Yes," I said curtly. Then I bethought me that even if I didn't stay I might as well have a drink. I picked my way forward. "Got any whiskey?"

"Sure have." He waited until he'd poured me a horn full before he fired his next shot. It was a telling one. "What does your old woman think about you traipsin' off here all by yourself?"

I had the liquor halfway to my mouth, and I spilled a little, a thing I rarely do, as my head came up. "I didn't ask her," I said grimly.

The whiskey was raw, but it at once comforted my travel-weary bones and settled my stomach, which the stench had rendered uneasy. The proprietor had seemingly watched me, but his mind was engrossed with my domestic problems.

"It's the best way," he decided. "Ask 'em an' they always squall and kick up a fuss. You goin' back to her?"

Resignation was beginning to enfeeble my resistance. "Would you?" I managed.

Asking his counsel called out the man in him, but he didn't advise me hastily. He was silent a full minute, letting me refill from the bottle he'd left handy. Then he spat again and struck the makeshift bar with his fist.

"No, by God! She'd have to meet me halfway anyhow or I'm damned if I'd stir an inch."

Setting back the bottle I'd rescued from his vehemence, I forlornly decided that it was useless to pretend that I had any choice. Many miles stood probably between me and the next shelter. If this one was no very wholesome fence against the elements, I was not yet prepared to bed down on the soggy forest floor. The landlord was getting ready to investigate another facet of my private affairs, but I forestalled his next question with one of my own.

"Got any rooms for the night?"

I didn't have the courage to examine the accommodations he claimed until after I'd curried Goober as best I could and fed both him and Talisman. The guest quarters of this tavern were in a windowless extension opening off the taproom. It was airier than the bar in as much as there was no chinking between the logs framing the solitary chamber. By the light thus admitted I could make out two bunks, each with a jumble of nondescript bedclothes, and a lame table. There was a pannikin on the table and a rat in the pannikin. The rat left upon our arrival, but the vessel and the smell that emanated from it remained.

"Which one is mine?" I asked hopelessly.

"Either one, stranger. You got here first, didn't you?"

"Do I have it all to myself?" I was trying to build some heart on the foundation of this tiny sarcasm, but he struck it out from under me.

"You can file claim on either side of one. I'll likely have some people on the way back from camp meetin' later."

"I'll pay double," I said desperately. "I want to rent the whole thing."

He shook his head like a judge regretfully turning down a plea for pardon. "How can I claim a bed is all took when anybody can come in and see you're only usin' part? It would ruin the repertation of this establishment."

The magnificence of that assertion silenced me, but he returned to the subject when he brought in the cold salt pork we shared. "You see, I couldn't lie, with my old woman comin' back from camp meetin'." While making this remark he lit a pine torch that gave some illumination but contrived to make the hutch look even more dismal. "That's where she is or we'd have better victuals than this," he said as he took his place. "There'd be hell to pay if she found I'd lied within a week or so of her gettin' religion. It takes awhile for a thing like that to wear off."

Seeing that I spoke little he cheerfully carried the burden of conversation himself. The camp meeting had stripped the vicinity of tipplers, and he was free to give me his undivided attention.

"Why didn't you go to camp meeting yourself?" I finally asked, wishing that he had before I was lured into his wretched box.

"I can't afford religion myself," he sighed. "I like it as well as the next hoss, but it just ain't for a man in my position. Last time I got it we all agreed Christians hadn't ought to drink at all, let alone run a doggery. So they all helped me burn mine down. Everybody said I'd done the right thing, an' I felt pretty good till I noticed all the men who'd helped me wreck my place was takin' their back-slidin' thirsts to a new grocery that'd just opened up. So I licked everybody I could an' cussed everybody I couldn't an' moved here. I ain't dared go near a camp meetin' since."

With intent to hide in oblivion I dosed myself with liquor and turned in early. I had been prepared for some sort of man-eating bed companions but not for their numbers and voracity. Yet in spite of them my weariness at length induced fretful slumber, a series of bad dreams from which I'd wake to an even more distressing reality.

Then I had additional company. From a sleep of comparative soundness I was awakened by the sound of a firm but friendly voice. "Shove your tail over and make room for some of my fleas."

Groaning, I sat up. The revivalists the proprietor had been expecting had evidently arrived. Aside from the bearded fellow preparing to hop into bed with me the torchlight disclosed three others, a man and two plump women. These latter three were clearly to share the other bunk, a little larger and a little more rickety than the one I'd selected. Shutting my eyes against this spectacle, I groaned again and moved to lie along the wall.

Previously I had been able to shift position and make the bugs work for what they got. Now I was cornered and pinioned, cupped from toes to ears by creatures which knew not the meaning of satiety. My body burned in spots, yet I was chilled through by the damp night breeze, which was sifted rather than impeded by the wall. For my bunkmate didn't idle away his time while asleep. He not only succeeded in cocooning himself in most of the covers, but he snored with an obscene rasp, appalling in volume, and he flung his arms about in vestigial camp meeting frenzy.

It had started to rain when I fled the place early, dallying only long enough for a horn of whiskey and a crust of corn pone. I felt brittle from sleeplessness, soggy inside, and I itched agonizingly. But from the one eye not closed by bites I viewed the dripping forest with favor. The very bog holes were comparatively in my good graces, for they were not the place of my suffering.

Nevertheless, as the sky cleared and the day warmed I found I could look back on the previous night with a degree of detachment.

While the subject of Mississippi taverns was no longer, alas, a closed book to me, its most revelatory chapter was not the doggery itself. The episode had been peculiarly horrifying because it had caught me so completely unawares. After all nothing had really happened to me except that I had eaten indifferent food and shared a poor bed. The man beside me, though he doubtless ate no better and was certainly no less exposed to insect attack than I, had retired good-humoredly and slept soundly. It was my first searching lesson in the massive extent of frontier acceptance.

That is not to say that I came to terms with backwoods hostelries. Now I knew them, though, I had fortitude for a friend. Also, I should add, my fortune at such way stops of chance wasn't always dismal.

Just beyond the river I identified as the Big Black I came in sight of an edifice built like saddlebags. The roof ran out from each of two cabins to join and form the only connecting link between them. Even before I drew near enough to see the sign I guessed it to be a tavern by the group of men loafing around outside.

Having learned wariness, I approached in a mood of sober caution. My anxiety was probably reflected in my face. At any rate my salute was acknowledged with subdued murmurs instead of the customary heartiness, and the men stared at me with the blank stolidity of cows.

Not paying much attention I walked inside. When I reappeared a couple of minutes later I was feeling more cheerful, having found the whiskey good and the premises reasonably clean. With Talisman at heel I was leading Goober around to the shed that had been pointed out to me when a man stepped into my path. He was whittling with a hunting knife, glancing up at me only momentarily now and then.

"Stranger," he said mildly, "I'd like to ask you a question."

That from a Westerner was too much. I had already stopped to avoid colliding with him. Now I braced my feet, and Talisman dropped by one boot as if he, too, was expecting a colloquy of some duration. I didn't know what was coming, but I had caught a gleam in his eye and glimpsed an onlooker trying to smooth away his grin.

"If you didn't want to ask a question," I carried it to him, seeking to smother him with words, "you'd be the only Mississippian that didn't have inordinate personal curiosity."

"I reckon I got it just like you said," he agreed equably. He stopped whittling, but whether or not he pointed the long blade at me merely for emphasis was more than I could decide. "Now here's my question, stranger. Did you lose the hoss that used to go with that hat or are you lookin' for a hat to go with that hoss?"

The incongruity between Goober and my fashionable apparel was a thing I had long taken for granted. In an effort to save as much as possible out of the modest sum McConnell had advanced me, I simply used the clothes I had. Meanwhile I derived a degree of amusement from the situation without conceding that it was the right of anybody else to call attention to it. Stroking Goober's nose, I looked at my accoster sidewise. He was a rangy, yellow-haired fellow with pale green eyes. His nose turned down, his chin tried to meet it, and inside the crescent thus formed there drooped a corn-silk moustache.

"I don't talk too well out of a dry throat," I said finally. "Of course, if you want to buy me a drink——"

He grinned a little. "Sort of got the jump on me, didn't you? But I'll tell you the way we do it around here. When a new thirst comes we give him a chance to find out if the drinks are on him or us." This time when the knife pointed it indicated Goober. "My hoss'll beat yours in a quarter race."

I hadn't seen his mount, but the thought of Goober in a speed contest was a monstrous absurdity. "My horse has been on the road all day, and he's done in."

"All right, my dog will whip yours."

"That dog's still a pup, as you can see for yourself."

He gazed up into the sky, speaking as if to himself. "His hoss is too tired, and his hound's too young."

"But I'm neither," I pointed out. In this my irritation betrayed me, for a day on that road was all the exercise I needed or desired.

"Oh, you want it to be between you and me," the fellow drawled musingly. "Well, that's fair enough. We likely wouldn't treat the hosses and dogs anyhow." He cut one more sliver from the stick he carried and sheathed the big blade. "Do you want to jump or run?"

Neither of these activities invited me at the moment, though I was a little relieved he hadn't suggested wrestling. I looked at the boots on my feet and the moccasins on his and chose the lesser of two evils. "I'll race you as soon as I've put up my horse."

He was using the stick to mark a starting line when I approached again a few minutes later. Then he used it to point to our goal. "Do you see that big sycamore just past the bend of the branch?"

The tree in question had the lambent pallor of its kind, and I could not fail to mark where it stood a couple of hundred yards away and just beyond the creek he had referred to. I removed my beaver and jacket, placing them on a rustic bench that fronted the tavern. I didn't expect to win, but the course could be easily negotiated, which was all that honor required. "There and back?" I asked.

"Right." He looked around at the diverted group of spectators huddled together the better to share their enjoyment. "You start us, Sam."

The man referred to carried lots of hard meat on a wide, short frame. He had a round, flat face that had been clean shaven within the week. "I'm goin' to see there's a neat start," he announced, "because I get a free drink no matter who wins. I'll count to three."

My antagonist, I noticed, was so confident he didn't bother to discard the stick he'd been carving. I determined to let him take the lead, keep as close behind as I could, then pass him in a final surge if it proved possible.

At Sam's cry of "three!" we got off together and stayed that way for about twenty-five yards. Then, having tried my pace, my opponent stretched his enough to pull ahead by a yard, no more. I began to feel more confident. My saddle-stiffened legs were loosening, as if glad of new service, and it felt pretty good to be running. He wasn't increasing his lead, perhaps he wasn't able to, and I was still loping easily with plenty in reserve.

The footing was soft but on the whole not bad. However, up ahead a little way I saw a large patch of oozy mud directly athwart our path. I expected my rival to swerve to avoid it, but he evidently felt that an accepted course must be followed for better or for worse. He was still just a stride ahead when he reached it.

At that precise instant he turned and deftly inserted the stick between my legs. Desperately and vainly I tried to leap it. Breaking my stride only made me fall the more awkwardly and joltingly. One end of the stick scraped along my right shin bone and the other caught under my left knee. I spun half around and ploughed through that muck on one shoulder.

The wrath of Achilles was no wilder than mine when I floundered out and charged after my convulsed antagonist. Behind me, too, there were howls of delight from his appreciative colleagues.

If he hadn't been laughing so hard he would have lengthened his lead more than he actually succeeded in doing. I was burdened with mud and had had half the wind knocked out of me. Only rage kept me going. He had reached the sycamore and was on his way back before I'd got to the bend in the creek. Watching him pound nearer I saw we'd actually meet there if I slowed a little. Heavy underbrush narrowed the course to a few feet at that point, and I knew the sudden blessing of hope.

Putting my head down to emphasize doggedness, I slowed, making sure at the same time that I blocked the track on the outside along the bushes. He was still gurgling boisterously when I looked up to see him just a few feet away. Nevertheless, he was wary of coming within arm's reach of me, giving my just anger such a wide berth that his feet were on the brink of the bank. It was then that I whirled to fall upon him.

It doesn't take much of a shove to throw a running man off balance if he's caught from the side. The bank was abrupt and there was no obstacle to his six-foot descent. I watched him disappear in the muddy water and then sped on. Before I attained the sycamore I heard the roars of laughter rolling after me from the vicinity of the tavern. If ours was a partisan audience it was not prejudiced against mirth.

When I reached the bend on the way back my opponent was still in the water, one arm draped over a half-sunken log. "Help me out; I can't swim!" he called.

[112]

"Stay there and drink water the rest of your life," I gasped. All the same I was relieved when he stroked smoothly for the bank.

"Damned if I do that!" he declared and started to clamber out. My heart was appeased, now that I had scored him off, but I wanted to cap my triumph with victory. Moreover, I had a natural nervousness about having him draw up from the rear. So much favored swiftness, but my body was against it. My early zest for running I had lost in the mire along with my wind, and I had to force myself to make every stride. My breath was burning my throat raw, and the crowd around the finish line was a shimmering blur.

In spite of his handicap of soaked clothes he was gaining and was about on me at the end. Still I had the race in my pocket when Talisman, breaking loose from the man who had been holding him, ran to meet me. In an effort to avoid his attentions I staggered into my rival's path. His velocity wasn't great, but my legs were gone. I crumpled when we collided, and he pitched over me onto the finish line, winner by a skinned nose.

The applause of the profoundly moved spectators reached only faintly to my state of demi-existence. For a while I was too sick with heat, and my breath entered my parched mouth too haltingly for me to do anything but lie miserably where I was. Finally I managed to push myself up and put an arm around the anxious Talisman, half in affection, half by way of finding support. When the dizziness appendix to that effort had passed I saw my opponent was likewise sitting up.

He grinned at me, and the mud on my face cracked as I responded. "The drinks are on me," I wheezed.

Struggling to his feet, he gave me his hand. "I always like to know a man's handle afore I drink his liquor. Mine's Tim Durham."

On the verge of introducing myself in the normal manner, I hesitated. I had won the right to my beaver hat, but a name to match its formality was an unnecessary burden here. "Daunt Godolphin," I said, using an abbreviation I hadn't used since boyhood.

It was thus I was presented to the friendly crew waiting to be treated and to treat in return. If any of them remembered my patronymic they did not trouble to use it. "Daunt" came easily to their lips and fell upon my ears with all the insidious power of intimacy. There are no syllables in the language to match a man's own name for compelling sweetness; and when the sound is made further bewitching by a familiar shortening its persuasive force is immeasurable. I had no more power to resist this simple incantation than anyone else and felt at home among friends as I had not since Cartwright intercepted my bullet.

The whiskey helped to bridge the gap of strangeness that normally lies between mere acquaintances, of course. There were ten or a dozen of us, each eager to stand his shot and equally eager to show appreciation of the next fellow's hospitality. It made for a pleasant evening even before we started to play Wahoo.

I had never heard of this pastime until Durham suggested it, but the general acclaim showed that I stood alone in my ignorance. Sam, now wearing my tall, white beaver, was enthroned as master of ceremonies on a stool placed upon the single large table in the taproom. At his feet was a gallon jug of whiskey, full but uncorked. The rest dragged up benches and stools until everyone could get his elbows on the table, while I stood apart, watching the preparations with great interest. Tim, however, would have none of this.

"Daunt's got to be in on it. Shove over and make room for him."

"I don't know how to play," I objected.

"You know how to spell, don't you?"

Orthography was one field in which I felt that I could certainly hold my own there. "Yes," I said confidently.

"All right, here's the way it goes. Sam sings three-four lines, and the last word of the last line is the one that counts. He points to one of us, and the one he points to has to start spellin' the word. If you can't think of the right letter you can say 'wahoo' and pass the buck. But if you say the wrong letter we all take a drink, and you pay for it. Got it?"

"I reckon so," I said, not too enthusiastically. I didn't see how, with such a convenient alternative, we were going to have misspelling enough to warrant many drinks. "Let's start it off and see what happens."

Shoving my hat on the back of his head Sam spread his thick legs, clamped a beefy hand on each knee and commenced to intone:

"Oh, clever Mr. Turtle, what's your way of gettin' to it:
I've thinked and thought about it an' I can't think how you do it.
A petticoat as stiff as boards would make my life a hell:
Do you yank out Mrs. Turtle or just prise up the shell?"

I had never thought of a turtle's carapace as a chastity belt, and I had little time to consider the matter then. Sam was pointing sternly at Tim. "Shell!" he repeated.

"Wahoo!" the latter said.

His promptness caught me flat-footed. Having counted on him for an "s," my "h" was out before I was aware. As we drank the round I bought I saw that the game was a better one than i had at first thought.

This time Sam moved my hat forward over his brow and proceeded to philosophize as follows:

"I don't like Mrs. Rattlesnake, she sets my hair arisin',
She ain't got all the legs I like an' she is full of pison,
But if I was a he-snake I'd sure be on her track——
Just let her shake her tail at me an' watch me rattle back!"

"Back!" he repeated.

We got through that word dry, spelled though it was with an extra "c" and a supernumerary "e." "Rump," however, yielded us a drink when Tim recklessly tried to insert a "w." Sam permitted a great deal of leeway but not rank improbabilities.

His store of zoological staves was endless, and the game went on and on. Tim, following his one stab in the dark, stuck to wahoos; but others grew more determined to show their erudition as the drink waxed in them. Among this number I myself might justly be classed. I found myself contributing my letters to the simple words with a heavy determination not to be found wanting.

Meanwhile the wahoos first became more numerous and loud, then commenced to come feebly and infrequently. One by one our companions laid their heads on the table or disappeared without ceremony of farewell beneath it. Tim had side-slipped to let his head fall on one of my arms, and I had no power to move him. My own head started drooping until it would almost hit the table, then I'd pull myself partially erect.

[115]

"Love!" I heard Sam call out. His flaming, round face, crowned by my beaver and swaying on his shoulders like an inverted pendulum, was turned directly toward me. Looking hazily around I saw why. Nobody else was there except in the body.

"Love!" Sam said again.

It seemed to me terrifically important—I had forgotten my original mistake—to preserve my record of never having missed. I goggled at him in an agony of concentration, then gave up. Yet there was a word which would save me from the ignominy of defeat. Suddenly I smiled the victor's smile as it came to me.

"Wahoo!" I said.

"Yes, that's right, wahoo," Sam muttered.

Carefully removing my hat, he stretched himself out on the table and began snoring. The game was over.

CHAPTER XII

I DIDN'T GET on my way the next morning as early as a traveler should who expects to journey to another haven in a sparsely settled country. Durham was still lucky enough to be asleep when I decided my head wasn't going to improve no matter how still I kept or how piously I hoped. My other bottle brothers had disappeared, although in what mystery of strength they had found the energy I couldn't imagine. I myself didn't want to go anywhere, but the thought of remaining was even more intolerable. Only by the illusion of travel, which in itself is the illusion of leaving one's worser self behind, could I so much as glimpse betterment. It seemed reasonable that the hapless vagabondage of the Wandering Jew could be simply accounted for. The poor old fellow was a chronic wahoo player.

The landlord watched in humorous sympathy while I pondered this point and toyed ineptly with my breakfast. "They say," he reminded me, "that if you live till four o'clock you'll live forever."

As it was then only about ten this was like promising a child a Christmas present on Ash Wednesday. Yet five or thereabouts did find me not only alive but in a much better frame of mind. The exercise had rubbed off the worst of my misery, leaving me still sluggish but in a mood to envisage hope. All I needed to regain the pulse of life was a stiff drink, which I proceeded to have. Then while Goober browsed I enjoyed my first cigar of the day.

There were problems left. Following the advice of my landlord I was riding up the valley of the Big Black, intending to cut across the intervening highlands to the Yazoo when far enough upstream. Due to my tardiness in starting and my lethargy throughout the day, I was still a long ways short of the village to which he had directed me. Where was I to spend the night?

[117]

Until one has actually encountered highwaymen they stand in the category of hobgoblins—beings that have no entity outside of darkness. Although I wasn't exactly alarmed I remembered nightfall was near and grew watchful when I heard the sound of a horse slopping along the mud of the road. He was coming from the direction whence I myself had ridden, a roughly dressed cavalier astride a bony grey horse. His face was largely concealed from me by an aged planter's-style hat, whose drooping brim was pulled well down. In consequence he recognized me first.

"Howdy, Daunt!"

"Tim, how are you?" I rose, smiling my pleasure. "Have a drink?"

This was never an invitation, as I had learned, to startle a Mississippian; but my great-grandfather's liquor kit really impressed him. He dismounted and watched admiringly while I filled the two noggins.

"What do you know about that?" he wondered. "Tendin' bar in the Devil's lost lot and pourin' drinkin' liquor out of a pretty bottle the size of a molasses barrel." His Adam's apple moved once to drink and twice more in appreciation. "How come you didn't wait for me?"

"I didn't know where you were going and you snored too loudly for me to find out."

"Oh, I'm headin' up the valley, then I'm goin' t' cut off for the New Purchase and fix me a trap line."

I didn't see fit to mention my own plans. There was, however, a topic I was most anxious to discuss. "Speaking of snoring, where were you figuring on doing it tonight?"

"Gettin' about that time, ain't it?" He spat confidently. "We ain't passed anybody's shanty for quite a spell now. There'd ought to be one up the road a piece."

His vagueness dashed my hopes, and his implication appalled me. "But we can't just stop at anybody's house and tell them we're going to spend the night."

I might as well have told him it was an imposition to climb on to a horse's back. He stared at me in astonishment. "Why not? We ain't goin' to find any other place to roost."

Within two miles, and just as the forest dark was thickening into night his faith in the existence of a cabin was justified. There was one in a rough-hewn clearing some fifty yards back from the road, and Durham turned into the path that led to it. Not too proud of myself, I followed. I was standing ready to profit by a brazenness in which I had too delicate a stomach to take a hand.

A few feet from the door Tim dismounted, shoved an arm casually through the bridle and slouched forward to knock. There was somebody within, as shown by the blurred light glowing through the oiled paper of the window. As I waited uneasily for the result of my companion's temerity I appraised the building doubtfully, not seeing how it could house us even if the owner was amenable. It was neatly built from the sills to the top of the log and mud chimney, but there wasn't much of it.

After a moment I heard the bar being removed, then the door opened enough for a man to look out. "Howdy," Tim said. "My name's Durham and that's Daunt Go something or other. We're moseyin' up the valley and reckoned on spendin' the night with you all."

The overweening forthrightness of this greeting startled only myself. The householder seemed to consider the remark in good order, for the door opened wider. "Just you two?" he asked quietly. Then he called over his shoulder. "Take a couple of more hacks at that venison, Bess, while I show the strangers where to put their hosses."

That was all there was to it. I still didn't see how we could be entertained there, and the mystery wasn't explained when I finally stepped inside. The cabin's one room was perhaps the right size for the honeymoon of a couple that didn't like to walk very far. Furthermore, there was already a third party hunched on a stool in one corner. My theory that he was a well-loved parent lasted until he was introduced as another stranger. Up to that moment I had thought the meaning of hospitality was known to me.

They contrived to make the occasion appear usual, possibly by virtue of the fact that to them it was. My host, a lanky, fair-haired youngster named Cameron, still working at his first beard, lugged in the chopping block. He and I sat on that while Durham pre-empted one of the two remaining stools. Thus accommodated, we huddled together as far away from Mrs. Cameron's hearthside kitchen as the bed would permit.

Tim was unaffected by any feeling of oppression. "Daunt," he prompted me as soon as he'd adjusted his legs comfortably, "show 'em what you got in the leather box." Then he turned to where our hostess was busy with supper. "Bess," he said with the license of an acquaintance not three minutes old, "you don't mind if we give your old man a drink, do you?"

Bess was as blonde as her "old man" and appeared if anything a couple of years younger. Nevertheless, she had an answer. "I reckon," she said with brisk friendliness, "that if he's man enough to take care of me he's man enough to take care of his liquor."

Her husband grinned proudly at this vote of confidence. "There now!" he exclaimed. "I'll be glad to have a horn with you, but what's the box got to do with it?"

For my part I was glad of the chance to contribute something and felt more at ease as I produced my heirloom. If Durham had been impressed, Cameron was dumbfounded.

"Well, if that ain't the prettiest thing I ever did see!" He admired it as I filled a silver noggin. In his desire to compound his enthusiasm by sharing it he addressed the other guest. "Did you ever see anything like that before, Mr. Holley?"

Mr. Holley looked to me as if he had seen plenty of things like that, as well as about everything else, before. He was a wiry man of indeterminate age whose face looked pickled in years of salty living. "I've encountered such things," he confirmed my estimate in an accent I took to be that of Maryland, "but never more opportunely."

I saw by the relish with which he imbibed that he spoke sincerely. Tim and I drank from the flask direct and after we had done so I filled the cups again.

"Are you headed north or south, Holley?" Durham wanted to know.

The man worked the whiskey around in his mouth to make sure he was missing none of the flavor before he swallowed. "Without caring too much which point of the compass it favors I'm making my way toward Natchez."

He said this in a manner that told me he was surfeited with idle questioning, too. His dryness was lost on Tim.

"Goin' there and don't know where the hell it is, eh?" Then he continued to satisfy the curiosity that everybody else seemed to arouse in the trans-Appalachian mind. "Got any folks there?"

Holley looked at him quizzically, but his voice was pleasant. "No, as it happens. As a matter of fact, just by way of saving you time, I've come to this part of the world to collect flowers."

Having loosed that broadside, he finished his liquor and leaned back, humming to himself. Durham looked at me to see whether I believed this, and our host eyed Holley as he himself might have eyed a new and wholly unsuspected species. There was complete silence while his statement was considered, then Cameron cleared his throat.

"Well, that's nice," he said politely. "You must like 'em right well to come this far."

Durham wasn't quite satisfied. "Don't they have none where you was reared?"

"Yes," Holley admitted, "but not necessarily the same kinds you have here. I've already found quite a few in Mississippi I never saw before."

This intelligence overwhelmed Cameron. "I want to know," he murmured. "What do you think, Bess? The stranger says things is different other places."

I couldn't decide whether he really thought all localities were botanically similar or whether he'd never previously considered the matter; but his wife was not in the least surprised. "Of course, things is different here, honey. If things other places was as *good* as in Mississippi folks wouldn't leave their own truck an' come here crowdin' us out."

Opening my mouth, I shut it on wordless air. They might have neighbors up the road, but to my personal knowledge there was none for ten miles down river. Then I tried again.

"Aren't there still parts of the state where you wouldn't find it crowded?"

She was taking the coffee off the hob, and she settled it with cold water before she answered. "There was plenty of open land when we was born, but by the time we'd growed up all the best of it had been grabbed up and picked over. Speculators got most of it."

I knew that real-estate pools had in truth partitioned much of the unsettled lands, securing them for nominal fees and denying squatter sovereignty until the eventual growth of the state would render their holdings profitable. I wasn't in favor of the average absentee land speculator, but I didn't have much sympathy for the average squatter, who could usually have good land if he stuck by it. The trouble about permitting the practice of squatting is that most of its practitioners not only want the privilege of claiming land but the license to abandon it, in the manner of children going through a box of bonbons and taking a bite out of each. The vexed problems of ownership left by claim and run drifters is one of the terrors of American freehold. Not wanting to go into this matter with my host, I changed the subject.

"What do you grow, Mr. Cameron?"

"Oh, I'll have a small crop next year," and I took him to mean cotton, "but, by the time I get it in, the New Purchase will be open an' we're goin' to move there. We'll have our chance at prime land then, and I'm goin' to be a real planter."

Once more I looked at this couple, estimating they didn't have forty years between them. Yet they planned on striking into a raw wilderness and were completely confident of the outcome. I tried to imagine how I'd feel, if to my personal problems was added the responsibility of establishing a home, and shook my head.

"How are you going to get by the first year?"

Cameron hadn't accepted the second drink, but the first had given his youth extra heartiness. He laughed and stretched out his arms.

"Why wouldn't we get along? Bess has a spinnin' wheel, a kettle, a fryin' pan an' a cow, an' I got a rifle, an axe, a hoss and two dogs. Between us we can do everythin' we need to."

"How you goin' to freshen the cow?" Durham asked, guffawing.

"We'll find some wild stud like you that ain't got sense enough to have a wife," Bess told him. "Bring yourselves over to the table now." Then as we gathered around the tiny board she added, "Goodness, we'd be crowded if there was any more of us."

I looked to see whether she was being sarcastic, but she wasn't. If anything she seemed pleased at this forced entertainment and was realistically undismayed at the manner in which it was served. There were more people than there were utensils and that fact, as anybody could see for himself, called for a certain amount of swapping around. As near as I could read her attitude she recognized our need for food and their need for the novelty of company as a fair exchange, and hang the inconvenience to both parties.

The food itself was something else again. It was plentiful and well cooked, facts of which she was comfortably aware. Cameron was not content with this silent display of ability.

"My wife's the best damn cook in the state," he bragged. "As a matter of fact it's got so it's a point of pride for a critter to be fixed by her. When I go huntin' I don't have to track down a deer no more. No, sir, they look *me* up, wantin' to know which one's next on Bess' list."

"That must have been pretty good whiskey, too," his wife observed.

The youngster patted her hand. "Bound to be good whiskey come out of a silver bottle. Daunt," he said again, "that's the prettiest thing I ever seen."

During the talk that followed supper I began to worry about the sleeping arrangements, but our hosts were not at a loss. When conversation bogged down in drowsiness they dragged down a couple of bearskins and some extra blankets from the rafters and spread them on the floor. They were for giving the bed to any two of us, but this extension of hospitality we firmly resisted.

Cameron brusquely spurned any proffer of payment the next morning, but after thinking it over I decided there was a way. He and Tim had gone to the shed to get our horses and Holley was outside, smoking a slender pipe and sorting out botanical specimens. I had been busying myself gathering my belongings, but now I stepped over to where Bess was busy with a broom.

"Mrs. Cameron," I said, holding out my leather case, "would you give this to your husband after we're gone?"

She thought she ought to refuse, but I saw she could not bring herself to turn down something that would so pleasure her man. In the end she chuckled excitedly and reached for it.

"That's right nice, Daunt. When he sees it he'll be like a coon in a cornfield."

On my part I was of the opinion that my great-grandfather would agree that it was well bestowed. As I stooped for my saddlebags I felt my black bottle, the hip-fitting flask of the country, now for the first time full.

The botanist had made no preparations for an early start, I found when I stepped outside. "I think I'll look around here for a couple of hours," he explained as we shook hands. "To one in my trade all localities are alike fruitful."

"You'll find Natchez rich in flowers," I said on the strength of casual observation and by way of making some sort of a rejoinder.

"And I should fare as well were I to follow you—better, of course, where company is concerned." He waved his pipe toward the north. "I believe I understood you to say when you were being put through your catechism last night, that you were bound for the fabulous New Purchase of the Choctaws?"

"That's right, sir."

"Then we may meet again on wilder heaths and ringed by more savage horizons. For if it is unknown country it must have unknown blossoms for my picking." His face remained his mask, but for the first time he let his passion show through his words. "I must find and know them all, you see."

In the course of the cross-examining to which he had referred Durham had learned that we were headed for the same general destination. Now as we rode forth, fellows of the road for the second day, there was an unspoken question in my mind. How were we to disembarrass ourselves of each other? It was a dilemma of a kind frequently afflicting people who previously bore each other no ill will, but it was one which usually resolved itself in an hour or so. This seemed likely to last for days unless one of us thought of a graceful out.

I couldn't think of any all that day and by nightfall I was glad of it. We passed through a village about noon, then saw no break in the forest for hours. Once again I was concerned about a place to spend the night, and once again Tim was not.

"There's a settlement up the road a piece, so quit worryin', Daunt. As a matter of fact, I got some folks that moved somewheres near here a year or so ago, and we can stay there if they ain't pushed on."

Mentally I determined not to stay with them if a tavern offered me an alternative. The night with the Camerons had been pleasant, but it had not won me over to a liking for imposing on strangers in one-room cabins. There was no alternative, and by the time we belatedly arrived I was so tired I'd shucked most of my squeamishness.

Tim had spoken accurately when he used the word "settlement." The community was not a village in any normal sense but a spatter of residences peppering a general area. The first shack we came to stood alone, and thence we were directed a mile down a side path to the cabin of Durham's relatives.

Present at the moment were Tim's Aunt Molly and her husband, Mr. Galtin, who made us as welcome as if the visit had been anticipated. The younger Galtins, our hostess told us, were attending a quilting party given by a neighbor. "You and Daunt ought to go, Tim," she suggested as she served us supper. " 'T ain't more'n half a mile off, and your cousins'll be just awful glad to see you."

"Good idea," Durham said, and I groaned in my samp. I had already had more traveling than I enjoyed that day. Moreover, in my catalogue of recreations a quilting party ranked just below hopscotch and just above pulling wings off flies.

Yet the idea of being left alone to answer the incessant questions of my hosts was even less bearable, so I went. It may have been no more than a half mile to the scene of festivities, but strange distances always seem longer. We footed it to give our mounts their deserved rest; and although my legs protested at first I found they'd limbered up by the time we sighted the squares of light that marked the cabin. For the second time Durham stopped and suggested that we drink from his flask.

"We've got to get in trim," he insisted, though I needed no persuading. I wanted some armor against the ambushed ennui. It did seem to me that the voices we heard were more excited than the making of quilts would warrant; but literature had often told me of the glee yokels could work up over simple pleasures. Then the fiddle started.

The effect on my companion was remarkable. We were still a few feet from the door when the first bar was being played. Before its conclusion he had flung the door open and was through it. With one bound he was in the middle of the floor, exploding into a breakdown as soon as he landed, his flask in one hand, his hat in the other. Betimes he leapt up and crowed, slapping his buttocks with his hat, marvelously like a rooster that has just trod a hen and is damn glad of it. Then he spun around and stopped, pointing to me, with words that froze me in the doorway.

"Here we are, Tim Durham and Daunt there, come to kiss all the girls, drink all the whiskey and whip all the men. Howdy, folks."

Several couples that had been preparing to take the floor when he entered had waited patiently for him to finish; and the fiddler had increased his tempo as if to abet Durham's frenzy. Rather than being antagonized everyone had seemed entertained. The girls were pleasantly interested and the men watchful, as if appreciative of a technique.

One of the latter who'd been lounging next to the doorway spat past me out into the dark, then grinned at me. "How are you tonight?" he enquired, pulling a bottle from his pocket. "Have a horn?"

"Thanks. I need one," I told him.

That and Tim's announcement of our intentions was all the introduction I got. I had been told my host's name by Mrs. Galtin but as I never identified him it is immaterial to the record. However, he had a larger than average cabin, which made it a suitable gathering place for the young people of the countryside, and either he or somebody had provided a stupendous amount of whiskey.

Presumably Durham had a reunion with his cousins, but I never knew who they were either. A girl called Ellie Lou was present and another called Katie, at least one of whom I was probably with part of the time. Yet if the characters are dimly remembered the dramatic structure of the evening is more or less clear in my mind.

Right after Tim had staged his entrance he walked over to a girl and yanked her to her feet. Then the fiddler bawled for a set to be formed, and the dancing went on. I located the whiskey barrel and an unclaimed tin cup and leaned in a corner, quite satisfied to be a spectator at first.

The violinist was a sombre individual who never changed expression and opened his eyes only when he spat. This he did regularly between stanzas of the songs with which he accompanied himself. The different stanzas in turn signalled certain movements of the dance, and the choruses, in which the dancers sometimes joined, still others. There was no calling.

Basically the dance itself was a reel, not unlike the ones I had been taught as a child. However, it had notable features that were perhaps unknown to the prim little woman who had instructed me. One was the interspersion of solo antics that never really interrupted the dance but blended into it as grace notes blend with an air. For the rest, the pace was terrific and the execution reckless.

A man balancing toward his partner might suddenly jump up, click his heels and gobble like a turkey, walk on his hands, spin and scratch himself, get down on all fours and bark, cut little circles flapping his wings or prance forward pawing the air like a horse standing on its hind legs. These activities did not disconcert their partners, who would squeal, hoist their skirts and do an intricate buck and wing until their dancing mates sprang forward to swing them. And swing them they did, snatching them clear of the floor, or handing them in a grand right and left that was more like snap-the-whip. Then at some signal I couldn't detect everybody would kiss whoever they happened to be dancing with at the time.

The reel was interminable. By the time it finally ended reason had connived with liquor to convince me that as long as I had to stay there it was silly to hold aloof. There was an interim for refreshment, during which the girls drank on one side of the room and the men on the other, before the next set was called for. I'd marked a fresh-faced, chubby little brunette and, getting in the forefront of the rush, asked her if she'd like to dance.

"Stranger," she not unreasonably asked, "what the hell do you think I'm here for?"

She didn't move, and I hesitated, nonplussed. "Stranger," she suggested after a moment, "would you either do something or get out of the way of a man that maybe means business?" Reaching out gingerly, I grasped her wrist as I had seen the others do and found she came docilely along. This may have been Ellie Lou.

I found that I remembered the steps well enough, and though I wasn't skilled in improvising I inserted a double shuffle at appropriate intervals. After I'd got used to tossing my partners around I had a fine time. As reel followed reel the ballads with which the fiddler accompanied himself had become progressively less decorous. Finally he sang one I partially remember because it was taken up and sung over and over by most of the dancers.

My partner at this time was a lissome redhead who may also have been Ellie Lou. I certainly heard the name from someone that night. She was at once no burden at all and a warmly solid armful as I swept her from the floor to whirl her. Her excited eyes blazed, perhaps for every man, but surely for me, as I snatched her hand and slung her toward the next that reached for her. And her kiss, I found to my gratification, was the kiss of the lichen for the rock.

The fiddler's voice was hoarse but still had plenty of volume:

"My true love went to Vicksburg town,
Good-bye, my darlin' lover;
I love her more than I done before,
For now there's lots more of her."

He spat as a sign that the chorus was about to begin, and I flung the girl away in preparation for balancing.

"Oh, a heifer gets to be a cow
By more'n gettin' older,
An' a pullet likes to fly the fence
If you ain't there to hold her."

I dutifully went into my war dance, but my partner's charade was more appropriate. Turning her back and flouncing up her skirts, she pranced away, looking invitingly over her shoulder. I felt the blood crowding to an already stimulated brain.

It was just then that the music abruptly stopped. This was evidently done at someone's request, for a man shouted: "Let's play hide an' seek!"

The anticlimax was too much for me. I stared bewilderedly around to find the others filtering through both the front door and the one leading out through the kitchen shed. "Come on!" my partner cried, putting her hand in mine, and I shrugged resignedly. If I had to play this child's game, at least I'd have her company.

Outside we scampered away through the woods. She seemed to know just where she wanted to hide, which turned out to be the prostrate hulk of a huge tree. "Nobody's beat us to it," she whispered after peering inside.

The tree was capaciously hollow with a soft floor of dry wood rotted to powder. When we were inside, snuggled together, I began to think less hardly of hide and seek. Suddenly knowing, I waited until I saw the white blur of her face turned to mine. "Nobody else thought of this," she said breathlessly.

All the churned-up passions that had been beating around inside of me now fused to wreak the desperate accomplishment of their purpose. And she was no less implacably driven. The body I grappled was as powerfully limber as a snake's, but much more fun.

So much for the doing. The bleak moment connected with an act of impersonal lechery follows completion. People who have wrought intimately ought to have something to say to one another, and there is nothing to say. She, I thought, managed it well.

"Stranger," she said, "you can't dance worth a damn, but that was mighty nice. Now you wait here a little an' let me find my way back by myself."

I was glad to let her go. I wanted no more of her nor of anything then save a drink and rest. The first I had with me, and after a couple of pulls on my flask I, too, made for the cabin. By this time, I hoped, even Durham would be willing to leave.

Others had returned before me, but they did not share my longing for quiet. First I heard the shouts and screeches, then I saw parts of the actual combat. Two men were slugging it out toe to toe, another pair were rolling on the ground, and three girls were busy tearing at each other's hair and clothes. Further advertisements of wrath sounded from behind the cabin.

From this point on I don't claim an accurate recording of events. Such parts as I definitely remember were no doubt complemented by others I have lost. At any rate I was drawing uncertainly near the strife when a figure loomed beside me.

"You been triflin' with Katie?" he demanded.

I couldn't honestly say, and my hesitation convicted me. "You been triflin' with Katie," he decided.

The last thing I wanted was violence, but seeing that he was going to hit me I struck him first. Before he could retaliate Tim materialized from somewhere and knocked him down. Well and good, but unfortunately the man had friends. I don't know where they came from, but I exchanged blows with a couple and ended up scuffling on the ground with a third. Neither of us was in condition to wrestle effectually; but he had a female partisan, who danced around beseeching him to hold me still long enough for her to let me have it. "It" was a log she was brandishing, and a blow from it, I retained the awareness to know, would bash in my skull. Finally she tried to do just that, missed us both and fell on top of us. In the resultant confusion I scrambled to my feet.

As if by fiat it was all over. The one unconscious victim started to come to when water was poured over him. Everybody else laughed and had a valedictory drink, and it was on this note of good fellowship that we left, as unceremoniously as we had come.

I never knew a man to be as delighted with an evening as Tim was with that one. He chuckled all the way back, recalling zestful moments aloud, heedless of my lack of response. I was thinking only of the chance to lie down that was just ahead. I was half asleep and bumped into my companion when he abruptly halted.

"You get the hosses, Daunt," he said, "and I'll sneak in and fetch our plunder."

I blinked at him uncomprehendingly. "But we're going to bed."

"Not here," he chuckled. "You know that fellow that was knocked out? That was my cousin, and I done it."

"But he won't mind that," I pleaded, out of my need. "It's all over now. He probably won't even remember."

"Maybe not," he conceded, "but my cousin Ellie Lou will tell Aunt Molly when she catches up, and Aunt Molly won't want me in the house till she simmers down."

"Oh, your cousin Ellie Lou," I said. "I reckon you're right," I added after a second and shambled toward the stables.

We got the rest we craved several miles up the road and didn't awake until noon. Aside from being parched and hungry I felt reasonably good. I had gained a black eye and lost a white hat and felt cheerfully inclined toward this evidence of nature's eternal striving for a balancing of accounts. Considering the night before, I turned it over several times before storing it away among my memorial treasures.

"Tim," I asked, "when do they make the quilts?"

CHAPTER XIII

"I USED ALWAYS to ride an alligator," one of the hunters said through a mouthful of venison. "His hide was a leetle hard on saddle blankets, but he had a nice gait, and he was so fond of me I wouldn't have swapped him for a prime quarter horse. Used to feed him on hominy and bald-face whiskey, and he wouldn't eat unless I give it to him with my own hands." He belched and sighed. "I'd have him right now if we hadn't went to Louisiana one winter. He caught the ague, and I had to shoot him."

"Stranger," I said, "please pass the salt."

Taking a pinch of the crystals from the hickory leaf that was handed to me, I sprinkled it on the gobbet of meat skewered on my great-grandfather's knife. When I had finished eating I cleansed the blade in the ground beside me and sheathed it.

Just beyond reach of the fire Talisman and the other dogs growled unseen over stag bones. Within its nimbus there were five of us. Tim lay stretched out beside me, and across the flames lounged the two strangers we'd encountered late in the day. The fifth was more than a stranger, for to me he was alien beyond hope of comprehension. This was a Choctaw who had strayed into our camp at nightfall. Insisting on gathering wood for us and silently ignoring protests that we didn't want his services, he had asked only for a little whiskey we could hardly refuse. Now he was asleep.

Below the ridge on which we were was the Yazoo. From time to time I could hear the wind riffling the cane brakes that lined its channel. But the black, unhurried water with its meringue of mist was for the moment merely something I believed in. Aside from our party there were only a few things of which I had sensual proof. These included the trees which loomed insubstantially when the blaze waxed, the wolves that were calling to each other not far away, and the run that gurgled down toward the river.

That we were at this particular spot had no more significance than that we were not elsewhere. The morrow would see us move on, or it would not. Place and time are only of importance to people who must think beyond themselves; we had no tryst with anything but accident, no obligation to anything save our stomachs. If this was grasshopper morality, I was in the mood to make the most of it. I had been independent before, but the concomitant boon of self-dependence was a stimulant of a rarer sort. I smacked my mouth on it and found that no sour reminder of ill days came through.

There were occasional encounters, such as the ones this evening, but the realizable population had shrunk to number only Durham and myself. All others seemed to be just floaters. There had been no formal agreement when he and I had entered partnership; not so much as mention of the association had been made. Yet when we might have parted we had not, and after two weeks we took the sexless matrimony for granted. Now he stirred beside me.

"You say you just got here, too?" He sent the question across the fire to either of the two who might want to take it up. Both brought their faces, all hair, flame and shadow, to bear upon him.

"That's right," the bereaved owner of the alligator said. "It's gettin' so crowded up Tennessee way the folks have to take turns breathin'. We stood it till they passed a law a man had to pick up his footprints after him to save room and then we figured it was time to go."

A wolf howled again and somewhere farther off a panther screamed. Rubbing the stubble on my face, I pursed my lips. No doubt Tennessee, where they were forced to pass such drastic laws, had recently been as raw a wilderness. Now I, among others, was plotting the end of this one.

Talisman sauntered out of the dark and stretched out in the warmth beside me. Putting a hand on his ribs, I glanced to where the Choctaw still breathed heavily in sleep. The building of the port fouls the harbor for some; but what was for the hunters a matter of taste was organic with him. Unlike them he wouldn't adapt himself or slip away but would stay fixed like a poisoned mollusk until he was scooped up, along with a bucketful of his peers, to be moved out of the way. If I had no antagonism toward him, neither did I see what anybody could do for him. Like it who will, as I had found myself, the man who can't pull the cork can't expect to keep the bottle.

Tim caught me eyeing the aborigine and shrugged. "Lend me that scalper of yours, Daunt."

Wondering somewhat, for of course he had a knife of his own, I complied. My great-grandfather's weapon had always fascinated Tim because of its antique fashioning as well as because it was supposed to have known Indian blood. Now he curled his fingers in the grooves of the ivory.

"Did you ever meet Mike Fink?" he demanded. I had never heard of Mr. Fink, but the others looked up as if they'd been asked if they'd ever met Pericles or the Black Prince. One of them promptly shook his head, but the man who had formerly ridden an alligator hesitated.

"I just missed him once," he recalled. "They figured if two men like me and him was both trompin' around the same county we'd shake the crops out of the ground, so the governor asked me personal to wait till Mike had gone.

"Well, I went up the Big Muddy with him and spent a year trappin' with him afore he died. He give me this knife, which I like a fool lost to Daunt here playin' black jack. Did you ever see a handle like that?"

He flipped the knife across the fire to stick in the ground between the Tennesseans. The ivory genuinely puzzled them, and they examined it with interest.

"What is it?" one of them wanted to know.

"Injun skull," Durham said matter-of-factly. "Takes a nice polish, don't it? That's because it's from a prairie Injun, always out in the sun without a hat on. Bleaches the skull right on the hoof and makes for a finer grain." He picked the knife out of the air as it came back to him and handed it to me. "You got to give me a chance to win that back some day, though I don't deserve it. A man that'll gamble a friend's gift is lower than a snake's belly in a wheel rut."

"Any time," I said mildly.

I was still waiting to hear about the man Fink and how he had become possessed of my great-grandfather's knife; and the others looked as if they were also. It was a moment, however, before Tim's troubled conscience allowed him to go on.

"Back in Kaintuck when I was a little shaver," he began at last, "we was havin' a feud with a family called the Hankinsons. I wasn't in on the start of it, but my grandpap left it to me along with a musket and a patch for my pants in case I should ever get any. They come direct to me on account of the Hankinsons had got Daddy and Uncle Ned and Uncle Dan. Did you ever go feudin'?"

"Well, in a way," the alligator fancier began. "I——"

Tim realized his mistake. "I can see you have," he said hurriedly. "I was damn near ready to call this one off, but Mammy wouldn't let me. Allowed she'd lick me if I didn't stand to it, so I said all right if she'd let me cut school."

He paused to shift his quid. "I only had one ball for the musket, and there was four Hankinsons left, but Mammy said it'd be all right for me to dig it out of each body and use it again. It was a cold day when I started. It don't often get real cold in Kaintuck, but that day the sun stuck and couldn't slide up the sky. It got just so far and couldn't budge. Stayed half past nine most of the day. There was four buzzards had been sailin' around that froze tight in the sky, too. I noticed 'em partickerler because I never seen nothin' like that only once or twice before."

"Weren't you frozen without any trousers on?" I suggested.

"I was chilly," he admitted, "but every time I got right cold I'd think of the Hankinsons and get mad and that'd thaw me out." He chuckled self-deprecatingly. "I got a terrible temper. Well, I dodged along like a man does feudin', lookin' for somebody to shoot behind every tree, but I didn't rouse nothin'. It was too cold for old Ebenezer and his boys, and they was holed up in their shanty. I could hear 'em havin' a high old time when I got there, singin' and laughin' whilst Cain Hankinson sawed on his fiddle.

[135]

It sure made me mad to see how I was havin' to do the feudin' for both families."

A gust of wind flattened the flames a moment. It brought something of the rank dampness of the river bottoms mixed with the hard freshness of the autumn woods. Talisman stirred and went to sleep again.

"I tried to look into the window," Tim went on, "but it was froze clear across and I couldn't see 'em any better'n you can see fish under the ice. So I got back to the edge of the clearin' behind a big gum tree, yelled I was there, and dared 'em to come out. "I'll say this for the Hankinsons." Here he looked around at us as if they were known to us. "There wasn't one of 'em that didn't have sand. Out they come in a hurry—old Ebenezer and Cain and Abel and Henry Clay. 'There'd ought to be only one of 'em, seein' as how we've killed all the rest,' Ebenezer yells. 'Spread out, and he won't have a chance.'

"Well, it didn't look good at that, but I figured anyways to make 'em pay for my funeral. So while they was sneakin' into position I changed loads and crammed every bit of powder I had behind my one bullet. Then I pulled the trigger and started lookin' for a target. Those old snap guns give a man plenty of time."

The more silent of the strangers laughed. "They sure do. Had one as a brat myself. Used to aim it an' then do all my chores whilst waitin' for it to go off."

"That's the way of it," Tim nodded. "Well, old Ebenezer was the meanest and had killed the most Durhams, so I aimed at what I could see of his beard stickin' out from behind a tree. The gun froze true in position, so I took my hands away to warm 'em up. While the primin' powder was fizzin' and sputterin' I picked out Cain peekin' from behind the cabin, Abel lookin' around a stump and Henry Clay's shirt tail in a clump of brush. They hadn't located me yet, and I hugged that tree mighty close."

Without warning Durham struck his hands together. The resultant sharp crack made me jump. Talisman sprang up, barked, looked sheepish when he found no excitement, and sank down once more. Tim looked gratified.

"That old musket, full to the muzzle of powder, went off just like that, sendin' the bullet faster'n a shootin' star with a bear chasin' it. It must have rattled around in old Ebenezer's skull some, for when it found its way out it had changed direction. It hit Cain skulkin' behind the shack, skidded on the frozen air, drilled Abel through the back, bounced off the stump in front of him and went right between Henry Clay's fifth and sixth ribs.

"The worst of it is," he concluded while we were still stunned by this massacre, "I didn't get to see what was happenin'. All that powder goin' off kicked me up into a butternut tree, and I would have had a mean fall if that patch hadn't caught on a stumpy limb. But the bang was so loud that it shook the sun loose. It got up a little higher, and things started to warm up. By the time I'd got down the buzzards had thawed free, and there was one on each Hankinson. Mammy was plumb proud of me."

In the ensuing silence he seemed to be the only one unaware that something was missing. At length I shouldered the burden. "Where does this Fink come in?"

"What?" He took his eyes away from the fire as if roused from a trance. "Oh, the Injun reminded me of the knife and the knife of Mike. He was a good shot, too."

Before there could be any more personal narratives I asked that Mike Fink be given less casual mention. He seemed to have many of the properties of Heracles, Daniel Boone and Friar Tuck, with a dash or so of Bluebeard and another of Jonathan Wild. For quite a while I was interested in this evidence of gods in our time, then I grew drowsy. I was still not used to life in the forest and sleep came early and easily. When the others started playing cards I begged off and sought my blankets. The wind blew over me, the fire napped, a fox barked, I slept.

The Choctaw had gone by the time the rest of us wakened, vanishing into the void whence he had come upon us. Taking inventory to see what he might have stolen, we found the only thing missing was the pack of cards. I supposed that the colors and pictures appealed to him and thought us cheaply rid of such a visitant.

Tim in his own way took a similar view. "An Injun's got to steal somethin' whether he wants it or not, just like a weasel kills whether it's hungry or not."

"What do you reckon he'll do with the cards?"

He didn't hold with my theory of colors and pictures. "Swap 'em off for whiskey, like he does everythin' else including his squaws and children." Tim was busy mixing hoe cake and didn't look up. "An Injun's the same about whiskey as a tomcat is—only not about whiskey. He's just got to have it, and he don't give a damn."

"They shouldn't be given whiskey, then," I said firmly.

"It's a waste of liquor," he agreed, "but they want it."

Not having had breakfast yet, I was in a mood to be troubled by the ills of the world. "But if it destroys them—" I was starting to argue.

Durham slapped the hoe cake into the pan. "They don't want to go on a reservation, but until they do they got to take their chance in the pit along with us other roosters. Now quit fussin' about Injuns and water the hosses."

After breakfast the Tennesseans went on, leaving with us the two dogs Tim had won from them the night before. Adding Talisman and the hound he had when I met him we had quite a little pack. My companion surveyed them with satisfaction. "Now," he declared, "we've got enough for a bear hunt."

It was a season of clear, clean weather, sharp in the early morning, but only then to the man who stayed still. There was frost promised but seldom delivered and then just enough to add such pleasant lacing as ice gives to a julep. There hadn't been enough sharp weather to transmute the leaves; they were fading gently. Many were on the forest floor, though, and others were sifting down wherever a man looked. Then when the sun got higher there was genuine warmth that never quite lost its autumn temper. It was a superb time to be adrift, and in such a country.

It was one of round ridges, seamed with water runs, of which the Yazoo was the master channel. There were mighty hardwoods on the uplands, swamps and cane in the bottoms. On the high ground traveling conditions were perfect. After the Choctaw custom, underbrush that would otherwise furnish too much cover for game in that land of lush growth had been burned away no longer ago than the year before.

Nevertheless, wild life held its own. It was a country of deer, wolves, wild turkey, raccoons, grouse, foxes, opossums, quail and wildcats by land. It was a district of geese, cotton-mouths, ducks, bass, giant gars, otter, trout and huge snapping turtles by water. Respectively each element boasted a redoubtable champion, the panther and the alligator. Then, classed alone, hunted and admired alike for his usefulness, cleverness and strength, there was the bear.

To a Mississippian, as I had come to find, the bear hunt was a thing apart. Ordinary hunting, though necessary and a pleasant occupation, was without spice of danger. Hunting panthers offered the danger but was otherwise unrewarding. The bear was completely satisfactory. In the contest between him and the hunter he could and sometimes did win. And if the hunter succeeded he had prime food and a skin he could use as well as a triumph to be the seed of great lies for ever after.

Next to the craving of the addict is that of the neophyte, and I had been noting all bear signs with eagerness. Not before this day, however, did Durham show more than conversational interest. That a man shouldn't hunt bear without dogs was an article of faith with him, nor did he consider our two—one of them untried— adequate for the quarry. Now that he deemed us prepared, though, he was keener than I.

With a scratch pack there isn't apt to be unanimity of purpose. We were hunting bear, but the dogs were just hunting, each one whatever he ran across. Sometimes one would follow a scent a little ways, then quit when it found we were riding on.

Within limits it was easy to see what they had picked up. If the yelp was completely light hearted the track belonged to a rabbit; if a little deeper, to a fox or deer; if there was a fiercer note, to a raccoon; if with growling undertones, to a wolf. We amused ourselves by interpreting, then verifying through examination of the tracks.

It was several hours before we heard what we were waiting for: a harsh excited baying with fear and anger in it. One of the new dogs picked it up, to be shortly joined by his mate. They weren't following very fast, we saw as we plunged toward them, and they kept looking back at us to see what we intended to do.

"It's a bear, all right," Tim announced after we'd trailed them a little ways. I had seen nothing, but he pointed at what to me were indecipherable scratches on the ground. "Call your hound, Daunt."

I did, though with some misgivings. The constant life of movement had done much for Talisman just when he was ready for it. Gaining in strength, weight, agility and woodcraft, he had left puppyhood behind him, but this was his first mortal test. Regretting his inexperience, I yet recognized that there was only this one way to overcome it.

As the pace quickened, I thought of other chases in Tidewater. Then, finely mounted and caparisoned, I had pursued a helpless, useless quarry. Now, hunting for food, I was a nondescript figure prodding an ugly little beast into a conflict of some peril. Or to be exact I didn't have to prod Goober. Evincing a Mississippian's flair for catching at the drama of the moment he put on more speed than I would have believed possible. If he couldn't jump such obstacles as the open woods furnished he was adept at scrambling. Tim's more capable mount gained on us but slowly.

In the general frenzy the one factor I neglected to assess was myself. I was accustomed to horse chasing. I had been taught to shoot as soon as I was large enough to hold a gun, and then I had been in the Army. I was a good shot and considered myself, though admittedly a greenhorn as compared with frontiersmen, a capable hunter. With Tim to guide me I had no doubt of being able to give a satisfactory account of myself.

My only real concern was that we would eventually drop too far behind. I would not drive a mount that was giving so earnestly, but the dogs were well out of sight, and I now caught only occasional glimpses of Durham.

We were stumbling down a ridge when I saw him dismount and run forward. "Wait, wait up!" I howled, convinced the bear was at bay, but Tim suddenly disappeared.

It was only then that I realized that what looked like a peculiarly foreshortened vista was no illusion. Riding up, I found myself confronted with a twenty-foot wall of cane. The huge stalks were as close to each other as the palings of a picket fence and visibility in depth had a maximum limit of ten or so feet.

Durham's horse stood with hanging reins near by. Seemingly

Tim had thought it too weary to stray, and I didn't bother to hitch Goober when I flung myself off to find a path of entry. There was none, though I wasted valuable moments convincing myself of this. How a creature the size of a bear could have penetrated without breaking a swath was a mystery, and how Tim had followed was another. None the less, I had seen the latter go in, and the bear had also gained entry. Quite faintly now, I could hear the hounds.

Furious at finding myself thus thwarted, I finally threw myself at the cane. This worked until I was exhausted, by which time I had gained about thirty feet. Meanwhile, I had found why my predecessors had left no trail. The cane sturdily sprang back into position. Looking behind me, I couldn't see whence I had come, nor even point out the direction with certainty.

Extricating my rifle, and the arm that held it, from a traplike clump of stalks, I disgustedly studied the situation. Then I began experimenting. Close to the ground the brake was more open, though I found crawling hard on both the body and the disposition. Next I found that irregularities in the growth made passage easier at certain intervals. Again I learned that backing could be accomplished where ordinary advancing was too painful.

The fact that my goal was itself in motion didn't simplify things at first. All this while the hunt, presumably slowed down, too, had been cutting some sort of arc. Then it passed its zenith and seemed to be curving back toward me. Taking hope anew I tried even harder in the face of new difficulties. As cane grows by kind in bottom lands, the farther in I got the soggier grew the footing. At last I was sloshing through little pools of water with a flooring of tenacious mud.

Then, to my incredulous delight, I heard a crashing through the cane just ahead of me. It would be inexact to say I assumed it was the bear. No other creature inhabited my consciousness. I chortled breathlessly as I plunged forward. Tim might have deserved the bear, but if there were men to keep their hands in their pockets while fortune was passing out gifts, I wasn't one of them.

Rather than detour I floundered through a pool and was knee deep in it when I glimpsed the moving body. It wasn't until I'd thrown my gun and pulled the trigger that I realized it wasn't a bear. Instead it was a deer, frightened out by the hounds, and in any case it did not stop for me. My rifle didn't so much as flash.

Thoroughly disconcerted, I waded out, only to find new depths of humility. An examination showed that the rifle hadn't gone off because in beating my way through the brake I'd allowed the cap to be knocked out. Worse, if the gun had gone off it would have exploded, because while scrabbling around I'd let it get clogged with mud. Worst of all was the reflection that I hadn't even known what I was shooting at when I aimed.

While I was dumping water out of my boots and somberly pondering these facts the dogs, now close at hand, changed from baying to barking. Next I heard growling, squealing, yelping and a heavy, hoarse roaring. The bear had evidently run as far as he was going to and was fighting it out.

Hastily clearing my rifle, I was reloading it when I heard Tim's shot. The roaring ceased, although the excited hounds still made enough racket to guide me. In a little while I made my way to where a huge oak had fought off the cane, and there they all were.

This, I winced to remind myself, was my first actual sight of the animal I had pursued so long and painfully. He was stretched out on the ground, a big black fellow, passively relinquishing his hide as Durham worked on him. Three of the dogs, including Talisman, were bleeding, but not so grievously as to interfere with their appetites. They were quarrelling noisily as they gobbled the mountain of entrails the bear was no longer using.

Miserably tired, sweaty, and mud caked, and more miserably aware of the ignominious part I had played, I stood there a minute before Tim looked up. One glance told him all there was to know about me then.

"Howdy, Daunt," he called, "where've you been keepin' yourself?"

His cheerfulness was almost as much of an insult as his sarcasm. Defenseless, I looked at him stonily.

He plied his knife with deftness and ripped free another segment of the pelt. "Too bad you didn't come along earlier," he went on chattily. "I would've invited you on a bear hunt."

I couldn't take my salted wound out of his reach for the aggravating reason I was depending on him to find the way out. Silently limping over to Talisman, I found he was no more than badly scratched. Then, as silently I limped over to the oak bole, resolving to shuck my boots in favor of moccasins at the first opportunity.

It was when I lowered myself to the sitting position that I learned the full wisdom of what McConnell had once told me. As a camel carries its own protection against the desert, so I, feeling the flask press into my hip, knew myself armed with the one thing that could solace me.

The long pull restored me to grace of spirit. Arising stiffly, I limped over to give Tim a drink and a helping hand.

"What's a bear hunt like?" I enquired.

CHAPTER XIV

I HAD NOT, as McConnell had breezily informed me that I would, mastered the craft of surveying en route to the Yazoo. But after I'd been there a few weeks I'd learned enough of the basic principles to make, if not maps in the strict sense, oriented sketches to serve as guides. For one inexperienced man to have attempted to do more in that vastness would have meant to do nothing.

A true map is an accretion of exactitudes embodying all there is of philosophy, which can be no more than a fixing of relationships. The exactitudes were beyond me, but I had cause to marvel at the relationships I found in the course of even such rough work as I did. At times I had the feeling that I knew that country's precise niche along the road from the sea's floor to the roof of Heaven.

The only precursor's work to hand was a chart as empty as a map of the ocean without soundings. The great rivers framing the territory were shown, along with a few other points thrown in as if to give a façade of accuracy. The task of filling this void, at once tedious and exhilarating, was my unusual fortune. As all good work is the creation of what was not I sometimes had the sense of inventing the land and stood in awe of what I was doing.

Withal I found that this part of my labor was in a sense secondary. To make the useful report for which I had primarily been hired I had to learn to comprehend the potentialities of the country in sum and in its separate parts. It was awhile before I realized this phase with any completeness. I was accustomed to evaluating land in districts where the solution to such problems as transportation and markets had long been worked out. Here the rivers would probably serve as roads as well as seaways for years to come. Cotton raised out of reach of a navigable stream might as well be cockleburs. It would find its way to no more buyers.

But, and this was the hardest thing for me to visualize, there would be other activities than those of a planter. There would be towns, and as in other parts of the world the propinquity of towns would affect the value of the land. Therefore, to attempt to guess where villages would spring up was indispensable to any judgment of a district's worth in waiting.

A man who could tell in advance where the great towns and cities of an undeveloped country would be built could tell where a flea was going to hop next or indicate where blowing thistledown would alight. Many a town whose site had been chosen with care and calculation by knowledgeable men shriveled in the shadow of a city that owed its origin to the fact that some ignoramus had tired of drifting.

I recognized that much; yet certain requisites seemed indispensable. Here again until highways multiplied the territory's capabilities the river was the all-important factor. A town thrives on accessibility, and the only avenues of access were the Yazoo and the navigable reaches of its larger arms. On the other hand, to survive it had to be out of reach of the river at its spring rising. Then to be healthy it had to stand, like Natchez, high enough for winds to wipe it free of the fever airs generated from bottom lands in a hot region. These narrowed the possibilities to make the picking no more a matter of guesswork than selecting horse-race winners. On the south bank there were not too many high points that didn't have disqualifying buffers of swamp between them and the channel. On the northern bank there was none.

To look over a wooded hill and visualize it as the core of a new land's business and cultural life seemed dangerously near to daydreaming. Yet the transmutation would take place, if not in the case of one spot, then of another. Still it was just as well to be able to balance these godlike piercings of the future with a healthy understanding of present reality. I had seen enough frontier towns to know that, if they were indeed destined to produce fair cities, they gave no more promise of the miracle than any other wrinkled seeds. Nor was it probable that anything more attractive would soon appear on the banks of the Yazoo.

Meanwhile, there were days now when cold rains and sharp

winds made shelter at night desirable. Then, too, having made a partial survey, we began to feel the need of a permanent base from which to conduct our respective enterprises. Tim was anxious to organize an otter trap line, and I was ready to establish a base of operations from which to make more exact explorations up and down the river. We decided, therefore, to knock together some sort of a cabin at the next suitable spot.

On our way to investigate a likely looking knoll we were dipping down into a shallow intervening draw when Talisman barked. At the sound a man scrambled from the bed of the creek that ran through the draw. I guessed him to be a Choctaw, but the face he turned toward us as he caught up his rifle was white.

His act was merely defensive, witness the fact that he made no threatening gesture as we approached. I felt that I myself would have been nervous about meeting strangers in the wilderness, but Durham chuckled. He made no comment, though, until we were just across the stream from the other. Then he turned to me.

"Scary lot around here," he observed loudly.

As this was the first white man we'd seen since leaving the Tennesseans I felt that he was drawing conclusions from insufficient data. The big, shaggy fellow awaiting us took an even more critical view of the remark.

"I ain't ascared of you, mister," he said heatedly, "nor of the other fellow who looks as ornery as you be, nor of anybody that's fool enough to like either of you. I ain't afraid of your guns, which I bet can't shoot straight, nor of your dogs, which I bet ain't got fleas that's critter enough to bite me. Want to fight?"

"I'd just as lief," Tim said cheerfully.

Pushing his horse through the branch forthwith, he leapt to the ground. His challenger sprang at him, and for a moment they pounded each other solidly. Then, while our dogs, joined by two more dashing down from the knoll, yelped enthusiastically, they clinched for the throw. As each was unable to unbalance the other the result was akin to a high wind in a box. The tugging, stamping, straining, whirling, grunting and twisting were frightful—but nothing happened until both toppled together down the bank into the two or more feet of water below.

My own emotions varied during this conflict. First I was startled at the savage suddenness of its joining, then I was concerned lest Tim should encounter some gouging or maiming tactics. When I saw that neither could make much headway I became more interested and less partisan. The upshot left me delighted but determined that the matter should end in the water. By the time they'd regained the bank I'd maneuvered Goober across.

"Let's have a horn," I suggested.

Looking at each other to make sure assent would not be mistaken for craven withdrawal, both started laughing. "Stranger," the stranger declared, "that's the first thing making sense any of us have said. I'll thank you for that drink, too. The water's cold."

He meant business, as I saw when he shoved the mouth of the bottle into his black beard and squared his wide shoulders. He took nearly half the flask and Tim, not to be outdone, left me to drain one modest drink.

"Yancey Shevlin," the fellow said when he could breathe. "Come on up to my wigwam, where there's a fire."

Among a fine stand of hickory at the crest of the knoll was the residence to which he had referred. This, if not exactly a wigwam was as casual an edifice. It was a cross between a cabin and a lean-to, an open-faced log structure with its back turned north and west toward bad weather. There was a thinly smoking clay hearth in front. Twenty-five yards farther on the knoll fell away to a fringe of cane brake. Then there was a twist of river, resembling a crescent-shaped lake.

I had time to appreciate these things while my shivering companions shucked their soaked clothes and Shevlin built up the fire. The abundance of seasoned hardwood handy was only one evidence that he had been there for some time. The blaze gave a blue smoke that barely thickened the atmosphere and soon threw off a luxurious amount of heat. Lapped in sensuousness, I lay on a bearskin and listened to the other two talk.

Durham started off with the usual Western gambit of asking personal questions. Shevlin, however, wasn't showing the frankness usual in such discussions, an attitude Tim saw fit to challenge.

"What state you hidin' out from?" he blandly demanded.

Our host considered this point. "Left it so long ago I done forgot," he decided. "How's your folks which ain't been hung?"

If Durham remembered that they'd all been killed off in a feud he refrained from mentioning it. "Middlin'. Of course, a state governor has to work pretty hard and it keeps Mammy humpin' keepin' the capitol in order." I thought he had exhausted his store of personal queries, but he dragged out one that had been previously overlooked. "Your old woman recovered from the shock of marryin' you yet?"

In place of answering him Shevlin sighed resoundingly. Then he turned to me. "Could you tell a squaw from a mule out fire huntin'?"

There were several aspects of this query. I started with the point I thought it easiest to deal with.

"What's fire hunting?"

He glanced at Durham enquiringly. "He means it," Tim said. "There's not much to fire huntin', Daunt. You just put a chunk of lightwood in a fryin' pan, go out at night and shoot at the shine of a deer's eyes."

"That's it," Shevlin nodded. "I used to couldn't do enough of it an' most every night me an' an Injun—you got to have somebody to carry the pan—would go out. The old woman always suspicioned I was triflin' on her, but I never was that kind of a man."

In truth he didn't look to be the light of any woman's bower. Finding his fidelity was not in question, he proceeded.

"Durham's right that the idea is to shoot venison; but what you actually do is shoot at a pair of eyes, then find out what was carryin' 'em. Takes practice, like everythin' else. At first I'd sometimes bag a wildcat or an owl, an' once I had my sights on a deacon, but he cleared his throat just in time."

"Well, sure, that kind of thing happens," Tim averred.

"After the deacon, I took it slower," Shevlin remarked. "I used to study the eyes pretty careful, an' I got so's I could tell most every time whether it was a wolf, a snake, or a polecat, say, even before I shot it."

I didn't want to ask him anything, but I had to for my own peace of mind. "What did you shoot varmints like that for?"

"Only way to prove I was right an' catch up my mistakes. Besides, I had to make sure I had somethin' to bring home or my wife would never believe me. She still had it up her nose I was cheatin' on her an' kept beggin' me not to go; but I was havin' fun an' couldn't see no harm in it.

"Well, you know how it is sometimes when you hunt, you just can't find nothin'. Hunted for hours an' didn't see even a June bug. Me an' the Injun was gettin' awful tired an' the lightwood was about to burn out; but I was scared to come home with nothin' to prove I'd been huntin', so I kept on. Then when I'd just about give up I saw a pair of shinin' balls lookin' like fox fire in the light the way a critter's eyes do."

"That's just so," Tim nodded.

"By that time," Shevlin said, nudging a log farther into the fire, "I'd got pretty sure of myself. I couldn't just tell what kind of critter it was by its eyes, but how much it weighed and how it was feelin'. So I says to myself: 'That there's a mule sixteen hands high, it's lame in the off hind leg an' has a mean disposition.'

"Well, if I hadn't been ascared of gettin' in trouble at home, of course, I wouldn't have shot. But I had to look after myself, an' I figured that mule had ought to look after himself, too, if he could. So I up with Old Flinders an' pulled the trigger, whango!"

"How'd you get the mule home to show your old woman?" Tim ask interestedly.

With a sweep of his hand Shevlin removed Durham's floppy headgear. "Take your hat off when you speak of her! She was awful big an' awful bug-eyed, but she's an angel now. When I didn't get home she come out lookin' for me, an' as those jealous but lovin' peepers shined out at me from the night I drilled her right between 'em."

That was as much as I ever knew of his history, though we stayed with him all that fine winter of rough work in foul weather. In common with Durham and the Tennesseans we'd met he was a hunter and trapper, but with a difference. They ranged the woods to maintain the particular if sometimes tenuous relationship to society they found desirable. He had no detectable part in the human scheme as ordinarily understood. He hunted as a panther does, because it was his method of existing. For the rest, because he had an alert mind which had no other place to go, he was exhaustively concerned with even the most minor details of outdoor phenomena.

The three of us fraternized as our respective pursuits permitted. Sometimes all of us together, but more often only two at a time found a joint expedition possible. As often as not it was Shevlin rather than Tim that I went with, and a master educator I found him. He knew the soil from the stomach contents of the bugs in it out; and from this profundity I drew accuracies else beyond me.

By volunteering to be the flame bearer I early induced him to take me on a fire hunt. I found it a grotesque kind of chase oddly blended with a dash of poetry. Lightwood is a pretty name for a chunk of resinous pine, but it is exactly descriptive in that the wood flares brilliantly. A frying pan tied to a long stick is an unusual seat for a beacon, but, keeping as it does the flame far enough away to save the hands from sparks, it is practical. Lastly, to pass through the benighted woods bearing a death lure fashioned of such elements is a thoroughly fantastic business.

But it worked. If light does not actually draw most creatures it transfixes them. From time to time I saw eyes suspended at all levels in mid-air. No other portion of the animal was in most cases discernible, but the eyes shone with a cold, live flame, giving the impression that the fire came from within. To my unaccustomed mind it appeared impossible to identify the owners. Failure to discriminate between the prominent eyeballs of a large woman and those of a mule seemed a forgivable error.

My companion, however, had lived to regain the self-confidence that must have been shaken by that tragic mistake. He strolled along a few yards ahead of me, maintaining a relative position that kept the light on his sights without dazzling him. Still, for all the inflamed eyes we passed he never raised his gun for two hours. About the time I was kicking myself for having insisted on this nonsense he snapped Old Flinders to his shoulder and fired at something my wandering attention had failed to perceive.

It was a doe and very good eating, too, but having convinced myself that it could be done I lost interest in fire hunting. Among the things of more lasting value which Shevlin taught me was how to manage that treacherous but useful craft, a log canoe. It could literally float where a goose was forced to use its legs, and under

Yancey's guidance it could move as quietly as the water that bore it.

My motive in taking to the water was to get some understanding of the extent of the channel as well as to investigate possible town sites from the river approach. Secondarily, I recognized that the Yazoo was the key to more than the accessibility of the region. In a country of rare springs, the streams supplied the drinking water for most people. This fact, or the poisonous effluvia from hot swamps, or both, seemed likely to account for the agues and fevers that were said to curse many southwestern communities. I was still physician enough to consider these matters, though apparently neither I nor anyone else was physician enough to do anything about the proximity of the source of wealth to the source of ill-health. My own immediate contribution was the makeshift one of plotting the stretches where water was apt to lie stagnant.

Incidentally, there was the Yazoo as an entity. Its chief quality was darkness. The stream itself, its banks, the swamps into which it periodically overflowed, and the boles of the ambient trees were alike somber. The cane brakes, though lighter in themselves, conspired with the great roofing branches to hold out the sun. Occasional patches and stretches of brightness only accentuated the basic tone. Even the smell of the river was crepuscular.

The creatures that swam in the muddy waters were suitable, if largely invisible. The most formidable, such as the alligator, the snapping turtle and the water moccasin were coddled in mire at that season. The great gar, the carp, the giant catfish and the horrendous water puppy kept their dark bodies in the depths. It was rather the river's shore haunters—the raucous birds and the silent animals—that gave a leaven of movement to the half light.

Once we rounded one of the incessant bends to see what looked like a waterlogged chunk of wood moving somehow athwart the channel. I couldn't hazard identification, distant and low in the water as it was, but Shevlin excitedly put a name to it.

"That's a b'ar," he cried, sending us toward it with a powerful thrust of his paddle. "Dig in!"

Mistrusting his statement, I complied with but half a heart. While realizing that the laws governing human conduct were subject to endless exceptions, I clung to the novice's belief that nature regulated things more strictly for animals. "It can't be a bear," I protested. "They've all hibernated."

"I don't know about that," he grunted, "but most of 'em are asleep. This one ain't though. Dig in!"

The bear was almost across by the time we got near enough for detailed observation. The banks at this point were too steep for ascent, and it turned down stream until, some fifty yards below, a slough made a break in the shore. We were thirty yards or so behind at this point, but it was still in sight when we reached the inlet ourselves. Gaining, we saw the traces of blood, then we noted the broken arrow protruding from the animal's back.

"That's it, then," Shevlin said, and I saw that he had had to know. "Some Injun caught him asleep in his nest."

The bear turned once to look at us, then applied himself more vigorously to the business of swimming. The big paws drove him through the water with surprising speed, notwithstanding the deepening color of the froth in his wake. However, we pulled up until we were right behind him.

"Do you think the Indian chased him into the river?" I queried.

"I expect he climbed a tree, if he was spry enough, as soon as he found he hadn't made a kill. No, I reckon the b'ar's just runnin' from pain, the same as anybody else that can't cure hisself."

For nearly two hundred yards it churned inland between the reeds, and Shevlin from his stern position guided us after him. The animal, which had exerted itself to the utmost in an effort to outdistance us, was getting winded. We could hear its snorting become a wheeze. I found the pursuit interesting, but my companion was completely absorbed.

"'T ain't very often you get to see a b'ar close up," he remarked, "when you ain't so busy fightin' you don't much care for it. You know, he'd be as big a varmint as I ever seen if he wasn't so leaned down by winterin'."

I was no judge of such matters, but the creature did look immense. Glancing ahead to see just when he might have a chance to escape from the water, I saw the slough was broadening to form a small, swampy pond with shallow edges. If it didn't offer good footing it was a feasible bridge to sounder earth, and the weary animal made for it.

Yards before reaching the swampy shore he sank into soft mud, belly deep. There was still water enough for the canoe, it developed, for to my shocked amazement Shevlin sent us swirling in an arc that took me right in front of the bear's fanged snout.

No better prepared for this than myself, the creature jerked his front legs out of the mud and reared back. By this time I had swept ten feet beyond his fright and anger. The rear of the canoe whipped by him, right beneath his upraised forepaws; and as he passed, Shevlin drove his knife into the soft spot under the near shoulder.

Dropping my paddle, I reached frantically for my gun. Dropping on all fours the bear lunged venomously for us. We were both belated. The animal just missed the stern of the canoe, and Yancey sped it safely ahead of his dying charge with a drive of the paddle he had to leave in the mud where he'd shoved it. By the time I'd lined up my sights the bear had lost his thrashing impetus. With a final hoarse gasp he sank down, to drown as much in his own blood as in water.

Lowering my weapon without firing, I let us drift until I was sure my voice wouldn't shake. Shevlin was still watching the beast broodingly.

"What the devil did you do that for?" I asked at length. I had passed from fright through indignation at being frightened to a feeling of helpless incomprehension.

He looked at me as stolidly as if he hadn't needlessly risked his life and—which I took a great deal more to heart—my own. "Well, I wouldn't have killed him at this time of year when he's so poorly, but I figured he'd likely die from that arrow anyhow."

"I don't care whether you killed him or not!" I cried, my exasperation returning. "But if you wanted to kill him, why didn't you shoot him?"

He searched his soul while I fumed. "I couldn't shoot him while he was stuck in the mud," he decided. "I'd have done it with another critter but not a b'ar."

I couldn't come any nearer to the matter than that. At the same time it was my closest glimpse into the profoundly divergent manner of thinking developed in the wilderness. This differed from giving a stag space and law as noted by Scott and from the ceremonious fox chasing practiced in Virginia. It took in a recognition of animal worth that perhaps borrowed something from religion but of that I couldn't be sure either. The only thing I could clearly see was that Shevlin looked from the forest out, like a wolf's eyes at a clearing.

CHAPTER XV

IT WAS IN MIDWINTER that we went to Turkey Run, the first town down river from the New Purchase border. One reason for the undertaking was the need for replenishing our staples. That in itself might not have driven Tim, as we were well supplied with bear meat, venison, turkey, ducks, geese, nuts and honey; but our whiskey ration had long been only a memory.

"I'd oughtn't to leave my traps," Durham remarked while making his decision, "but I'm so damn dry I'm scared to go near a fire, and I'm shiverin' so I'm scared I'll shake to dust."

"I'll take care of your traps," Shevlin offered. He had from the beginning voiced his intention of remaining. "The only reason for goin' to a damn town," he pointed out, "is to buy what's needed. You all can do that."

As for myself, I was avid for news, any news of a world I'd been out of touch with for months. Moreover, as the riverhead for shipping, Turkey Run was the town through which McConnell and I had agreed to communicate. Sooner or later, in any case, I'd have to leave directions there as to just how I might be located when he came north.

The trip, once it was definitely scheduled, took on the air of an exciting adventure into a Babylon of luxury. My exact memories of frontier towns had faded to softness, and anything in the way of a community stood for opulent ease.

It required three days of ambling through the forest to take us into the Old Choctaw Purchase. Early in the afternoon of the third we came to a little square cabin with a roof that looked as if it had been mashed down on top of it. A clearing had been made by the crude ruse of killing the trees on it by fire. This, by making the trees incapable of bearing leaves, let down the sunlight to whatever crops the owner might plant. This particular owner hadn't got around to doing any planting yet, though he might have been contemplating a crop as he sat in his doorway.

"Howdy, stranger," Tim called out to him, "where's Turkey Run?"

Inevitably the man pondered and spat before he spoke. "Reckon you must be in it, stranger. I am."

I gazed down the wheeltracks to where they switched out of sight into the woods. "How far is it to the main part of town?" I asked hopefully.

"Not more 'n a frog hop. Of course, you got to have a dependable frog. What you lookin' for, the store or the doggery?"

"How about the doggery?" Tim enquired.

"Oh, you'll find that all right," the man said confidently. "I just wanted to tell you that if you're lookin' for the store it's in the same buildin'."

On the way we passed several well-spaced shacks. Then we came to one, larger than the rest but no less solitary, which had a tavern sign pendent in front. We were in the business section of Turkey Run.

My visions of urban bustle had vanished during that first encounter with a local citizen. I was already resigned to what was not and glad of what there actually was by the time we dismounted at The Horsethief's Head. Both the lettering that gave the name and the illustrating portrait were crude. The latter, however, challenged attention, what with the protruding tongue and the gore dripping from the severed neck.

Tim glanced up at it disapprovingly as he shoved in against the door. "Don't look like he can hold his liquor," he observed.

Those within were doing better. There were only two customers, who broke off conversation to eye us quietly. Not so the bartender.

"Howdy, strangers," he said as he shuffled over to lean across the plank toward us, "what kind of tanglefoot do you want?" He jerked his head toward the barrel that apparently made up his entire stock. "I'll call it whatever you want me to."

With the sighs of men home at last we leaned on the bar ourselves. "How's your drinkin' liquor?" Tim wanted to know.

"Stranger, I don't like to brag," our host said, "but it's like lightnin' an' a tornado held together by a widow's kiss. Of course, it ain't for boys. A little fell in the river when we was gettin' it off the boat, an' the Yazoo got tight an' run backwards for an hour an' twelve minutes. Think you'd like to try some?"

We would and did. It was strong, untrammeled whiskey, but we had gusto to match it. We had two to clear the passage, a third for the good feel of it going down, then lingered comfortably over the fourth. The landlord watched us genially the while, asking questions with the rapidity of an expert.

"I reckon you come to town to meet the boat," he suggested when he'd made all the usual queries.

"We came in to buy supplies," I informed him.

"Then you did come to meet the boat," he said. "I won't have nothin' to sell till the steamer paddles up. Won't even have whiskey enough to serve the welcomin' party till they roll it down the gangplank."

Tim looked around at the empty shelves behind us. "You're cleaned out for a fact. When's the boat comin'?"

"Well, it was due yesterday, an' I've about give it up for today. I got a boy up a tree watchin' for it though, an' he'll fire a gun as soon as he spots it."

On the chance that McConnell might have written to me I enquired for mail. "How long has it been since the last steamer?" I asked when assured I had no letter.

"Three months ago there was one. The skipper was to have been back by Christmas time, but he sent word by a rider passin' through that he couldn't make it till now. He'll be here for sure this time, though."

"How do you figure that?"

"Well, you may not have noticed, but the head on that sign out front has been bleedin'. It only does that when a steamboat or a white woman comes near, an' steamboats is all I've seen so far. Have one on me?"

"Any time," Tim assured him. "Who was the hossthief anyhow?"

"Nobody knows," one of the other customers spoke up. "Nat wishes he did, and he'll give a hundred dollars to the man who can tell him."

"That's right." Our host lifted one with us and went on. "You see, just when I was about to open this place a man borrowed Rockaway, an' I lost three days' trade findin' 'em both. I didn't have a shovel, an' it was too much work bringin' him back, so I just toted his head. It's buried out yonder, but I'll dig him up if you think you might know him."

"I don't know many people in Mississippi," I said, "but all I've met so far have had bodies attached. Have one with us and serve the two gentlemen down the line."

We got reasonably drunk, enjoyed a meal we didn't ourselves cook, and retired early to sleep like hibernating bears. We were enjoying a smoke and a glass after a late breakfast when I heard a shot. The landlord smacked his hands together.

"He seen the smoke! She'll be here in a couple of hours now."

A fellow lounger suddenly came to life and bolted out. While we were toasting fortune's kept promise he galloped away on an errand kindred to that of Paul Revere. Durham gave out a war whoop to send him on his way, and the landlord cried out some directions. Though more silent, I was party to the excitement myself.

What I or any of them expected could not be compassed in words. But there is nothing to match the drama of an arrival of unknown portent. The boat winding along through the all but unbroken forest could hold anything. The eager mind of isolation grasped the possibilities and promptly convinced itself that the craft did in fact hold treasures. I yearned for that steamer and would have thrown away as worthless the hours of my own life that kept us apart.

Finding passive waiting no longer bearable we walked down to where a few men already stood on the little wharf. An hour after the signal shot the wharf and the adjacent clearing held the entire population of the vicinity, and outliers came drifting in every few minutes. There was well on toward a hundred of them, but I saw why the thief's head didn't bleed more frequently than its wont. A few Choctaw squaws had emerged from somewhere, but I saw no white women. Until the Indians were largely removed from the New Purchase it wouldn't be a family country upriver in the Old.

What the squaws were there for it was easy to guess; but the rest of us were waiting for the world we'd deliberately left to be brought to us in some form. My own chief hope was that the ship would include a variety of newspapers and journals—I didn't care from what city, state or county—in its marvellous cargo. I felt a craving for information about any event, place or person that would serve to blend me once more with the main stream of human existence. My mind felt as painfully empty as a starved man's belly, with as basic a need for something on which to grip.

"There she is!" somebody cried. Far down the river, where it disappeared among the trees, we saw the prow. For a minute the ship was broadside to us as it crossed to follow the channel, then it approached head on. We could hear the engines now, and stemming from the funnel was a lank, black cloud of smoke. We could see one or two men moving about, and several tried to reach them with shouting. The half dozen or so who fired shots got better results. The steamer acknowledged the courtesy with three long exhilarating blasts of its whistle.

That was no such imposing packet as brought me from New Orleans to Natchez. It was small, old and dirty, a stray relegated to secondary streams because it could no longer compete on the main runs. But it was only in retrospect that I saw this. At the moment it was a symbol of man's daring in concept and power to execute. It filled the eye and ear satisfyingly, and everyone aboard her was a man of no ordinary mark.

When it at last worked its way alongside the dock the crew had more helpers than they could use. The citizens of Turkey Run shoved each other in their eagerness to help unload. They were equally zealous in volunteering to carry aboard wood from a great pile which had been waiting since the vessel was first expected weeks before.

Standing well out of the way of this form of activity, I watched for newcomers, hoping for I knew not what. Of course, every arriving vehicle is potentially the bearer of an old friend or a new one. I wouldn't have been surprised at finding almost anybody I had once known on a boat like that. Yet in the upshot I was. Of the three identifiable as passengers by the luggage they carried ashore one was the little gambler—Jack Garland, the big fellow had named him—whom I had last seen at his moment of triumph after the successful raid he had engineered against Natchez.

As my enmity had no personal basis it was dead away from the situation that had made us hostile. If he was a rogue, he was now among men used to taking care of themselves. Many of them, for all I knew, might be professional knaves also. From the beginning I had taken the blazonry of the tavern to have significance. Save in a district with a special clientele such a display of robust humor couldn't be a profitable advertisement.

Watching the gambler as he considered the port of Turkey Run, I speculated about him out of the wealth of my entertained idleness. Had he come to survey the possibilities of profit hereabouts, or had he been driven to a place generally regarded as an outlaws' haven? The latter seemed the more probable case. A man of his trade, accustomed to the raffish opulence of Natchez Underhill or the luxuries of a Mississippi packet wouldn't abandon them voluntarily. Filing this thought for future consideration I moved to where the captain of the steamer was indulging eager enquirers concerning the outside world.

"Old Hickory," he was saying, "is havin' a balloon made. He aims to find out if there's anybody livin' on the moon, and if there is he's goin' to send word he can whip 'em."

"I bet he can, too," a hearer vowed. "What in hell's a balloon?"

When I finally followed the tail of the crowd up the bluff I found the rest gathered in front of the tavern. Enthroned on a whiskey barrel under the sign, the landlord was calling out names as he read them from a dwindling parcel of letters.

It was strange for me to reflect that there was now only one person in the world from whom I might anticipate mail. When my name was actually shouted, I saw the missive was indeed from McConnell; but I didn't open it right away. Waiting till the mail was all distributed, I borrowed a newspaper from the landlord and went off to enjoy my prizes in solitude.

The date of the note showed it had been written in time to make the cancelled Christmas run. Few people can transmit their personality in writing. McConnell succeeded as well as most through what he didn't say rather than through any turn of phrase:

THE WILD YAZOO

Godolphin——
This is just to tell you Pace is back and is satisfied with our arrangement. I'll be along in time to beat the spring floods. Leave a sketch map at the bar I suppose there is.

T. McConnell

The paper was more fulsome. It was a New Orleans sheet containing, in addition to some international and more national news, notices and personality items of local interest only. I read it page by page, finding it at all points absorbing. Soberly intent, I read, for instance, of the nuptials of two people with French names and hosts of equally Gallic witnesses. With no slackening of interest I familiarized myself with the ships that had entered and left the port a month ago. Then there were such arresting articles as the one that weighed theories concerning the Garden of Eden's location. The most barren declaration had a magic because it was a link with a familiar world of more varied horizons.

When I was through I sauntered back to the tavern in a better frame of mind toward actuality. A right lively actuality it turned out to be. The Horsethief's Head had been doing a rush business, and action was the order of the moment. A quarter race was being organized by the owners of as curious an assembly of nags as I had ever seen. Several men were already engaged in shooting at a small target with a crude cross for bull's-eye. There were two wrestling matches, one of which had passed the stage of being a friendly test of strength. One of the new arrivals was operating a shell game. A man was leading his horse around beseeching somebody or anybody to swap with him. Another was doing a breakdown, careless of the fact that there was no cork in the bottle he was flourishing. Flasks were being tipped by shifting groups who discussed news items, the steamboat, and President Jackson's lunar challenge.

By the joint exercise of patience and force I secured a drink at the bar, had my flask filled and squeezed outside again. The quarter race was just thundering to a conclusion, nearly overrunning one pair of rough-and-tumble practitioners and their cheering audience. The race was won by a nose, but there were two opinions as to whose mount the nose belonged to. I left the claimants threatening each other with knives and strolled on in search of Durham.

[161]

When I found him he was leaning on his rifle, watching the shell game. Thimblerig is a midge among games of chance, designed to afflict only those who believe in the sporting instincts of professional gamblers. A number of this hardy breed were gathered to play, and the manipulator was taking their money so fast he hardly had time to use any of the usual methods of persuasion.

Among the onlookers and occasional players was Jack Garland. As a Mississippi River operator, and therefore a buzzard with a bigger wing spread, he was above playing shill for a shell game. In fact it seemed to me that he was deliberately posing as a sucker. The twice I saw him play he lost.

Durham wasn't playing but was having a fine time drinking and joshing everyone else about their bad guesses. Finally a victim of his humor rebelled.

"Why don't you play an' take all his money away if you think it's so easy?"

"Well, I would," Tim said, "but he may have to look after a widowed mother with a busted arm and twins to suck. Of course, I know where that little pill is right this minute and every minute."

His statement hurt the pride of the operator, a fellow with a broken nose betwixt surly black eyes. "You don't need to worry about me, mister," he barked. "If you think you can find the ball, put your cash down. If you ain't goin' to play, cut stick."

"Oh, I'll play if that's the way you feel," Tim said mildly.

"Well, you better if you know what's good for you," the gambler retorted nastily. "All right, what'll you bet?"

"How about an otter skin against a dollar?"

The man's eyes gleamed, and I opened my mouth to protest before I thought better of it. Many of the bets were made in pelts, but an otter skin was worth far more than a dollar. Pleasantly aware of this himself, the gambler worked his legerdemain, shuttling the pellet from one little wooden thimble to another with marvelous address.

"Now," he grinned when he lifted his hands to leave the shells neatly aligned, "which one is it under?"

"That one, I reckon."

"Oh, you do?" the manipulator sneered. He lifted the indicated thimble to prove it concealed nothing.

This turn of events manifestly dumbfounded Durham. "Well, what do you know?" he muttered, shaking his head. "Come on, Daunt, let's go watch the shootin' match."

"Now hold on!" the gambler said. "None of that, now! Where's that otter skin?"

"Oh, the otter skin," Tim said. "Why the one I had in mind is on an otter. Lives two—three miles upriver at the foot of a hollow gum tree. Has one white foreleg and answers to the name of Jake. Tell him I sent you."

There was some laughter, but some disapproval, too. After all, a bet was a bet, and on the terms specified the operator had won. The latter was furious and with a certain amount of public opinion to back him he became menacing. Removing the board from his knees, he drew his knife.

"Give me the price," he blustered, "or I'll take it out of your hide."

Whereupon, to my astonishment, Tim was conciliatory. "Well, maybe I oughtn't to have bet something I didn't have," he admitted. "I'll tell you what. We priced that skin at a dollar. I'll give you a chance to double your money if you'll match these." To show he was in earnest he clinked two silver coins, and the thimblerigger's growl died to a mumble. Still grumbling a little, he reseated himself, replaced the board on his lap, and extracted the money called for from his own pocket.

"Put 'em down first," he said.

"If I find it, I win?" Tim asked.

"Naturally," the other snapped. "That's the game, to find it. Put 'em down first."

When Tim complied, he placed his own money on top and glanced up with a look of vengeful triumph. Once more he maneuvered the pellet through a series of lightning rebounds and split-second pauses. He was just lifting his hands with a smile of satisfaction when Durham thrust the muzzle of his rifle under one of the gambler's armpits and fired.

My first horrified thought was that Tim had shot him. The operator, greatly more horrified, was sure of it. Throwing up his hands he pitched over backwards, dropping the little ball he had palmed, kicking over the board, scattering the shells, and spilling the dollars.

Ignoring all these objects, Durham flung himself on the thimble-rigger, relieving the latter of his knife while he was still dazed. Then he scooped up the ball.

"I found it," he announced.

This I noted out of one eye, busy as I was making sure that the gambler didn't have any confederate or spur-of-the-moment ally who might join him in an attack on Tim. As I turned my head I found myself face to face with Garland. A professional gambler in a frontier region must be prepared for occasional violence; but possibly Durham had introduced him to a new procedure. In any event he was looking very thoughtful. When our eyes met, though, his expression lightened.

"Your friend plays games his own way," he murmured. "Is that the custom here?"

"Yes," I said curtly. Satisfied no one was taking the operator's part I once more watched him and Durham.

The gambler was outraged beyond all measure but felt the loss of his knife too keenly to make any save a verbal protest. As he struggled to his feet he invoked the technicalities, appealing loudly to anyone who might incline to sympathy.

"He didn't win right, damn it! That isn't the way to play. He had to guess where it was!"

"The bet was I'd find the ball," Tim retorted, displaying the pellet between a thumb and forefinger, "and here it is. Watch him, Daunt."

Bending over, he picked up the stakes. "Come on," he invited me when he'd pocketed the silver and jingled it for the benefit of the now apoplectic thimblerigger. "Let's buy us a few drinks with this."

"How about my knife?" his antagonist asked, finally reduced to pleading. The next instant he jumped just in time. The blade stuck in the ground where one of his feet had been.

"Careful what you do with that," Tim warned. "And next time you want to cheat anybody along the Yazoo use some God-damn manners!"

Swinging around to go with him, I bumped into Garland. "Sorry," I said.

He eyed me brightly. "No," he protested, with an innuendo I thought I understood, though I don't believe he intended me to, "excuse *me*, and tell your friend I said so."

The night was merry and hectic. Tim and I thoroughly enjoyed both qualities after the long nights of silence in the forest. We drank the night into morning; drank ourselves first drunk and then sober; and at the end felt a deliberate quietness of being to match the coming of day. We had needed that night as a spiritual purgative and experienced all the limp calmness of convalescence.

The crew of the steamer, be it noted, had been no large sharer in our revelry. Our Babylon was their exile, and they were up early to hasten from us. Those of us who had lasted through went down to see the boat drop down river into the mist. Watching it do so I realized as never before how slender was the tendril that held us to the rest of the world. I knew then that we had to bring the world to us through reaching back; of its own accord it would touch us as gingerly and leave us as offhandedly as the crew of the dirty little river boat. And until we could show better cause why, I could not especially blame it.

Durham had had enough, too. "This place is only good for one drunk," he commented. "Let's catch a little sleep, buy what we need, and get the devil out of here."

CHAPTER XVI

WE WERE PREPARING supper when the hounds suddenly rushed from us giving tongue with the rare barking that presaged strangers. Shevlin sprang for his gun and promptly took a course through the woods parallel to the path the dogs followed. Tim and I remained crouched by the fire, contenting ourselves with glancing to make sure our weapons were handy.

The hounds were in an ecstasy of excitement, not menacing but hopeful of being talked into it. Durham listened as he turned the big gobbler on the hickory spit. "They've got somebody treed down by the branch."

"Yancey'll bring him in alive or dead."

We were both more interested than we sounded. A stranger was an event. If I hadn't acquired all the brazen curiosity that had first startled me in the West, I had learned to know the starvation that begot it. Contented and self-dependent though I was, the craving for a more developed society was never far below the surface and was easily stirred to the top. Just as in the case of the newspaper items dealing with persons unknown to me, the elements of anyone's life took on an unnatural importance. However trivial, they were lines from the human epic in which I myself sometimes seemed to be playing no part but only hearing brokenly from a distance.

While indulging in these reflections I had been scraping a plug to collect a pipeful of tobacco. From this occupation I looked up from under my floppy-brimmed hat as the dogs returned to the fire, still talking to each other about all the excitement they'd had. Behind them came Shevlin and a man leading a horse.

"Man claims he knows you, Daunt," Yancey announced.

"The man wouldn't have bragged about it if he'd known what

you looked like," McConnell declared. "Godolphin, how are you; and, by the way, which one are you?"

I was not especially surprised, although he'd come a little earlier than I'd expected. "At least you can read maps, which not every greenhorn can manage."

It was the first time anybody had been called upon to follow a sketch of mine, and I noted the fact as I rose to stride toward him. I was glad to see him, and he acknowledged the welcome with a grin of his own.

"You look like a bear that needs a shave."

"It isn't too thick to drink through," I said, pulling out my pocket pistol. "Fire a shot out of that and pass it to my friends, Durham and Shevlin here."

Following the drink of salute, I observed Tim walking all around McConnell's mount. "It's interestin'," he finally announced, "but what is it?"

McConnell, who'd been standing with his back to him, now looked around. "When it was sold to me I was told it was a horse," he responded in a politely informative tone.

The statement seemed to impress Tim. "Why sure! I might have knowed it by the bridle. Would you want to swap him?"

"For another horse?" McConnell said doubtfully.

"Naturally." Tim looked startled. "You didn't figure I wanted to cheat you, did you?"

"No. But if it's a dead horse you have in mind you'll have to bury it before I consider a trade."

"Well, I done my best for you, Yancey," Durham said, "but it looks like you'll have to dig a grave for that old plug yourself."

Shevlin grunted. Durham and McConnell were ready for companionship after that by-play, but Yancey waited and watched while he made up his mind. The ice hadn't been broken for him as it had when we first arrived, and his primary reaction was to be on guard.

I felt finely satisfied as we lounged around the fire, listening to McConnell's report of the rest of the world. Friendship and good company were luxuries I'd been fortunate enough to enjoy all winter; but the pull of kind is as subtly all powerful for me as for most. People and not landscapes are the essence of home; and a stranger can create the illusion by virtue of sharing habits and mannerisms. I was nearer friend to both Durham and Shevlin, I think, than was either to the other; but they shared a mutual understanding that was forever denied me. In like measure McConnell was of my own sort and would supply my lack. Aside from his physical properties a man in general uses only so much of his power as is evoked. Much of a man's personality may be dormant away from his own ilk, among whom alone it can fully expand.

It wasn't until the next morning that he and I had a chance to talk as we would. The others had gone off about the day's business, Durham trotting jauntily away and Shevlin slipping off afoot.

"Good men and a good place," McConnell commented, strolling over to admire the river prospect. He returned to where I had unconsciously assumed the woodsman's squat, a painfully acquired position of ease. He grinned at me. "It'll take me awhile to learn to do that again."

This was his recognition of our changed relationship. I was a full-fledged Mississippian, no longer in need of his mentorship and as such things were reckoned along the Yazoo, I was an old-timer.

"You'll have to learn to get along without cigars, too," I said. "Let me help you get used to it by burning one up for you."

When we were smoking, seated on the sill log of the shack, McConnell blew a ring into the still, brisk air. "Tell me what you know," he suggested.

At this I drew the long breath of hunger surveying a feast. It is not too often that a man is invited to talk at length about the thing uppermost in his mind. The Yazoo country had obsessed me for months to the exclusion of almost every other interest. Deliberately and by assimilation, I had been storing facts about a district with which I had wholeheartedly identified myself. Now at last I could give my enthusiasm form and coherence.

"I'll know lots more by the end of summer," I began. "I've only seen two sides of the four, but this is what I have so far."

In commencing, as was inevitable in all geographies of that land, I started with the river, its depth, channel, width, current, tributaries, its intrinsic fauna and floating bird life, as well as its flood

and low as reported by Shevlin. I dealt with it as a traffic artery, a
drainage duct, a drinking supply, as a source of food, a source of
disease, a source of sport, a source of beauty and a source of destruction. Then from the point where it seeped over its normal
banks to create swamps I built the land up, stratum by stratum,
giving each its present flora and agricultural potential. As well as I
was able I put the birds in the branches, moved the life crawling at
the roots, tracked the mammals that lived beneath and in the trees,
blew the winds through the forest and beat the sun and rain down
upon it.

All these things I dealt with in parallel, first as they existed and
were of interest to me and secondly as I conceived them to affect
the economy of a pioneer development. Until I put it all together I
had not realized myself how much information I had accumulated.
When I was through I was happy, not so much from any sense of
personal accomplishment but because I had been able to speak of
something I considered wonderful.

McConnell had asked but a few questions and those only at the
beginning. "Good," he said at length. "You'd never think so much
passion could lurk behind a beard like that." He leaned toward the
river, dreaming over my report, and I was content to let him do so.
"It's all there, isn't it, Daunt?"

He had picked up the nickname from Durham the night before.
I nodded. "All there but the people to make what they will of it,
Tom."

"They're coming," he promised me. "Vice can't wait for honest
toil to take root before it moves in to corrupt it; evangelists can't
wait for people to be corrupted so they can move in and save 'em
again; thieves can't wait for settlers to acquire property before they
move in to take it away; politicians can't wait for communities to
be organized so they can run them and represent 'em in Jackson and
Washington; and editors can't wait for the politicians who haven't
been elected to make mistakes in operating towns that haven't been
built so they can bear-bait them in so far imaginary newspapers.

"Oh, they're on the way. They've been arriving by boat all winter, and summer will flood the traces with oxcarts and Conestoga

wagons. Yes, and a good part of the already established population of the state will leave their holdings either in the hope of something better or just because they can't resist the excitement."

"Like you," I remarked.

"That's right," he chuckled. "I couldn't sleep well of nights if I missed the scramble for property and power. Of course, my presence will have its useful aspect; for once I will be able to add public service to business and pleasure. We lawyers, bitterly as we are condemned, are the only human agency that has yet quelled chaos."

"The cloth would hate to hear you say that," I cautioned him.

"Time was when the cloth had to turn lawyer itself to get the same thing accomplished. Four hundred years ago I'd be getting my liquor free and be called 'father' into the bargain." He sighed. "Now if a mateless lawyer is called 'father' he moves to Texas."

My cigar had gone out long ago, but I hadn't relighted it out of a reluctance to interrupt myself and to risk loosening my grip on his attention. Now I picked up the stub from beside me to smoke what was left. "And what of your client and my employer?"

"Oh, Harry Pace is back with plans enough to organize two such empires as Alexander ruled. More to the point, he secured enough financial backing during his trip East to make him a figure to be reckoned with when the rules are made here."

I tried to call up the man I had known so briefly and who had yet affected so strongly the course of my affairs. "Can he execute, or does he just get enthusiastic?"

"He's a man to do what he wants to." McConnell looked at me to make sure I was heeding. "In the suggestive metaphor of the country he's an alligator by water and a horse by land. He is also a hawk in the sky, a mole in the earth, and the best card player in Mississippi."

I digested this praise. "With whom is he swimming, running, flying, tunneling or playing cards now?"

"With the politically influential wherever found, to clear the way for whatever lands he may see fit to buy when the New Purchase is opened in the fall. Let's take a look at your maps."

"Sketches," I corrected him diffidently.

But he liked my work better even than I had hoped he might.

"Good," he pronounced again when he had examined them all in detail. "This will give us something better to work with than most people will have." Taking up an over-all sketch of the upper valley he put his finger on Turkey Run. "The men who will really make money out of speculating, as Harry plans to do, will be the men who manage to found dominant communities—or get control of them. What do you think of this one's chances of survival?"

"Its location isn't bad, though I've seen better." I shrugged. "You were there yourself."

"I didn't stay long enough to see how much of a population it served; but it at least has the advantage of being started. It's all very well to declare the existence of a town, but it doesn't do much good if you can't get anybody to live there."

An implication disturbed me. My visions called strictly for choosing an untouched site and watching it emerge from the forest.

"Pace isn't thinking about taking over Turkey Run, is he?"

"I don't know what Harry will decide. The upper half of the Old Purchase will be really developed for the first time, too, you know, and he controls a lot of land in the Turkey Run vicinity."

McConnell picked up a stick of kindling and started whittling it aimlessly. "Many towns will be started and lots of them won't last. It may be necessary to back several horses to find a winner, so one that's already foaled and got to its legs isn't to be overlooked."

He was right, but the idea remained more than distasteful to me. Whether Pace had interests in both purchases or not I was only concerned with the development of the New.

"It's true you've got to get people to want to live in a town," I said, "but it makes some difference what kind of people they are. Do you remember Jack Garland, the man they all cheered the night we watched by the beacons at Underhill?"

"Garland!" McConnell looked at me sharply. "Is he in Turkey Run?"

"He was a few weeks ago, and there were some others I wouldn't choose as settlers for anything but a penal colony."

Throwing the stick away he stuck the knife in the log beside him. "There'll be a lot like that, understood; and if Turkey Run isn't their headquarters some other place will be. Felony in the

[171]

gross, like hard work, is just one of the afflictions common to new countries."

"How about Garland and the other gamblers?" I asked curiously. "Did you ever catch up with any of them to square accounts for that raid?"

"They couldn't resist coming up on the bluff to strut and laugh up their sleeves at us. We took indemnity out of their hides they haven't forgotten."

"From the big one, too—the one that actually led the expedition?"

"Oh, Alexander Pope Cummins; yes, he was there on reckoning day. Did you run across him also?"

"No, just Garland." My cigar was endangering my whiskers, so I reluctantly discarded it. "I don't see what draws that sort to the Yazoo."

"The same thing that draws us—rich returns on small or no investments. The only difference is their method of procedure."

It still didn't fit my idea of a gambler's activities. "He won't find much money to take away from people along here."

"Not in cash," McConnell agreed, "but he can fleece people of purchases, claims and leases; play brag for towns and faro for counties. Then there's always politics, which is the boss gambling game of the lot." He stretched with animal content. "No doubt our friend Garland has some or all of the possibilities in mind."

Previously I had regarded the Yazoo as a prize for the bold and the ambitious. That it could also be a prize for the criminal was a contingency to which I hadn't given thought. A certain amount of lawlessness on the part of drifters and fugitive outlaws I had taken for granted; but not organized lawlessness equipped to seize power in a major sense.

"That could be the case," I admitted.

"Oh, that's all a part of it," he said briskly. "You can't go through a forest and meet nothing but rabbits. And speaking of that, how soon are you going to take me hunting?"

Hunting in that country meant for bear or panther; other creatures were merely pursued in a routine quest of food. "Perhaps tomorrow," I answered, "if we can get the use of all the dogs. I'll ask this evening."

The opportunity came sooner than that. The fascination of a newcomer to exchange words with was too much for Durham, and Shevlin made his kill early. Contrary to their wont, therefore, they had both returned by late morning, each with his little train of hounds.

"Tom would like to go hunting, Yancey," I announced while we were smoking after lunch. "Do you think we could scare something up for him in the morning?"

Shevlin gazed up through the still bare branches to a half-clouded sky. "It'll likely rain tomorrow." He was silent a moment and even Tim waited him out. "I couldn't promise a bear today," he said at last, looking at McConnell. "Would a painter do you?"

Only simplicity can acknowledge magnificence. A person might exclaim over a squirrel, but what words could deal with the proffer of a panther?

"Yes," Tom said, "that'll be fine, Yancey."

The woodsman nodded. "There's been one messin' around a little south of us. I run across his trail this mornin' again."

"Are you pretty sure he's staying around and wasn't on his way somewhere?"

"He's holed up for the day," Shevlin said confidently, "and not very far from where I cut his sign. The tracks was so new I could smell cat."

Shevlin was capable of Mississippi hyperbole, but I knew that wasn't one. His faculties had an incredible acuteness.

"You in this, Tim?" I asked.

"I was hopin' you wasn't goin' to ask that." He shook his head sorrowfully. "How's a man goin' to make a livin' when he's all the time bein' coaxed away from work by his no-count friends?"

Yancey's mount, which he never used except when he anticipated a burden too heavy for a man, was a huge one-eyed mule. If it had ever hurried it had learned better, and the rest of us dawdled in its wake. As Shevlin knew exactly where he wanted to go there was none of the intense questing attendant upon seeking for sign. The dogs seemed to understand that nothing was expected of them for the time being and sniffed all intermediary scents with no more than connoisseur curiosity.

There was no use in plying Shevlin with questions so we contented ourselves with conversation until, at the end of four or five miles, he halted us. "Hitch your nags and bunch the dogs," he ordered.

The hounds now knew that serious hunting was afoot. They came readily at call, whining in nervous excitement; nor did they forge very far ahead of us when we started walking. Nevertheless, they picked up what we were looking for in a few minutes. We heard one growl, then they all got together, snarling and mumbling. They were pretty sure this was what we wanted but waited for confirmation.

The scuffed humus to which Yancey pointed when we'd almost caught up didn't tell me much. Tim on the other hand read it at a glance.

"Big he," was his deduction.

"What I figured," Shevlin said. "Come on!"

He loped toward the fidgeting hounds, his gun at trail. He was speaking to them as he went in a jumble of half words and sounds, possibly Indian speech. It was startlingly effective. Exploding into excitement, they broke before him, voicing their passion as they surged toward the lurking catamount.

I grinned at McConnell, "How's your wind?"

"Not as good as I'll probably wish it was," he confessed.

As a matter of fact neither of us had breath for talk thereafter. The pace Yancey set was a pelting trot that didn't change for uphill or down. We kept within range of the dogs, for the very good reason that the dogs saw to it that we did. They were enthusiastic, but they wanted lots of company. Perhaps we could have kept up with them if we slowed to a shuffle, but Shevlin knew what he was doing. A running hound feels much more confident.

The dogs breathed us as they temporarily lost the scent where the panther had taken to the trees. "Tried for his kill and missed," Shevlin commented. "Soon as we find where he made it we won't have far to go."

The evidence of success was near. A few hundred yards farther on the beast had claw-marked a giant oak in making his ascent.

Beneath a far-reaching limb that swept out beyond it were torn bits of hide, the only available remains of a deer.

"That'll hold him," Tim said. "We'd ought to find him in the next good cover."

The dogs led away over a ridge, then turned down the draw at the bottom. The pounding of my heart as I followed was not just from exercise. For all the time that I'd been in the forest I was hunting my first panther. But over and above this was the knowledge that here was combat as well as hunting. My rifle held one bullet. Should the furious, cornered animal charge toward me I had one chance only to stop him. I wondered if I had loaded my weapon as carefully as I might have. It was a business I had attended to so matter-of-factly back at the camp.

I never did know where the beast was hidden. Of a sudden it was just in sight, a comet of tawny power. Involuntarily my voice swelled the joint cry of men and dogs. What the others meant I don't know, but I was hailing embodied desire, voicing awe, calling out my recognition of peril, and shouting the excitement invoked by all these.

The end of my yell was almost a wail, though, for it seemed impossible that we could ever catch that darting fugitive. It did not seem to me that he either ran or bounded. He described an arc over the ridge and in a moment was gone, drawing the frantic hounds after him.

To my astonishment Shevlin and Durham slowed down. "The dogs won't leave him now," the latter explained, "and he'll tree sooner if he don't see no men."

By then I needed the rest and McConnell was frankly blown. Still even he knew more about panthers than I did.

"They're quarter racers," he gasped. "Haven't got the wind for a steeplechase any more 'n I have now."

Striding briskly up the next ridge, we heard the baying change to the yelping, barking and growling that meant the quarry was halted but not engaged. "Treed," Shevlin grunted. "Spread out an' see how near you can get without lettin' the critter know."

The panther didn't wait for us, or possibly it was upon sighting one of us that he acted. One moment the hounds were cavorting around the base of the tree, joyously defiant. The next instant they scattered, yelping, as the great cat dropped to earth in their midst.

They were at once craven and bold as only hounds can be. The dog being threatened fled shamelessly, his tail between his legs, howling his mortal fear. Yet as soon as his mates closed in on the panther's rear to draw its attention the frightened whine would change to a threatening snarl, the fleeing dog would twist with snakelike agility, and in it would dart for its own distracting bite.

They were swift, and only their swiftness saved any of them. The catamount was deadly fast also; and he was desperate to be rid of them and on his way. Two he gashed and one he ripped open while we were leaping to close in.

Anxiously looking for Talisman, I saw him dashing in for a hamstringing snap, then the panther and the other surviving dogs were a whorl of furious bodies. We men were all close but had to hold our fire. Shift for position though we would in search of a clear shot, the risk of hitting a dog was always too great.

The free-for-all, though it seemed prolonged, only lasted a second or so. The beast rolled over on its back to get the full use of its terribly armed paws, and the dogs had to leave it. On its feet again, it started to streak away with a spurt the hounds couldn't match. It didn't choose a direction; it followed its eyes with all the drive and power of its wonderful body.

There was almost no time at all to realize it was making directly at me. I happened to be in its path, and neither of us would have time to side-step before we met. Of the two leaps that separated us it had taken one before I knew what I was up against. It was in mid-course of the other when I fired.

There had been no time to lift my rifle, but I'd been holding it at the ready, pointed toward the animal in the hope of being able to make a more deliberate shot. I couldn't well miss at that range, but that wasn't good enough. I hit high on one shoulder, knocking it back to stop just in front of me, staggered but by no means fatally wounded.

If before I had been merely an obstacle to be overrun, such was not now the case. It was a badly hurt beast, recognizing me as its chief enemy and seeking not escape but vengeance for pain endured. It sprang with sweeping forepaws, capable of bashing in my head and tearing out the splintered bone from the torn flesh.

Just how I felt was something I could only reconstruct later. The eyes, I think, horrified me more than the claws, the paws, the snarling and the great fangs. Reading them was to read the absolute in implacability. At that instant I penetrated the farthest possible into the wildness of my country.

But this, as I say, was emotion rather than thinking. What I did wasn't based on thought, either, for there was no time for planned action. Once I hit it with my gun but could not get into position for a second blow when it came at me again. I dropped the rifle when it bore me over and reached for my knife.

The savagely driven blade sank into it, but its claws were through my leather shirt, finding one shoulder and the opposite set of ribs as we hit the ground. The awful mouth was nuzzling for my throat when the panther collapsed on top of me.

I wasn't seriously hurt, and I didn't lose consciousness. But I had simply given all there was to me then with the exception of quick being. When they pulled the beast off me I just lay there, letting them ascertain for themselves that I was comparatively unharmed.

Schooled to take injuries for granted, Durham and Shevlin didn't give me much attention. "He's just clawed a little and had the wind knocked out of him," Tim commented, then they both turned to the more interesting business of examining the catamount.

McConnell, more solicitous, lifted me up so I wouldn't choke on the whiskey he was dribbling into my mouth. The others, meanwhile, were puzzled as to just who had slain the animal. Though I hadn't realized it, each had sent one bullet home in addition to the one with which I had originally stopped it. The point at issue was which of the shots, none in itself apparently fatal, had caused death.

Finally the whiskey took effect enough to give my vitality coherence. "My knife," I said quietly.

Shevlin threw me a quick glance, then lifted up a paw to find the ivory hilt of my great-grandfather's weapon. "By God! that's it," he acknowledged. "Couldn't see you do it from where I stood."

"It's Daunt's kill," Durham agreed.

Perforce I thought of Artenay and how he had once transfixed my imagination by using almost the same phrase. Sitting up, I looked around. This was a level spot between several trees, indistinguishable from thousands of others. I wouldn't mark it on any map as Artenay had suggested; nevertheless, it would be a sighting point in the topography of my life.

That panther would have immortality as long as I did. For every time I had to shoot my first horse, for every time I learned that my parents were lost at sea, for every time I saw Cartwright fall, or surrendered mastery of Spring Hill, so many times would that beast leap from where it also lurked in my mind, glare terribly and be stabbed.

CHAPTER XVII

For a few days after the panther hunt I suffered reaction. My stomach was queazy the first two days, I ached all over where I didn't pain, and nothing interested me. By the afternoon of the third day, though, I began to pull myself together. My physical demands were still limited to assuming a position that wouldn't irritate my wounds, but I found my mind avid for entertainment.

Of my few books I had read all but one at least twice in the course of the winter. Craving something new, I fished in my slender effects for the volume my cousin Edward had passed on to me and shuffled away to comfortable solitude. I had glanced at this book a few times before without finding that it held my attention. In the past months my reading had been done in periods of semitorpor following vigorous outdoor activity. Literature that didn't slip into my mind oiled with simplicity had been too much for me. Now I was hungered of untasted reading as I had been of news when at Turkey Run.

The fact that the collection of pamphlets dealt largely with Virginia had at first irritated me. It had seemed more suitable to leave the book behind along with the state it dealt with. If it hadn't been a generously tendered heirloom, probably prized by Edward Godolphin himself, I would have done so.

Then the presentation of the matter had rebuffed me in the past. The typography was archaic, but that was a minor obstacle. Spelling with Smith was often not so much a matter of delineating words as it was a challenge to the reader's ingenuity. His syntax often ranged from the turgid to the mysterious. Yet once I had engaged the fire beneath this smoke I became Captain John's man.

Some would have it that he is the father of American romance rather than the parent of its soberer literature; but I could use his eyes for seeing and believed him. I, too, had been to a strange new country, and I was aware that any report I might make of it would neither be credible to those who hadn't seen it nor acceptable to the inhabitants.

Scandal aside, dullness is the general passport to credulity. The fictions of a drab mind will get ten votes for every one polled by a fact with the suspect quality of richness. Of course, Smith was no man to let a lovely fact go unattended and in a slut's attire. He would have made a good Mississippian.

But in point of fact he had become a Virginian, and I had been one myself. Allowing for the quirks of individuality, a man is made up of the things he's aware of. It is the alien concept rather than the alien speech that makes the foreigner; and I had developed ways of thinking and points of view as different from those of Tidewater as Smith's must have seemed to untraveled Britons. And this, he made me see, was but the begining of an ever more far-reaching process. I could not shuck my roots, if I would, but what grew out of them was also the product of soil, weather and winds.

The equinoctial rains took place while I was recuperating. The downpours were torrential, but in the absence of melting snows the river was only moderately gorged. It rose to flood the adjacent cane brakes and hollows, then started to recede, leaving replenished swamps and temporary ponds behind. By then it was full spring along the Yazoo, and I was but one of many to come out of retirement.

Up from the ooze where they had mysteriously held life in check rose the great alligators, the beaked snapping turtles, and the baby-handed frogs. Fish ceased to hover near the sludge of the stream beds and came up to meet the sun. Snakes left their lairs as if drawn out of the earth by the warmth and lizards did likewise. Though some birds left, many more came to brighten the quickening trees. Ground flowers unfolded, too, but in chief there was the dogwood blossom, the true spring flower of the South.

It was in such a repopulated and redecorated land that McConnell and I made an expedition the first day I was able. We went afoot, as the jogging of Goober would have been too hard on my lacerated ribs, and in any case it was a time for walking. We had no purpose except enjoying what our fine country had to show us, and there was no destination to limit our rambling.

We had gone perhaps four stop-and-go miles when we heard a shout. "Company in the offing," Tom remarked. Then he laughed. "Don't you like neighbors, squatter?"

It was only when he said this that I realized I had automatically slipped a cap into my rifle. I had become of the frontier faith that although a stranger should be welcomed as a friend he should be prepared for as an enemy. I looked at Talisman, but he took men for granted whom he couldn't see or smell and was absently nosing a cold scent. After a minute or so, however, something must have come to him on the wind. He gave a growl of warning and stood fast until we could catch up with him.

"Indians," I said, peering ahead. "Do you want to meet them?"

"Not especially, but I'm not going to hide." McConnell shrugged. "We didn't come here because we had delicate sensibilities. If they point out they're still the owners of the land we can point out that we don't give a damn. But I doubt if they're any more anxious to talk to us than we are to confab with them."

"Likely enough," I agreed, but I felt my pulse increase. To me, as to most Americans, the Indian ranked with the bear and the panther as a big-game inhabitant of the forest, and I had never encountered a large crowd before. There had been groups of Choctaws but no sizeable villages in our section of the Purchase, and they stayed localized during the winter.

In this party there were about fifty, a dozen or so on horses and mules, the rest—assorted as to sex and age—straggling along on foot. They were a tatterdemalion, pitiable lot, and I watched them with mixed feelings. In so far as they were wretched I was sorry for them. But their demands for survival asked too little of themselves and too much of others, myself included.

Their path took them close to where McConnell leaned against a tree and I crouched, holding a growling Talisman. Used to interlopers, the Choctaws looked at us sullenly, curiously or just blankly. Only one rider turned toward us. Weathered as he was, it was not until then that I noticed he was a white man. Above the homespun of his long, loose-limbed body there were muddy eyes in a horse face.

Neither of us moved as he approached, and the Choctaws became motionless to watch. "What're you all doin' here?" the man demanded brusquely.

"Do you want to find out or do you want to fight?" McConnell took him up.

The man considered, then he half grinned. "Reckon I want to find out, first off."

Tom remained uncompromising. The other had taken the aggressive and it was up to him to find an easier meeting ground if he would. "We're here because we damn well want to be."

After a pause the fellow tried again. "Figure on stayin'?"

"If we like it better than other places."

This time the man shook his head. "Not around here. I'm tellin' you."

At this I straightened, checking Talisman with my knees. "You've made your brag," McConnell said. "Lay 'em down."

Taking up the symbolism, the other made a card-spreading gesture. "I'm gettin' me an option on this whole stretch of land. Soon as the treaty's in effect I get title. I'm tellin' you to save you time an' trouble. Don't squat around here."

Tom looked past him to the watching Indians and nodded. "You might get a small pot with that hand if you know a state senator."

The man chuckled. "I am a state senator."

I would have doubted that statement from such a source, but I saw McConnell didn't. "All right, Piney Woods," he said dismissingly, "we know all about you. Get out of our light."

The self-styled senator looked back at the Choctaws, then evidently decided they'd be of no help. If he was discomfited about retreating, he didn't show it. He gave us that half of a grin again.

"Well, I got to be leavin', but I'll look you up if you're still around when I get back. Truesdale's the name; Senator Guy Truesdale."

As he rejoined the Choctaws my interest swung from him to them. During this talk about property rights they, the true possessors, had said nothing. I watched them bemusedly as they trooped off. Alive but unconsidered, they reminded me of the days when I was the discredited titular owner of Spring Hill.

McConnell's reflection had been more to the point, as he showed with the remark that roused me. "That sort of speculator is going to bring me a lot of business if I don't get shot by a zealous litigant."

I hadn't taken Truesdale's pretensions seriously and was surprised to find that he was doing so. "How can he establish a claim now any more than you or I can?"

He sighed and sat down, leaning against the tree. "It's a legal powder train. The treaty, with an eye to some sort of fairness, gives every Choctaw who wants to stay a chance to claim land before the territory's thrown open. Well, if a man can own land he also has the privilege of transferring ownership."

"Yes, but can an Indian turn over rights in land he doesn't intend to possess?"

"Who the hell can prove intent in an Indian?" He waved an arm irritably. "Half of 'em don't speak English, and the rest only do so when they feel like it. And it's worse than that. The Choctaws don't think of land as an individual possession. There are exceptions, but mostly they can't be made to think in those terms. Whether they decide they want to stay here or figure on clearing out has nothing to do with the case either. The point is that for two drinks of forty rod they will designate any piece of land you ask 'em to, claim it's theirs, and turn it over to you. And mark you, nobody has standardized the spelling of Indian names—the rendition is at the discretion of the recorder—and the varmints themselves all look about as much alike as the Xs with which they sign. One of 'em's apt to file on several sections, and by the same token, several are apt to file on one claim."

As well as I could I grasped the appalling complications he'd sketched. "How can their claims have any standing?"

"Any claim on real estate has standing until it's disposed of. Land can't just fall down a crack or be lost like a picayune. It's always there and title's got to be established." He saw all the difficulties so clearly he was impatient of my legal obtuseness. "Land the government falls heir to starts from scratch, but the Indian titles—"

He looked to where the last of the Choctaws was barely in sight down a long vista of trees. "Those redskins are going to haunt this land as a place has never been haunted. For every whiskey-begging, louse-infested horsethief in the tribe at least two palefaces will die with their boots on, and we may be among 'em."

His earnestness had dissolved my skepticism except concerning one point. "Can that man Truesdale really be a state senator?"

"There was one of that name elected last fall, and it might as well be he as any other peckerwood." McConnell rose, and we started walking again. "Did you think politicians would keep their hands out of this Jack Horner pie?"

I merely grunted. If there was trouble ahead I saw no reason to let it mar such a fair day.

"Did you notice how many of the Choctaws had bows instead of guns?" I asked by way of changing the subject. I hadn't forgotten the arrow in the bear Shevlin had slain; but even with that evidence it had been hard for me to believe that the primitive weapon was in general use.

Tom nodded. "Most of them have had guns at one time or another, but as they never clean them the rifles don't usually function very long. But, of course, there's a special reason for bows at this time of year."

"Don't say 'of course' to the ignorant. What reason?"

"Why arrow fishing—but that's right, you haven't been here in the spring before. Wait till this evening. I bet Yancey has the equipment tucked away somewhere."

This turned out to be so, for on request Shevlin took down a buckskin bundle from behind the rooftree and displayed the tackle in question. This consisted of a bow, short in the Indian fashion, and two long arrows with barbed, detachable heads, looped for lines. My amazement that this aboriginal gear was used by white men was only equalled by Yancey's at the fact I had never seen anything like it before.

The business didn't look practical to me. Besides, it was upsetting to my idea of angling. "But that isn't fishing," I declared.

"What do you want to do when you go fishing," Shevlin challenged, "get a piece of string wet or catch fish?"

"Catch fish," I conceded feebly.

"All right. This time of the year a fish has so much food in his gut he wouldn't budge for a mess of bacon and greens with whiskey on the side. Well, if the fish don't come to the hook you got to take the hook to the fish." He looked off toward the river. "It'll be right for it any day now and you can find out whether it's fishin' or not yourself."

Within a week my shoulder was ready to swing a paddle again. The current was still swift and full of eddies, but the river had dropped well below the flood stage, stranding many pools and ponds. In general these were still accessible to a vessel of such light draft as a pirogue, though in time all would be cut off from the source to shrivel under the summer sun.

It was the first time I'd been on the Yazoo since the change of the year, so I was content to let us ride down with the stream. The low, northern bank was largely awash, so we hugged the southern shore except once when we detoured around a shoal of alligators catching the sun in the muddy shallows. Some of them were big rascals, fully capable of upsetting the canoe by a charge, a thrash of the tail, or by simply rising beneath us.

About two miles downstream we found a place McConnell pronounced ideal. Our paddles took mud for several strokes as we left the river for a lagoon full of trees. Here the unmoved water had dropped its silt, and the forest floor was clearly visible three or four feet below. Also visible were swarms of fish ranging from fingerlings to the fattening giants which preyed on the lesser fry.

McConnell, who was in the prow, picked up the bow and an arrow with a stout line dangling from it. "Don't push her any more; just inveigle her through the water. I'll signal you where to go."

By dint of an occasional wriggle of the paddle I made just enough speed to assure control. We passed over a few larger fish, three pounders or so, but McConnell didn't notice them. At his whim we wove through the water-beleaguered trees in an irregular course. Then he signalled me for a sharp swing left.

Half rising to see what he'd found, I saw a dark bulk below the surface near a tupelo tree. I thought I could glimpse a big fluke as it languidly held itself in suspense, but I couldn't be sure. Sinking back to my knees, I moved us without a whisper. From that position I could only gauge developments by watching my companion.

He was leaning forward, holding the arrow nocked with his left hand so he'd be ready for a quick draw. Then he signalled for me to halt. As I silently dragged, he drew without shifting position. The twang of the string blended with the splash of the water.

Before I had time to speculate on his success there was four feet of writhing fish in the air. "Let him take us!" Tom yelled. "Just keep us clear."

He was paying out line swiftly, unwilling to pull against the harpoon-like arrow until it was firmly wedged in the flesh. I didn't have much leisure to watch, however. There were too many places where an earnest fish could break a line to make it wise to give it much play. McConnell snubbed for a test, and the pirogue yawed sharply. I shoved us away from a tree, then dug in frantically to keep us from being dragged over a sunken deadfall.

But the blow was too nearly mortal for the struggle to last. Our catch broke water once again, then had no more to give. It was almost dead when my companion hauled the big, gleaming body inboard.

"Forty pounds of sturgeon and two ounces of steel," he said with satisfaction as he gaffed it with a forked stick and held it up. "Want to try it?"

I had already swung around so we could retrieve the arrow. It had shaken loose from its head at the sturgeon's first leap and was floating some yards away.

"Sure," I said incautiously.

In two tries I had nothing to show for this enthusiasm except a skinned and benumbed forearm. McConnell had the bow again when the pond literally exploded fish. A horde swept toward us with a frenzied splashing. Fish seemed to tumble out of the water as if the pond had been inverted. One good-sized bass actually landed in the canoe just as a monster sped beneath us.

"Good God!" I gasped. "What was that?"

"An alligator gar—and seven feet if an inch."

"Is it a fish?"

"Well, they wear fish shirt and pants, but they've got some of a 'gator's equipment, too, and a lot of his disposition. Once one gets in an aquarium like this it's like a weasel in a hen yard. Do you want him? We can always tell Yancey we're sorry about smashing his pirogue."

With such a quarry present, all other fishing lost savor, so after him we went, tracing his progress by the furor he created. He was wreaking slaughter in the shallows when McConnell's arrow caught up with him.

In an instant there was a froth of blood, muddy whipped water and convulsive fish. "Back up!" Tom yelled, and I dug ground, complying.

The gar had a similar desire to seek more maneuverable waters. He came toward us in a lunge, and I saw he'd have little if any clearance passing underneath. Just as he scraped the canoe's bottom I succeeded in swinging so we were riding with the direction of his rush. We shipped water but righted, and McConnell managed to whip the line over the prow so we wouldn't be tripped.

By the time Tom had paid out all the free line he could do no more without getting a hand cut to the bone. He jammed the stick the line was on into the prow and held it with one foot.

"Your move, Daunt," he grinned at me.

We were both moving, but I didn't have time to point that out. The pirogue careened around a tree, and I thought I was going to break the paddle giving us the inch of leeway I earned. Thereafter we skimmed precariously, weaving among the trees but heading more or less straight inland. I expected to have the canoe ripped open by a snag any moment, but it didn't happen.

"He'd make a good quarter racer," McConnell said. "What do you reckon he'll do when he gets ashore?"

A second after he'd asked that question the gar hit shoal water, floundered around a little and headed back. But it'd given me a respite in the form of slack line, and I'd had enough of its gambols. To snub it I spun the pirogue about a black oak.

"Let him fight it out with that," I said, taking my paddle inboard and flexing my aching arms.

It took the gar a minute to find it was no longer hitched to anything tractable. The line didn't give even when it started thrashing, so it leapt. A buzzard not excepted, a more hideous creature never took to air. A foot of length was teeth, the rest was knotty scales, and the whole was evil fury. We watched between awe and admiration until the struggles grew weaker.

"Let's go ashore for a drink and a smoke," Tom said. "We don't want those teeth in the boat while he can still use 'em, and it'll take awhile for that much meanness to die."

After anchoring the line, we dumped the water out of the pirogue and sought drier ground for a resting place. Within a few yards we struck what looked like an old Indian trail, and as it led up out of the bottom lands I followed it. Suddenly I stopped, looked back at McConnell and pointed. What I thought I saw was an old barn, but the improbability kept me from saying so.

My companion was interested but not startled. "An old council lodge," he remarked.

His matter-of-factness didn't lessen the impact of the discovery on me. I had seen Choctaw buildings, if their miserable huts could be dignified by such a term, but nothing to prepare me for this. It was about seventy-five feet long and fifteen high. The just budding vines were matted so thickly it was impossible to tell what it was made of, but that wasn't important. It was an achievement and so announced itself.

But the tone of it was inexpressibly forlorn. That houses reflect the quality of their relationship to man is a truism. Yet perhaps it was my knowledge of the facts that made me believe it looked more deserted than other abandoned structures. A deserted building can always be told; but here was one bereft of the civilization that had created it.

Closer inspection showed that the lodge was made of heavy bark lashed to a frame of poles. Undoubtedly the walls would have fallen away but for the vines. As it was there were only a few large gaps in addition to the two doors and the smoke hole.

"I've run across a few earthworks like this," I said, "but never knew what they were for. I should say that this whole mound the thing stands on is artificial."

"Your friend Artenay, who's an amateur on the subject, will tell you just how these places were built. I heard a paper he read with a great deal of pleasure, for he serves an excellent punch." McConnell signalled me to drink first. "There are various theories for the purpose, ranging from the realm of the priest to that of the undertaker. It's always looked like war and politics to me."

Within we found nothing but ancient wood ashes, but in the undergrowth outside we kicked up some broken pottery. In the process of doing so we noticed an ancient trail that led down from the terrace and up to a bluff that overlooked it. It was after climbing this bluff in vain quest of other Choctaw antiquities that we had our smoke.

The habit of appraisal I had cultivated kept me at work even as I sucked on my pipe. While McConnell continued to lounge I arose in a couple of minutes and started looking around. There were a few dogwoods in bloom, but the leaflessness of the dominant oak and ash permitted ready orientation.

The spot pleased my horse sense as much as my imagination. In form it was a high, level promontory overlooking the Indian mound and the lagoon on one side and falling away more gently to the river on the other. My admiration for the site was completed by the discovery of a spring, and at that I called Tom. A drink of clean water was a pleasant novelty after the muddy branches from which we usually drank.

"Clear as a dewdrop," McConnell approved. He, too, looked around. "It's too small for a town site, but this would be a good place for somebody to put up a house."

While he had been drinking I had been consulting my notebook. I found that I had marked the vicinity especially well adapted to planting.

"It would," I agreed, when I realized he had spoken. I had been thinking that I would call the place Council Lodge.

When our tobacco had burned down we recrossed the Choctaw mound and descended to our pirogue. The gar was belly up, and we hauled his armored carcass ashore. After I'd examined the hundreds of long teeth McConnell cut out the barbed arrow point. "Is the old ruffian edible?" I but then thought to ask.

I was somewhat relieved when Tom shook his head. "No, he's like the old lodge up there—no use to anybody, but he flavors the country."

CHAPTER XVIII

ONE MORNING when full-blown spring was musk in the valley I waked very early to find Shevlin busy with his belongings. Steam showed the coffee pot was at work, so I rolled out of my blankets and strolled over to join him.

"Where're you going?" I yawned.

He looked a little embarrassed. "Just goin', Daunt." He'd finished breakfast, but he poured an extra cup of coffee for himself as well as one for me. "No sense in stickin' around. This here place'll be too crowded for me come fall."

Not having noted the extent of his preparations I had only figured on a lone hunt. The change I was planning to help bring about was bound to be distasteful to a man of his leanings, but the loss of a friend is never to be lightly borne.

"I suppose it will be," I said soberly. We sipped in silence, eyeing each other. "Why don't you stay out the summer with us anyway?"

He shook his head. "Met an old she-b'ar yesterday, an' before I knowed it I'd whistled at her. Figured it was time I found me a woman an' shacked up."

"Maybe you're right in that case." Still I couldn't envision Shevlin in a domestic role. "You're not going to settle down, are you?"

"Well," he said evasively, "there ain't no use stayin' with a woman longer 'n you an' she both want it."

"And then?"

"Find somebody I don't like who's got a good horse, borrow it and head west." He rose in sign of departure. "You can have the pirogue, Daunt."

I myself was the next to leave. By summer the opening of the territory was only a few months away, and it became imperative for me to report to Pace. I retraced my route from Natchez, but anybody who'd noticed me ride north could have now recognized me only by my horse and my dog. I had hair reaching halfway to my shoulders and bangs above a full, brown beard. In place of the tailored garments I'd worn the previous fall, I had a shapeless hat, a buckskin hunting shirt, a pair of linsey-woolsey trousers I'd bought on my visit to Turkey Run, and moccasins.

The footing was much better but the atmosphere far worse than when I had come that way before. The foliage tempered the heat somewhat in the uplands; in the bottoms nothing could help. The mire crusted around shrinking pools smelling as foul as they looked. But whether the air was rank or brittle it held mosquitoes, gnats, midges and flies for horse and man. I carried a leafy bug chaser to protect Goober and myself and rejoiced at the providence that made me hairy.

But neither the heat nor the insects aswarm in it could flatten my zest for the trip. I was newly broken out of the woods, taking the whole category of starved appetites to a town famous for its exuberant luxury. Other places intervened, but I didn't intend to pay much attention to them. I was holding my breath till I reached Natchez.

Halfway down the valley of the Big Black I found the road unwontedly crowded, and from overheard conversation I gathered that a camp meeting was toward. Had it happened at noon I would have ridden on by, but it was just at evening that I reached the vicinity of the prairie where it was being held. Having the leisure I simply couldn't stay away from any gathering then, so when Goober had rested I left Talisman in charge of my camp and rode over.

There were hundreds of people stirring about the prairie or in the fringes of the woods adjacent. Only a minority were so far engaged in the spiritual business of the evening. The rest wandered around afoot, on horseback or in vehicles, enjoying the spectacle of which they were a part and waiting for the sunset to make frenzy more appealing.

The more industrious zealots, nevertheless, were already crowding around a dozen scattered evangelists. I could not believe that anyone who'd braved the Mississippi sun would be terrified by threats of hell fire; and in truth they didn't seem to be. They were having a good time, still only mildly excited, applauding the speakers' attacks on sin but not yet taking them personally.

A little later the glare gave way to twilight. The prairie continued to swelter, but the fierce impingement of heat eased with the sun's going. It was at this point that I emerged from the shelter of the trees to join one of the groups. Several dozen other people were gathered around the barrelhead this particular evangelist used as a pulpit. A few like myself watched from horseback, but his real audience sat on the ground. I took notice that the ambient grass had been burned. Chiggers were apparently less susceptible to exorcism than the Devil.

The congregation was such as I would have expected on the frontier, but the preacher was a source of astonishment to me. Though I could not claim to be a regular communicant I yet belonged to a church whose ministry was recognizable by a certain dignity of costume and bearing. Scholarship, too, though often absent in fact, was an ideal among clergymen of my acquaintance. The man exhorting us had none of these conventional attributes.

For surplice he had galluses and for cassock a red shirt. The fact that it was open to his diaphragm was partially concealed by his tangled black beard. Where Demosthenes used pebbles for practice speaking only, this orator had brought his tobacco quid to the rostrum. He did, however, clutch a book in his hand which I assumed to be a Bible or a Testament.

While I was wondering who had ordained him or where he had studied to equip himself to give the word, he touched on these matters himself. "God told me to be a saint," he said simply, "so I'm adoin' it."

"Good work, old hoss!" a settler applauded.

"I'm adoin' it," the evangelist repeated, "but I'm adoin' it by savin' souls an' not by makin' out I'm better off than anybody else." He held out the tattered, coverless volume. "Do you see this book?" I was expecting him to proceed with some eulogy of Holy Writ but he confounded me. "I can't read a word of it. It may be the Bible an' it may not. I don't know."

He seemed pleased to be able to make this admission, and the crowd was pleased with him. "Bless the man!" a woman said.

The preacher spat, snapped his suspenders and followed the gesture through to slap the book scornfully with the back of his hand. "I figure that anybody who's got to find out from a book that sin ain't right don't know nothin' and never will. So what we need ain't books, it's clean hearts. You! Have you got a clean heart?"

I started guiltily, but the finger he pointed wasn't directed at me. After a moment a gangling youngster spoke up uneasily. "You ain't got no call to ask me a thing like that. I ain't doin' nothin'."

The evangelist snorted at this feeble protest and appealed to the rest with a look. "'T aint what you're adoin', but what you'd like to be adoin', an' what you'd keep on likin' to be adoin' if I hadn't come here to save your no-count soul." Dropping his book, he put both hands on his hips. He had his victim on the spit and now he was ready to roast and baste him. "Young man, I don't know you, but I can see from right here that if God made any lower critter it couldn't have been many. Your soul's as black with sin right now as the inside of a nigger's hat on a foggy night. But like I said I'm agoin' to save you. I'm agoin' to take that dirty soul of yourn an' wash it white as a catfish's belly an' hang it out to dry."

This proposed public soul-cleansing delighted the others, but his chosen victim was revolted. "You leave my soul alone!" he yelled. "I'm gettin' out of here."

He reckoned without the implacability of the dedicated. As he rose to flee the evangelist leaped from the barrel and was on him like a wildcat on a rabbit. One powerful swing battered the youngster to the ground, then he was borne off bodily to the pulpit.

"The fact he didn't want to be saved shows how far gone he is," the preacher opined. "We'll pray for him first off."

There was too much going on for me to spend much time with any one group. I nudged Goober away, and we moved over to listen to some mass singing. Here a skinny old fellow was leading while a fat woman clapped her hands by way of providing the only accompaniment. The tune was jollier than that of the hymns to which I was accustomed, but there was no levity among the singers. As they rendered them, the words had the earnestness of passion served up with the volume of hog calling. Of the several songs I audited I recall only one refrain.

> "Oh, take your needin' from Adam's fall;
> Play possum when the Devil comes to call
> Till an angel takes you by the hand
> And leads you straight to Beulah land."

As twilight deepened more and more of them drifted down to one end of the big meadow where log seats made salvation more comfortable. Here was the real revival of which the other groups were only outposts. Two shouting men were spelling each other in frenzied appeals from a trestle table. Their words didn't make much sense to me, but they didn't need my support. Their congregation was so enthralled it had passed the point where it could listen in silence. Like members of a classical chorus they exclaimed, echoed and commented in periods left for the purpose by the preachers.

It was obvious to me that they were half hysterical, but I wasn't prepared for the explosion. All of a sudden a woman screamed and started running forward down an aisle between the logs.

"I've got it!" she squealed. "Oh, my God! I've got it! I'm goin' to be saved!"

In front of the table there was a pile of leaves and weeds whose purpose I hadn't previously determined. She pitched headlong into this, groveled energetically, then rose to her knees, shouting a confessional. She was posting her claim to be the vilest member of the human species, but the competition was prompt and severe. Before she had got very far a dozen others were running forward, each claiming to be the most depraved.

At first there were only women, then the men started feeling the call. Soon there were scores rolling around and shrieking self-denunciations, and those who had not yet gone forward could not remain seated. They all rose, swaying and shuffling around, shouting and moaning. And over it all I heard one or the other of the high priests of this hypnotism crying: "It's workin'! Oh, thank God! The blessed spirit is workin'!"

Admittedly I felt uneasy. Distaste at seeing others loosed from control of their faculties is cousin to fear that the substance of one's own character might dissolve. I stayed out of fascination in the spectacle, but I would have been glad of someone with whom to share my sanity. Looking around for a person capable of bearing this responsibility, I saw one other observer on horseback not far away.

It was a woman, and moreover a woman I knew. The real or self-styled countess I had met at Natchez Underhill was as desirable as I had remembered her to be, and all my months in the woods came back upon me in a rush. If I had not quite got to the point of flirting with female bears I had been sufficiently aware of my celibacy for some while. Now the recollection of how she had looked when I first met her overwhelmed me.

My first thought was to curse the hair, beard and costume which prevented me from making a suitable appearance. My second thought was the better one that this was hardly the time to present myself, even were the circumstances favorable. Weird as the rites seemed to me, I was yet on the scene of a religious ceremony—and one, for all I knew, that she herself was viewing sympathetically. Thoughts of carnality were surely out of place.

It was a little while before I discovered the congregation did not share my belief. The already risen moon brightened as night took the place of dusk, so it was never really dark. Yet even before this substitution of half lights the change in emphasis had taken place.

Only a few cherish emotion as an entity. Most look upon it as the natural prelude to action. The intensity of these people had to be completed by some sort of accomplishment. They could not then actually go to Beulah land. Yet they were not without recourse.

One of the evangelists started it. "God is love!" he shouted. "If you want to be saved you've got to love each other!"

At the time I didn't know it was a familiar step in ritual and was startled at the results. The cry was taken up and salvation ceased to be an individual bargain between man and his maker. With something just a little too acute for blind attraction they started groping for each other.

A few of the older matrons were content with the embraces of their own sex, but the men seemed to feel an obligation to seek out only women. Squeals and hysterical laughter began to mingle with the prayers, protestations of faith, and exhortations.

Love is a word of divers meanings, and the letter of Platonism is best preserved in solitude. First one couple then another broke for the privacy of darkness offered by the woods. Meanwhile, those who hadn't yet found a partner floundered around in the moonlight for someone to clutch. To disentangle myself from the orgy I sidled away to the fringe of shadow among the bordering trees and noticed while so doing that the countess was following my example.

It seemed to me that this was a time she could use guardian retainers, and I wondered where hers were. Sharply aware of her as I was, I was quick to notice when one of the men did finally mark her. I heard him beseech her to be saved and, greatly to my relief, her curt refusal. But missionary zeal is overweening. The fellow, whoever he was, had pulled her off her horse by the time I got there. There was one part of dog in the manger to one part of chivalry as I jumped to the ground to intervene.

I did so just in time to save the man's life. The shove I gave him cleared him of the knife with which she was in the act of slashing at him.

"Cut stick!" I growled at him, but it was not of me that he was in awe.

Religious fervor had temporarily given way to defeated amazement. "Never did see a woman with a bowie knife before!" was all he could manage.

"You do not know the right people," the countess explained with the peculiar accent concerning whose authenticity I could never make up my mind. "Will you go?"

He didn't answer her directly but turned away, muttering to himself. "She hadn't ought to pull a knife at camp meetin'. She sure needs savin'!" Then he regained his spiritual stride with a phrase. "Oh, bless the Lord!" he yelled, starting to run in quest of another soul to help. "I ain't never goin' to do nothin' but right no more!"

Feeling silly about butting in where my help was so little needed, I was trying to contrive some word of farewell. The fact that I didn't want to leave her made it all the more difficult to think of anything to say; and my hesitation put me in her hands. She was well enough acquainted with men's motives to unravel mine swiftly.

"Thank you for wanting to help. You do not have to go unless there's someone whose company you want more."

I still couldn't say anything. The fragrance of some scent she used reached my nostrils with searching effect. My throat vein was pounding, and for the life of me I couldn't refrain from audible breathing. She let me cook for a moment before she stirred me again.

"Once," she said reflectively, "you did not want much to be with me. Yet tonight I think you do—Mr. Godolphin."

The fact that she remembered me did not please me. A man doesn't feel so bad about being made a fool of if only it is accomplished by someone who doesn't know his name. I wanted to get off the hook, but she kept a taut line.

"What has changed you?" she persisted.

Suddenly I wasn't having any more of this. "Ten months in the New Purchase with no bedmates but wood ticks. Now do you wish me to stay?"

"Ten months?" she said interestedly. "Of course, I am not a wood tick," she continued after a few seconds. "Still I do the best I can."

If she had planned further discussion I cancelled it. Before I could conceive of the action myself I'd scooped her up and plunged into the woods after the revivalists. She laughed briefly and lightly but made no comment until we'd gone a few paces.

"I always ask do you like me first," she said in a dreamy voice.

"I like you," I said grimly. But I would almost have been willing to make it stronger. She'd adjusted her head on my shoulder so that her cheek was partially in contact with mine. A strand of her soft hair was across my face, and her body seemed to meet my hands through her thin summer costume.

Again I felt moved to the piety of fondness when we lay nested together in a shadowed copse. The affair with the girl at the quilting party had been pleasant, but this was graced with a delightful fillip of personal desire. Only when quiescence at last came upon us did I know for certain that we had nothing else to give each other.

It was then that I got around to asking her how she happened to be there. "Oh, I am on business." In the darkness the hand she lifted was a pale blur.

"Where are you singing?"

"Singing?" She snapped her fingers in dismissal of the idea. "The Old Purchase is not Natchez Underhill. Our camp-meeting friends would burn a place where there is my type of singing. Besides, I have retired. There is no future for a young singer but to be an old whore."

"Oh," I said, because I thought some word was called for. "What became of your troupe?"

"Now I travel with a young couple who are somewhere in this mixture of people." She gestured once more. "I have saved money, and I am ready to be a credit to my family again. Here in this valley or along the Yazoo I shall be a landholder like all my ancestors."

I couldn't imagine her operating a plantation, though I believed her capable of finding someone who could do it for her. For the time being, it occurred to me, I had some trifling responsibility toward her myself.

"Do you know how to find the place where you're spending the night?"

This time a bare leg glimmered in the air as she stretched luxuriously. "I have found it."

Relieved that I would not be called on to squire her anywhere, I stretched drowsily myself. She was gone by the time I waked, though that was very early in the morning.

With belated anxiety I commenced looking for the horse I'd recklessly abandoned. Fortunately, Goober had found no better place to browse than the prairie, and any horsethieves who might have been at the revival hadn't yet had time to backslide. I found my mount a half mile away, and about a week later we reached Natchez.

CHAPTER XIX

THE TOWN WAS NOT the busy metropolis I had found it the previous fall. Summer was the neutral season when trade was slackest, and there were neither carriages nor carts on the streets. Plantation owners were afield on their holdings, taking their families with them or sending them to cooler latitudes.

I secured refreshment for both Goober and Talisman at a livery stable, washed the dust from my throat down into my stomach with a cool punch and, without further ablutions, made for my employer's place of business. As a traveler in a hot country must, I had become so used to discomfort as not to consider it important; and I had my own reasons for wanting Pace to see me as I was.

He had an office on the ground floor of a high-ceilinged, two-story brick building. It was, by comparison with the outdoors, blessedly cool. The open door sucked a slight breeze through windows facing toward the river. Even the flies found it a soothing haven and were motionless on the wall.

The only other occupant of the simply furnished chamber was Pace himself. His feet were on the desk, his chin was on his chest, his breathing was easy and regular. After observing him a moment, I leaned my rifle in the corner. Then pulling up a chair and pulling down my hat brim, I put my feet on the desk also. The liquor had soothed me, and the position was comfortable. Shortly I slept.

It was perhaps a quarter of an hour later that a hand on my ankle roused me. I was immediately alert, a faculty I'd acquired in the woods.

"What can I do for you?" I enquired.

"Do for *me!*" Pace was a little irritated. "Nothin', damn it!"

Carefully dusting my beard, I closed my eyes again. "Then let me alone, stranger."

He did so for perhaps a minute. Then he tapped my shin. "Listen, hoss," he said firmly, "there ain't no use tryin' to stake out a preemption claim here. I've got clear title."

I reopened my eyes. "You must be Harry Pace then," I stated, swinging my feet to the floor. "Here, I've got a note for you."

One glance at McConnell's writing told him the truth. He looked at me searchingly, chuckled, then guffawed. "Sort of took out naturalization papers, ain't you?"

"Reckon I have," I nodded with a smile designed to show I was in earnest but not cocksure. I wanted him to feel that way, and the bit of foolery I'd enjoyed was useful for coloring. I wished my words to have weight with him, and all indications that I wasn't still a greenhorn sight-seer from the East were important.

"Tom says you got some good maps," he said when he had finished the note. Pulling out a big watch, he flipped open the case. "I'm waitin' here for somebody due on the upriver packet, but it must be late. Where're you stayin'?"

I named a hotel other than the one I'd patronized on my former stay at Natchez. It was not to be expected that that outraged house had forgotten what Talisman had accomplished. Pace nodded when I reported my choice.

"You'll want to get the bark taken off and let the sap run tonight. I'll pick you up there late tomorrow mornin'!"

In sequence I was barbered, purchased a straw hat, took a room at the hotel in question, sent a darky to the livery stable for my luggage, and ordered a bath. Then I arranged for my one remaining presentable outfit to be pressed while I sipped juleps in my tub. This was a satisfactory business, and I didn't hurry it. Every pore in my skin seemed to rejoice individually at that steaming bath, whereas the juleps, aside from keeping me entertained, maintained my body temperature at a pleasant level.

When I was once more dressed in something approaching fashion I felt resplendent and eyed the mirror with earnest approval. Save to see it in a pool of water this was the first time I'd viewed my face for months, and it was like meeting an old friend. True, the lower part, which my lost beard had sheltered, looked startlingly white, but the sun would soon cure that.

I had a fine supper, then with an excellent cigar for company took a carriage for Underhill. That unusual suburb was also half shut down for the summer. Nevertheless, the remaining night life was exhilarating after the long stay in the wilderness. I had a busy voyage and rolled into port late with a full cargo.

To a man a solid drunk often does what a good cry is said to do for a woman. It rakes away the ashes and leaves the fire of life burning with a clearer flame. I felt a little wan but cleansed as I pottered about the room the next day, chuckling over what I could remember of the night before. Still only half dressed, I was enjoying a big breakfast when Pace knocked.

"See you shed the Spanish moss," he said after we'd exchanged greetings. "I don't have to ask how you're doin'. You got high, acted low, and feel mighty good about it."

He sailed his hat onto the bed, threw his coat on a chair, kicked off his jack boots, wriggled his toes, spat out the window, emptied my water tumbler into the spittoon, filled it from the bottle of brandy I'd somewhere acquired the night before, and downed it at a gulp. "Just give me your maps and go on with your breakfast," he advised as he adjusted himself on the bed. "We'll talk it over later."

He was deliberate in his examination, moving a finger from point to point and reading all names and notes. When it came time to talk I did not expatiate as I had with McConnell. He was interested in facts not reactions, and his questions shrewdly covered the economic probabilities.

"How about you?" he asked at length. "Are you countin' on goin' back there?"

The question astonished me, for in my own mind I'd been identified with the country since shortly after reaching the Yazoo. "Why naturally."

"What do you want to do when you get there, speculate, push niggers, pettifog, get sent to Jackson, or keep a doggery?"

One of the things that had happened to me during the winter past was that I had attained certainty as to my vocation. Having land of my own to love and develop was what I most desired.

"I hope to become a planter."

"All right," he said with a lordly wave of the arm. "Of course, I'm payin' you, too, but just let me know when you get ready to do your plantin', and I'll see that you get a fine patch of land. This work you've done is worth a lot to me."

"What's your method of procedure?" I asked curiously.

"First off I'm goin' to the capital and be an expert. To do it in a capital you don't have to know a damned thing. Just every now and then I'll call some branch or otter slide by the tag you gave it, and before long they'll be convinced I've made every snake hole on the Yazoo a personal visit. About the time they're convinced of that it'll be time to play euchre, usin' state representatives for counters."

He flourished the over-all sketch of the upper Yazoo so I could identify it. "Now these likely lookin' town sites you got marked: I'll be in a position to pick up a couple of 'em anyways by openin' day, and I can horseswap for others later if it looks necessary."

I was relieved at this sign of interest in the sites I'd selected, for I'd shown none outside of the New Purchase. "McConnell thought you might prefer to locate your headquarters in the old territory."

"I thought about it," he admitted, "but the Old Purchase is like a bull in the springtime: all that's needed is one good shove, and the job's done. Folks don't have to know what they're doin' to build up from the start that place has, and my land there will sell pretty good. But if I'm to pull anything out of the New Purchase I've got to make somethin' out of nothin' before somebody else beats me to it."

"Most villages just grow around a tavern or a ferry landing," I observed. "Not many will think of actually starting one in the round."

He was frowning at the map again. "I'd know better what I was doin' if the territory was already split into counties. In a new district a village has got to be a county town or it's nothin'. The county town's where the boats land and the cotton brokers operate; it's where folks go to hang horsethieves and blow their crop money. Well, that's part of the gamble."

"What are you going to call the place?" I asked. As the site had not so much as been determined the question struck me as mildly humorous, but he snapped his fingers and jumped from the bed to pick up his coat from the chair where he'd thrown it.

"Glad you thought of that," he said, making a notation on a piece of paper he found in one pocket. "Names are important. Leave it to some squatter and he'll name a town Dirty Ear or Chiggerville, and you'll have a hell of a time gettin' any woman to agree to bring her family up there." He replaced the paper, threw the coat on the bed, and sat down on the chair. "What's Tom doin'?"

"Oh, I left him figuring out what Yazoo lands, according to the documentary evidence available, had been given away by the French, Spanish and British governments as well as by the State of Georgia before the United States cancelled the titles on the ground that only the Choctaws had sovereignty. Now that the Choctaws won't have sovereignty these titles may be valid again or at least some people may think so. He says it's complicated."

"That's somethin' I want to talk to him about. He's supposed to meet me in Jackson at the tag end of summer, so if he hasn't taken off by the time you get back put a burr under his tail."

I spent some additional time in Pace's company, but he was busy while I was all for leisure and pleasure. However, it did not take me long to get a surfeit of what Natchez and Underhill had to provide at that season. There was little congenial company of any sort and none like-minded. I would have enjoyed calling on the Artenays but found they were out of town at their plantation house.

When I did leave it was not by way of the Trace. If I couldn't enjoy my holiday I could at least pamper myself. I stowed Goober and Talisman aboard a fast packet, booked the best cabin available, and sailed for Vicksburg. I'd have to go overland from there in all probability, but the distance would be comparatively short and much of the route new.

The river was torrid by day. After sunset, what with the alleviating breeze created by the boat's passage, it was contrastingly delightful. The passengers, who had endured with a kind of submissive torpor until then, came to life, and I along with the rest. The ship had seemed rather empty, but the night brought people out like moths, and the saloons were soon full.

The passenger list ran the usual frontier gamut, which is to say it included everything from moccasins to monocles and assayed about three men to every woman. The men had the normal interest in the pleasant pursuits of drinking, smoking, gambling and making statements which, if true, were remarkable. Those who showed their deeper side had but one topic. Politics, the banking situation, and even cotton had yielded to the New Purchase, the imminence of its settlement and the ultimate effect on the state at large.

Music had been coming from the ladies' saloon for some time before I got around to watching the dancing. This turned out to be a rash act for a lone male. They were forming for a new cotillion, and before I'd grasped the risks I was pressed into service by a forceful dowager. I didn't mind too much, but I was about to make my escape at the completion of the dance when I noticed a lady who looked familiar.

She was sitting alone and in an attitude that suggested she considered herself a spectator. I couldn't remember when I had seen her before or where, but she unmistakably stirred recollections. They should have been pleasant recollections, for a finer face I never saw, but they remained aggravatingly vague. Then it was that I saw the true uses of an executive dowager. I approached the one who had kidnapped me, pointed out the object of my interest, and asked to be introduced.

"I don't know her name myself," said the dowager, whom I now fully admired, "but I reckon she'll tell me if I ask her."

She did tell, but as she murmured the name, while the dowager persisted in talking, I did not catch it. It is embarrassing to ask people to repeat their names, and it is useless if one doesn't expect to see them again. Even before our go-between left us I had arrived at the awkward conviction that I had not really seen the lady before; she merely reminded me of somebody or other. I could not, however, retreat without asking her to dance, and I did so, not caring whether she accepted or not.

She was a trim, bright-eyed woman, poised to coolness. For a moment she looked at me as if she were staring at something through clear water. Then she smiled.

"I was hoping somebody would pluck me off the wall. I love to dance."

So did I with her. And we managed as easily with our conversation as with our feet. She was neither shy nor the least bit interested in impressing me, and I found we could talk without inventing topics. At the intermission I asked permission to bring her some of the champagne punch that was being served.

"Whereabouts in Mississippi did you settle?" she asked during some desultory conversation in which I had revealed that I was a comparative newcomer.

If I told her I didn't live anywhere she'd naturally think I was either rebuffing her or trying to be mysterious. I chose instead to amuse myself with words.

"When you see me in my working clothes I'm a Choctawland squatter."

She had a way of watching the eyes as if comparing what a person said with what he meant. Now she seemed satisfied the two were congruent.

"I wish you could meet Charles—my husband—but he's not feeling well. He'd love to hear about the country from someone who has lived there."

I'd been about to ask her to repeat her name after all, but I dropped the idea for good. Harriet Cartwright had cured me of wanting to know other men's wives.

"I'd like to meet him," I lied politely.

She grasped the lack of warmth but misunderstood. "But all that's valuable information you naturally wish to keep to yourself; I wasn't thinking. You see, I couldn't help getting excited when you mentioned the New Purchase. We're going to live there ourselves."

I was so startled I absently drank some of the saccharine punch myself. Women had been and would continue to be pioneers in America. I realized it was inevitable that many would suffer the hectic drudgery offered them by the Yazoo country. But a slim, young woman in fashionable summer attire always suggests a fragility she probably doesn't possess. It was impossible for me to visualize her floundering through a sultry cane brake, living in a mud-floor lean-to, or shopping at The Horsethief's Head.

"What do you intend to do there?" I asked.

"My husband's a planter—or he's going to be." She must have

caught my concern, for she added: "We know it'll be hard work, but it'll be interesting."

"Yes'm." I thought of what I had already encountered in Choctawland. Then I recalled McConnell's grim expectations. "I'll be delighted to talk to your husband and give him any information I have that he might consider useful."

Again she gave me the look that weighed words against motive. "That's very kind," she decided, "but he probably won't be up and about before we reach Vicksburg. He hasn't been well lately, which is one reason we left Natchez. We think the outdoor life will be good for him."

Frontier life is like frontier cooking. It's nourishing if one can build up the constitution to stand it.

"I hope he finds it so," I said ineffectually.

A few minutes later she left me to find out whether her husband had need of anything, and I sought the bar to wash the champagne punch out of my mouth with an honest drink. On the way I at last remembered who my dancing partner had reminded me of. She looked somewhat like a more mature and less exuberant version of Corinna Artenay.

The passengers in the men's saloon had been weeded out. Those who retired by the clock had done so; the rest had settled down to some sort of occupation. Gambling was the most popular, followed by the philosophical pursuit of watching gambling. Most of the spectators hovered around a faro table operated by a blonde, detached professional. There were also a couple of tables of brag and one of high-low-jack. Because the players of this last game seemed to be enjoying themselves rather than trying to cut each other's throats I took my stand there. Eventually I was invited to take a hand and accepted, ordering a round of drinks for all by way of initiation fee.

Before the cards could be dealt there was a diversion which turned all our heads toward the faro game. A foppishly dressed youngster, overdrunk and underbred, was pushing his way through the onlookers, dragging a well-set-up house darky after him.

"Damn it all," he was crying, "you said my I.O.U.'s no good! I'm going to show you it's always good!"

THE WILD YAZOO

The gambler paid off some bets before he gave any heed to this clamor. "What's on your mind?" he finally asked.

Observing that everybody was watching him, the boy raised his voice another notch. "What's on my mind? Why I want to pay what I owe you—even though you wouldn't take my word I would—and then go on playing." Imperiously he slapped the table twice. "Here, Josh, jump up here."

The darky, who must have been worth close to a thousand dollars, did so unhesitatingly. He, too, was enjoying the drama of the occasion and grinned around.

"All right," the lad shouted triumphantly, "play me for my nigger, double or quits!"

The gambler didn't so much as lift his pale eyebrows. After giving the slave a glance of appraisal he piled up some money and shoved it forward in sign of accepting the wager. Then while everyone waited he deliberately sprung his box, flipping out a card. I couldn't see the play from where I sat, but the returns were in a moment later, reported by the young dude himself.

"No damn luck, but I can take my losses!" he cried as he turned away.

Although many beside myself appeared to disapprove of this vulgarity, nobody else appeared to be surprised. I shrugged and cut the cards for the man next to me.

It was one of those blue moon evenings when all I had to do to win was to put down the cards dealt me. Winning is fun, but eventually, in view of the fact I was a stranger on a river notorious for card sharpers, my good fortune grew embarrassing. Yet gambling has its own morality, and the two occasions when it is impossible to quit are when one is winning or losing.

The stakes had originally not been high, but inevitably they mounted as the rest strove to retrieve their losses. Of the other four players I broke them all except one in a couple of hours. Their good nature had yielded to morose silence, and they sat watchfully to see how I made out with the last of them.

Beneath a haystack of light hair the man in question had a round face that didn't go with his thin, angular body. He looked blankly solemn except when he smiled, which he did all at once and all over. Then a sort of comic intelligence was alive in his eyes.

He should never have been allowed near a deck of cards, though. In addition to overbidding and recklessly backing his bad judgment he played execrably. Only the fact that he was well supplied with cash sustained him. At last, however, he gave a groan of mock anguish.

"You've emptied my wallet, Mr. Godolphin."

"I'm sorry, Mr. Caradock," I told him, and I meant it. A more cheerful loser never played a game so badly.

He leaned back and gazed at me in earnest appeal. "Would you be sport enough to let me have one more try? My luck can't have the blind staggers forever."

"Why—yes." My hesitation was not due to reluctance to give him a chance to recoup but to a conviction that he'd only hang himself from a higher tree. I expected him to bring forth a watch or some such handy collateral, but instead he said: "I'm going to put up Eli."

I wasn't ready to believe he was imitating the noisy young fop we'd recently seen fleeced. "What and where's Eli?" I asked to be sure.

He took the parts of my question up in order. "He's inky black, tireless, docile and can do anything within reason that you ask of him. Just now he's below decks. Of course, if you doubt his existence——"

"I take your word for it," I said vexedly. I didn't like any part of such a business or have a high opinion of anybody who'd propose it, and I didn't mind showing it. "I'm used to playing for cash only," I said curtly.

He tried to melt my opposition with a smile. "You've got everything else I own except my share of the family burial plot. My luck isn't bad, it's just misguided. Give it a chance to reform."

Magnanimity is expected of a winner in a so-called friendly game. I was no longer feeling friendly; but I recognized what was expected of me, and the others did, too. "Sure, moneybags, let him try to come back," one of them growled.

My very disgust at the idea of gambling for a slave operated to make me concede. A man that would do such a thing couldn't be a good master, and I felt that I'd be doing the negro a favor to get him out of such hands.

"All right," I said ungraciously, "but I'm calling his value, take it or leave it. You can put him up against just what I've won from you and not a cent over. What's more, this is the last hand I play, win or lose."

"That's just fine!" he cheered. "I know I shouldn't have squeezed you, but you know how it is when a man feels his luck coming around."

Annoyed as I was, I still didn't want to take anything more from the fool because of his muddled playing. "We'll have a hand that will give your luck a chance," I told him, tossing the pack to one of the players who'd dropped out. "Will you shuffle them, please? High card pays off."

There was an approving murmur from the bystanders as the fellow obliged. I had a drink and yawned, more or less indifferent to what was happening. If I lost, why I would still leave the game winners. If I won, I'd have a slave who might or might not be an asset.

The man shuffling finished and at my request cut for me. The card was a six of clubs, and everybody was delighted. My petulant gesture had cleared me of suspicion, but the general feeling was that it was time for my comeuppance.

I felt relieved that it was turning out that way myself. "You ought to be able to beat that," I told Caradock.

He wasn't listening. Deliberately he rose to walk thrice around his chair, muttering what mystic words I could only imagine. When he had reseated himself he stared at the cards as if he would hypnotize them, rubbed his hands as though to cleanse them of all but good fortune. Then with the deft movement of a prestidigitator he turned the trey of hearts.

Everybody groaned save Caradock himself. He stared fixedly at the card as if he expected the pips to increase. When they failed to do so he threw up his hands and laughed.

Nothing is more winning than good humor in misfortune, and my displeasure with him was largely dissipated. "I'm sorry," I told him for the second time that evening. At the same time I had no intention of remitting the stakes of the game he'd forced upon me. "When do I get possession of Eli?"

He sobered somewhat and drew out a paper I took to be a certificate of ownership such as people traveling with slaves usually carry. "You can have this now, but you'll have to wait until they unload him before you can see him."

"*Unload* a darky?"

He helped himself to a drink as if to brace himself. "I never said he was a darky," he pointed out. "He's an Eli Hitchcock printing press—mostly known as just an Eli in the trade."

This was the kind of thing to please the Western funnybone, the more so as the joke was at the expense of my previously all-victorious self. After I'd had time to catch my breath I joined the roar of mirth.

"What the devil will I do with a printing press?" I wondered, fingering the bill of lading he'd handed me.

He looked owlishly concerned. "Better than I'll do without one. Neither Eli nor myself is any good apart from the other, so you'd better take me along with him." Now he assumed a confidingly interested expression as if the matter had been all settled. "Where are we going?"

Thinking of my destination reminded me of Harry Pace, and a thread from his mantle descended upon my shoulders. Newspapers would be needed along the Yazoo, and one would be an asset to that epitome of civilization, a county town.

"I don't know about you," I said. "Eli and I are going to the New Purchase."

CHAPTER XX

VICKSBURG WAS A SMALLER and cruder facsimile of Natchez, what with its dockside cutthroat and amusement area and its residential section high on the bluff. I had no reason for lingering there and didn't once I'd made arrangements for the printing press to be shipped to Turkey Run in the fall. Caradock wasn't so easily disposed of. He placidly made it clear that he considered me the controller of his destiny. Certainly he seemed to have no other means of support.

I didn't want to be shackled with him, yet could not deny his claims upon me. In the upshot I gave him some money and told him to take passage for the New Purchase or anywhere else when he could and if he was so inclined. I didn't expect to see him again when I rode forth upriver.

The portents of change were evident as soon as I was deep in the Old Purchase. In contrast to my former experiences along the Yazoo I never knew when I would encounter some wayfarer nosing about for a site on which to file a claim. Turkey Run, through which I passed early one morning, was also crammed with potential settlers of both the Old Purchase and the New. Yet of all the people I encountered at that time, I never saw the face of the only man I remember. It was only recently that he had been shot through the head, but the buzzards had pretty well picked his features over.

Fortunately I was upwind of him, and I came no closer; but the fact that his clothes had been partly removed suggested that the motive was robbery. Thereafter the lonesome trail often didn't seem lonesome enough. To the casual dangers of the wilderness the spectre of wanton treachery had been added. I was alert for ambush and rode around anything I couldn't see through.

When I reached Shevlin's old camp all that was waiting was a note from McConnell stuck in a blazed hickory:

Daunt:

Tim's finished curing his otter, so we've loaded them plus a few bearskins, the hounds, the nags and ourselves on a Vicksburg bound raft. Thence I'm going to Jackson to meet Harry. See you at Turkey Run on claim filing day.

T.

As this was about what I had expected I didn't mind it at first. I spent a week making a survey of Council Lodge. This included not only locating the boundaries of the section I was going to claim but picking out the fields I first intended to clear and deciding just where—when I was ready to build—I would put my house.

That was pleasing, but when I had finished I didn't know what to do with myself. Into the vacancy created by idleness and prolonged solitude moved a mawkish despond. I was lonely not so much for the men I'd known as for a way of life. Thinking of all the pleasant times I'd had in that vicinity only the past seemed worth while and the future as planned a foolish denial of what I had found good. The knowledge of things already done should nourish the consciousness as food does the blood, but that wisdom isn't always handy. I wasn't savoring the old days, I was longing for them as something known in an otherwise chartless world.

For all my mooning I hadn't forgotten the lesson of the dead man in the forest, though. When I heard a sound I didn't recognize while I was about to cook supper I grabbed my rifle and got out of camp with a speed that would have done credit to Yancey Shevlin. Talisman was off on some project of his own, so I was able to circle silently.

When I approached my bivouac again a man was crouched among my belongings, showing more curiosity than is expected of a visitor. Specifically he was in the act of putting the stopper back in the small molasses jug. I stepped forward, my rifle cocked.

"The whiskey's in the larger jug," I remarked.

A hunter would have whirled to see what I meant to do, or he would have frozen where he was, awaiting eventualities. At the least he would have looked embarrassed at being caught unawares even if he didn't blush for what he was doing. This fellow did none of these things.

"Thank you," he said, reaching for the larger jug. He was used to drinking from one and didn't dribble as he took a couple of vigorous swallows.

Amused as well as annoyed, I watched him deliberately recork it. "That's an easy way to get yourself shot," I pointed out.

He gently grounded the liquor. "I'd rather be shot for an accomplishment than for an intention," he said as he rose and turned to look at me. "Philosophically it's undignified to desist from crime only because one is observed. Theory has it that if the reproachful eye of conscience doesn't deter you nothing should. Reaching deeper than mere philosophy, it's bad for the spirit to interrupt an action once the will has decided upon it. Furthermore I had a hankering. Are you going to drink?"

Lowering the hammer of my weapon, I leaned it against a tree. "It won't be the first time we've shared my whiskey." I swung the jug over my shoulder. "How's the flower-gathering business?" I asked when I had drunk.

Holley had the look I remembered, hinting that he was both aware of and careless of everything that existed. "Now at last you shame me," he said. "It's far more grievous to forget a man than to steal from him, which, viewed from certain angles, is a compliment."

I was glad to see him; in fact I would have been glad to see almost anybody then. "We were guests of a young couple down along the Big Black," I reminded him. "I had a silver decanter."

"Enshrining prime Monongahela," he finished. "Why, surely. Godolphin, that is the name—or did it belong to your friend with the Punch-like profile?" While I was assuring him of my identity he examined the camp, then turned back to me enquiringly. "Before we go any further with the amenities am I invited to supper?"

I wanted company, but I was not above meeting insolence with bargaining power. "The jug and I will be glad to have you if you can cook."

"I am an excellent cook," he declared, "and as soon as I've unburdened my mount I'll prove it."

While I contentedly leaned against a tree and smoked, he worked and talked with equal vigor. "I remember telling you that I planned visiting the New Purchase, and though I'm glad I've come," here he paused and sloshed a little whiskey into a sauce he was preparing, "I find myself overwhelmed with awe."

To be awed isn't within everybody's capacity, calling as it does for certain wholesome perceptions. However, I didn't challenge his statement. "Are the flowers here that unusual?"

"For once they weren't uppermost in my mind." He turned from his sauce and started hacking collops from my haunch of venison. "No, it's from being in a country at the exquisite moment of its loss of identity. One isn't often privileged to look on the face of history at the instant of one of its tragic gestures. Usually it's more like a mosquito—one never knows it is around until the damage has been done."

The fact that I had been afflicted with pessimistic qualms had no effect upon my thinking now that I was recovering cheer. I was sure in rebuttal, even though I didn't believe him to be very serious.

"Change doesn't necessarily imply worsening." I replaced the pipe with my pocket flask then the flask in turn with my pipe. "Take the case of the egg and the swan, or consider the noble transmutation awaiting that venison when it becomes yourself."

He held a collop up and inspected it. "I'll pass that, even though realizing a buck might differ as to the true uses of doe flesh. But the debauching of a marvelous wilderness so that the land will sprout a weed called cotton is something else again. Tearing down this forest is an act of aesthetic wantonness akin to scalping a beautiful woman. And the land will look very much like the head from which the scalp has been torn once the sun is free to work on it.

"In place of these trees and all the intricacies of wonder and beauty they bulwark you will have a district warty with tree stumps. To each five stumps there will be a lean, lousy woods hog, to each five woods hogs there will be a dirty, lousy squatter, and to each five squatters there will be a ramshackle and still again verminous cabin. Yet all of you strive to wreak this disenchantment, to produce a sorry changeling out of embodied loveliness, dignity and quietude."

He had talked himself into an approximation of earnestness. Nor did I argue with his prophecy of evil. I had seen the frontier. But I had also seen enough of the power of the wilderness to admire the ability of men able to take anything from it. Survival was an accomplishment; anything more than that an achievement.

"You can't expect man to build like God," I observed. "In the first place there wouldn't be any sense in such encroachment on prerogative; in the second place he doesn't live long enough to acquire the knack of instant perfection."

He put the coffee on and sat back. "We're talking somewhat at cross purposes. You are eyeing the problem from the point of view of what man will build, while I am thinking of what he will destroy."

"You can't make a ripple without heaving a stone," I said carelessly. "Would you have men stay put and do nothing like your flowers?"

"Barring yourself—for I never insult the owner of the liquor—I wouldn't have men at all. If flowers do nothing they do it with unutterable perfection. Consider the quality of their existence, from cool seed to lone growth to quiet blossoming to slow fading as a prelude to sure immortality. Per contra man is born of a struggle, lives in hectic confusion, destroys what he touches, and dies corruptly."

I had learned during my medical studies that to the scientific mind, insatiable of clear patterns, man's dynamic insouciance is infuriating. "No doubt plants lead more regular lives," I murmured, "but I've lived in Mississippi too long to consider that a virtue."

If I didn't agree with him, I did enjoy his cooking. Moreover, I found him a stimulating and instructive companion in the days which followed. One of the ironic facets of a true cynicism is that, like atheism, it's a passion and a faith in itself. Another one is that it is seldom bestowed upon lazy people, the only ones equipped to enjoy it. So in spite of Holley's disillusionment with humanity, which is to say himself, he yet found it worth while to obey man's most tremendous urge.

He worked unstintingly, careless of trouble, effort and weather, at the one thing he really cared about. He had studied all phases of botany, and like anybody else who has labored for recherché knowledge he rejoiced at an attentive listener. I was one such, for he was telling me things about my country, supplementing Shevlin's factual accuracy with the economics of science.

If I didn't retain too much of what he gave me I did follow him closely when he dealt with the medical properties of plants. There would be much sickness along the Yazoo as in other Southern valleys, and I made notes on everything Holley could tell me concerning the healing uses of flora.

So when one morning he slipped away from me, taking the last of the whiskey, I wasn't too wrathful. I was in his debt for information painstakingly transmitted as well as for company in passage through what would have otherwise been a morbid hiatus.

It was almost a year since I had made my forced retreat from Spring Hill that I saddled Goober early, intent on claiming another property. But as I rode, conscious that I was moving toward the new way of life about to develop in the valley, that way of life met me more than halfway. Long before I reached the Choctawland border it came piling through the forest like a wave, with all of water's aimless force.

The land seekers were loose in the woods. Settlers they could not be called, for nothing less settled was imaginable. Squatters they could not be called, for they could not bring themselves to a long halt anywhere. Probably waiting for official permission and guidance had grown irksome to some, and the rest had stampeded after them, fearful of being left out. They didn't know the country, they had no maps, they had no information, no idea as to where they were going. All they knew was that here was reputedly rich land to be had for a song. They wanted it, and they knew that everybody else wanted it. The combination of greed, rivalry, and the excitement of the treasure hunt was overpowering.

Among so much that was desirable many couldn't decide on a preference. They dashed from one location to another, their ecstasy at what they found poisoned by the fear that there was something better of which they were depriving themselves through delay.

Others, more sluggish, would stay on a so-called claim overnight or possibly even a couple of days before they could stand it no longer and move on.

There was also a dogged type that marked out a section and promptly started building a cabin, as if there could or would be no challenge to his ownership. Suspicion and quarrelsomeness were concomitants of the hysteria; but this last group, because more fixed of purpose, was the most difficult to deal with.

On one occasion I approached what looked to be a harmless family group. The man was not in evidence, but a bony woman, squatting on her heels, was milking a bony cow. A tumble of children and dogs were in the foreground and a partially loaded oxcart in the background. As soon as I was near enough for Goober to be audible the woman rose, the cow ambled away, the children ran behind the cart, and the dogs ran toward me. I didn't pay much attention to any of this, for a man had stepped out from behind a tree, aiming a rifle.

"Get off my land!" he ordered.

I didn't like to have a gun pointed at me, but I didn't like to irritate the man who was doing it. I halted Goober abruptly. "I'm not on your land, stranger. I'm following this old Indian trail down the valley."

He held his weapon where it was. "Goin' to file on land?" he demanded.

I was becoming angered in spite of the need for discretion. "What I want to claim is none of your business, though it doesn't happen to be this section. Now you want me to go, and I want to leave. How about pointing that damned gun somewhere else and letting me ride ahead?"

I think it was because he grew tired of holding the heavy weapon to his shoulder that he complied. "Well, I'd ought to make you go around—I can't have people ridin', through here all the time, and you crossed my line twenty—thirty rods back—but I'll let it go this time. Now get movin' an' don't look back or I might figure you're tryin' to start somethin'."

I didn't look back either, but I believe he trailed me for about a quarter of a mile to make sure I was the transient I claimed to be.

The incident made me fume for awhile, but it taught me how to conduct myself in the future.

Turkey Run, as I found when I reached there, was also full of excitable people. The surrounding forest was a sprawling, disorganized camp where men and their animals bedded down and foraged while they waited to be unleashed.

I saw every sort of bivouac from the dirty blanket of the lone hunter to the elaborate camp of the family with a dozen slaves. But the hopes of the owners were alike and high. Before them was the chance to reverse their fortunes, recoup past losses and make good past mistakes. I knew how they felt, for the feeling was my own. Here was the exile's gamble, the chance, so often prayed for and so seldom granted, to start life anew.

If these were pious hopes, there was not necessarily the motif of piety in their interim employment. True, there were the inescapable preachers, but they had to compete on a fair basis of entertainment offered with pit dogs, thimblerig, cock fights, faro, man fights, horse races and stolidly industrious Choctaw squaws. There were also two new taverns whose rivalry The Horsethief's Head could hardly resent. There was more business than all three could conveniently handle.

All in all it was a lively gathering, and I enjoyed being part of it as I waited for chance to show me McConnell. Very likely I would have seen him eventually if I'd taken my stand somewhere, but it wasn't the course I adopted. After paying my respects to The Horsethief's Head, I lost a few dollars on a quarter race. Then after investigating the premises of The Yazoo Queen I won back part of what I had lost at a cock fight. It was at The Bear Hunter's Rest that I first saw somebody I knew.

Jack Garland was seated in a corner with his associate in gambling and other enterprises, the redoubtable Alexander Pope Cummins. I got my drink and drew back so I wouldn't be jostled by the crowd at the bar and happened to take a position near them. I had just drained my glass when Garland spoke to me.

"I've seen you before, haven't I?"

"That's right," I said, "we were both watching the thimblerig game."

"The day of my arrival," he assented. "What'll you have?"

"A little branch water on the side, thanks." It amused me as I seated myself and was introduced to Cummins that I was a guest in the enemy camp. "Have you settled in Turkey Run?" I asked.

An indispensable part of the gambler's craft is the ability to be ingratiating. "Well settled, I hope," Garland rejoined smilingly. "In fact I like to consider myself one of the valley's leading merchants."

I had already noted that they were dressed far more soberly than when I had last seen them together. "Merchants?" I repeated questioningly.

"The Turkey Run Emporium," he nodded, "the largest mercantile house in Mississippi east of Vicksburg and north of the Big Black. If we haven't got it, we'll order it; if we can't obtain it for you it doesn't exist."

I had seen no such establishment. "Where's it located?"

"At present in a wing, so to speak, of The Bear Hunter's Rest here, which I also own. Incidentally, we'd appreciate your custom."

It was conceivable, I thought as I lit a cigar, that he was acting in good faith, but it was at least as probable that he wasn't. The man who could plan such a raid as he had directed against Natchez was capable of using a business, even one that was prosperous in itself, as a blind for other activities. The presence of Cummins, who had acted as his field executive on that other occasion, lent color to this theory. Had I intended to remain in the Old Purchase I would have been more concerned.

As it was, I was just about to excuse myself to go in search of McConnell when he came through the door. He didn't see us, as his eyes weren't adjusted to the comparative gloom of the tavern, and as I now found the company I was in a matter of embarrassment, I didn't hail him. I had hopes that the gamblers wouldn't notice Tom, but he had just reached the bar when Cummins yelled: "You won't be served here, McConnell. Get out!"

The taproom had been busy but calm. This was like a rock through a closed window. McConnell whirled and peered, and all three of us at the table jumped to our feet. Everybody else there, obviously learned in such matters, got out of the way. I kept my eyes on the gamblers, but I didn't have to take action. Cummins started to reach for either a pistol or a knife, but Garland, who was clearly the dominant partner, restrained him.

"I could have sworn," McConnell said after a moment, "that one of you told me to get out. If you want to raise any dust with that wind you'll find me right behind my drink here." He glanced toward the puzzled barkeep and tossed a coin on the plank. "Give me ten fingers of storm cloud in a buffalo horn."

"I'll join you in one of those elsewhere," I spoke up. "This place belongs to them."

Tom scooped up the money as if rescuing it from contamination. "The devil it does! Come on, then!"

Garland's eyes ran quickly from McConnell to me. His face retained its smile but not its pleasantness as I started to back away. "Don't worry; I don't want any trouble in my place," he told me. "But forget what I said about wanting your trade."

No buffalo horns were available at The Horsethief's Head, but we found adequate vessels. "Looks like the gamblers' guild has taken over here," Tom commented after he had cleared the channel. "I've seen quite a few of the citizenry of Natchez Underhill since I arrived."

"It'll be a sore spot," I acquiesced, "and maybe not a safe one for you."

"I know it," he admitted. "It was my testimony that got those two a flogging. They'll certainly kill me if they can."

"Watch yourself at night," I admonished him. "When's Pace going to arrive?"

"The next boat, I imagine." McConnell accepted a cigar and rolled it into position. "He left Jackson before I did to make some last-minute preparations at Natchez. Tim hasn't shown up, has he?"

"Haven't see him."

"I reckon he hasn't finished spending all his money. He—" McConnell was chuckling in advance of his anecdote but stopped as three men came in. They were carrying a fourth who was past getting much good out of the liquor they doubtless meant to give him. The fellow was partially disembowelled by a knife thrust and was, I believe, already dead. Tom lifted his drink again. "Lots going on and more to come," he observed.

CHAPTER XXI

McConnell would not join the line of land claimers. "I'll have enough real estate thrust upon me by shifty clients, Daunt." He flourished his cigar. " 'To Thomas McConnell, in payment for valuable services rendered, my estate called Emperor's Jewel, consisting of one cabin, jerry built, one barn, built in my imagination only, and 640 acres of land that would doubtless be arable if anybody could find a means of hoisting them above the encumbering waters. For good measure I also throw in all equipment and stock, consisting of one clasp knife, lost while trolling in the garden, and a pig whose whereabouts can be ascertained by asking the alligator with which he was last seen.' " Tom settled himself more comfortably against a supporting tree. "Go ahead, planter. I'll wait for you here."

After standing in line for hours I at last found myself, hot, tired and annoyed, before a clerk who had all those afflictions plus that of boredom. My specifications as to the location of my claim were naturally more exact than those of most people. I felt he should be relieved to find somebody who knew the country, but he made no comment until he'd consulted an assortment of rough sketches.

"I can't be sure—all these claims will have to be officially surveyed before there's a final settlement—but it looks to me like a Choctaw or so has put in ahead of you. Got any second choice?"

Indignant and baffled, I glared at him. I knew that no Choctaw had shown any interest in locating there; but I couldn't tell how I knew without disclosing my illegal status as a treaty-jumping squatter. In my irritation I wanted someone to have it out with. I would have liked to accuse the clerk of complicity in some nameless plot to defraud me, but he obviously didn't care.

"You say you can't be sure," I said sharply. "What have you got in back of your statement?"

He shoved forward a sketch with squares marked off on it here and there. "Pick out your spot," he directed.

The drawing was crude, but the principal local features were discernible. I put my finger on a point where two squares touched and waited while the clerk consulted some notes.

"You'll have to argue it out with Peter Stinking Crow and Jack Shuffle Bones," he announced. The preposterous declaration seemed to please him. He brightened up and became more communicative. "Their mothers likely didn't call 'em that, but the clerk who filed their claims probably couldn't spell Choctaw names and made free translations. Anyhow they're Injuns and had a chance to put in their claims months ago."

I bit my lip. "Can you file my claim to establish priority over anybody but the Choctaws in case the Indians don't stay settled?"

"I can put your counter claim on record." He put down his pen and flexed his cramped fingers. "But why in Hell don't you find some other wood lot? God knows there's plenty of them here. What difference does it make?"

His position was reasonable, but that's a luxury detachment can afford. I had seen what I wanted, I felt I had earned the right to it, and I knew that I was being cheated.

"It makes a God damned lot of difference!" I cried, trying to convince with heat where I could not with argument. "Record it, please."

So after a year of the hardest and best work I had ever done I had nothing to show. My counter claim didn't take the form of a tentative deed or receipt: it was merely a notarized statement scribbled on the Federal books.

I was outraged rather than discouraged. As the clerk had pointed out, there was other property available and Harry Pace had promised me land; but I had my back up and wanted what I wanted. I felt, because I insisted on so feeling, that I would get my chosen section even if I had to buy it. Meanwhile, I had to decide what to do with myself.

Those who succeeded in establishing uncontested claims were

leaving Turkey Run. They acted, I observed sourly, as if there wasn't a moment to be spared from the business of turning a patch of wilderness into a prosperous plantation. Still there were enough idle people left to form a crowd around any entertainment or disaster. I was walking slowly back to rejoin McConnell when I passed such a group.

"A dollar gets you two he's dead," a man was wagering.

Nobody seemed willing to contradict, but someone else had a different suggestion. "Well, don't you think we'd ought to find out some way?"

While my medical studies hadn't gone beyond the middle stage I felt I could at least distinguish between the quick and the dead. I pushed my way through the crowd. "Let me look at him," I said authoritatively.

The man lying inert on the ground was Mr. Philips, with whom I'd toured Natchez Underhill my first night in Mississippi. He certainly looked in bad shape, but a swift examination convinced me that life in him wasn't yet extinct.

"He's alive," I said. "Back away and give him a chance to get some air."

The fellow who had risked money on Philips' mortality wasn't willing to comply. He straddled the body.

"I know a goner when I see one," he insisted. "A buck gets you two he's a stiff. Goin' to put up?" With the words he tossed his money on my helpless patient, spat, grinned at me, and pulled out a knife. "Whether you bet or not I aim to show I know what I'm talking about. If you stick a knife in a man and he don't bleed he's dead, ain't he?"

The author of this medical theory was a big, buck-toothed young fellow. He didn't look quite as barbarous as his proposal, but he was sure he was right and wanted the satisfaction of proving it. I started to argue with him but saw by the gleam of arrogance in his eyes he wasn't subject to mental persuasion.

With one hand I tossed down a dollar to confront his two; with the other I drew my pistol from inside my shirt. "You'll get the stakes if you're right, but we're going to find out just what's wrong before we play mumblety-peg. Now if you don't stand back there won't be a betting doubt as to whether you're dead or not."

He looked around indignantly, but he didn't have the sympathy of the crowd. One of them gave him the out he needed, though.

"Quit bein' a chigger-brained pig louse, Jake. Stand back and let the doc work on him."

"Aw, I didn't know he was a doctor," Jake muttered. He sheathed his weapon, lifted a foot carefully over the invalid, and backed away.

The pulse was slow but not dangerously faint. I loosened the stock below the pale, handsome features and propped his head up a little. Fortunately, someone had had sense enough to take him into the shade. There wasn't much I could do, but more to hold the audience at bay than anything else, I went through a sort of physician's charade while I waited for the tide to turn. As I had judged, the disorder was transient, however deep-seated the cause. His strength began to come back as mysteriously as it had ebbed. He groaned and opened his eyes.

For this entirely normal course of events I won a magician's credit. As far as the witnesses were concerned I was a veritable Aesculapius of the Yazoo, and the praise was fulsome. I promptly made use of the power of which I found myself possessed.

Picking the money up from where it lay on Philips' stomach, I pocketed it, smiling good-naturedly at the loser. "Jake," I said confidentially, "we ought to get this poor devil back to his camp where he can rest comfortably. Could you and a friend or so give me a hand?"

He was all eagerness to show himself in a better light than before, and he had zealous volunteer assistants. I didn't have to do any of the carrying but walked ahead with a fellow who professed to know where the sick man's bivouac was located.

It was a camp for settlers of the more prosperous sort. Several darkies were asleep near the two Conestoga wagons that were its most prominent feature. A white woman sat reading in the driver's seat of one of these vehicles.

Before she could possibly have identified the patient she recognized trouble. I saw her go limp, then pull herself up straight. Next, I was interested to notice, she took a flower from her hair and deliberately marked the place before she jumped down. I took my hat off as she stalked by me. The last time I'd seen her we had danced on shipboard.

"Is he yours, ma'am?" Jake asked. Then he called to me. "Say, Doc, where'll we put him?"

She had made sure her man wasn't dead. The professional title turned her head to me.

"He stood too long in line in this sun," I told her. "Is there an easy place for him to rest in one of the wagons?"

"Yes. I'll show you." It was the first sound she had made.

Jake and the others lifted Philips in, then, at my word, gladly made off. I hadn't any more stomach for wifely grief than they had; but, having assumed the post of medical advisor, I couldn't very well leave. I gave the patient some water, refraining from adding the drop of whiskey I would have thought wise in some cases. The liquor he'd already swallowed had done him no good.

By the time Mrs. Philips had bathed his face he was in condition to talk. "I'll wait outside if you want any suggestions," I said. "Don't keep him from sleep now."

For the few minutes it took her to get him settled I leaned unhappily against a tree. She needed real help, and all I had to offer was some probably useless advice.

"I didn't know you were a doctor," she said when she rejoined me.

"They just called me that," I dismissed the subject. "But I know a little. Your husband doesn't belong in these woods. It's no place for a weak heart."

She looked at me sombrely. "It wasn't good for him at Natchez either."

Her tone wasn't exactly defensive, but I thought I saw. She had been the one responsible for bringing him away from the certainties of town life to the chanciness of the frontier. Except for one thing Natchez had an unusually healthful location.

"Underhill isn't good for a man in his condition," I conceded.

She flushed painfully. "I didn't know you knew him. Doctors told me that living outdoors would be good for him. He'd been inside so much at Natchez and getting no stronger. A planter's life will—I thought it would—restore him and build him up."

It was on the tip of my tongue to say that there was no use trying to season rotted wood. "I've known it to happen," I agreed. "But life on the frontier is hard enough for the robust. It might kill him in short order. You have a right to know that."

As soon as I said it I saw that she did know it and had placed the stakes against hope. "A woman who can't keep her husband from Natchez Underhill has to try something else," she said at length.

I thought she wouldn't have said that unless she was desperate. In any case she wasn't really talking to me, she was telling herself that action in crisis is often its own and sole justification. I knew without asking that she wasn't going back to Natchez. Probably she couldn't for more reasons than those involving morale.

"Have you any capital?"

She looked to see what I meant in that searching way I remembered. I was glad I had no ulterior motive; I had the feeling she would have picked it out of me as easily as scooping an oyster out of its shell.

"A little," she said finally.

"Then don't try to file on a claim," I told her out of the wisdom I'd acquired not an hour before. "Buy from some speculator who has arranged for whatever dealings may be necessary and can give you clear title. Otherwise you may find yourself shoved from pillar to post—or your claim disallowed just about the time you get a few acres cleared. It'll cost you something, but if you can afford it, it's worth it."

I thought of recommending her to Harry Pace, but I didn't want her to think I was a speculator's shill. Possibly she suspected I might make such a specific suggestion, for she waited a moment before answering.

"We may have to," she said. "Things haven't worked out too well so far, and it's a fact we don't know much about land."

"Don't let them sell you any swamps—take a look after a heavy rain, if possible, before you buy—and be sure you have access to the river, and—" I brought myself up short, feeling foolish. Like a hanger-on at the races, I had an abundance of advice but no record of ever having backed a winner myself.

"Thank you, Mr. or Dr. Godolphin—whichever it is. I'll tell Charles what you said. What would you advise for him now?"

"He'll probably be normal tomorrow." I shrugged. "The best thing is to get settled and let the country work on him. From now on you'll never find a better climate, so if he's going to mend, and wants to, now's his time." I edged away a little to signify that I thought I'd been there long enough. "Good luck, ma'am."

I'd been afraid she might attempt to pay me for my pseudo-professional services, but instead she gave me her hand. "It's been good luck for me both times I've met you."

She achieved a smile as she said this that swept her face clear of everything except pleasant liking; but I knew she was desolate as I walked away. Fortunately, the woes of most other people don't haunt a man or the world would be filled with grieving to the neglect of more worth-while pursuits. Yet for almost anybody there are persons, as often as not comparative strangers, who have the instant power to challenge the imagination. She was such a one for me. The fact that she was in desperate straits was a depressing if transient reality.

McConnell was asleep when I returned to our bivouac but he waked before I could nudge his ribs with the toe of my moccasin. It was a day of disappointments, and I sat down resignedly as he sat up. "I thought you must be wooing The Yazoo Queen and couldn't find your way back," he greeted me. "Have a horn?"

"What time is it?" I asked as ritual demanded.

"Earlier than moonrise but later than sunrise. The sands of time run, but moistened sand not so fast."

"Let's slow down a minute so we can take a look at it," I decided.

"Well," he enquired after the toasting, "are you a master of broad acres?"

"No." I consulted a scrap of paper. "But Peter Stinking Crow and Jack Shuffle Bones are. They each have a pre-emption on about half of my claim." I looked at him to see what he thought.

He didn't seem surprised, nor did he waste breath on commiseration. "That sounds like Senator Truesdale's work. I've seen him around here, and I have no doubt he's selling land titles."

"I haven't seen him, but I thought of him when this happened."

"Oh, well, there's lots of other sections."

"But that's the one I want," I said grimly, "and I intend to have it in spite of every Choctaw and dirty-necked senator in Mississippi."

He listened patiently to this rhetoric. "What are you going to do now?"

This was a matter to which I'd been giving some thought. I snickered. "Just about what I would have done in the long run even if I had got my land. Surveying ought to be profitable this winter and I'll have to build up capital. I found out some years ago that a farmer who can't be his own banker might as well go to the slave market and put himself up for auction."

"There'll be money in surveying," he agreed. "Why don't you put your shingle under mine? The possum still hangs from the tree of which my office will be built, but you're welcome to share it."

A village would have to be headquarters for my activities, and for both personal and practical reasons I intended to settle where my friends were. "Let me know when the possum moves out. Meanwhile, the word's passing around that steamboat smoke has been sighted. How about seeing if Pace is aboard?"

On the way to the landing we passed the spot where I had found my patient prostrate. "By the way," I asked, "do you know a citizen called Charles Philips?"

"The dude you were with that night at Underhill? Yes. As a matter of fact he married one of old Artenay's nieces—or perhaps you knew that."

So that was why Mrs. Philips always made me think of Corinna. "No, he was just a chance acquaintance. I mentioned him because I happened to run across him here."

"How much did he borrow?"

"Nothing," I said, giving him a quick look, "but I wouldn't have minded if he'd touched me. He was certainly a lavish host the night to which you referred."

"Oh, he'll spend his money, too," Tom granted. "It just doesn't make any difference whose it is, and these days he hasn't got it any longer. That night he entertained you so royally he'd probably sold Emily's—his wife's—necklace."

That random phrase stabbed me. Maybe Mrs. Philips was as much at fault as her husband. Perhaps a woman who would drag a sick man into the wilderness, knowing it might kill him, wasn't the kind to contrive a home a man would want to stay in. But she had won me, and I chose not to think so. It was senseless to dwell on a matter that couldn't concern me, but for a little I did. I was starting to wonder how anybody who seemed so intelligent could get involved with a shiftless weakling when I thought of Harriet and stopped. There was no reason why she—Emily, McConnell had called her—couldn't have the same license to act the damned fool.

The crowd that watched for the boat with me this time differed from the buckskin group that had waited the previous winter. It was a larger and more varied gathering with some evidences of wealth and fashion. The most significant difference, however, lay in the presence of some white women and their children. A bachelor community can dissolve in the time it takes to kick the door open and saddle up, but when men bring their wives they mean to hold somewhere. If Turkey Run could keep a few of these it was on its way to being a permanent town.

When the steamer drew near I was delighted to descry Harry Pace, legs braced and arms akimbo, gazing ahead toward his empire. Nobody who marked him would have given the engines their due credit. He looked as if he was forcing the ship upstream by the power of his concentration.

McConnell noticed it, too, and nudged me. "I never knew a man that chewed to such good advantage," he chuckled. "Every time that jaw comes down on his quid it generates a plan complete with whereases and footnotes and a decision as to who's going to foot the bill."

Pace didn't give any sign of seeing us when he turned away, but he came directly toward us when he strode down the gangplank a stride ahead of the mate. "Howdy, Tom; Godolphin, how are you?" He looked at us enquiringly as we shook hands. "Where's your luggage? We're sailin' on up to Roseville as soon as they've unloaded whatever they're goin' to at this muskrat den."

"Our luggage includes a couple of nags and a bear hound," Tom reminded him. "Where's Roseville?"

His client peered upstream. "You can't quite make it out from here, so I'd better tell you about it. But you can't do justice to a great subject with a dry gullet. Where's the doggery?"

The bartender at The Yazoo Queen, along with the owner and everybody else in town, was still down by the landing. McConnell served us and tossed some coins in the till. Pace, meanwhile, was spreading one of my maps out on the bar. He put his finger on some lettering which undoubtedly spelled "Roseville."

"There she is," he declared.

As I recalled the locality it was thickly covered by hardwoods, with no other conspicuous flora but an undergrowth of seedlings. "Where did you get the name?" I demanded.

"That's just the right name," he vowed. "It's respectable and ain't fancy; it's homey and yet pretty; and it makes the place sound like it's already all settled." He grinned at me. "Is there a rose anywheres around?"

"There're rows of alligators sunning themselves not far away," I grunted. The place was about a day's journey downstream from Council Lodge. It was a good site and, I was pleased to note, one that I had especially recommended. It stood clear of the bottom lands, had a firm approach to the river where the channel cut the bank, and there was good drinking water handy. As the place was known to have my endorsement I made no comment.

Pace flipped his drink past his quid. I was always curious to know whether he made an impromptu cocktail of whiskey and tobacco juice or whether he had some occult system of keeping the liquids apart. Next he reached into his coat and flicked out another map.

"There's Roseville," he said again.

It indubitably was. The name was printed in the lower right-hand corner. Above was a waffle of streets, each with a name. Beyond the town limits roads ran up and down stream, as well as

THE WILD YAZOO

into the back country. They ran, it was indicated, to such far cities as Nashville, New Orleans and Mobile.

While we were inspecting this he further dazzled us with a manifesto. Among other advantages, it spoke of stores, schools, churches, and regular steamboat and stage-coach service. Roseville itself was boldly referred to as the cotton capital of the New Purchase.

The author was gratified at the impression his effort made upon us. "Of course," he said, "I've got a couple of other towns ready to plant in case Roseville don't happen to sprout. I left 'em aboard or I'd show 'em to you now."

"Roseville will be all the city we can manage in one afternoon," McConnell said.

Pace poured a final round. "Well, get your nags as soon as we've downed this. I'll hold the boat for you."

I had my own ideas as to how I myself was going to travel. So far all my exploration of the territory had been confined to the southern bank of the river. Now that I had no pressing business, it was a good opportunity to indulge my curiosity about the swampy depths of the north shore. "I'd rather go overland," I said. "Blaze a few trees, so I'll know where the town is when I get there."

By the time we returned to the landing the crowd was beginning to stream up hill. As we were working our way through the advance guard of these I felt a hand on my elbow.

"Oh, hello, Caradock," I said.

If I was less than cordial it was because I foresaw problems and was wondering what to do. There was no such obstacle to his enthusiasm.

"It's mighty good to see you again, Godolphin. Nobody seemed to know you, and I was afraid you weren't here."

"I am," I reassured him awkwardly. McConnell and Pace were waiting for me, and I had to make some move toward finality. "I'm in a hurry now, but where are you going to be available?"

"Where?" Caradock was pleased at this evidence of interest. "Why wherever you install us."

"Oh," I said, remembering the time when I had spoken more confidently of the printing press. "You mean Eli?"

[232]

"We came by the same boat." He pointed to a jumble of impedimenta piled up by the landing. "There's Eli yonder," he chortled. He was getting a lot of fun out of my perplexity and was generally very pleased with himself. Perhaps he even thought he might goad me into giving my winnings back. The thought ordered my mind.

I glanced at Harry Pace inquisitively waiting, then up to where the Yazoo vanished darkly in the overhanging trees. "Get them to put Eli back and hop aboard with it," I directed. "Tell them you're going to Roseville."

He looked puzzled, though he had less reason than I to consider that order remarkable. "Where's Roseville?"

"It's where I'll meet you." I pointed at Pace. "Look him up when you get aboard. He'll keep you from getting lost when you arrive."

Caradock was vainly trying to keep track of me. "It couldn't be that big," he scoffed.

"It isn't the size," I told him. "It's the way it's laid out."

CHAPTER XXII

I SWAM GOOBER across the river with Talisman churning in our wake. The line of bluffs and rolling hills ran up to the Yazoo from the south and there stopped. From the river north and west the country was a flat, bodiless fill. It was rich soil to any depth, but there were serious flood and drainage problems. Whenever the Mississippi kicked over its banks the Yazoo backed up over these lowlands. Much of it was permanent swampland, and the whole area was poisonously unhealthy in cold weather or extremes of heat.

Now, however, a medial crispness had followed the equinoctial rains. The air was relatively clean if the footing was often under water. Generally there was no skirting the swamps, and we had to pick our way between bog holes and quagmires. Fortunately both Goober and I were used to wet faring. The eye can learn to find terra firma in a variety of unlikely guises. The eye first had to become used to dusk at midday, though. The cypress rose to knit a sunless welkin. The vines swooped from tree to tree, limiting visibility, and the moss drooped heavily over black pools and sombre bayous.

On the higher ground, as I had suspected, there were settlers. After all there was rich, easily tilled soil to draw people who either didn't know about floods and the ague or who considered them the normal hazards of the country. So far there weren't very many of them, though, and there were no through trails I could use for any distance.

At the same time a path wasn't so unusual that I was surprised to run across one when I'd worked my way through a bad stretch of swamp toward the end of the second day. I also took the empty cabin to which it soon led me for granted. Building a shack was the usual way a land claimant took to show he was in earnest. As often as not these were mere monuments left to prove the builder had a right to return if he didn't find anything better.

I only investigated enough to be sure it wasn't still in use. As long as it wasn't raining I wasn't interested in sleeping indoors, for dirt-floors cabins are musty at best, but the branch that slipped by the shanty looked comparatively clear. Water that wasn't pure elixir of the bog was scarce thereabouts, so I went upstream in search of a place to bivouac.

By dim dusk I was settled for the night. Goober was hobbled, foraging for himself not far away. Talisman was stretched out near the fire. I was leaning against a tree in the mid stage betwixt dream and catalepsy. As soon as it was fully night I intended to have a final smoke and turn in.

About that time a wolf started yelping. It must have been a bitch, for Talisman didn't growl. Instead he wagged his tail, then after a moment got to his feet. I dozed before I got around to my smoke, and when I opened my eyes again Talisman was gone. I envied him, but as it seemed unlikely there would be any siren call for me I had my smoke and turned in.

Life in the woods had given me the matched boons of easy sleep and quick rousing. Goober's whinny brought me wide awake. Horses didn't call like that unless there were other horses around. I thought about that a couple of minutes, and while I was thinking I heard a slight scuffing of the leaves. Slithering out of my blankets I grabbed my weapons and got away from what was left of the fire. This was nothing but flickering coals, but it would throw a Judas halo into the dark for anybody's guidance.

I had no reason to believe the visit was necessarily hostile. A man returning to his cabin and finding, through Goober's whinny, that somebody was in the vicinity would naturally want to investigate. Flattened behind a big root, I waited.

There was more than one of them, but they knew the rules of caution, too. I could not see them across the glow of the fire, but I heard them from time to time. They must have been trying to determine whether I was still in my blankets, visible but indistinct on the edge of the fire glow. Eventually one of them found a way.

Something thudded into the blankets, and though I couldn't see it I was sure I knew what it was. One of my visitors had thrown a bowie knife by way of feeler. All my questions being answered, I started out to find Goober, wondering now why I'd waited so long. He hadn't whinnied since that second time.

Stealing to the next tree in a direct line away from the fire, I ducked around it and met a man just scrambling to his feet.

"Alex?" he whispered.

The knife I aimed at the blur of his face grazed it only, but the fist that held the knife snapped up his jaw, overbalancing him. I jumped on the fellow once for luck and started legging it. His yell was taken up and several men started crashing toward me, but once I had a start I wasn't worried about being caught in the woods at night. They stayed around until they saw the futility of it themselves, then I didn't hear them again.

So far it had been exciting rather than serious. But I couldn't find Goober, although I spent a lot of energy trying. I knew where I'd left him, but he'd been hobbled, not hitched, and the yelling and scurrying might well have frightened him into moving out of the way. By the time I admitted to myself that he must have been stolen I'd lost my bearings, and it was a couple of more hours before I found a landmark in the form of the cabin. After laboriously making certain that no guards were posted I eventually found that there was nothing to guard.

Chilled through and wretchedly tired and sleepy, I found my way back to my camp. No comfort was to be had there either, for all my food and equipment had been stolen also.

After awhile I gathered strength enough to stoke the coals. It was there Talisman found me, asleep in the sitting position, my head in my arms. He was tired, too, but he'd had a better night. After acknowledging his cheerful greeting I dozed fitfully till sunup.

It wasn't until I saw all the tracks around the cabin that I could concoct a theory as to just what had happened to me. There'd been several more horses than men. Adding in the loss of Goober it looked like an organized horse-thieving expedition which used the cabin as a way stop. Unsuccessful in bagging me they'd got clear before daylight should give me a chance to identify or snipe at them.

That was the past. The present found me hungry and worn out; the future offered me dangerous traveling conditions in a choice of three directions. I took care of the present first, finding a rabbit with Talisman's aid; then while it was baking in mud I caught up on my sleep.

Rest and food improved my physical condition but not the outlook. Had I been on the other side of the river, reaching Roseville would have meant no more than a day and night or so of hardship. But I hated to think of traveling north of the Yazoo without a horse. It meant the difference between riding through mud and countless shallow pools and wading through them. It meant the difference between riding through slimy bayous and fording them. It meant the difference between being comparatively dry and being weighted down with water and mud to the hips or even the armpits. Then there was the Yazoo itself to cross. Although I could swim well enough, I had my rifle to ferry, and there were alligators.

The only thing to do was to get going. I was starting to leave when I noticed the buzzards. Nothing was dead, for none was dropping; but something was dying, for they were flying low. The attraction might have been a moribund deer or bear. Or, conceivably, I had wounded the man I met far worse than I thought, leaving him to wander, dazed and helpless. After watching irresolutely I had to see. It was only about a mile.

The way toward the wheeling birds was the way taken by the horsethieves. This in turn was the path which I had unluckily stumbled across the night before and followed to the raiders' cabin. Just below where I had cut into it the trail wound past the rims of a series of evil-looking quagmires. Approaching, I heard a splashing and a horrible sucking sound. Somebody or something was stuck in the quicksand, and the buzzards knew it wouldn't get out. I was hampered by nausea as I hurried forward.

The horse lay on its side with only the head and a part of one flank showing above the film of water which covered the ooze in which it was sinking. Even the eyes were covered with mud, and as it breathed I saw dirty foam come from the mouth and nostrils. As I watched, the creature made another vain effort. There was that terrible sucking as it heaved itself up a little and twisted its head, sobbing. It couldn't see me, but, mud or no mud, I recognized that head as it turned in my direction. Goober must have tried to escape from his captors and had chosen the wrong spot.

After I'd shot him I had a senseless desire to try to follow the thieves. Or again I half decided to wait around until they should return to their rendezvous. In either case I was wistful of murder. But when I'd finished cursing and had got the lump out of my throat, I knew there was only one thing to do for the time being. I would have enough to do getting out of that district alive.

There were no readily discernible landmarks in these tree-blanketed flatlands. I had traveled by dead reckoning and as the country would let me. I had only a general idea of how far I was from the Yazoo and not a much clearer one as to how far I had come since leaving Turkey Run.

Miles were the least of the obstacles that stood between me and the river, as it turned out. After a couple of hours floundering in a villainous swamp I encountered a cane brake. Knowing I'd have to have some guide in that reed jungle I skirted it laboriously until I found a bayou that coursed through it. By following the stream, if that was possible, I'd reach the Yazoo.

Scattered among the common days when creation is a stolid fact there are days when it has special aspects. That afternoon it was hostile. I had not much belief in good of any kind and plodded on with a sort of defiant hopelessness. Mud was not just soft earth to me that day. It was a lurking evil which made by flesh crawl. The cane was an endless series of small cages. The swamp-infused air seemed too rank for my lungs.

To keep the stream in sight through the thick cane I had to stay within a few feet of it. At that proximity the floor of the brake was as often water as earth. I was mud-caked to the knees, water soaked to the waist, and weary to the top of my head. Only necessity kept me going. Only the knowledge that the river could not forever dodge the stream's pursuit kept despair at arm's length.

It was already getting dark under the thick foliage when I got clear of the brake. I was in the open and at last had a chance to sit down; but there was nothing else to give me cheer. Slackly I surveyed the prospect.

Where the cane ended the twisted trees of the river bottoms began. The ground beneath them was insubstantial slime. The branches they thrust at each other locked out what was left of the sun. Looking down the sombre grottoes thus formed I could see the dark Yazoo fifty yards away. This was Limbo if any man ever saw it. There were even alligators moving about in convincing facsimile of damned souls.

After awhile, because I didn't have enough energy for more forceful expression, I sighed. The river was not to be crossed here— or anywhere that day. Now I'd have to find a place to survive the night, before it grew too dark. There was only one spot that looked like it might be well enough drained for bivouacking. Un- luckily, it was on the other side of the bayou.

Rising, I looked with loathing on the sluggish water and began to strip. I hated the thought of entering that fluid mud nude, but I couldn't afford to get my clothes wet above the hips as well as below. It was already cool and would soon be sharp. If I came down with the ague I'd probably stay on the north bank.

The mud let me down until it gripped me just below the knees, and the water lazed by my armpits. Just past midstream I saw the water moccasin angling across current in my general direction. Now had I observed a man in such a predicament I would have sagely counselled him that there was no cause for alarm. A snake cannot conveniently strike from the water, and a water moccasin will not attack a man unless provoked. How comforting my knowl- edge would have been to that hypothetical other man.

As it was, I discovered that to know a thing positively is not necessarily to be convinced. That reptile bearing down on me at almost eye level looked deliberately vicious. I plunged wildly for the bank, stumbled in the mud, managed to keep my gun and powder dry, but soaked my clothes after all.

I was bitterly hungry, but fire was more important than food, and there wasn't much light left in which to hunt for wood. For an hour I drove myself, gathering anything that looked inflammable, knowing that heat was my only ward against fatal exposure. By the time I got the fire going I was shivering violently, and the bottom-lands miasma was cold and heavy in my throat.

After I'd more or less dried out I tried to sleep. With the aid of a stupefying weariness I finally succeeded; then Talisman's barking aroused me. Clutching my gun, I became aware of heavy, dragging footfalls such as I'd never heard before. And Talisman, who'd attack a bear or a panther, wouldn't leave the firelight to offer a challege. I understood when I glimpsed the blaze redly reflected in an eye close to the ground. It hadn't occurred to me that light at night would have an overpowering attraction for alligators too.

This addition to my lore cost me my sleep until it got light enough for me to be certain the great lizards had gone. When I waked we breakfasted on an opossum Talisman treed. I didn't have the time and condiments to make the strong meat palatable; but after some uncertainty it stayed down, and I was ready to go on.

It was well past noon when I found a place where the channel clipped the bank. Here the Yazoo was at once accessible and unsuited to the lounging purposes of alligators. After about an hour I'd contrived enough of a raft of driftwood and vines to support my weapons and clothes if not myself. A last-minute survey disclosing nothing hostile, I shoved off.

The current was not strong, and the opposite shore was invitingly firm. I swam along, pushing my little raft and rather enjoying myself until, within a few strokes of the south bank, I heard Talisman yelp. When I looked he'd gone under; then he came up, paddling frantically, only to submerge again. It couldn't have been an alligator, for there was no bloody explosion of destruction, but some beast of the water had him.

Groaning, I reached on the raft for my knife and stroked over to where my dog had disappeared. Feeling for him, I found I could pull his head to the surface, though he felt as if he was tied to the bottom. Naturally he was panic stricken. He tried to climb on my head, and we both sank. As we were going under my knee struck something hard and smooth. It felt like a rock; but that was a land of no stone and at last I knew what was the matter. A huge snapping turtle had clamped on one of Talisman's hind legs. Once again I got us above water for air, then I dived and went to work.

There was only one way I could see of handling the matter with the right promptness. I yanked the turtle and with it Talisman's leg to the surface. This forced the dog's head down, and he was already drowning. But I got in a hack at the snapper's stretched, leathery neck, then, after sinking and rising, another. Fortunately, the heavy blade was of prime steel, and I'd taken pride in keeping it sharp. Even in death the fatal jaws kept their grip, but on the fourth attack I cut the body away from them.

Not sure whether or not I was clutching a carcass, I towed my dog ashore. There I propped his mouth open with a stick and went forlornly about the business of squeezing water out of him. The disaster, timed for the moment when I had high hopes of leaving the worst of my troubles behind, looked to me like cosmic persecution.

When I'd almost given up in desolate exhaustion the water started to gurgle out of Talisman. Then he got sick, and I knew he'd be all right. That was more than I knew about myself. My clothes and, which was for worse, my rifle and my means of making fire were out of sight down river.

My only hope of survival was to retrieve my gear. I wasn't swimmer enough to overtake it by water even if I was inclined to dangle my toes and masculinity before who knew what other voracious turtles of the Yazoo. The overland route would be rough on my bare feet, but I could eventually come abreast of the raft unless a cane brake intervened. Prying the snapper's jaws free from the leg, I left Talisman to the pangs of convalescence.

Occasionally my unaccustomed soles would find a sharp branch or root lurking in the leaves; but I made better time than I had counted on, and I began to feel more cheerful. In a mile or so, at the rate I was going, I would pull level with the raft. Then I could simply walk along with it until the channel swept within a few strokes of the shore.

Atop the ridge around which the Yazoo made a second bend I obtained a long prospect of the river. My raft was in sight, still a good distance ahead but undisturbed. When I next caught sight of it, however, I was bewildered with alarm. A man was swimming his horse out into midstream to salvage the derelict.

I gave a yell of anguished protest, but he either didn't hear or didn't heed. Even as I started to run he scooped up my rifle and clothes and turned his mount back toward the south bank. Intercepting that fellow was what I had to do, and I postponed even cursing about the toe I stubbed and the heel I twice painfully scraped. If I failed to catch up with him my feet wouldn't hurt very long. I'd probably die of exposure that night.

I reached him in plenty of time, for he had remained at the edge of the river. From a hundred yards away I marked him, afoot now, alternately examining my rifle and stirring my garments with one dripping moccasin. His back was toward me, but my relief was so great I almost couldn't go on.

"Tim!" I called out. I wanted to add some jaunty remark but had to stop there. I didn't realize how much of my strength I'd been using to hold myself together in the face of persistent disaster until now that trouble was behind me. He spun alertly. Having, of course, recognized my gun and clothing, he was not too surprised to see me without them. Peering at me, he must have guessed my condition. For once he didn't say a word but reached in his pocket and had the flask uncorked by the time I reached him.

The lovely whiskey made me jell again. I drank once for my soul and a second time for pleasure. Then I let out my breath.

"What's new?" I asked coolly.

Finding I was unhurt, his nose and chin drew together in mirth. "How come your pants travel by water and you go by land?" He took his drink and turned back to me inquisitively. "And what's your hoss doin', flyin'?"

Some misfortune is easily forgotten bad luck. Much that had just happened to me was in that category and with a little help from the imagination would make a good yarn for camp fire and doggery. But when I told that story I wouldn't say how my horse died.

"Goober's hell diving, not flying," I said explicitly. Drawing another deep breath, I looked soberly back across the river. My curiosity had cost me a lot, and I couldn't think of anything I'd got in exchange.

CHAPTER XXIII

APPROACHING ROSEVILLE, we met Harry Pace in what I at first took to be the neighboring forest. "Where's the town?" I enquired politely after I had introduced Tim.

He glanced around to get his bearings, then consulted a piece of paper. "You're at October and Ram Streets. I haven't got all the signs up yet; but, just so's you won't get misled, Durham, the streets runnin' with the river are months and the ones runnin' from the river got zodiac names. If a hoss can read the calendar or the almanac he'll know from one street just where all the others are at. Of course, that's only good for a dozen each way, but I figured that'd be enough to start with."

I looked around at the gum and tulip trees. "It should," I agreed.

He grinned. "This is a residential neighborhood. You're as far from the city and as near to a church as any place in town. A fine place to rear children."

"It'd be a pretty good place to raise coons or possums, too," Tim said. "You got a doggery?"

"There's a tavern fit for a congressman on payday night at January and Virgin Streets, smack in the heart of the downtown mercantile section. It's The Merchants Meetin', H. Pace, Prop., open but not for business until we get there. Wait just a minute till I locate a marker, and we'll go right along."

I wouldn't have recognized Roseville as the town described in Pace's prospectus, but neither was it the shady bluff I'd marked on the map some months before. Many of the trees which had furnished that shade were down. Some of them were already incorporated in more or less completed log structures. The day's operations had halted by the time we arrived, though. We passed several bivouacs where the evening meal was being prepared.

"January's the stalk street," Pace said, waving a hand at that stump-lined thoroughfare. "That squirrel may not know it, but he's spang in the middle of the cotton market. Do you aim to settle here, too, Durham? We'd sure like to have you."

"I had an uncle that was asked to live in a town once," Tim said thoughtfully. "The man just begged him to settle; he was so damned anxious he bought the drinks while he told what a fine piece of land in a fine city he was tryin' to get my uncle to take. Uncle Willie was awful soft hearted, and the man was so heart set on it that my uncle said all right just to oblige him. Twasn't till he'd already agreed to it that he found the polecat wanted to get paid for it." Durham looked at Pace enquiringly. "Did you ever hear of a thing like that?"

Harry shook his head. "Must've been a scalawag," he said disapprovingly.

"Just what Uncle Willie figured, but he'd done said he'd stay so he asked the fellow polite how the trappin' in that town was. 'Oh, you can't trap here,' the critter said. As my uncle told the judge, he thought it only right to shoot a varmint who'd sell a man land and then tell him he didn't have no right to make a livin' on it."

Taking out a notebook, Pace thumbed through it to a certain page. "There ain't no Roseville law against trappin', and as a matter of fact, I shot a bear at December and Twins Streets yesterday myself. Still you'd likely do better in the suburbs."

"That's what I reckoned, though I might drop in once in a while to look over that doggery you was talkin' about."

I understood the phrase "open but not for business" when I saw the tavern. The unroofed walls were perhaps four feet high. Nevertheless, a pole planted outside bore a picture of two prosperous-looking men shaking hands. Within there was a makeshift bar, a sufficient stock of potables, Tom, Caradock, and one or two other thirsts. A good house can be known by the satisfaction of its customers. The Merchants Meeting was a good house. It was very pleasant to lean on the bar in the autumn dusk and gaze down through the trees at the darkling Yazoo while leaves rustled high overhead.

"Welcome to Roseville," Harry said after he'd drawn a bottle-full from a cask and placed it before us. "Fill your horns as high as they go and as deep as you can swallow. And don't forget the name of the tavern."

After we'd drunk Tim nodded toward the sign. "How come you named a doggery a thing like that?"

"The Merchants Meetin'? It took me two—three weeks to think of that." Pace refilled all glasses in acknowledgment of the fact that he was taking the floor. "Roseville ain't just a center of commerce, it's a city of homes where a hoss can live in peaceful comfort with his squaw and as many little hellions as he's man enough to make. But the time comes when a hoss has to bust out of his stall or founder from livin' right too long.

"Just how often that comes depends on how many Saturday nights he counts in his week. Now maybe he don't want to quite tell the ol' woman he's headin' for the nearest doggery; but he can allow he's goin' to The Merchants Meetin' without chokin' on it. It sort of suggests he's goin' out to meet other leadin' citizens busy buildin' the prosperity of this great town. Lookin' at it that way he ain't goin' out to raise hell but to work the lightnin'-bug shift, tired as he already is."

He pointed over the wall to an unfinished edifice on the opposite corner of January and Virgin. "One of the merchants who'll do his meetin' here bought that place as is today. I threw in the good will. In case you ain't acquainted around these parts, that's one of Roseville's dry goods and general merchandise emporiums—everythin' for the house but the wife; everythin' for the plantation but the nigger."

"Are you going to sell this tavern, too?" I asked.

Pace used his bowie knife to cut himself a fresh plug. "After awhile and to the right bungstarter," he nodded. "The kind of doggery a place has when it's born points to the kind of town it's goin' to be when it's weaned. For instance, from what you told me about The Hossthief's Head I figure that's what started Turkey Run drawin' flies."

I hadn't thought of a tavern as the moral index of a community, but I found the idea acceptable. Harry meanwhile worked diligently to soften his quid.

"If things go right, Daunt," he at length observed to me because everybody else was watching Caradock palm a coin, "we'll have nothin' but brick all along here; but that load you seen back there on February 's for the courthouse."

"Have you got a court here already?"

"No, but when you put out a trap for a mouse it don't do no hurt to throw in a piece of cheese. We need that court and them bricks are my personal gamble for it. Of course, if it don't work out I'll rig a steeple on it and sell it to some bunch just after they've been rained out of camp meetin'."

Shortly after we'd finished a steak from the bear Pace had shot, the others turned in, but Tom and I sat up by the fire for an extra smoke while I told him what had happened to me. "So now I'm about where I was when I was robbed at Natchez Underhill," I concluded. "My money's gone, and so are the surveying instruments I was going to make a living with."

"A land of opportunity always includes the opportunity to get into trouble," he reminded me.

"I took full advantage." My misfortunes weren't far enough in the past for me to be philosophical about them. Also I was genuinely irked at the whole situation. After a year of hard work during which I'd had the inside track I had nothing to show for it, whereas raw newcomers were rapidly taking hold of the district's riches.

McConnell meanwhile had been thinking my story over. "The only thing you know about the thieves beyond the fact that they robbed you and failed in their efforts to kill you is that one of them was named Alex. Alexander Pope Cummins?"

"That occurred to me, naturally." I shrugged. "A dim suspicion doesn't go far toward convicting a man."

"On the other hand the annals of law show very few men who were convicted without first being suspected. We'll keep him in mind." Tom yawned and rose. "Have you had enough of Roseville's night life?"

By the end of a week he and I had a log-cabin residence at April and Scorpion and a log-cabin office at January and Balance. There was a shingle nailed on the latter for Thomas McConnell, attorney, and another for Mordaunt Godolphin, surveyor. That last was a flag over an empty fort. Until I could procure a new set of instruments I could do no more than promise my services for the future. The boat that would start my order on its way hadn't arrived yet and would not for weeks. Meanwhile, I was bored and conscious of marking time while everybody else was doing something toward building up the community.

Pending the moment I could use my half of the office, I told Caradock he could set up his press there, and, not having anything else to do, I helped him unlimber it. He was happier than I had ever seen him, which is saying much, for he was normally as jaunty as a catbird. He sang with all the carefree gaiety, if with none of the skill of that mocker, as he cleaned and oiled the machine. Then he proceeded to smear the plate with ink.

I watched him absorbedly, as it is always interesting to observe a new craft. Ignorance is as often prepared for miracles as it is surprised at achievements. I would not have been too amazed if he'd published a book during the time it took me to smoke a couple of McConnell's cigars. However, when the press was readied, it was not to drawers of type he turned but to me.

"Eli's fixed to go," he announced. "What'll we print?"

Astonished, I took the cigar out of my mouth. "Don't you know what you want to print?"

He gestured impatiently. "You're the owner. What jobs have you in mind?"

There was only one thing in that line that had occurred to me, though I'd visualized it as a job for the future when Roseville was all put together. Actually, I saw on consideration, there was no valid reason for delay. I replaced my cigar.

"As long as you haven't got anything else on your mind you can start a newspaper," I said comfortably.

It was Caradock's turn to look incredulous. Then he slapped the press, and the blow was a bond. "You might as well tell that to Eli as to me. Damn it, man! We're teeth—we don't make food, we work on it." He slapped the press again. "We're mud, Daunt; we'll hold footprints till the Devil gets religion, but somebody else has got to put on the boots and do the walking."

As I looked taken aback he pursued his advantage, fixing me with an indignant eye and pointing an inky finger. "I'm a journeyman printer. If I had nothing better on my mind than writing I wouldn't have spent fifteen years learning to read type upside down. If you want a newspaper, write it yourself."

Well, I'd wanted something to do. I examined the press with renewed fascination. For the first time it was really brought home to me that I had the power to decree what was produced by this mysterious engine.

"Do you think I could?" I asked anxiously.

He shrugged, personifying mechanical indifference toward the products of the intellect. "Anybody could, I reckon, that's got past using wampum belts and picture messages. All there is to it is to find out what's going on and put it down." He unbent a little. "Of course, if you can't get enough to fill out the pages I can steal stuff from an almanac or something."

While I finished my cigar I thought it over. I didn't know anything about the rules of conducting a newspaper, but neither did the first man who started one.

"How do we stand on paper?" I finally asked.

He brightened, and I saw that he'd been afraid I'd give up the undertaking. Now that he had Eli housed and unpacked he couldn't wait to get to work.

"Oh, we've got enough for quite a few issues for a town of this size."

When he showed me his stock I regarded it dubiously. It was standard folio, but I thought I'd never beheld so much unoccupied space.

"You can start in setting whatever you can find to lift," I told him. "I'll see what's going on around town."

Roseville had developed in the week since I'd arrived. A blacksmith, another storekeeper, and a veterinary, each bringing his family, had come with the declared intention of settling. Several wandering bachelors were bunking in the dormitory of The Merchants Meeting, and a number of others were camped in the vicinity. These could not all be counted upon, but certain ones could be expected to find the place suited to their respective wants. Then planters were moving into the neighborhood, multiplying the business potential. Roseville was not yet sure of itself, but there were grounds for believing it might hold its own against the crowding forest.

There was the excitement attendant upon growth, and much other excitement too. For every man that sought the New Purchase in pursuit of peace, there was a fugitive from peace, if not actually from the law. In the absence of any form of constabulary, those who felt like it stepped high and swam free. I had, therefore, greater hopes of finding items for my paper than I would have while touring the ordinary small town.

At Lion Street I happened to glance south from January and saw two men confronting each other belligerently. Ordinarily I would not have paused to watch. I was not given to intruding on the affairs of others, no matter how public they chose to make them. Now, however, I was a servant of the people and could indulge my curiosity without loss of dignity. With a fine sense of being untrammeled I hurried toward them.

There was a pile of logs handy, so I seated myself, took out a piece of paper and a chunk of lead to write with and conscientiously observed the scene. Two burly woodsmen, more or less indistinguishable except for their respective black and brown beards, were the principals. Lion Street was a mud wallow at this point, although by keeping to the center one person at a time could pass dry shod. It was at either end of this slender passage that the contestants stood.

"If you don't get out of the way," Brown Beard said, "tell me is your widow good lookin'. She might like to have a man around for a change."

"I ain't agoin' to move for you and a case of smallpox," the other stated doggedly. "I got here first; not that I give a damn who got here first, 'cause I'm agoin' through first."

"Maybe you would," his opponent admitted, "if you had Andy Jackson, the United States Army, Mike Fink and a couple of he-b'ars to back you. Just by yourself I don't pay you no more mind than a high wind does to a June bug."

I knew enough of frontier ways to be sure they weren't just making noise. They were working themselves up to battle frenzy as deliberately as tomcats.

"You ain't agoin' to stop me," Black Beard spoke up again, "no more'n a snake hole does a streak of lightnin'. But I'm givin' you one more chance before I rest my quid so's I won't get it nasty when I chaw you up. You mightn't know it, but I'm Talapoosa Jim Townsend, half painter on my mammy's side an' full-blooded earthquake on my old man's."

At last I had a couple of cardinal facts. "Mr. James Townsend, former resident of Alabama," I wrote.

"I ain't never heard of you," his foe declared, "but if I had heard tell I wouldn't 've believed it. We ain't got nothin' lower'n wart toads in the Smokies." Suddenly he leapt up, beating his chest and kicking his feet together. "You're fixin' to tangle with Charlie Timbers, you poor damn fool! I'm a bear in a fight, an' a deer on the run, an' a buzzard for seein', an' a hog for eatin', an' a 'gator for bitin', an' a mule for kickin', an' a fish for swimmin', an' a wildcat for gougin' an' a woman for hatin'. Yeouw!"

"——encountered Mr. Charles Timbers, a native of North Carolina, on Lion Street, Thursday morning," I continued my story.

Townsend, true to his promise, placed his chew of tobacco on a near-by stump. "Now I know what you are I'm agoin' to whip you," he said, drawing a knife. "Do you want this or do you want me to pick you apart like a roast chicken?"

Timbers was undaunted. "I can whip you with a knife, but I kind of hate to spoil the blade by stickin' it in you. I can whip you with my hands, or I can outbutt you."

I didn't grasp the literal intent behind this offer, but his antagonist did. He brightened as if welcoming a sound suggestion. "Never saw the buck I couldn't outbutt. I'll crack you like a hoss steppin' on a mud turtle."

"Not with words you won't," Mr. Timbers cautioned. "How far do you want to back up?"

"Twenty-five or thirty paces."

"Make it thirty."

"Unable to decide which should have the courtesy of the road," I scribbled while they were counting off their steps, "they decided to contest the issue."

By the time I'd written that much the two were ready for their trial of strength. "How about it?" Townsend called deeply.

Bent at the waist, Timbers shuffled his feet and wiggled his buttocks, convincingly like a bull about to charge. "Ready," he called.

Townsend meanwhile had started to count. Then, grotesquely stooped, they started lumbering toward each other, bellowing defiance.

The difficulty with thirty or any number of steps is that two men are unlikely to travel the same distance while taking them. Nor are two men likely to rush to crush each other's skulls at the same speed. The pair did not meet as planned on the little strip of dry ground but on Townsend's side of it. I had foreseen that, running as they did with their heads down, they might also miss each other. These, though, showed themselves to be expert butters.

The two bulletheads, each one with a holder of thick neck and the weight of a broad body behind it, met. They met as unerringly as lovers' lips but with considerably more noise. I felt the crash at the pit of my stomach and held my breath, expecting the even more terrible sound of smashing bone. I didn't hear it.

Both men staggered back and collapsed, but only the black-bearded Townsend rose again. He stumbled around, then, disoriented, started walking back where he came from.

Holding my chunk of lead poised, I pondered. Townsend had won the combat, but Timbers had actually crossed the contested passage. I was trying to distill some sort of moral from these circumstances when it occurred to me that readers might prefer to draw their own. I jotted down the facts of the struggle, headed it "Traffic Altercation on Lion Street," and rose much cheered. I was launched on a new, and so far diverting, career.

As a journalist and a former student of medicine I had meant to examine Timbers when I was through writing, but he recovered too fast. He was on his feet by the time I was ready, and I left in search of other items of interest.

While following the blazes that marked June Street near Crab a blond young fellow hailed me. Assuming that his worn but tailored clothes hadn't shrunk, he himself had done so since they were fitted. Certainly he was thin and wan; even the lank hair looked faded.

"Good evening, sir," he called. "Could you tell me where I could find a doctor?"

Drawing near where he leaned against a tree for support, I shook my head. The hazel eyes were the only thing about him that had any lustre, and they had too much.

"There's no doctor in town," I told him, "but I'm physician enough to know that you oughtn't to be up and about. The best medicine for you is the flat of your back."

"Oh, I'm all right now," he declared. "I just run a little fever still when I get excited. I wanted the doctor for——" He was interrupted by a cry and had no need to finish.

"How long has your wife been in labor?" I asked.

"My sister," he said. "It started a couple of hours ago, but I thought it best to get to this town if we could. Then she couldn't go any farther, so we camped here." Perhaps he thought it awkward that there had been no mention of a husband. "My brother-in-law was killed by robbers a few days ago. It makes it hard."

"Yes," I said, trying to make up my mind. I didn't consider myself competent, but I couldn't think of anybody else who was as well qualified. "I know what to do," I told him, "but that isn't the same thing as being able to do it. I'll try if you like."

The young woman had gone through the ordeal before, witness a wailing infant. Pitiful as it was, I was glad to see it. A traveled passage is easier for all concerned. Whether nature bungled or not there wasn't much I could do for the mother now. My service would be to receive the baby. It didn't look to me as if there would be long to wait.

"The best thing you can do," I told the man, "is to take the child out of the way—if you're strong enough, that is."

"I'm all right," he assured me once more. "Fortunately, the bullet went all the way through me, but it took quite a lot of blood with it. As soon as I get it back I'll be fine." He reached out a thin hand. "Carruthers Blaine. If you live here in Roseville you must visit us." Next he waved toward the young woman gasping on a makeshift pallet on the ground. "Mrs. Walters and I aren't settled yet, but we'll be glad to see you any time. Meanwhile, thank you, sir."

Under the circumstances I found the invitation unusual. "And where will I find you?" I asked curiously when I had presented myself.

"We just got here, so I don't know," he confessed, "but there can't be too many cotton brokers in so new a city. You'll find my office along the river front. Just ask along there."

I blinked at this invalid who could speak so surely of a non-existent office in a town he had not yet actually seen. It would have interested me to find out how he was going to be a broker for cotton that wasn't yet planted, but his sister had another seizure.

"Take the child out of hearing," I repeated. "I'll call you when it's over."

The pains were coming rapidly, but after I'd started water heating I had time to give thought to my primary work. Novice though I was, I could see that the significant character from Roseville's point of view was the baby. It was the first local birth, a veritable symbol of the hopes of a new community. I toyed with such phrases as "The Virginia Dare of the New Purchase" until I made myself see that my public had never heard of that most mysterious of the world's heroines. Their interest would lie not in metaphors but in the fact of the first native-born citizen.

As such things go Mrs. Walters didn't have too rough a time, but such things go hard. She was of the same make as her brother, however, and never admitted that she was other than all right. In the end her fortitude was rewarded by a little boy, and I was glad I'd already dismissed the bad poetry. Fortunately, there were no complications to tax my ineptitude.

By midafternoon I had the baby washed and wrapped in a towel. The mother was sleeping from exhaustion. There was food in camp, but she'd need some broth, and I found that Blaine luckily had a fowling piece. There were still more turkeys, rabbits and quail in Roseville than there were people.

While I was hunting I thought more about the news story. The most engaging aspect of it I couldn't write. The things that had happened to Blaine and his sister could be told, but not their intrepid acceptance, because my prospective readers would take it too much for granted.

I was lucky enough to run across a covey of quail on the near side of December Street. After I'd cleaned the six I bagged I left Blaine preparing the broth and hurried away. There was barely time to catch a drink at The Merchants Meeting before I went behind it to provide the press with an eye-witness account of Roseville's first cock fight.

CHAPTER XXIV

I'D INTENDED to call the paper *The Roseville Gazette*, but Caradock had lost the only "Z" in the appropriate font. This left the field open, and at McConnell's suggestion I dubbed it *The New Purchase Surveyor*. After about a week the first issue was run off.

Pace had taken a tremendous interest in the enterprise and had gladly agreed to contribute. His article on the business prospects of the town read like an American postscript to The Book of Revelation; but I didn't touch it. Like the book itself it contained a power that could not be watered without being dissolved. I used it as a salute editorial and ran it down the middle of the front page. There was a small space left at the bottom and Caradock had filled it at his discretion. He had mentioned borrowing from almanacs, but I hadn't been well enough acquainted with that branch of literature to know what was in store.

This item read as follows: "When Davy Crockett first went to Washington as a congressman John Randolph of Roanoke happened to mention Cleopatra to him. 'What county is she from?' Davy asked. Mr. Randolph then proceeded to relate the history of the beautiful Egyptian Queen, concluding: 'She kissed an asp and died.' 'Well!' said Davy, 'if she'd had any proper rearin' she'd 've died afore she done it.'"

There were other shrewd observations of Representative Crockett and one ballad which linked him with the redoubtable Mike Fink:

> When Davy Crockett met Mike Fink
> They started in to bicker
> And swore the least man of the two
> Would have to buy the liquor.

They wrestled in amongst the trees
    And pushed 'em down like clover,
They turned the rivers wrong side up
    And kicked the ridges over.

But Davy couldn't get his hold,
    And Mike he couldn't throw him.
"We'll shoot to see who buys," said Mike,
    And Davy vowed he'd show him.

Mike shot the taste from sugar cane
    And left it awful bitter;
Dave shot the smell from off a skunk
    And never touched the critter.

They both were good and neither one
    Could claim that he was winners.
"The hell with shootin'," Davy yelled.
    "We're dry as fryin' sinners."

They took some whiskey and the moon
    And plunked 'em in the dipper,
Then stirred in half the milky way
    And soon were on a ripper.

They caught two good-sized hurricanes
    And tied their tails together,
Then cried alaughing at the way
    They'd scrambled up the weather.

From then on Mike and Dave were friends
    And never had a quarrel,
They drank instead—and thank the Lord
    There isn't any moral.

Still there was a considerable quantity of local news on the first three pages. By way of balance to the citation of facts and aspirations I'd devoted quite a section of the last page to that lay of the backwoods, a bear story. Harry had told it to us over the whiskey as we lay around the fire one night, and I'd done my best to render it truly, using the names of all known parties to give it local interest:

"Speakin' of what we wasn't speakin' about," Pace said, "did I ever tell you about the b'ar that wished I'd killed him?"

"No," McConnell admitted.

"Well, I'd just helped Andy Jackson whip the Creeks, and when I see he didn't need me no more I moseyed back to Mississippi and Sue Margaret."

"I didn't know you were married," Caradock said.

Pace reflected. "As I remember it we wasn't exactly married, but we was so friendly a stranger wouldn't notice the difference. Sue Margaret was impatient, though, and while I was savin' the United States from the united Creek Injuns she wiped her little feet on the heart I'd left behind with her and skedaddled." He sighed. "There wasn't no love left inside the cottage, but there was prime b'ar huntin' outside, and I took what I could get.

"I had a good bunch of dogs and done right well till late one afternoon I spotted a he that made any other b'ar I ever seen look like a runt coon. I put a bullet in his heart, but it looked like he wasn't dyin', for he come right at me, battin' the dogs out of the way like flies. I figured out the direction he was runnin' in and run the same way."

"How was that bullet in his heart getting along?" McConnell wanted to know.

"I was wonderin' about that myself at the time; but I found out later he was a left-handed b'ar and of course had his heart on his right side, so all I'd done was to make him mean and unforgivin'. And he meant business, for a fact. I kept tryin' to get enough of a lead on him to give me time to reload, but he matched my best paces. My tracks was so hot he'd yelp with pain when he stepped on one, but he kept crowdin' me, and I decided to head for Sour Mash, which was the nearest town. I was awful lonesome for people with loaded rifles in their hands, and that was my best chance of findin' any.

"I don't know if you all are acquainted around Sour Mash, but as you follow the trace in from the north the first cabin belongs to Mrs. Bagley. It used to belong to old Flint Bagley, too, until she jawed him to death. Anyhow when I busted out of the woods I was right behind the Bagley shanty, and the widow herself was astandin' there with a dishpan in her hands. After what had happened to old Flint she couldn't get any other takers, and when she seen a man actually runnin' her way she grinned like a dead possum and flung the back door wide open.

"B'ar or no b'ar, I shied away, aimin' to go around. I give a smart hitch and dodge, but just when the critter tried to follow suit he stepped in a patch of slick mud where Mrs. Bagley had emptied the slop. For a second his feet whizzed without movin' him, then he lost his ground grip and rode on his tail right up that mud patch and through the widow's door. And, gentlemen, she give a whoop and slammed it on him."

Harry spat and drank. "Did you ever hear a b'ar scream? I never felt so sorry for a critter in my born days. I hated to have to listen, but my conscience was botherin' me so much I couldn't drag myself away. I stayed around, wishing I could help but ascared to, and along about dawn the b'ar sneaked out. I didn't have no reason to like that b'ar, but when I seen it I could've cried. That fine lookin' varmint had shrunk to the size of a hound pup. And do you know that when he didn't come back that ornery woman sued him for breach of promise?"

Here Pace fell silent, showing no intention of going on. Blaine weakened first.

"How'd the case come out?"

"Oh, I'd done a little pettifoggin', and I thought the least I could do was to defend the b'ar. The widow's lawyer based his case on *res gestae,* meanin' the b'ar done it; but we won, and collected damages, too, on the ground of *reductio ad absurdum,* meanin' the b'ar couldn't no more."

Whether or not *The New Purchase Surveyor* conformed to the canons of newspaper journalism it was very well received. Shortly its circulation was limited only by our ability to distribute it, and I began to see prospects of profit. When a steamer finally arrived I put in a large order for paper along with the one for surveying instruments.

Roseville meanwhile was growing in more ways than its well-wishers favored. The hopeful, the ambitious and the boldly talented kept coming because they wanted to. But the shiftless, the forever dissatisfied and the outlaw came, too. They came because the energy of chaos is essentially dependent. Its owners need the building of others as the worm needs the apple.

We had more of them than we could comfortably ignore by the time most people had picked their stand for the winter. If the worst of them weren't tolerated at The Merchants Meeting there were soon other places for their friendless carousing. There was no control of them beyond the combat skill of the individual, and fights became frequent. Before long death was a commonplace on January Street.

It began to look as if Roseville might go the way of Turkey Run, and McConnell and Pace were both away. The former had taken some pressing cases to the nearest court, a hundred or so miles down the Yazoo, while the latter was in Jackson attempting to jockey the legislature into adopting locally useful measures. For a while I stewed futilely in my sense of responsibility, then it occurred to me to use the newspaper. Previously I'd thought of it as a medium for information and a certain amount of entertainment; now I tried it as a weapon. I wrote a strongly worded censure directed at all to whom it was applicable—and it drew no reaction whatever.

After thinking it over, I picked out the fellow I considered the most objectionable, ran a log of his activities, and appended a libelous critique. This time I did better. Citizens who could not get worked up over a general condition could, I found, get incensed toward a publicly accused individual. In turn the individual who could stamp a man to death and brag about it could, I also found, become outraged when somebody else referred to the business. Having ascertained so much from various sources just after the paper came out, I returned to the office and waited.

The man I'd accused was not the sort to brood in silence over his wrongs. He enjoyed being in a murderous rage, and sharing his savage humor with others served to increase his pleasure. I could hear him telling what he was going to do to me while he was still a full square away. Perhaps, in view of my public method of arraigning him, he was justified in making his own public statement. But if a man is in the right he shouldn't crowd his luck by bragging about it too loudly. George Munger's protestations and threats drew a large crowd, including many who despised him.

He was still the dominant figure when he arrived before the office of *The New Purchase Surveyor,* though. The counter faction had yet to find a guiding force. Watching from out of sight back in the cabin, I saw Munger halt and promise my destruction anew to what looked like most of the population of Roseville. While he was still at it I walked over to pick up my pistol from beside my editorial pen.

"Stand back, boys!" Munger ordered. "Stand way back or you'll get his guts in your eyes when I start trompin' him into the mud."

"Maybe he's not there," somebody nervously suggested.

"Then I'll bust the goddam word machine and wait for him."

He had turned his head to give this message to his audience and was not ready, when he faced around, to see my pistol pointed at his forehead. The window out of which I leaned was close to the door, so the distance between the muzzle and his eyes was not great. Involuntarily he stepped back before he started to curse me. Yet in the end he saw that words, however unpleasant, were not accomplishing his vengeance.

He fell silent, looking at me in baleful uncertainty. I could see the crooked teeth lurking in the hair below his broken nose. His arms hung down along the mighty frame that gave him his license to be arrogant. The hands ending them were not clenched, however, or he would have impaled his palms on the long, thick nails he'd developed for gouging.

With my free hand I slipped the bar from the door which was immediately at my left. Then I jerked the door open and sprang sideways to stand in the jamb. Having him at the end of my pistol was like having a bear or a panther at the end of a rifle. He was as vicious as the one or the other and would fight in much the same way if allowed to seize the advantage.

"Munger," I said, loud enough for everybody to hear, "you've called me a lot of names I don't like. Is that all you came here to do?"

"No, I come to whip you."

"You came to kill me," I corrected him. "Why?"

"All right," he growled. "I come to kill you for sayin' what you done said about me in the paper."

"Did I mention anything you didn't do?"

He took this for quibbling and stirred impatiently. "I don't know whether you done it or not. But I don't like the way you put it."

"There's no nice way of saying a man is a murdering bastard of a louse. I don't want you in this town, alive that is, and I'm prepared to shoot you if necessary." That was the truth. Something the like of this interview had been foreseen when I wrote my diatribe. Moreover, I'd had enough military training not to point a weapon where I wasn't willing to send a bullet. "You've come here threatening my life," I concluded. "I'm not going to stand at bay the rest of it. Go away or I'll fire."

He saw I was in earnest, but he couldn't bring himself to accept the fact I was in a position to dictate. A subtler man would have retreated to wait for a more favorable chance, but he didn't know how to break off. He'd sworn publicly to annihilate me and had invited spectators. Regardless of the fact that I'd caught him at a disadvantage he only saw that withdrawal meant humiliation.

Only one move was left to him, and he made it. "You shoot me while I'm unarmed and my friends will cut you down."

I held my breath. This was the crucial moment I'd faced in contemplation without being able to guess what would come after. If Munger's cronies chose to back him up, at best there would be a bloody skirmish and at worst a passive acceptance of defeat by the well-intentioned citizenry.

Up to that moment nobody else had taken shares in the argument. Now Carruthers Blaine spoke up. "If anybody points a gun at Godolphin I'll put a ball in him." His voice had his usual casual confidence. "I'm a very good shot. Anyone who doesn't believe me can tell me about it."

Now that a stand had been taken by somebody several others declared they were with me. Possibly because they did not see the incident as critically affecting them, Munger's friends made no move to intervene. They had come to watch a fight, not to join one in which they could see no return for the risks.

The absence of support plainly upset my foe. He made one final effort. "If you're a man you'll fight me with hands or a knife."

I didn't care what he said any more. In the first open trial of determination the men who wanted the town as a home had won out. I permitted myself a smile.

"Munger, I'm tired of holding this pistol but won't put it down while you stand there. I'm going to whistle a little tune, and if you're still facing me when I'm through, I'll pull the trigger."

He folded his arms. "Damn you, I won't go!" he cried. But when I'd whistled a few lugubrious bars he did. "Look for the article in next week's paper," I called, still watching him carefully.

"I'll shoot anybody who lends him a pistol," Blaine announced. But Munger, as I had suspected all along, didn't need to borrow a pistol. When he reached the ringed audience he ducked behind a man to reappear with a weapon he'd drawn from his hunting shirt. The knowledge that my own pistol was already pointed at him made him too hasty. Snap shooting, he missed me.

Of no mind to let him off, I put a hole in his right shoulder, thereby making sure he wouldn't be shooting at me again in the near future. While he was pulling himself together I reloaded.

"I'm going to whistle that tune again," I warned. "Better get moving."

The wound wasn't desperate, but he was. In his galled fury all he could think to do was to start howling insults again. Finally one of his own associates grew tired of him.

"Shut up, George! You fit and got whipped. You're lucky that hole ain't in your head." And that stood as the verdict.

Munger shuffled away, his disappointed colleagues dribbling after him. I don't think any of them understood the significance of what was happening, but as I eyed them I felt that they had let slip their chance to become a menacing faction. The men who remained with me had a little clearer idea of what was going on.

"That's one 'gator had his teeth pulled," a man laughed. "Goin' to write about any more of 'em, Daunt?"

Now that it was all over I was a little shaky. I took a swallow from the flask Blaine passed before I answered.

"Gentlemen," I said. "I expressed what I took to be the sentiments of all of you when I stated Munger would have to behave or leave town."

"Why sure," another said. "We all figure you told that hoss just what he ought to know, Godolphin."

"You've just told me what I want to know," I retorted. "If we all feel that way I see no reason why I should elect myself to get shot at while the rest of you watch." I looked at them all in turn. "The columns of *The New Purchase Surveyor* are open to you all if you've got any good ideas."

The upshot of that remark was an article hatched that evening at The Merchants Meeting and printed in the next issue. It was directed at a second obstreperous ruffian and was signed by some twenty names. This time there was no public demonstration. That night, though, the rogue in question tried to burn the office.

He only succeeded in charring a few of the logs. Caradock, who slept next to Eli in anticipation of just such a gesture of protest, waked in good time. The next morning I put Talisman on the tracks of the arsonist and found out just who he was. The same day he was asked by the twenty signers of the article to go, and he did go.

Two or three others, fearing they might be cited in the next issue, left before it came out. About that time Munger grew hopeless of turning the tables. When he took his glum face and lame arm elsewhere Roseville was, by frontier standards, a law-abiding community. Transients frequently brought violence to town with them. There were brawls, often vicious enough, between citizens who found time for it after working hours. But there was no longer a resident group whose main occupation was to flout the peace.

About the time such a *pax Mississippiana* was established Pace returned with a provisional charter for Roseville and its vicinity. It would be superseded and possibly revoked entirely when the New Purchase was divided into counties. Meanwhile, the charter represented formal authority in a vast tract where it was previously unknown. The fact that the authority was largely nominal did not impair what it stood for. This was a recognition from the state and through it from the rest of the world. The inhabitants were pleased, and as the strength of a town is the confidence of its citizenry, Roseville profited.

Harry also brought back an appointment as magistrate pending the extension of state, and the organization of county, courts. He called on *The New Purchase Surveyor* to carry the information that he would sit every Sunday to arbitrate such legal disputes as weren't settled out of court or by an appeal to arms.

I made a note of the day and hours. "It's a fine idea," I said bluntly, "but what the devil possessed them to make you a magistrate?"

"Why I reckon I did."

My mind was back in Virginia where law is one of the humanities, not lightly approached. "But you haven't got any qualifications!"

He looked injured. "What do you mean, I ain't? I thought you heard me say once that I've done some pettifoggin'."

As it turned out I was entirely wrong. He was shrewd and without malice. He had enough respect for law to credit it with common sense. Above all he had the supreme qualification of knowing his people.

Aside from having genuine civic worth the court was extremely popular and drew people to the town who wouldn't have traveled that far for drink or religion. If they weren't interested in the philosophy of law they were fascinated by litigation. The interest in a well-argued case surpassed that aroused by a quarter race or a shooting match. The audience was not backward about expressing its opinion of court decisions, and the judge was held responsible to the individual as well as the commonwealth. It followed that the role of magistrate required courage in addition to good humor and a firm grasp of what was going on.

In one of the early sessions one man accused another of shooting a cow on the misapprehension that it was a deer. The complainant chose to present his own case and insisted, with a considerable amount of technical verbiage, in inserting the clause about mistaken identity in his charge.

Harry Pace shook his head. "Let him say that if he has a mind to. What the hell do you care what he mistook your critter for, or if he mistook it at all? 'T wasn't the mistakin' that done the damage but the bullet. Come back next week with a true bill."

Samuel Burgess, the complainant, flushed and bristled. He was a local planter, a man of some parts but not quite as many as he thought he had.

"I don't need any instructions as to how a charge should be written. This is a true bill, your honor."

"Not accordin' to this court," Pace said crisply.

Burgess argued loudly, then he argued insultingly. He checked, though, when Pace pointed a finger at him.

"Mr. Burgess," Harry said, "I've allowed you a long tether because I know that cow was valuable, and it hurt you to lose her. Now, just to get it off your chest, tell me why you think it's important to try to read Mr. Simmons' mind when he let fly at your critter?"

There was a gleam in Burgess' eye as he looked around to be sure everybody was listening. "I don't expect justice here where law might as well be Choctaw, and I don't expect damages from a man with too many friends; but I do hope to prove that Simmons is such a star-spangled idiot that he shouldn't be allowed to carry a gun in the future. Any damn fool who'd mistake a cow for a deer is just as apt to mistake a man for a deer. The next thing I know he may be shooting at me."

Some of the audience found this speech diverting. Pace was an exception. He looked at Burgess broodingly. "I should reckon you'd be safe, Sam. Nobody ain't goin' to try to shoot a deer in the only part he could get mixed up with you."

This comment from the bench sent Burgess into a rage. "True bill or no bill," he shouted, "I'm not leavin' this brothel of prosti—goddam—tuted justice until my case is tried!"

Harry's expression didn't change. "Sam," he said, "you're like the tomcat at the taxidermy shop. You're tryin' awful hard, but you ain't doin' no good. You got anythin' else to say before I have you throwed out?"

"Yes," Burgess roared. "How's this for an argument?" And drawing a pistol, he aimed it.

The clamor and the stirring as most of us rose halted when Pace put up his hand. As unhurriedly as if he was not mortally menaced, he thumbed through the Blackstone on the desk at which he sat.

Then, as if failing to find guidance in the commentaries, he opened a drawer. Instantaneously two pistols appeared, leveled at Burgess' one.

"Overruled!" Pace barked. Burgess *vs.* Simmons was scheduled for a future meeting, and the next case was called.

I had been thinking how much McConnell would have enjoyed that interlude when I walked outside to find him just returned from down river. He was talking to a stranger, a sharp-looking man, slender, big beaked and freckled to the bushy brown eyebrows. After the latter had been introduced as O'Rourke we all chuckled over the court session just past.

"Well, Daunt," Tom said, "that gives you a good story for your last issue." Then, before I could quiz him about that remark, he asked: "Your surveying instruments came, didn't they?"

"Yes." I was still looking at him enquiringly. "About ten days ago."

"Now that I'm back it's time you used them. O'Rourke wants to run a paper hereabouts. I told him yours would probably be for sale."

For lack of an intelligent rejoinder I grunted. I had become so engrossed in *The New Purchase Surveyor* I had forgotten it was started as a stopgap. Of all man's occupations there is nothing so insidious as work. If it's good work it always seems much too important to be left to anybody else. "If he wants a paper," I said finally, "he'd better do what I did—start his own."

O'Rourke himself sensibly said nothing. He looked at Tom who looked at me. "This section needed an editor, but it doesn't need two. It does need a surveyor, and one who knows the country. You're the only one I know of. The prime thing now, Daunt, is to get property boundaries more or less settled. I'm not above saying you'll make a lot of money out of it if the crops don't fail."

Of the two reasons for work I no longer knew which had more force. Originally I had come there to make what profit I could; and that was still important. But the curse of John Smith and all lovers of new lands had come upon me. The great captain had come to seek his fortune, lost his shirt, and found a passion. That had been my fate, and the surveying, as McConnell had pointed out, would be a contribution to the welfare of the district.

The newspaper was not going to be my life's work. Now that I thought of it, I would rather have *The New Purchase Surveyor* carried on by somebody than to have it lapse when, in a few months at most, I'd have to give it up. All the same it was a damp, chill time of the year to begin traipsing around the woods. I sighed.

"Let's go over to the office and talk it over," I suggested.

CHAPTER XXV

I LET O'ROURKE sell himself the paper while I only
answered direct questions. In part I was diffident in the presence of
a professional, feeling uncertain as to how he'd regard both my
equipment and what I'd done with it. In part I was determined not
to push the sale until I'd made up my mind about him. I wasn't going to turn my work over to a man who either wouldn't see or
wouldn't care what had to be done.

He on his side was brisk, inquisitive and thorough. While Caradock was showing him Eli I stood by the window, alternately
watching them and gazing through the glassless opening while I
listened to them. Tom, who was standing with me, pointed at a man
riding by.

"There goes a friend of yours," he said bitingly.

I had seen Charles Philips at The Merchants Meeting several
times during the past month or so. We had exchanged drinks and
in spite of what I knew about him I had found him good company
while he had charge of himself. I nodded noncommittally.

"He's been around quite a bit lately."

"That means he's settled in the vicinity. Do you know where?"

"No," I said firmly. At least Philips wasn't the kind of drunk that
talked about his personal affairs and aired his home life; and I had
purposely refrained from finding out where he lived.

"I suppose I ought to find out and call on Emily," McConnell
pursued.

To this I could think of no response. Knowing that she was somewhere in the neighborhood, I frequently thought of her. A man
without a woman to think of has a void in his mind where any
flotsam of the imagination is apt to find haven. It was a vague, impersonal business, and I didn't intend for it to go any further than
that.

Annoyingly, Tom dwelt on the subject. "I bet she's having a rough time of it this winter, doing all the work and getting no help from him."

I knew this must be so, but I also knew that the one nook in Purgatory where no help can reach is the one reserved for the grossly mismated. "I'm sorry," I shrugged, feeling silly about even referring to the subject. To make sure that would be the end of it I walked over to rejoin O'Rourke.

The latter seemed more or less satisfied, though he still had questions. "Do you find your readers genuinely interested?" he asked me at one point.

"They're kind enough to say so."

He swept that away with the back of his hand. "Do people here really act as if they know and care what you put in the rag?"

After a moment's consideration I led him outside. I hadn't previously probed for Munger's pistol ball, but now I dug it out from where it was imbedded head high in the door post.

"Some of them care," I remarked as I handed it to him.

O'Rourke grinned and pulled up his sleeve to show a scar. "I got this for disagreeing in print with the fiscal policies of Henry Clay. The editor who can't get himself shot at in Mississippi isn't worth his salt."

From there on we got along well, and I made the sale. The rest of the winter McConnell and I worked our way down river from town, trying to clarify the status of claims in the extensive Roseville orbit. As Tom had stated, the settling of boundaries was essential to the shaking down of a country still wild eyed with land-grabbing fever. Once holdings had been more or less defined, the owners could at last turn all their energies to the necessary business of making them yield.

The fact that this was sound economics didn't simplify the matter of unraveling claims filed on the basis of small-scale, inaccurate maps. It didn't help with the claims sketched by rule of thumb and then sold. It was of no use in the case of land seized by personal proclamation. Still less was it a guide for land acquired from the Indians. Not all believed in the original validity of their titles, but all believed unfalteringly in the authority of possession, whether or not their claims overlapped those of others.

But no matter how savagely obdurate some settlers proved about their own holdings the time had come when everybody realized that there had to be legal sanction for permanent ownership. We progressed because most people believed McConnell knew what he was talking about and because I had geography and mathematics for allies. All claims abutted on the river or one of its navigable branches, and a section contained just so many acres.

Whereas the winter before I had sketched the wilderness, now we were mapping the backwoods. All along the valley there were jagged holes in the forest where men fought to clear the giant hardwoods and painfully quarried their roots. It was a mighty struggle but not inspiring except on second thought. This was the awkward stage of the great gamble. There were felled trees, but not cotton. There were hearths, but very little to cook on them. There wasn't enough game to feed that many people, and there was nothing growing. To pinch the last cry from desperation, animals stole everything from cornmeal to cattle; stray Choctaws stole all these and horses, too; while roving whites extended the range to take the lives of the owners.

We always camped in hiding, and to meet a fellow traveler was to cock the trigger. Naturally many that we warily passed were just as skittish about us. Preparedness may have saved us trouble on more than one occasion, but once there was no doubt about it.

In the cold half light of late afternoon in the forest we saw a group of riders. Not being able to appraise them in the dimness, we halted. When we stopped, they did. Then one of them came trotting toward us. It was apparently his intention to join us, but he pulled up when I slapped the stock of my rifle.

As he had seen us in our hunting shirts and beards before, while we had never seen him out of store clothes, Alexander Pope Cummins recognized us first. "Well, if it ain't McConnell and Mr. Godolphin. How are you all?"

Both recognizing him by his voice, we glanced at each other. His greeting was ironic rather than friendly. On the other hand it wasn't as hostile as we had every reason to expect.

"We're all right so far, Cummins," I said in a voice that invited him to state his business.

He made no effort to. "Where're you headed?"

It so happened at the time that we were faring down the valley and they up the Yazoo. "The opposite direction from you," Tom said, and again we waited.

Cummins cleared his throat. "I reckon we could say the same thing," he remarked after a minute. "Where'd you come from?"

Curiosity was a Western norm, but idle questioning from such a source was something else again. Moreover, he wasn't interested in the answers. He was just pushing phrases at us as if to hold our attention. McConnell and I glanced at each other again, then I looked at Talisman. There was a cross wind, and the hound had smelled nothing, but a Yazoo valley man wasn't likely to make the mistake of circling in the wrong direction.

"Tell your bushwhacking friends that we're riding up the breeze," I said.

"And," McConnell added, "be careful how you wiggle that rifle of yours till we're well gone."

Leaving the trail, we cut around so as to end up down wind of any possible trackers. It was by then getting dark, so we made camp in the shelter of a windfall. While McConnell, whose turn it was, cooked, I stood watch; and as I watched I had time to consider and brood. A group acting in the manner of the men we'd just met were not just casually encountered ruffians. They were an organized raiding party with a premeditated plan for disposing of horse owners who were not foolish enough to ride right up to them. I had suspected Cummins of complicity the time Goober was stolen; now I had evidence that he was active in a similar type of marauding.

Although I had fared better this time I was more indignant about being attacked by Turkey Run raiders when I was in the New Purchase than when I had been in the Old. At the moment we were near the Old Purchase border and at the extreme outside of the Roseville orbit. But if they had come so far they might go farther and terrorize the whole upper Yazoo valley. It was a nasty possibility for the future.

For the time being, however, the infuriating part was that now when I should be resting I was shiveringly furtive lest I be surprised and murdered. That night there would be no fire to ease our winter-stiffened muscles. When we had eaten we would move camp. Then we'd bed coldly in the damp dark.

It was a wretched night, though we would have rested better if we hadn't been so angry. Having slept ill, we felt seedy the next day, and feeling seedy, we moped. We made stupid mistakes, and the work progressed slowly. One night of broken slumber shouldn't so affect healthy men and wouldn't have bothered us two weeks before. We were getting stale from uninterrupted drudgery, or we wouldn't have permitted such an incident to aggravate us into uselessness.

What is noble, considered as a whole, may lose all aspect of grandeur when examined in detail. When I had sketched large sections of the Yazoo system the winter before I had been exalted, feeling half as if I was creating the country. But surveying land claims was a matter of dull precision. I was much more skilled than I had been when I dealt exuberantly with vastness. But my imagination took no comfort from my increase in accuracy. It was highly necessary work, but its unalleviated tedium was making the spirit sodden.

Early that afternoon we reached a tract overlooking the Yazoo and went doggedly to work. Some time later Tom tapped my shoulder as I pored fuzzily over some miscalculations.

"I've been looking through the transit," he announced.

As he helped me in all phases of the work this was not worth remarking, but I wasn't alert enough for wondering. "I hope you're able to see through it better than I can."

"Much better," he nodded. "You never saw a boat through one, did you?"

"Where?" I brightened for the first time that day. A boat represented novelty, and the mere sight of one could count for pleasure.

"South yonder." He pointed and led the way to where the telescopic instrument stood on its three wooden legs. "It's stopped, possibly to take on wood."

Having been told it was there I could descry the bow of the steamer with the naked eye. Through the transit I could see the texas and the smoke rising behind it. The vessel certainly wasn't moving, and I thought I could detect a list.

"It's stranded!" I beamed.

"Do you reckon so?" Tom was as much cheered by this disaster as I. "By God! you're right, Daunt!" he cried when he had looked for himself. "Hide all this damned stuff, while I go for our nags."

We rode the steep nose of the ridge we were on to the edge of the bottoms. Striking down river from there we trotted, then galloped. It was at this pace that we again caught sight of the steamer. Here the channel cut so close to the bank that we were directly above the river, and nothing obstructed our view. Pulling our mounts back on their haunches as we found ourselves where we wanted to be, we stared with naive interest.

It was a river packet of the lesser order. Apparently it had been trying to follow the channel on one of its sharp switches across the stream. About fifty yards from us, however, it had found a sand bar in the muddy, uncharted waters. It must have happened some time ago. There were no frantic attempts to back the boat free, and the few crew members we could see moved about with the slowness of resignation.

But while we looked on with satisfaction we were ourselves objects of attention. A few passengers emerged from the upper cabin and stared at us curiously. Among them we were pleased to note two young women. Just how attractive they would have been to us at another time is not worth considering. We had been in the woods for a couple of months, and Roseville itself was a haven of unwilling celibates. They seemed very pretty indeed.

No doubt we looked to them like veritable wild men of the forest. At any rate everybody stared at us as unabashedly as we gazed at them. This was satisfying so far as it went, but I could look forward to the time when it would pall. And when we'd found out that they'd been low on steam as they hit the sand bar and that a wood-gathering party was now ashore to remedy the fuel deficit there seemed nothing more to say.

We waited around in hopes of seeing the woodcutters return so we could watch the boat extricate itself, but nothing happened. We were turning away in deep disappointment when we heard one of the young women shriek. As we looked quickly around, a down-river breeze was just depositing a feminine hat on the river.

McConnell was over the bank first only by virtue of being nearer to begin with. The splash made by his steed caught me while I and mine were in mid-air. The first water race of the upper Yazoo had begun.

Our observers, being Mississippians, were swift to note and appreciate. Cheers and cries of encouragement filled the air. The woman shrieked gleefully, the crew came to life and joined in the applause. The boat whistle blew. Shots were fired. Bets were recklessly exchanged.

Even without this we were creating more stir than speed. The horses thrashed, puffed and splashed, and the cold water burled around our waists in a burlesque of fast motion. The explosion into absurdity after the unbroken weeks of drudging reached to our beings. We laughed, whooped, waved our hats, and insulted each other's horses. Tom pretended to drink from his long-empty flask and tossed it to me for imitation. This brought more cheers, shots and whistles. I doubt if the hush of the shadowed river had ever been so joyously violated.

The Yazoo was gentle with the little feathered hat and bore it away from us slowly. All things considered, we were catching up fast, my horse still behind by a yard. Tom's mount was the better by land, but ground speed is no proof of aquatic ability. We had gained a little, and I had great hopes.

It was the other of the women who decreed that the race should not be completed. Apparently it was borne in upon her that all this excitement was redounding to the greater glory of her companion; meanwhile, she was relegated to the post of envious bystander. Of a sudden, above all the other noises, I heard a petulant squeal.

"Oh, Lordy, that old wind has taken mine, too."

Her millinery fell short of the first, and, as I was upstream of McConnell, nearest to me. I glanced from one to the other. I hated to give up the race, but to ignore the second hat would be pointedly ungallant. Besides, the gratitude of two girls was needed. With a yell and a wave of my free arm I turned my horse toward it.

A few minutes later my mount found bottom on the sand bar.

With Tom behind I sloshed along beside the boat, holding the hat by a dripping ribbon, the while I looked eagerly for the owner. The whole ship's crew and small passenger list were our welcoming committee as we came abreast of the gangplank port. The hatless young women were apparently the only female members.

They turned out to be satisfactorily comely upon closer inspection. I had already gathered they weren't the bashful type, and they laughed frankly back at us as each indicated her respective top piece. The one I held belonged to a dimply little blonde whose brashness hadn't yet passed beyond the bounds of being winsome.

"Oh," she simpered, wriggling her hips, "you're so most awfully kind, Mr. Man. I could just kiss you for that."

If she didn't mean it I wasn't the one she should have said it to at that time. The shallow-draft boat listed toward us, and the gate of the gangplank port was just above me. In a second I had climbed on the saddle, got my grip, braced one foot and swung over the gate. I had just time to notice the startled look on her face before I caught her to me. Remembering how she'd flirted with her hips, and knowing it wouldn't last long, I took in all the territory I could when I gripped her. While I was kissing her I perceived out of one wary eye that Tom had followed my lead.

The roar of appreciation was loud but was not this time universal. McConnell's girl had a jealous admirer. He tore McConnell away and slugged him, whereupon Tom caught him around the thighs and pitched him overboard. The man in the water had a friend still aboard who had a knife. He was going to use it on Tom when the barrel of my pistol hit his blade. As he turned on me the barrel moved up to clip him under the chin.

It didn't knock him out, but he wandered dazedly off to be alone with his grief. The man who was fished out of the river had also lost interest in combat. We looked around, but everybody else, the young women included, seemed to consider the interlude entertaining.

"Alligator horses!" a hunter yelled, holding out his flask. "Here, drink out of mine first."

We could have made a session out of it and would like to have done so, but our horses were still shivering in the river. It was just as well, for an episode needs a cork to keep the flavor in. We stayed long enough to get our flasks filled, clambered over the side, and swam our mounts away. The whistle tooted five times and there was a fusillade by way of final salute. On the bank we lifted our flasks in toast to our well-wishers, fired our own weapons, and trotted into the forest. We were tired, wet and cold and McConnell had a sore jaw. But we were out of the dumps and ready to work again.

When the freshet brought the rivers up and the Mississippi backed the Yazoo over the bottom lands, we laid off, returning to Roseville until we could better determine what was land and what was water. I had plenty to do, completing the maps of the properties I'd surveyed, and Tom had reams of data about conflicting claims to draw up into legal form.

All winter we'd longed to be housed, but now that we were the weather was becoming alluringly mild. The sweet forest breezes swept past our stuffy office and made staying indoors an act of stubborn folly. One day I ceased to be stubborn.

My pretext for a holiday was to look over the land which Harry Pace had bought for me with the money I'd received for *The New Purchase Surveyor*. I'd asked him to try to buy Council Lodge, but when Tom and I returned from our expedition he reported failure. He had, however, succeeded in getting the tract immediately up-river from it. This included about half the section I had originally tried to claim, although not the bluff overlooking the old Choctaw mound where I had once confidently planned to build my house.

Having ranged the vicinity for months, I didn't need to get acquainted with my property, but, as I say, it was as good an excuse for loafing as any. Leaving McConnell to flounder among his depositions and whereases, I rode happily up the valley. First of all I intended to spend a few days with Tim Durham, whom I'd only seen now and then during his periodic visits to town; but halfway to the claim from which he operated I met him heading for Roseville. That dampened my enthusiasm, for I'd looked forward to doing some hunting with him; but as I couldn't face the thought of returning to my drawing board I rode on.

When I neared Council Lodge I hesitated, then, unable to resist, rode off the trail to take another look at the place I so coveted.

I proceeded cautiously in case the owner was touchy about trespassers, but no one challenged me as I found my way to the spot where I had hoped to live. Those now in possession had passed the site by for one down in the flatlands between the bluff and an adjacent ridge. After casting around I reached a vantage point dominating the new clearing.

It was a sad spot at this season. Like so many others I had seen recently it was neither tillage nor wilderness. There were a few cleared acres and several others where trees had been burnt to death on the stand. The ground was so far merely torn and disheveled. It had not yet been ploughed and couldn't be until a few days more of steady sun should dry it out somewhat. Meanwhile, the rains of spring staled in every hollow.

On the edge of this sodden desolation was the cabin. It was primary stuff, no more than a cave above ground—and such ground! Except that it was convenient to the work in hand there was no excuse for putting it where it was. There was a glitter of puddles around, though there had been no rain for forty-eight hours. It could have served as a barn for a sea cow, say. For the family it probably housed it was an unhealthy, cheerless box.

I was about to go on to my own land when a rider came slowly across the mucky clearing. First I stared, then in spite of my chagrin I laughed. When I had learned Council Lodge wasn't for sale I hadn't bothered to ask who owned it, not dreaming I knew him. But that wasn't the ironical part. It was I who had advised Mrs. Philips to purchase from a speculator.

After watching Charles Philips disappear into the cabin, I turned away, casting only one look behind me. I was no longer laughing, even in wryness, as I did so. The hypothetical woman I had pitied for having to live there was the one I most hated to think of in such circumstances. Granting the improbability that there was a floor, I knew from experience the mustiness no fire could purge and the dampness to which every odor forever clung. It would be difficult to decide whether such a residence would be harder on the soul or on the body of a woman. Whatever it was doing to her I didn't want to see it.

Having reached my land I put in a week surveying it, but my

heart wasn't in the work. After all, that was what I had been doing all winter, and I had come away for a change. Why the deuce couldn't Tim have stayed put, or why the deuce couldn't I have stayed in Roseville where I would at least have had somebody to talk to when I was through working? I was unpleasantly reminded that my life as a planter would be almost as solitary until I should somehow acquire a family. Then I was irked at the thought of my nearest neighbors. Everything was wrong.

The day before I was planning to leave I walked over to Yancey Shevlin's old camp, which lay upriver a little from my holding, to get the pirogue he'd given me. It was still where I had left it suspended upside down from the branches of a white oak. It had collected some mold but was basically undamaged, and the buckskin-wrapped bundle I'd wedged in one end of it was also unharmed. This contained my few books, the skin of the panther I'd slain, and some other souvenirs of my first winter on the Yazoo. I meant to pack them back to Roseville after I'd paddled the canoe down to my own bailiwick.

If the next morning had been rainy I would have left promptly; but it was fair, and I hadn't spent any time on the river itself for months. I couldn't resist launching the pirogue again for a glide through the mist.

As usual at that season the flooding Yazoo had washed through the forest and ebbed to leave a series of ponds and inlets. This put me in mind of the day Tom and I had hunted the alligator gar and found the path to the Indian mound. Deciding that a smoke by the old council lodge would be as good a way as any to put a period to my trip, I paddled down to the big lagoon.

Atop the artificial hillock everything was as I remembered it. I poked around in search of arrowheads and pottery, then decided to go inside. As I started to step through the doorway, I knew, for these things are sometimes revealed in advance, that there was a presence within. Drawing back, I hesitated uneasily.

"Don't worry, Mr. Godolphin," a voice came out of the dimness, "though I'm in a position to shoot you, I won't."

I wasn't as surprised as I might have been. When a man has a woman on his mind he unconsciously looks for her on the other side of every door. "Words I like to hear in a voice I like to hear," I said after a moment. "Will you come out, Mrs. Philips, or would you prefer for me to leave?"

She answered by materializing, tucking her pistol in her sash. She was somewhat thin and looked tired, but she was by no means the haggard frontier wife of my troubled imaginings. Her expression retained the keenness, intelligence and poise that I so well remembered. She hadn't laughed enough, and her poise had too much the quality of still control, but it was a face I found it an enrichment to look upon.

"I'm glad to see you," she said, her eyes affirming, "but I didn't know this was one of your points of call."

The remark reminded me that I was actually, although I hadn't thought of the mound belonging to anybody but dead Choctaws, a trespasser on her property. But I was saved from embarrassment by the recollection that in theory I knew nothing about her affairs.

"Is this where you purchased? It's an old stamping ground of mine, and I forgot I could no longer just go where I pleased."

"Yes, we hold this section from the bottoms on back a mile." Then she waited, watching me while I got my pipe packed, lighted and going. "You must know this locality well if you've found another way here than the trail from the bluff. That other one drops into the water."

"Where I left my pirogue," I said, brightening. Standing around with no particular topic of conversation was awkward, and I didn't feel quite in a position to suggest finding some spot for a tête-à-tête. At the same time, once fate had ordained what my common sense had tried to avoid, I wasn't going to leave her then.

"It's a fine day for canoeing, if you think you might enjoy it."

She, too, brightened. "I don't know whether I might or not—I've never been in one—but I'm willing to find out."

CHAPTER XXVI

Being a Mississippian she had seen pirogues even if she had never before cruised in one. She stepped into the hollowed log gingerly but without any real show of squeamishness. I wet my moccasins making sure we were launched without accident; and once we were adrift the patent buoyancy of the canoe made doubting absurd. There were no seats, but she was comfortable enough half reclining in the bow. In this position she faced me, near enough for conversation but far enough to fend off any suggestion of intimacy. After a moment she was at ease.

To her, as a year ago to myself, the flooded forest was revealed as a place of beautifully pied creation. The clear still water below was more suggestive of the sky than the thickly knit foliage above. The tree boles soared out of the water, and the fish glided over the land. My companion was entranced, and I let her take it in.

"I think you made it all up," she said at last.

I had hoped she would like it, but her enjoyment was more vivid than I would have expected from someone so self-contained. It occurred to me that this was the first thing in the way of pleasure in which she'd been indulged in a long while.

"How did you yourself happen to be at the old lodge?" I at length asked.

She was watching a white heron rocket like a startled spirit and didn't answer until it had disappeared. "Riding's my dissipation hereabouts. The lodge is a place to go, and there aren't many. I happened to find it a few weeks ago and now I'm almost a tenant. Until today, as a matter of fact, I'd always considered myself the first visitor since the Choctaws."

"You're probably the first who's given the place a thorough examination," I told her. "I only——"

"Oh, I know all about you," she interrupted lightly. "You just appear every now and then to serve some useful purpose, and it might as well be there as any other place. I shouldn't have been surprised."

From under my pulled-down hat brim I glanced at her face covertly. This was the first time I realized that she on her part had given me more thought than our encounters in passing required. That brought to mind the last time I had seen her.

"How is my patient?" I asked.

I wanted more from that question than medical information, and I got it. "The life here did him good for awhile. The weather was fine, there was lots of game for him to hunt, and he was interested in the plantation at first." She shrugged. "The winter was hard on him and——"

Having seen Philips in Roseville I knew that the rest of that sentence was "and he was easy on himself," though she let it drop without completing it. "I think," I said, evading directness in the interest of consistency, "I must have passed your cabin yesterday. You've got a terrible location, ma'am. Living in a swamp is danger-ous for a man in indifferent health, and it's bad for anybody."

"I know it. It looks very silly now, but we simply didn't know any better. Last fall, as I say, it was fine, and Charles wanted a place where he could——"

This time I finished her remark. "Where he could stay inside by the fire and still keep an eye on the work."

In a moment she smiled. "To do him justice he didn't stay by the fire much of the winter—only when he was at home."

She had lived alone in a region precarious for the roughest and strongest. Meanwhile, the business of managing darkies through a winter of drudgery had fallen to her also. Of these things, however, I could say nothing.

"But," I repeated my former argument, "whether he stays in it or not that house isn't healthy for you."

"I decided that myself when our chairs started sinking in the mud. We broke up one of the Conestoga wagons to make some sort of floor; and we'll move before the next wet season, though Charles doesn't want to. In the first place he won't admit he made

[281]

a mistake to put the cabin where he did, and in the second he says it's not worth while to build elsewhere."

That was interesting. For the moment my hopes of obtaining Council Lodge were paramount.

"That doesn't sound like he figures on staying," I prompted.

"He says not. His idea is that we should stay just long enough to put a crop in the ground, then sell to some optimistic newcomer."

This was almost too much for me. I was within a breath of telling her she was talking to the buyer her husband wanted. Just in time, though, I realized it might be a touchy subject with her.

"He would find it easy to sell," was all I said.

She looked at me impatiently, as if I had been openly siding against her, then her face relaxed. "You know how we'd lose out. We'd be paid for the improvements only—no more than a jobber's fee."

In this she was right. On the improvements they'd made so far they'd hardly get their capital investment back, let alone get paid for their time and effort. I nodded agreement.

"Is he just dissatisfied with the particular section you own?"

"No, he wants to leave the New Purchase. He wants to go back to Natchez—or to go to any city: any place, that is, where he can find lots of people with whom not to work."

These were confidences not ordinarily expected of an acquaintance; but she made them, and I accepted them matter-of-factly. It wasn't only that she had been cut off from companionship for the past six months. We had always been of interest to one another and talked easily together. Now we'd reached the point where we could discuss personal matters as if they were intellectual problems.

"What's going to happen?"

"I've told him that I was staying in the New Purchase."

I would have liked to ask whether she thought her determination would hold Philips there, but I shut my teeth on that trespass. Starting to paddle more vigorously, I soon brought us to the edge of the inlet and pushed us through the shoal water into the Yazoo. The swollen river was a muddy roil of eddies in contrast to the calm clarity of the lagoon. My companion clutched the gunwhales, then laughed at herself.

"It's the first time I've been on the water except in a steamer. Where did you get the pirogue—or do you just produce them to be agreeable?"

I told her something about my winter with Tim and Yancey Shevlin, concluding with the latter's farewell gift. She listened absorbedly while I went on to speak of my mapping activities.

"Is that what you're interested in?"

"It's a way of living," I pointed out.

She considered the words. "Don't you want any of the land you've explored so much more thoroughly than the rest of us?"

"Yes," I admitted, "I do."

"Then why haven't you taken any?"

I ducked my head, making a long paddle stroke, so she wouldn't see me flush. When I was a neighbor our relations would have more problems than attended them now, and I saw no sense in reaching toward that time.

"I've been looking over land in the vicinity," I told her.

We had been paddling upstream close along the cane to avoid the full pull of the current. At first I thought it was the wind rustling through the brake in a manner suggestive of cadences. I stopped paddling, listened, then looked enquiringly at my companion. Finally I answered the enquiry in her own eyes.

"It's music right enough."

She was too full of wondering to express pleasure or astonishment. "Where from?" she asked as if I were well informed on the subject.

I harked again. "On the river, I should judge. It's coming nearer." The instrument was still too far away for me to identify it or the tune being wrung from it. "Do you have any musical neighbors?"

She shook her head. "Even the wolves here howl out of tune." Again the marvel was too much for her. "But it's coming from upstream!" she protested.

This was admittedly contrary to expectations. The Yazoo, in common with other rivers, tapered off in the direction of its source. The source lay in a country inhabited by Chickasaw Indians if by anybody at all. The region between was little better populated, as settlement hadn't pushed much farther than the district we were in. So there was no point up the valley from which navigation could reasonably be anticipated.

"Do you want to find out about it?"

"We've got to," she declared. "Wait till I turn the other way, or I'll tip us over craning to see what's going on."

I was somewhat afraid she'd capsize us in negotiating the shift of position, but, considering her inexperience, she did it featly. At about that time the music seemed to stop.

"Is it going away from us after all?" she asked disappointedly.

I was too well acquainted with the vagaries of river acoustics to believe so. "He's rounding a bend," I reassured her.

We heard it again as I drove the pirogue upstream. Then we heard nothing for about five minutes. Once Mrs. Philips turned her head to look at me as if to make sure I wasn't getting discouraged, but the rest of the time she gazed eagerly ahead. We had rounded into a straightaway when the raft came into view about a furlong away.

Judging a love for music no index to goodness of heart, I examined it carefully. I didn't want to take my companion into any situation from which I couldn't be sure of extricating her. There was a great deal of assorted gear on the raft, which was a sizeable one. As far as I could see there were only two people on it, although there could have been others in the tent at one end.

It looked safe enough, so I held us where we were by grasping a sturdy cane stalk. With the other hand I shipped my paddle and placed my gun across my knees. Busy watching the oncoming craft, Mrs. Philips didn't observe my preparations.

A raft doesn't rush, no matter how strong a current is bearing it. I heard my companion sigh impatiently; but the crew were either born to philosophy or had acquired it along the slow fortunes of the river. One of them started to play the fiddle—no doubt the instrument we heard originally. A second later the other began to jig.

Partly because of their occupations and partly because we were against the neutral background of a cane brake, we went unnoticed. They were almost abreast of us when I hailed them. At once it was evident that they were not strangers to the social customs of the New Purchase. The dancer, who I saw to be a darky, dove into the tent. The musician dropped his fiddle and bow and started to grab up a rifle.

Being ready, I had my gun on him a mile ahead. "Let it go!" I called, and he did. He looked more startled than aggressive, and I didn't reckon him hard to deal with.

"All I said," I pointed out good-humoredly, "was hello."

Mrs. Philips had glanced at me quickly when the fellow went for his weapon. She was at once astonished and relieved to see me already poised with my own rifle. Now she took a hand in the negotiations.

"We just wanted to hear you play," she said. "It's been so long since I've heard any music."

The man straightened, stared, uncovered his shaggy head and swept his coonskin cap across his stomach in a professional entertainer's bow. When he spoke it was in no accent meant for human ears. The imitation English speech might have sounded convincing in the back country of his native North Carolina, but it would have appalled Britain.

"Your pardon for acting the ruffian, madame. Whereas I'd have not the slightest objection to shooting your good man, don't you see, I'd be loath to bedew so lovely a face with a widow's tear."

Her laughter contained a tincture of acid. "It doesn't always follow," she observed.

"To be sure, madame," he said delightedly. "I ask your pardon again, this time for hesitating to shoot him." Once again he made as if to pick up his gun and once again, to forestall any foolishness, I raised mine first.

"I like you better with the fiddle," I informed him. Mrs. Philips looked at me appealingly, and I didn't want the incident to end there on my own account. "Do you mind if we board you?"

"I reckon not!" All pretense to England left him with the phrase. "Roust out, Defoe! We've got company."

The negro, who reappeared at the command, helped me haul the canoe onto a corner of the raft. Our host contented himself with helping Mrs. Philips to step aboard. He was a stringy fellow, resembling, with his luxuriance of red beard and hair, some rank species of flowering weed. Below a buckskin shirt there was a pair of black and green checked trousers patched with canvas. He was barefoot, but wore several jewelled rings.

"This is an honor such as the *Terrapin* has never had!" He was avid of our company and couldn't decide whether he wanted most to talk or to hear us talk. "Where did you all come from? My name's Geoffrey Conklin, of the where-you-find-'em Conklins. Are there any towns near here?"

Without waiting for answers, he drew up a box, dusted it off with his coonskin and ceremoniously offered it to my companion. "I wish I could proffer you tea, madame. A magician should be able to, don't you know, but every time I reach for a cup all I get is this." With the word he reached out into the air as if to pluck something passing. It turned out to be a jew's-harp, which he handed to her apologetically. "You see, it isn't tea."

She was delighted, and he was overjoyed with her delight. "Now that I've made you smile I can die happy." I was positive it was no toy that he drove at his breast, but it vanished upon contact. He shrugged. "As long as I must live, let me at least hear your name."

I threw in mine for good measure, and he listened intently. "Now that I know the names of everybody on the river, what river is it?"

We stared, then Mrs. Philips decided this must be part of his foolery. "I suppose you don't know where you're going, either."

"Madame," he said as impressively as he could in his vile pseudo-British, "in a broad sense, do you take me, this river is like existence itself. It's carrying me along, but I'd hesitate to say where."

"You're on the Yazoo," I said with a local resident's unthinking offhandedness.

"Is it on this continent?"

"All right," I smiled. "It flows into the Mississippi, which is also the state you're in."

He looked awed. "I reckon I must be a magician, even though I never could conjure up any tobacco." He looked at me sidewise as he said this but dropped his posing when I produced my pouch. His ecstasy even induced temporary silence while he filled his lungs with smoke. "I ran out of the divine weed some months back while I was crossing one of your provinces; I believe the one they call Alabama."

"Did it get washed off your raft?" Mrs. Philips asked.

"At the time, as it happened, I had a wagon drawn by mules and laden," he gestured toward the sundry boxes, "with musical instruments and books. In addition to tea and tobacco, a thing I never could create was money, so I set out to make my fortune in the rich new lands of the West. I've thought since that I'd have found a better market if the rich new lands had been inhabited.

"I lost two mules to thieves, and got lost in escaping with the other four, don't you see. Of these, one was shot by a Red Indian for a purpose I didn't wait to ascertain. Then two died to spite me, and one is a part of me forever."

At this implication Mrs. Philips looked skeptical. "Did you like it?"

. Conklin removed his pipe deferentially. "Madame, there is a strong popular prejudice against mule meat—and it's justified. Well, not far from where the last of the mules gave up its sterile ghost I found a creek. Making a raft, I loaded on everything it would take. As the channel widened we increased our comfort by enlarging the raft until we are as you see us. Yet up to this moment, by Jove, I haven't had any idea where this traveling mud puddle was taking me. I wouldn't have been too amazed if I'd rediscovered the Pacific."

He must have spent a rugged winter, but he had come out of it well. He looked in good health, he'd salvaged a quantity of his stock in trade, and he was nearing his destination. Moreover, allowing for a raft's limitations, he was living in comfort. What must have been the cover of the Conestoga wagon sufficed not only for a tent but to cover much of his cargo. The planking of the wagon made flooring for the unencumbered parts of the raft. It also served in the capacity of a stage for the darky's gyrations. I noticed a section where cornmeal had been liberally sprinkled.

"Now that you've arrived in Mississippi," I asked, "what are you going to do?"

[287]

He fondled his beard, looked startled, then with signs of embarrassment showed us a small turtle. "Forgot to use the comb this morning," he mumbled as he started to toss it in the river.

Little though it was, the turtle yet dared to resent this treatment. "Put me down," it squeaked angrily, "or I'll pulverize you!"

"I reckon I'd better," Conklin agreed, setting it carefully on the deck. He met our applauding laughter with a grin. "Well, I figured on peddling my stock, and now and then I can put on a show or I can play."

At this Mrs. Philips looked at me wistfully. I took out my flask, and Conklin, watching me, took off his cap.

"Maestro!" he breathed. "May I test its reality?"

When he had done so manfully I retrieved it. "Mrs. Philips enjoyed what she heard of your playing; so did I, as a matter of fact." I recorked the flask but left it in sight. "We were wondering if you'd be generous enough to perform for us."

With a bow that did not ignore the bottle he complied. There was an accordion aboard, and Conklin was master of its music. With the ease born of hard work he moved richly from one tune to another. After awhile he shifted to jig time, and Defoe went into a convulsive double shuffle.

Mrs. Philips sat tapping one foot, laughing appreciatively from time to time. I had never seen her gay before, and I watched her curiously. It is always unsettling to see a new facet of character in a person of whom one already has a strongly developed opinion.

Conklin had been watching her, too. Of a sudden he called Defoe from the floor and swung into a blood-warming waltz. "Mrs. Philips and Mr. Godolphin will now dance," he announced loudly.

She looked taken aback. I think she would have refused if I'd shown the least hesitancy, but such was not my mood. Leaping up, I employed tactics I'd learned at a certain quilting bee. Grasping her hand without parley, I pulled her to her feet and put my arm around her. For an instant she held back, then laughed and yielded as I swept her into a swirling glide. The darky caught up the violin to add backbone and pace to the music. So as the raft floated down the flooded river we danced.

The platform was small, the cornmeal couldn't gloss all the unevenness, and there were chinks in the planking. Neither the riding boots she wore nor the moccasins on my own feet were designed for the ball. The composition of the orchestra was unorthodox and by some standards too small. Yet that was dancing to glow pleasantly in the recollection forever.

We were an entity, so thought of ourselves, so performed. The music controlled us, and each movement was an inevitability. We did not know what we were going to do, but when we did it we had wrought beautifully. And this took place amidst a sharp awareness of each other that was just too particularized to be passion.

But if there was not quite passion between us, neither did impersonality attend the doing. We kept our eyes on each other and laughed with the mirth that seeks no footing in humor. If there was no searing fire there was yet warmth to burn away all reserve. I had known her ironic, perceptive, rebellious, bold, sharp, resigned, friendly, bitter and wistful—but always self-contained to the point of coldness. Now she took being in my arms as a woman whose swift vitality was barely in leash to her will. Furiously as I danced she had abandon to match me. For me, and I believe for her too, it was a spell and a healing. It temporarily sucked the starved loneliness out of us and left us, when Conklin finally stopped, just happy in the knowledge of each other's strong liking.

Conklin had earned his reward. While Emily and I browsed in a box of books he'd apparently opened for his own reading, he worked on the bottle with quiet diligence. To this we left him in our new delight. Emily was famished for books, and I was in like case. Neither of us had any money, but in exchange for the rest of my tobacco I secured *The Water Witch* for her and *The Misfortunes of Elphin* for myself.

By that time we had slipped quite far down the river, and I recognized it was time to start paddling back. By that time also Conklin had finished the whiskey. As often happens to one long unaccustomed to the impact of the liquor, it suddenly drove his faculties into abeyance. Abruptly he folded into himself, gazing at us silently as if through a clouded window. Thus we left him, a conquered djinn. But we had no more need of him.

We ourselves were merrily talkative as I shoved the pirogue

upstream toward the lagoon where I would leave her. The morning had been luxuriant with wonders, not least of which were the books to which we could still look forward. Emily clutched hers all the way, patting it every now and then as if to verify its reality.

The mood carried us up to the moment of parting but not quite through it. Had we been younger we would have kissed, but we were old enough to know that there's no sense in people starting a fire unless they're ready to burn the house down. The same cold wisdom shut out all thought of future meetings. Men and women who are put together right can't long endure each other's fondness without wanting to mate. She wasn't the sort to countenance adultery, and I'd had my own sour share of it.

"Good-bye, Daunt," she said with quiet finality.

CHAPTER XXVII

THE AGUE STRUCK in midsummer. Medicine has twenty theories, which is to say none, concerning its cause, but I wasn't the first to observe that the malady isn't common in virgin forests. Where the trees are down the heat appears to steam the concentrated damps of centuries out of the bared ground. Of this miasma men sicken. If that isn't a fact, this that follows is: The year before the wilderness seemed to be free of it and now it was ravaging the scattered clearings. For the first time *The New Purchase Surveyor* had material for a regular mortuary column.

There were no doctors in Roseville, which meant there wasn't one within several days' ride. Ranking in the probable order of medical knowledge, there was a veterinary and there was myself. I dropped my surveying, and in a desperate awareness of my inadequacy turned physician.

It was small comfort that no accredited doctor had discovered what to do for the plague either. Still that left the field open to the extent that an amateur could experiment with a clear conscience. When a man is dying something has to be tried. Treatment then stands flatly on the basis of everything to gain and, to a certainty, nothing further to lose.

Some tried to bleed the bad humors out of the body on the apparent theory that it was like a fish and would perish in a scarcity of its chosen element. Some gave quantities of spirits as though the disease could be expelled when too groggy to resist. Some tried to blast it out with dynamic cathartics. Some tried to steam it out of the system with artificially stimulated fevers. At times the patient survived these ministrations; at times it merely meant he was tortured on his deathbed. The trouble was that nobody knew the nature of what they were trying to get rid of or where it lodged.

My ignorance on these points matched that of everyone else. However, I had a few ideas and had picked up some useful herb medicine from my friend the thieving botanist. My premise was that as I didn't know what I was attempting to cure I'd mostly do what I could for the general comfort of the patient. Therefore, I took them away—bodily and with their families, if need be—from the bottom lands and the riverside clearings back to the freshness of the high ridges in the deep forest. There it was comparatively cool, the air was untainted and the streams ran clear.

As for medication, I simply gave them enough to keep their bowels and pores operative and, on occasion, to induce sleep. A few of my patients died, but most of them pulled through. Perhaps they would have done so anyhow. I wasn't sure that I saved any lives, but I did feel that I was making convalescence more rapid and more pleasant. And of a surety I made the effort. After awhile I was as worn and gaunt as if I'd been an ague victim myself. I covered hundreds of miles, working night and day, until, just as mysteriously as it had seized upon us, the plague lost power.

Plenty of people were still feeling the effects, but now I was no more than politely interested in their symptoms. I was only a doctor for the emergency, and when it passed I tossed my caduceus into the Yazoo and went to town to get drunk.

Roseville, which I had left to the ministrations of the horse doctor, had lost its share of inhabitants. These, however, had been replaced and more were coming. Cotton was ready for picking, and the town stood tiptoe on the threshold of prosperity. The ague was already an outmoded conversational topic, as I found when I entered The Merchants Meeting.

I was glad to forget the sickness myself except for one question I didn't like to ask. From time to time throughout the plague I couldn't help wondering whether Charles Philips had been one of its victims. From what I knew of his condition it was reasonably certain that if he contracted the malady he wouldn't survive. While engaged in my medical circuit riding I'd been haunted by the fear that I'd be called to attend him. Trying to save him would be an act of extreme hypocrisy I didn't relish. Neither did I want to risk tending him in vain and have him, no matter how well I had striven to pull him through, in the back of my thoughts forever.

Tom McConnell had gone to Jackson to argue some cases, but I found several acquaintances willing to enter my holiday mood. About the time I'd adjusted myself with a few horns Harry Pace came in. We were always glad to see each other, but it seemed to me his welcome was especially hearty. After we'd had one together and were working on a refill he took me aside.

"Daunt," he said, speaking as usual without preamble, "I can give you title to that land you hone for."

My mind was intent on frivolity, and I didn't immediately catch up with him. "What land," I asked, interested but not taking sides, "do I hone for?"

He bit on his quid impatiently. "The section by the old Choctaw shanty you got me to try to buy for you. The one Senator Truesdale slickered you out of with his fake Injun claims."

I was abreast of him from then on. Emptying my glass, I put it down.

"That belongs, I understand, to a man called Philips."

"It used to," he agreed. "Elsewise he couldn't have sold it to me."

"How did he happen to offer it to you?"

"When I found Truesdale had sold it I went to Philips direct. He put me off then, but when he got ready to turn loose of his property I was naturally the first one he come to."

Taking it for granted that Philips must have made this deal behind Emily's back, I thought of how she must feel. "What about —well, where's his family?"

Harry shrugged. "When I knew him in Natchez he had a wife. I suppose she's on the plantation and will stay there until it's definitely changed hands."

"But I thought you said it had."

"I've been waitin' to talk to you about it," he reminded me, "and ain't been out to take possession yet. As far as that's concerned, maybe she don't know nothin' about it. Philips wouldn't give a damn when he was short of cash and liquor both."

Up to that moment, if not showing all the enthusiasm he'd justifiably expected, I'd at least managed poise. This was too much for me, though.

"I'd like to shoot him!" I abruptly snarled.

Pace considered me, quite naturally finding something unusual in my attitude. "You'll have to dig him up to gratify that longin'," he said finally. "Didn't you know?"

I shoved a cigar into my face to hold my features in position. "No," I mumbled. I couldn't decide just how I felt, but by the time I'd got the cigar going I'd succeeded in stowing the problem out of sight until I had leisure to view it in privacy. "The ague?" I then asked.

He nodded. "Philips was fightin' the horrors and one of 'em turned out to be real. The shape he was in the sickness took him like a frog snappin' up a bug." He shrugged again and spat. "Even for friends I don't want land so bad I buy from the spifflicated, but he would have sold to anybody for any price, and there would've been plenty of takers."

"Yes," I said. The word as used meant nothing at all, accurately interpreting the state of my thoughts.

"Well, that's the story," he said when I added nothing to my monosyllable. My puzzling reaction had dampened the eagerness with which he had started to tell of the favor he had done me. "You still want that land, Daunt? I can hold it till you cash in on your surveying next month."

I knew he deserved better of me than I was giving, but my faculties had been overwhelmed. "Thanks, Harry," I tried. "Yes, of course, I want it, but I'd sort of given up hope. This came as a surprise, you see."

At last he had made his own diagnosis of my confusion. His eyes twinkled, and he slapped my chest with the back of his hand.

"Hell! I shouldn't try to talk business with a man feeling like you do, but I just couldn't keep it in my mouth. That was good work you done as a medicine man, and you've got a toot comin' to you. Ride that tiger, and when you fall off drop around and we can fix things up."

After he left me, so far was he from divining my state, I was so cold sober I shivered slightly. Taking a four-finger bracer, I stepped forth to where I could be confused in solitude. Without especially meaning to go there or anywhere I found myself down by the wharves. In a little while I sighed and sat down dangling my feet over the softly muttering river.

Charles Philips was dead. This was the point where the might-have-been faded and reality took over. It's one thing for a man to dream of a woman he can't possibly marry and quite another to be concerned with one he conceivably can. How Emily felt toward me I couldn't guess, but she, too, would have to make up her mind.

Complex as the problem of marriage between any two people necessarily is, it was simple compared to the other matter that was worrying me. That Indian gift of fortune was a mantrap.

For more than a year I had wanted a certain fine piece of land. Now I had it. Good—but for the fact that the land, by every right if not by actual title, was Emily's, and I didn't want to take it from her. At the same time I had to buy it or it would be sold to somebody else, dispossessing her and spiting myself to no avail. Having bought it, as I felt myself forced to do, how was I to proceed?

At this point both problems became one and the same. Of a certainty Emily wouldn't let me yield her the property as charity. If she did we would never be on an even footing again. Yet if I took possession she would have to move. Whether she would leave the district then was something I couldn't decide. She wouldn't have once, but things had changed. Perhaps she wouldn't mind returning to Natchez unembarrassed with a shiftless husband.

In some ways the most difficult point was that I could not claim that I had come into the property ignorant of who owned it. I knew her troubles well, and she might conclude that I had purchased the land deliberately for the power it might give me. Even a proposal of marriage might not clear that doubt from her mind.

Going over the whole business three or four times I got the same answers. It was by a wrench of will power that I pulled my mind out of this whirlpool and gave it a course of action to cling to. Whatever else happened there was one obligation I could not avoid. Having made my decision to take the land I had to tell Emily I'd done so. By telling her what I must I would also set the wheels of the matter in the swiftest possible motion. Thereafter things would fall into place even though the place might not be good.

During the night of restless speculation that followed, one additional thought came between me and my sleep. While Harry and I were settling the details of our business transaction the next morning I worked up my courage.

"You say you haven't notified Mrs. Philips of this business?"

Pace was putting a cap in his pistol, getting ready for his morning saunter around town. "No, aside from waitin' to talk to you, I didn't want to give her the idea I was hurryin' her off before she got her crop picked. Still that's up to you now. You're the man that's puttin' up the cash."

"Oh, you're right, she should have the cotton," I said hurriedly. Then, bracing myself, I let my question fly. "By the way, did anyone ever notify her she's a widow?"

He'd had his feet on the table while we were talking, but now he let them fall to the floor. "Why, Daunt, I don't know," he said soberly. "I never thought of it before."

"There'd be nobody regularly delegated?"

He shook his head. "We ain't that well organized. Whoever was with him when he turned up his toes might have, but at that it's a long ride to bring bad news to somebody you ain't never met." Again he reflected. "There was a lot of people kickin' off about then, and it could be nobody paid him any particular mind. Still she must've heard somethin'."

"Maybe," I said gloomily.

"Naturally you'd like to know for sure." Harry grimaced sympathetically. "Nobody'd like the idea of wavin' a deed at a female, then, when she asks what it's all about, have to tell her that her old man's buzzard food."

That started a new trend of disturbing thoughts. "Is he? I mean did anyone take care of burying him and——"

My companion looked pained. "Roseville's a civilized community. We protect our buzzards from anybody that's died of the ague. It might be catchin'." Nevertheless, he saw what I wanted. "It's all in the record, right enough. As a matter of fact, the town council appointed O'Rourke coroner when folks started droppin' off. See him about it."

O'Rourke was a good editor, but I didn't see that his abilities equipped him for the duties of coroner. "Why didn't they appoint the horse doctor?" I demanded. "He'd at least know something about how to make the findings."

Pace was always amused at my exasperated insistence on technical knowledge. "There ain't any trick to findin' out if a man's dead," he opined. "Just put him outside and see if the sun ripens him."

I knew I was fighting a losing battle, but I never could forego the struggle. "Yes, but," I pointed out, "a coroner's supposed to tell what caused the death."

He opened his eyes wide, then let his lids drop. "I reckon after a man's dead he don't much care what caused it, but maybe O'Rourke figures different. You go look in his book."

My relations with O'Rourke had been professional, amicable rather than friendly. Since he had come to town I had spent most of my time afield. He was good company, but I hadn't been in it long enough to determine, for instance, what lay behind his chronic acidity.

"I hear you're a coroner," I said diffidently after we'd exchanged some remarks about *The New Purchase Surveyor*.

His shrewd face crinkled about the eyes. "What more of an in could an editor ask?"

At another time I might have been amused, and then made my point. But because I was disturbed I chose to be highminded rudely.

"You might have passed it on to a man somewhat capable of handling the job. It's important, you know."

"The horse doctor?" His grin stiffened at my criticism. "As a matter of fact, he does do the actual work and gets feed for it; but he was so busy learning his trade he never had time to learn much about reading and writing. Then most of his technical terms are those of the Cherokee medicine men who taught him, and the others he made up himself. My part of it is to find out what he's talking about and make the book look like a respectable record."

I nodded and offered my flask. He accepted it and the tacit apology.

"There was a—no, not a friend of mine," I corrected myself. "A man I knew is supposed to have died. I want to find the record and locate the grave. It's believed his wife may not know of his demise, and I've been delegated to bring her the news."

"If he did die, he made the paper, too," O'Rourke promised me. "I'll give you a copy, so she can read the account. It'll save you from having to go into details yourself."

We found the name easily in the brief records of the Roseville coroner. The notation read simply: "Died of the ague impinging on a generally vitiated constitution."

The New Purchase Surveyor was less laconic. "Snapped off by the ague," the lead paragraph ran, "in a quarter race finish with the screaming horrors, heart failure and stomach rot, also rans in that order, Charles Philips died in a hog wallow on Goat Street last Friday. By paying man's mortal debt he spoiled an otherwise perfect record."

Thinking how Emily might feel about such pithy journalism, I doubtless look dismayed. "That's accurate reporting," O'Rourke commented. "Everybody in town knew him, so there was no use in trying to veil his character or gloss over his manner of leaving this world. You weren't around much this winter or you wouldn't purse your lips."

"Well, he's dead," I muttered.

"Look, he died owing me ten dollars he had a lot of fun spending. All I could do was to make a *bon mot* when it was too late for it to bite him. Who got the best of it?" O'Rourke tossed the paper I handed back to him aside. "You still want to see his grave?"

"I reckon I'd better. Just give me the directions if you're busy. By the way, is it marked?"

He chuckled. "That's another advantage of having me as coroner."

It was when I reached the potter's field, a patch of cracked earth in a stump lot, that I understood O'Rourke's last remark. A country without stone and one where paint was as yet unprocurable would be hard put, now that I thought of it, to mark its graves. Into the epigraphic breach thus created Eli had stepped. The inscriptions were printed on sheets of paper, which in turn were stuck to the headboards with pitch.

Starting my search, I promptly detected Caradock's almanac borrowings, wryly tailored by O'Rourke to fit the individual. I

was first confronted by a board jauntily askew and raked back.
This could have been the result of offhand placing or the work of
the wind while the ground was still soft. In any case the marker
illustrated that frank, factual reporting on which O'Rourke prided
himself.

> Somewhere below is David White,
> Too snake mean for a louse to bite;
> Started off in the right direction,
> He'd made six feet at the last inspection.

The second one beyond it was commemorative of the lone casual,
such as myself, who'd come to the New Purchase because no other
place seemed to have an altar for hope or to be a sanctuary from
despair. This pilgrim hadn't been long left in doubt as to what was
awaiting him.

> Here lies a fellow, we don't know who,
> But he caught the ague by the dank Yazoo;
> He came so far to see the sights
> We gave him permanent squatter's rights.

Not all were victims of swamp fever, however. One board re-
corded a tragedy of overwrought passions.

> John Bedore told Fox he lied.
> Tom Fox did when he denied;
> Both were skilled with bowie knives,
> Both lie here without their lives.

Then there was this note from the forest:

> Here lies the leg of James McGill,
> Who shot at a bear and missed his kill.
> The rest of him was eaten whole;
> We trust the bear belched up the soul.

O'Rourke had dealt with Philips as offhandedly as with the rest,

I found when I located the grave I came to see. It had rained since the marker was put there. The print on the affixed paper was streaked and the paper itself was stained and warped. Since the rain the sun had hardened the broken earth so that it lay there in a disorder of brittle chunks. Shoving my hat back from my forehead, I lit a cigar.

This was the end of the man who had greeted me so gaily when I first landed in Mississippi. He lay in a potter's field, not buried in the sense that a rite had been performed but tossed in a hole like a dead cat. His fellows considered their society improved by his passing. His wife would be relieved. His family probably would feel the same way.

Of all the people in the world I was perhaps the only one to whom his death, with its nasty legacy of conflicting obligations, gave concern. It was the devil that the same man could be a nuisance to me dead as well as alive.

Yet for all I knew and had come to feel about Philips I had, in my few tavern conversations with him, found him pleasant company. Up to the minute his liquor overcame him he was personable, friendly, anxious to be liked, witty, educated, and well mannered. If he was also selfish to the point of little principle, so were highly esteemed men in all communities, politics and callings. Except that he could not bring himself to work I could not see much in his character that warranted the general dislike he had aroused. If a man doesn't want to work about the only permissible activity is scolding the people who do. If he follows any other love in the desperate field of choice left to him, he had better be able to afford it physically as well as financially. Philips simply hadn't been able.

Perhaps I thought of him so charitably because I remembered how near I had been drawing to the end of all men's patience just before I left Virginia. Certainly I felt a humble kinship with him as the man who had failed at being Emily's husband. I wondered if I could do any better, granted the chance, and could flatter myself with no promises.

After awhile I turned away, waving vaguely with the hand which held the cigar. That was probably the only *requiescat* Charles Philips was given.

CHAPTER XXVIII

Although I had marriage on my mind I had decided not to mention it by the time I reached Council Lodge. I would, I felt, be fortunate to emerge from the forthcoming interview with any part of Emily's esteem. Also, while I did not respect false mourning I shied from the indelicacy of telling a woman she was a widow and proposing matrimony in the same paragraph. After all, if the bond between us was strong enough to warrant wedding it could stand a slight delay without withering.

It was a long day's ride out there, but I started the day before so I'd arrive early in the afternoon instead of toward evening. Taking my time as I did I had plenty of opportunity to think the matter over and every minute of it increased my certainty that, no matter how I tried to explain, she was bound to think nothing but the worst of me.

Fortunately, I wasn't left to dangle after I arrived. Emily was at home and advanced to meet me before I could alight to knock.

I took off my hat but couldn't think of a greeting or manage a smile. She was not the one to show how she felt for nothing and looked at me as coolly as she had when I first met her. Her first words told me one of the things I wanted to know, although they reminded me that we had said a final good-bye at our last meeting.

"How nice of you to drop in on us. I'm sorry Mr. Philips isn't at home."

The phrasing was too much for me. If she had looked worried about Philips or glad to see me or even disturbed that I was there I might have been able to produce one of the two dozen ways of breaking the news I'd polished in transit. But her detached composure left me no opening to be friendly or gentle.

"Mr. Philips," I said gruffly, "isn't going to be home—any time at all."

I let it drop like that because I had to get it out some way, then I met her eyes morosely. She returned my look fixedly, and I wasn't sure she'd comprehended.

"Are you trying to tell me," she asked at length, "that my husband has left me or that he's dead?"

"Dead—the ague; there's been a pestilence of it."

"I suppose I would have known if I'd cared more," she said, mostly to herself. "He was gone so much longer than usual. You were with him?"

"No, I only heard. Then it occurred to me that you might not have."

Having stretched the corpse out between us, I didn't know how either to walk around it or ignore it. I'd said all I knew how to on that subject and yet to introduce any other topic was unthinkable. It was Emily who put her finger on the trouble.

"It would be less embarrassing if I were decently grief-stricken and you could honestly feel sorry for me, wouldn't it? Please come in and have a cup of coffee with me, Daunt."

The little cabin was like dozens of others I had seen except that it had a floor, boasted some mahogany furniture and had glass instead of oiled paper in the two small windows. It seemed ridiculous to have a servant in a residence so tiny, but there was a negro woman in attendance. Emily sent her on an errand as soon as she had served us.

"I don't want the darkies to know yet," she commented when the slave had gone. "Maybe they don't belong to me any longer. Now let's get what has to be said out of the way. You say you heard Charles was dead. Do you know any more than that?"

Her acceptance of actualities made talking easier. "Yes. I knew you'd have to have more than hearsay, so I found the coroner's report and located the grave."

"That was in Roseville? His family will want to know."

I couldn't be said to be glad about anything, but I was pleased that she didn't speak as if she intended to visit it herself. Sipping my coffee, I stared vacantly, wondering how I was going to break my next piece of news.

"I suppose you will want to go to Natchez."

"I'll have to," she nodded. "I owe it to his family, I want to see mine, and I want to know how I stand as far as property is concerned."

"You say you're not sure he left you the slaves?"

"Oh, I just said that because I've never actually seen the will. I think he probably gave me everything—what little there is left."

Now it was coming. I scrunched my toes inside my moccasins.

"He didn't leave you the land," I said heavily.

The news hit her as word of her husband's death had not. Evidently it didn't occur to her to doubt what I had said, and indeed her mind leaped to a part of the truth.

"He sold it!"

When I nodded she jumped to her feet. The knowledge of what she was achieving with the land was the only thing she had. It was on this that her self-confidence was based. I could understand that, and it hurt me to see her knifed so unfairly.

"Damn him—damn him, dead!" she said fiercely. "He used to threaten to, but I never thought he would—not when I'd been doing all the work!"

When I was speechless she wouldn't let me remain so. "Do you know how it happened—who got the money?"

I rose also. "Apparently he was drunk, then got the ague, then wanted more liquor to keep from facing the fact he was dangerously sick. And it seems his credit wasn't too good."

"I know," she said wearily. "That's one of the reasons I insisted on leaving Natchez. But who would be mean enough to take advantage of a man out of his head with drink and disease?"

"A good friend of mine." I just managed to get it out. "He bought it for me."

It sounded even worse than I thought it would. And the explanation was too involved for me to attempt unless she was prepared to listen. That I didn't expect, and I steeled myself for recriminations or a fit of hysteria. To my astonishment she became, to all outward appearances, absolutely calm.

"And why," she asked, reseating herself, "did this excellent friend of yours buy my land for you?"

I preferred to talk on my feet. "Philips would have sold it to

[303]

anybody for a pint of forty rod. My friend knew that I'd wanted it. I'd always wanted it, you see. Oh, not just since you've had it but long before that when I was making the survey of the valley I told you about."

After I'd got started and saw that she was listening sympathetically, it was easy. I recounted the discovery of that tract and how the desire for it had seized and grown upon me. Then I explained how Senator Truesdale's maneuverings had blocked my pre-emption claim.

"I wouldn't buy from Truesdale direct because I didn't like the man. About then my money was stolen, and it wasn't till this past winter that I was in a position to buy. When I found this property belonged to you all I forgot about it—but Harry Pace didn't. So he bought it for me, and I had to take it or it would have gone to some third party."

"I'd always wondered why someone who loved this country so much hadn't taken up a claim." Emily mused a moment. "And now that I'm your tenant, what are your plans?"

"I don't want this land—I don't need it now," I disclaimed. "As a matter of fact, I've taken up a tract just north of here that's just about as good." In my gratitude for her tolerance I made wild offers she couldn't possibly accept. "Look, you take the deed back, or I'll pay you a fair price for the plantation, whichever you wish."

"And have you pay your friend, too?" She smiled a little but shook her head. "I can't let you be penalized for Charles' wrongheadedness."

Knowing she was right, I didn't persist. "Before I say anything further do you want to stay here, or would you really prefer to live in Natchez now?"

"Now that Charles is out of the way? No, that won't change my plans, Daunt. It'd be bad enough to return to live with some member of my family as a poor relation, but I'd have to go into mourning, too. Everybody there knows that Charles and I didn't get along well, but everybody would act—and expect me to act—as if I was irrecoverably crushed. I haven't got time for that nonsense. Charles made me miserable while he lived, but he shan't do it dead. I'm staying in the New Purchase somehow."

"Good!" I congratulated her. Feeling much better on all counts, I proceeded as I should have in the first place. I drew the deed out of my pocket and put it on the table in front of her. "As I say, I now have other land. You can pay me just what I had to give for this when your crops earn it."

She picked the document up and looked at it thoughtfully. Then she pushed it back toward me. "Perhaps I should take it now, but I won't. If I accept it at this time the land will revert to Charles' estate; and I haven't seen the will. This way the land won't be affected whether Charles left me what he owned or not."

"The executors," I pointed out, "might want to know the whereabouts of the money in payment."

"Let the executors find out where Charles spent the rest of his money and all of mine, too," she said tartly. "If they can contract to get it back from the cheap women, the wrong cards, the trailing horses and the empty bottles, I might tell what I know. Otherwise, so far as I'm concerned, it was simply a transaction made without my knowledge."

On the whole I was very well pleased with the interview. We were still on good terms in spite of the fact that I had told her everything; and her intention of staying in the valley left the way open for more intimate negotiations later. Relieved beyond expression, I felt that it would be silly to try to crowd my luck. I picked up my hat.

"Well, that's all I came to say. If you'd drop me a line at Roseville when you return I'd appreciate it, Emily. I hope you have a pleasant trip."

"Stop that!" she demanded. "I won't have a pleasant trip, and I'm not ready to say good-bye yet either." At a couple of points in our conversation I had anticipated that she might be angry with me, but now for the first time she was. "Do you remember the last time we were together?"

"I've thought of it every day since," I said simply.

"And this time," she fumed, "you expect to just toss me my property without giving me a chance to say what I think about it? Please sit down!

"All right," she said more softly when I had complied, "you're offering my land back to me on generous terms, Daunt, and I'm accepting because I think under the circumstances you should. But I like to think two things about it. I like to think you're the kind of man who'd do it anyhow, and I like to think you're doing it especially for me."

I grinned. "If I deny either I damn myself for a louse."

"Exactly," she agreed. "So as you're forced to be noble on both counts I'm going to admire you for your altruism and be grateful for the kindness you wouldn't have lavished on anybody else."

Now I could really laugh. If she had thanked me in the normal fashion I would have had to acknowledge the gratitude and flee under the guns of my own rectitude. As it was she had freed me from constraint.

In turn she giggled. "You had the weight of the world on your shoulders when you got here. I couldn't imagine what had happened to make you look like that. And how you must have hated to come!"

"There was no way of knowing you didn't have a suspicious mind," I chuckled. "You might have even thought I made away with Philips."

"For a moment I did," she said calmly.

Well, I had killed one man over a woman I didn't care about. This would have been far more reasonable. For an instant preoccupation with my sourest recollection kept me from grasping the important implication of her words. If she thought I cared enough for her to quarrel with Philips she had a clearer idea of my feelings for her than I thought. That was no warrant that she reciprocated, but it showed that the matter was on her mind.

Now I no longer wanted to leave right away, but I didn't want to stay where we were. As far as I was concerned that cabin belonged to Philips alive or dead. I would never feel comfortable in it.

"Would you like to go for a little ride before I start back, Emily?"

When we prepared to step forth I picked up the rifle I brought inside with me. My companion was amused that I hadn't left it in the saddle boot.

"What did you think I was going to do to you," she teased, "that you had to have a weapon?"

I'd been in the New Purchase too long to be laughed out of going armed. "In this country," I stated, "a rifle's like a lifeboat. That once you need one, it's too late to send for it."

We were halfway to the little log shed that sheltered her horse when we heard a turkey gobble somewhere beyond the fringe of the woods. "It's nice to have them tamed so they come right down to the edge of the fields and wait for you," I remarked. "You'd better send one of the hands after that bird a little later or he might think he isn't wanted."

She looked at me mournfully. "Charles sold all the guns except his pistol."

I took a couple of more strides, then stopped. "What do you do for fresh meat?"

"I drool for it," she said honestly.

"And with all the game in the woods and on the river——"

"I live on salt pork," she finished.

"Come with me," I said firmly, when I'd ordered Talisman to stay with my horse, "and I'll show you one advantage of always carrying a rifle right now."

"I know a little about turkey hunting," she objected. "You'll never get near enough to a lone cock until twilight when it roosts."

"But I can make the turkey get near me," I said rashly. "Come along, and I'll show you."

Before we had walked the brief way to the forest I half regretted putting myself so far out on a limb. Under Shevlin's tutelage I'd learned how to make a turkey call and to use it. Yet the best that can be said for any such device is that it works sometimes. Nevertheless, I cut myself a piece of dogwood with a brisk show of confidence. A man who won't bluff won't achieve anything, and a man who won't back his own bluff doesn't deserve to.

Emily watched me with skeptical interest. "Do you mean to say you're going to whistle for a turkey and expect it to come?"

"I'm going to imitate a hen," I said with dignity.

"Well, that's half the turkeys in the world that won't come right there."

"It's good for cocks only," I admitted.

While I was carving I was pleased to hear the gobbler sound off again. At least my quarry hadn't played me false by leaving the area. Softly testing my call I made a couple of minor adjustments, then touched my companion's arm.

"Now quietly," I admonished.

I didn't attempt to draw very near the bird we were stalking. If it would come at all it would come from as far as it could hear the call. There's nothing more skittish than a turkey, and there was no use in taking Emily's booted feet any farther through the dry leaves than was strictly necessary. About fifteen yards in we found a grounded ash, suitable for concealment, observation and the support of my rifle barrel. When we were stretched out comfortably behind it I went to work.

Emily was watching me, and I was very conscious of the fact. Silently praying for luck, I concentrated all my faculties on using the instrument, my breath, and my fingers just as Yancey had instructed me to. One of the things he had impressed on me was never to overdo it. My first note was a soft, ruminative cluck, the note of a hen that never dreamed there was a cock within miles.

I knew from experience how far the sound would carry, but Emily wasn't impressed. "Is that the best you can do?" she whispered.

Disregarding her, I waited a couple of minutes just as a busily scratching bird would do, then repeated the call. After a moment I was rewarded by a low, questioning gobble. The cock suspected the presence of an unattended female and wanted to be sure before investigating.

I left a tantalizing interval before I sounded again. The call wasn't much louder than the others, but it was no longer mere aimless commentary. It wasn't inviting, nothing so crude, but it was more positively and alluringly the note of a hen. The answering gobble was deeper, with a suggestion of bombast, and Emily's shoulders shook.

In five minutes the cock was near at hand. I couldn't yet see it, but I knew it to be furtively stepping through the woods, as alert for enemies as intent on courting. Meanwhile, the hen I was impersonating had admitted it was aware of a male in the offing and was tentatively responding to the cock's bold demand for an assignation. Both Emily and I were peering, heads close together, in an effort to pick it out of the forest. It was she who saw the bird first.

"There!" she pointed, squeezing my arm excitedly.

I gave an ecstatic chirp to tell the cock it was observed and admired. That was all that was needed. It knew the hen was in hiding close by, just waiting to be found; but first it aimed to make sure of an eager reception. Behold then it assumed magnificence. It swelled, it spread its tail feathers, it dragged its wings, its breast, comb and wattles took on lustre, and it strutted gloriously.

Knowing that it was a sight my companion hadn't witnessed before, I let her enjoy it for awhile, but I couldn't risk a last-minute failure by waiting too long. I was leading the bird with my barrel and when it had paraded and turned twice I blew its head off.

If the turkey cock had been proud of itself, what of me then? I'd made good my brag, and I didn't even try to look modest. There were any number of men along the Yazoo who could have stalked the bird as skillfully, but that didn't matter in the least as long as the art was new to my companion. In any case I turned my head to find that Emily's face, not a foot from my own, mirrored the unstinted admiration I felt for myself.

To have applause at the moment a man is acutely conscious of deserving it is a heady thing. I had started the interview feeling stubbornly righteous but on the defensive withal. Through Emily's acceptance of my motives I had regained my equanimity but felt that was all the good fortune I could ask for one day. Now for the first time I felt ahead of the game, sure of myself.

No more than the turkey cock was it possible for me to visualize a rebuff; but unlike that luckless bird I didn't waste time in sterile preening. Catching Emily to me, I gave her a kiss that let her know a man had hold of her.

For a few minutes she matched me heartily, then, at her instance, we drew apart to parley with passion. Somehow in that exchange we had both learned what we wanted to know. We were elated but no more surprised, now that it had come to pass, than if we had planned it months in advance. And so far not a word had been said.

As for any plans I had made, this was contrary to them. In addition to feeling that the day I announced Philips' death was not the day to propose, I had not felt ready on other grounds. I had meant to be cautious, not out of any doubt of her but until I was in a better position economically and domestically. In a word, I hadn't meant to say anything until I at least had a house of my own to which I could bring her. Still a man's private life is like the professional life of a general; he spends most of his time planning and at the last always has to improvise. Events had made all past notions obsolete, and I spoke accordingly.

"As long as you feel you have to go to Natchez there's no sense in our marrying until you've made your visit. Do you want me to come down there to get you?"

"No," she said, speaking as matter-of-factly as I myself, "I'd prefer to meet you back here. The family likes their widows to age awhile. We'll all be much happier if I'm brazen away from home."

"They might make it difficult for you to return," I worried. "How long will you stay?"

"They will—except for Uncle Henry, the one you met—but I'll come anyhow. I'll have to stay awhile, of course. For one thing, the will may take some time to unravel."

I was just as glad that I'd have a few months to get my affairs in better order. Now that it was officially some of my concern, I asked a question that had been bothering me ever since she mentioned going to Natchez.

"Who were you figuring on leaving in charge of the plantation? I don't want to interfere with any plans of yours, but——"

She chuckled. "When I first said I was going I was bothered about that, too, but I think I'll let you worry about that. You've got title to the land, and you can keep the work that goes with it, too."

If we talked further then, I don't recall what we said any more than I can imagine how we managed it. It was the long shadows, warning me that I had to find a place to bivouac, that started me on my way. While Emily was ordering her hair I retrieved the gobbler I'd shot. Then we walked slowly back to her cabin and my horse.

"I'm leaving you here, honey," I said, laying the turkey down just outside the door.

She didn't argue, divining something of the way I felt about the cabin and perhaps sharing my feeling that it had no place in our lives. "I'll be leaving in about ten days, Daunt. When the charter boat comes to pick up the cotton hereabouts, that is."

Feeling grateful that she didn't suggest any intermediate visit, I made the most of my farewell and rode off. When two adults are ready for marriage there's not much sense in their being together under any other circumstances. I put a reasonable number of miles between us, and it was nearly dark before I made camp. None the less, I had spared a little time for a side trip. Upon reinspection, the site for Council Lodge, the house, had looked more pleasing than ever.

CHAPTER XXIX

I SPENT THE HOURS before I slept, as well as those before I rolled out of my blanket late, in making plans for a future of new and pleasant complexities. Halfway home, however, I had an idea of another sort. I was in the vicinity of Tim Durham's camp, and suddenly I knew he was the man whose company I would then most enjoy. In a few days I would start in on what I hoped would be a lifetime of hard work. I was looking forward to it eagerly. Yet now, while I was still on the loose, I wanted to exercise my franchise.

Turning off the trail, I felt my way along the river until I reached the wild holding on which he had made good his claim. When Tim spoke of his land he always called it a plantation, but he had chosen it because it looked like a favorable headquarters for his trapping activities. To date he had cut no trees except for firewood.

Knowing the uselessness of arriving earlier, I dawdled until time for the evening meal. His dogs told me he was home a minute before I drew near enough to see the man himself. He put aside his gun, drew out a flask and turned it upside down.

"Looks like it's on you," he said. "Did you bring tobacco, too?"

I knew how it stood with him then. He'd been on his annual summer spending spree and had returned to the forest with nothing but his gun and his axe. He nuzzled my flask like a hot horse at a trough, then cut himself a huge chew.

"Catch yourself a smoke, Daunt," he suggested. "I'll have eats for us directly."

While he busied himself at the open fire place before his shanty I looked after my horse, then sat down to watch. Here on his premises it was still, to all appearances, as unchallenged a wilderness as the one he and I had found two years ago. Though a man has a new birth at every new phase of his life it is inevitable, if the abandoned phase has been good, that he should mourn it as a dead friend. Knowing that I was going on to something else, I had a gentle attack of melancholy. There would be hunting for sport and to eke out the larder, but wilderness life with its casual self-sufficiency would soon be only a recollection.

"How does the season look to you?" I asked halfway through the meal.

He hacked off a chunk of meat, flipped it into his mouth and chewed thoughtfully. "Not good. I likely should've spent some of my money on farm equipment instead of splitting it even-Stephen between Vicksburg bitches and Vicksburg tanglefoot."

"Otter getting scarce yet?"

"Partly that, though there's still quite a few on the other side of the river, but mostly more men after 'em. I don't reckon it makes much difference to an otter whether me or some peckerwood squatter takes his pelt, but I ain't so broad minded." After a pause he added: "Specially when the traps is mostly mine."

I was crunching hoe cake in one jaw but managed a warped look of interest. "It livened up the winter but didn't make for a good catch. I had to spend a lot of time trackin' borrowers and by the time I'd settled with a few, why others'd come along."

By this time my tongue was free again. "Some of those cotton mouths will bushwhack you," I warned. "You know that as well as I do."

"Better," he grinned. "One of 'em tried it. Of course, I'd been watching him sneak up and while he was gettin' his sights on me I snap fired. My traps wasn't bothered much after that, but there'll be a new batch of squatters this year, and there just ain't enough varmints to go around. This'll be my last season, for a fact."

"What'll you do then?" I asked.

He started shaving the plug I'd given him for a smoke. "Do what everybody else does," he asserted. "I've got this land. Next year I'll get me a woman to put me to work and make a planter out of me."

I had not bothered to tell him that I myself had already made arrangements to settle down. "You better start clearing now," I advised.

[313]

"Nope, I'm givin' myself this one more year of trappin' while the rest of you get the country whipped down so I can live in comfort. I hanker for a damn sight better roads before I risk the axles in my carriage when my old woman wants to traipse around doin' her callin'. And get that town built up so it amounts to somethin', and my old woman won't always be squallin' for me to take her to Natchez or New Orleans."

"Anything else?" I enquired.

"Well, you can get rid of the snakes. They'll scare my old woman and make her forget to tell the niggers the old man hankers for his mornin' dram." Tim looked at me earnestly. "The liquor's right in the house, and it's mine, and I know where it is, of course. But home'll be just like a doggery; I'll have to put in my order, and they'll raise hell if I help myself."

The picture of Tim as master of the mansion was too dazzling for me to contemplate. I blinked and drew away from it. Such things would happen in the New Purchase and would happen to men of narrower parts. But Durham stood for something of which I was most acutely aware at that, my moment of saying farewell to it. I stood up and sniffed the small wind, wet from the river.

"Tim, do you reckon we could scare up a bear in the morning?"

"If we can't we can at least tree us a squatter. Kick a chunk into the fire and see if you can find that flask again."

The smoke and the sparks as I threw the wood on, the smell of the whiskey as I pulled the cork, the rank whiff of the bottoms, the crisp odor of the forest, the roar of an alligator, the hunting cries of foxes and owls—these together with our talk and tobacco made the evening as of old. I missed only one thing: the howling of wolves. The enmity of farmers and the competition for game was already proving strong enough to drive them back from the Yazoo.

There were still bears, however. The dogs found the tracks of one that had come down to the river to drink during the night. It had just got nicely to sleep and was in no mind to move without fighting. It held the dogs off until we bore down on it on horseback. Then it slapped its way through the hounds, smoked through the underbrush and vanished.

Very few race horses could match the pace of a bear; none in such a steeplechase. Our mounts were far from being race horses, though they knew what to do with their feet coursing through vines, creepers, brush, deadfalls, roots, streams and gullies and slowed for nothing. Yet I knew we hadn't a chance of sighting the bear until it should once more turn for a stand.

Talisman, I could tell by his bay, was leading the chase. It was also easy to tell that the bear had distanced the dogs, too, and that the hounds had settled down for a long run. Such was the situation when something happened. It's easy to tell when dogs have overhauled the quarry they've been tracking, but this was no such thing. The baying changed to startled yelping, then to the combat snarl, all within the space of a second. Tim and I, riding abreast though about ten yards apart, exchanged looks.

"Somethin' else cut the trail," he called.

This was correct so far as it went. A minute later when we galloped on the scene there was a bear in the open, sparring, snapping and whirling to reach at dogs attempting to take him from the rear. There was also a bear swaying part way up a slender tree.

Neither of these was the animal we'd been pursuing. The fact that one had found no refuge and the other an inadequate one showed how abruptly they had just been alarmed from their daily rest. That much I simply knew, having no time for reason. I was making every effort to get toward the bears and my horse was trying just as strenuously to avoid doing so. It was important to quiet him lest he bolt when I dismounted. I did not quiet him.

One of the great points about bear hunting is that anything can happen. For one thing, a bear, although he fights dogs when they attack him, is never under any illusions as to who his real enemy is. While I was struggling with my mount the bear fought free of the dogs and charged.

I wasn't able to keep my rifle and my saddle, too. The horse sprang sidewise, just clear of the bear; I was bucked off to sail right over him, falling to my knees and one hand. Although the dogs were closing in on him again the beast kept me in mind. Six feet away he whirled and reared, red eyed, slavering and bleeding; but I had a knee under my elbow now. I was forced to shoot high to miss the leaping hounds, but I blasted it through the throat.

It was a death wound that would take a minute or two to mature. The bear had been in the act of throwing himself forward and actually struck my gun barrel before I could scramble out of the way. Then it and the dogs boiled around on the ground while Tim tried to get in a shot and I frantically reloaded. My shaking hand was measuring out powder when the creature caromed into the tree which bore its fellow.

The overloaded trunk could not withstand this assault of weight and desperate power. The slim bole swayed out so that the whole heft of the clinging animal was on the under side. The tree snapped, and the beast let go just as Tim gave the *coup de grâce* to the other.

The bear which had just hit the ground, not having been hurt, didn't want to fight; he only wanted to go away. I wasn't quite ready, the dogs weren't interested, busy as they were with the carcass of their late antagonist, and Durham hadn't even started to reload. Under the circumstances, I'd have stayed content with truce but, as the bear started to make a getaway, Tim reached out and slammed it on the nose with his rifle barrel.

The stunning pain stopped the animal so that it reared back, shaking its head like a man who has been knocked down. It was no longer pacific, however. It let out a roar which changed to a snarl as it took a blow between the eyes. Then it attacked.

The only dog to leave the passive satisfaction of a dead bear for the active danger of a live one was Talisman. He took a hamstring grip just when the bear got moving, deflecting its attention at a critical moment. Tim had dropped his gun and was springing in with his knife, but by that time I was reloaded. While the bear was lunging at my retreating dog I shot the beast through the eye.

Without pausing, Tim caught up his rifle and loped forward. I knew what he was looking for and followed at his heels. The odds were that the animal we'd originally pursued had taken advantage of the respite gained when he'd led the chase across the hide-out of the other bears to find a tree while he got his wind back. As we'd only lost a couple of minutes he should be still there.

Occasionally I could see a blurred suggestion of a track and Tim saw much more than that. He led on for about five hundred yards and then pointed to a claw-marked walnut. A moment later he shot the bear out of it and drew a knife across its throat for good measure.

While we were sitting on it, resting and passing the bottle back and forth, I shook my head at Tim. "What in God's name made you go after that second bear with an empty gun?"

To my surprise his answer was perfectly serious. "Daunt, there's too much huntin' and too little findin' these days. If you let a critter go now somebody else gets him or the varmints gets smart and hits for the hills. I'll eat somethin' besides birds and fish this winter, and I was beginning to wonder about that. Last spring it was hard enough."

"How about deer?"

"There's still some around, but they're awful bashful. Oh, I got one yesterday, but I spent the best part of two days lookin' for it that I'd ought to've spent settin' out my line. You can't trap if you've got to put in too much of your time chasin' meat."

We gutted the first two bears, then leaving the dogs to sleep off their feast of entrails, we went in search of our horses. They had been badly frightened but at a time when they had also been badly winded. We had them both back in an hour or so and used one to carry the third bear to where the other two lay.

By the time all three were skinned and butchered at our leisure the afternoon was largely gone. There was no point in comfortably tired men who had everything they needed going any farther than the nearest stream. There we made camp, which is to say we cut wood and tossed our respective saddle blankets down within reach. After a couple of belts of liquor we ate monstrously of the fresh meat of our kill, poured whiskey on top, then pillowed our heads on rolled bear hides to smoke.

Then my solaced body knew that it had been well used and gloated drowsily. The gorged dogs slept in the warmth of the fire. The flames let the night breeze bring us the forest scents and sounds but none of the evening chill. Having cleaned our hunting knives by three jabs in the ground we were faced with no chores. We didn't even talk for a while.

I spent the interim before the time came in reviewing the day with satisfaction. The high spot of the hunt was when Tim challenged the fleeing bear, but I had held up my end, too. That shot in the eye now—ho! ho!

"Tim," I said at last, "that was a damned fine piece of bear hunting."

He took his pipe out from under the hook of his nose and rolled his head toward me. "After this year there ain't goin' to be no hunts like that in this neck of the woods, and we was maybe on the last of 'em. Of course, I've been on better ones."

"Yes?" I said resignedly.

"Sure. When I was a young buck just growing my horns back in Tennessee——"

"I thought you came from Kentucky."

"Mostly I do," he admitted, "but not always. When I was a young turkey just growing my chest beard in Tennessee there was so many b'ars around you'd have to explain to 'em that if they wanted to be hunted they'd have to make an appointment for next year or the one after."

"Why did you leave there then?"

"I was just fixin' to tell you." Tim stimulated his memory and tossed me the flask so I could fortify myself for listening. "Well, the year I was talkin' about," he began, "I killed so many b'ars—four or five a day was nothin'—that I give all my friends all they needed for the winter and had enough left over to swap for a prime Chickasaw squaw.

"Well, I traded the squaw for a race hoss, the race hoss for a span of oxen, the span of oxen for a flat boat, and the flat boat for a butcher shop. Then I come to find out there wasn't much meat in the butcher shop, so I had to go back to b'ar huntin' to stock up. The trouble was that it was gettin' late in the season by then, and most b'ars was already in their hideaways for the winter."

Tim glanced at me, but I didn't bother to comment. "I hunted all mornin' without so much as findin' a claw mark, so when I come to where a bunch of hosses was fixin' to shoot for beef I signed up. There was a lot of awful good shots there, but the others was in for the fun of it, drinkin' a heap and laughin', you know. But me, I was in for business. I had to have some sort of meat or close up my shop. I won by a bug's whisker and started home with my quarter of beef.

"Now b'ars is like most other things, Daunt; not there when you want 'em and right where you'll stub your toe on 'em when you don't. I was most back to town when I heard somethin' followin' me. It was gettin' dark but not too dark to make out a b'ar close on my tail. That beef was makin' friends."

"Was it too dark to shoot?" I enquired when he glanced at me again.

"It could've been bright as the sun in a lookin' glass without doin' me much good. I'd fired all my bullets at the shootin' match, and though of course I'd saved the lead I'd have to mould 'em again afore they'd fit in the gun. I was out of powder, too, when I come to think of it, and I did come to think of it when I looked at that b'ar. He looked bigger than he had a right to be, and he had a mean way of sniffin' so's I wasn't always sure it was the meat he liked the smell of so much.

"I took a hitch in my pace, and the b'ar done the same. I pointed the gun at the b'ar, and he stopped; but when nothin' happened he come on again. I tried it again and yelled 'bang!' and it sounded awful like that varmint laughed. Anyhow he speeded up tryin' to get nearer, and I speeded up tryin' to get farther."

Tim looked at me appealingly. "I wasn't exactly runnin' away from the critter, you understand, though it would've taken some explainin' if anybody'd been watchin'. All I was doin' was hustlin' to my place of business, which a man has a right to do in a free country. And the b'ar had a perfect right to be goin' the same way—up to the second it hit the lot my store was on. Right there it done wrong, and I got mad."

Feeling that I'd need it, I took a deep one and threw Tim the flask again. "Well," he went on a moment later, "I zipped through the door of my shop, and so did the b'ar. I jumped the counter, and so did the b'ar. I whizzed into the cooler, and so did the b'ar. And I scooted out of the cooler, but the b'ar didn't quite, because I slammed the door on him. He took it hard for a while. I was bunkin' in the store, and every time I woke up that night I could hear him thumpin' and scratchin' and growlin'; but by day he'd got tired and gone to sleep."

Tim sucked at his pipe and finding it smoked out, put it aside. "Well, I had my b'ar meat; but I couldn't figure out how I was goin' to market it, so I opened up shop and started in with my beef. I done pretty well and had it about half sold when the sheriff come in. I'd had to whip him once to keep him from arrestin' me, and we hadn't been good friends since."

"What did he want to arrest you for?"

"Assaultin' him, I think he said. Anyhow he asked me what kind of meat I had.

" 'Beef,' I say.

" 'Got any b'ar meat?' he wants to know.

"About then I heard a little gruntin' in the cooler just behind me. 'Yes,' I allow.

" 'Let's take a look at it,' he says, just like that. He didn't smile or say please or ask me about my folks, so I shook my head, not smilin' either.

" 'Can't let you have any,' I say.

" 'Why not?' he says, gettin' mad.

"Daunt, I hated to admit I had a b'ar I didn't know how to handle, though I might've to a friend. 'Just got 'im,' I say. ' 'T ain't dressed yet.'

" 'I can dress my own God damn b'ar meat,' he cusses. 'Bring it out and let me take a look at it, I tell you.'

"The b'ar had started scratchin' a little, but the sheriff was so hotted up he didn't notice. 'I'm savin' it for somebody,' I tell him.

" 'You can't do that!' he yells. 'You're keepin' a store, and you got to sell to anybody that wants to buy. That's the law, and if you don't go along with it I'll get me a posse and arrest you.'

"I thought it over just long enough for him to come to a full boil. 'The law don't say I have to sell by the piece,' I say finally. 'I'll sell you the whole carcass or nothin'; and let's see your money first or you'll take beef and lump it.' "

Tim put the cold pipe in his mouth again. "As he'd only met me in the dark you can't really blame that b'ar for not bein' able to tell the sheriff from me, though it kind of hurt my feelin's. Of course, I was standin' behind the cooler door when I pulled it open, so the sheriff was the only one the varmint could see." He sighed gently. "Well, after they'd gone I took the money the sheriff had planked down, bought back the Chickasaw squaw, swapped her off for the race hoss again—and I never did get to sell the rest of that beef."

After awhile Tim pulled his saddle blanket over him, rolled over and went to sleep. Emulating him, I was soon ready for slumber myself. At such a time a man may think no thought at all or almost anything may come to him. In my half dream I thought of old Captain Smith and linked him with myself. The Johnny-come-latelies who followed us would not know the things we knew.

CHAPTER XXX

WHEN THE CHARTER BOAT called at Council Lodge to pick up Emily's cotton it brought me and the supplies I required for the winter. It wasn't nearly as much as I wanted. I would have liked to bring all sorts of equipment, too, but, in spite of reasonably careful planning to avoid it, I was land poor. The cash I'd received for *The New Purchase Surveyor* had gone for a tract I wouldn't now have time to develop for years to come. Much of the money I'd earned surveying would be diverted as received to Harry Pace in payment for Council Lodge.

Emily and I had only about an hour together before she embarked on the boat I had just left. The hands were having the harvest holiday that shouldn't be denied them, so I spent the first couple of days sizing up the job before me and taking inventory of my assets and my handicaps. I placed myself in both categories.

Having once failed at farming, I knew what it demanded of a man. But such professional skill as I'd picked up in a lifetime largely spent on a plantation didn't include any knowledge of cotton. Emily had done well, considering her inexperience and Philips' lack of co-operation, yet the acreage under cultivation was pitifully small. I had six field hands and could have used sixty. I had a few horses, whereas I needed mules and oxen. I had a minimum of tools and most of them the wrong ones. On the whole I figured that if I had a margin it lay in one thing only. This was the fact that I had done too many things in Mississippi to doubt that any work could be accomplished.

The first and most obvious of the hundreds of pressing tasks was clearing more land, and during the fine days of autumn we did nothing else. The Philips' hands were a good, cheerful group of darkies and had a winter of tree felling behind them. I handled the team, worked out solutions to the numerous small engineering problems and learned with them. For the rest I kept them in game—ducks and geese still swarmed on the river—tapped the whiskey for them once a week and didn't expect too much of them.

Occasionally, as I worked them, I pondered the fact that people had gone to a great deal of trouble to remove one primitive, alien group only to replace it with another. If the Choctaws, negroes and whites thought it over they should all be puzzled at what was going on. The answer was that what was happening was not the product of thought.

I suppose slave labor was always a frontier expedient just as it was with us on the Yazoo. It was the only labor available, and if a man wanted more work done than he could accomplish by his lone efforts he used it. In a land where every settler was a potential planter the man who didn't have gumption enough to build anything for himself was yet too conscious of his birthright to work for anybody else.

All things considered, my hands and I did well and got quite a stretch cleared. However, in time I had to stop this work and turn to the business of clearing out stumps and preparing the land for cultivation.

It was in the midst of this drudgery in the winter rains that McConnell came to see me, accompanied by a man called Williams. The latter belonged to that curious order of men who can do almost anything capably for somebody else but have no force on their own account. He was a sort of hanger-on of Tom's and occasionally employed by him.

"I brought Williams along to take charge of your operations," Tom said when we were through with preliminary exchanges. "I want you to come to Roseville for awhile."

The idea was tempting, for the months of lonely work were beginning to be oppressive. Nevertheless, I shook my head regretfully.

"That's nice of you, and even nicer of Williams, whose services you're so cheerfully offering, but this is work I'd better look after myself."

Knowing that he had not taken so much upon himself just to have my company, I grinned at him with a mixture of curiosity and challenge.

"There's no use in protesting, Colonel," he said calmly. "You're under orders."

When I simply raised my brows he reached in his pocket and handed me a piece of parchment. I examined it, put it down on my lap, then looked at it again. Shorn of the circumlocutions it favored, it stated that Mordaunt Fitzmaurice Godolphin had been appointed a colonel in the Mississippi State Militia.

I was not flattered. Having been regular army, I had acquired the professional's low opinion of the home guard.

"And why should the governor have done a damned thing like that?" I finally wondered. "I didn't know he was aware I existed."

Tom preened himself. "It's one of the many things you owe me."

"Including a root in the rump, not yet delivered." But I was too mystified to be really indignant. "What is it, some political scheme?"

Abruptly he grew serious. "We're having trouble with outlaws, Daunt. There've been raids not far down the river from Roseville."

I sat up. "You think they're directed from Turkey Run—that it's some of Garland's and Cummins' work?"

"That's the strongest possibility, but the main point is not who's doing it but that somebody's doing it. Last year they didn't get very far into our territory, and we must admit there wasn't the deuce of a lot to attract them. This year it's different. Taking slaves and stock, they're undermining the economy of the country. Also they've killed some settlers and scared off others."

"All right," I said, "what's going to be done about it? I see you've got it all worked out."

"We've got to find out just who and what we're up against and descend on them in force. We're not ready yet."

"Well, let me know when you are." I knew he wasn't through, but I flicked the parchment dismissingly. "Meanwhile, don't go around calling me names."

"I'm not calling you anything you're not entitled to," he persisted. "This can't be handled by a vigilante group, as you saw us handle things in Natchez. There the lines were clearly drawn. The citizens of the town were defending themselves from a known nest of criminals. No political power would dare champion Underhill openly. Our position isn't that unassailable. As far as the rest of the state is concerned we'd be only two quarreling towns nobody ever heard of before."

I nodded. "In other words, if the men from our district took the offensive the government wouldn't know whether they or we were really the outlaws. So?"

"So I went to the governor, making no specific accusations, least of all against any community. However, as his excellency was well aware—he probably was well aware, but I was careful to point it out—a newly opened territory draws the bully and the outlaw as well as the adventurous and the enterprising——"

"And the dreary hopefuls too shiftless for crime even," I finished.

"I didn't mention them," McConnell confessed, "but I went on to say that in the interests of local security and state prestige it would be advisable to start a regiment of militia drawn from Roseville and the adjacent rural districts."

"A regiment!" I snorted. "We couldn't raise more than a battalion if we took 'em from under the grave markers."

"I know it, but the political mind likes to deal in the large. Launching a regiment—I admitted it would be a skeleton, but declared we had to make a generous allowance for growth—tickles a governor much more than authorizing a battalion does. It sounds better when making his recommendation to the legislature, too. It shows that his excellency is taking prompt steps to nip a dangerous condition in the bud and that he isn't content to send a boy to do a man's work. And, of course, it helped when I assured him that the citizens of Roseville wouldn't consider asking a state subsidy for such a patriotic enterprise."

I was visited with sudden disquiet. "Before we go any further," I said, "just how many colonels are there to a skeleton militia regiment?"

He eyed me innocently. "There's just one to the Yazoo Invincibles."

Jumping up, I shook my commission under his nose. "Do you mean to say I'm the head of your scarecrow army?"

"I hadn't planned it that way," he said brazenly. "I'd counted on taking it myself, but the governor forced my hand. He started out by saying he wouldn't even consider granting our petition if the regiment wasn't going to be a credit to the state. He wasn't going to embarrass the state with any more undisciplined collections of backwoods boobies, etc. That's when I pulled you out of my hat. There was no danger of such a thing, I said. Why, we would be commanded by a distinguished professional soldier."

"There's no such thing as a distinguished lieutenant," I growled.

"I may have promoted you a notch or so," Tom admitted. "The thing was to get the business accomplished. You can readily see that it's one thing for a group of independent citizens to make a foray and quite another for a unit of the Mississippi Militia to invade a suspected headquarters of criminals."

"Wouldn't it require authorization every time we went into action?"

McConnell reached into his pocket again and took out a letter. "We've got orders—or at least you have—which authorize the use of the state's military might in case the lives and property of its citizenry can't be protected by any other means. If we need anything more specific than that we can get orders back from Jackson in a few days. I think his excellency will back us if we make weighty enough representations."

Perusing the letter, I found that it was addressed to me and gave blanket discretionary orders covering limited emergencies. "His excellency is a trusting man," I commented.

"His excellency is smart enough to know whom to trust." Tom wasn't, or at least didn't appear to be, especially impressed with what he had done. "He knows Harry Pace, who strongly backed the measure, and he knows me, too, as far as that's concerned."

"So I'm a colonel," I finally accepted the proposition. "What did you and Harry elect yourselves to be?"

"Oh, we're just majors. Harry's your second in command, and I," Tom picked up the flask that had stood untouched between us, "am your faithful adjutant."

"Well, don't try to drink before your superior officer," I warned, snatching the flask from him. After drinking, I consulted the gubernatorial letter again. "His excellency declares himself in favor of prompt organization."

"That's where I come in," Williams spoke up. His broad, good-humored face turned solemn as he regarded one of his feet intently. "I got a game leg and can't drill, but I can run your niggers for you while you're gettin' the regiment goin'."

"Williams knows how to boss your operations, and he's being paid for it," McConnell broke in. "We've got to get started now, for later in the season we'd never get the men away from their planting. It'll only take about a week, Daunt."

I had been so busy that for once I hadn't been aware of what was happening in the valley. In spite of the small crop that first fall, so insatiable was the demand for cotton that prosperity had come to the New Purchase. It came directly in the form of premium prices for the yield. It came indirectly as the report of a successful season brought new settlers and new capital to be invested.

Most of the original group had come with vague to cloudy notions of how they were going to proceed. As fortunes were being made out of cotton the fact that they were able to claim rich land looked like wealth in the hand. And if it turned out to be true for some, for others it only meant they were wretched in a new locality. At first the swarms of game had made living easier, but now that it was thinned out hard times had enveloped them once more. They were ready to sell their undeveloped claims and move on somewhere or to sink to the status of hopeless squatters on land they had once owned.

By and large those who bought from them were better prepared. By and large they weren't desperate colonizers but practical opportunists. They had the special knowledge and the equipment needed to run a large farm, and they had the labor, too. For the first time slaves were in the upper valley in any numbers.

The trend was reflected in Roseville, which had doubled in size and was reaching eagerly toward magnificence. Frame residences of some pretentiousness were going up here and there. Honest log cabins were cased in boards to hide the nature of their structure, and two stores on January Street were faced with brick.

Even my old home was radically changed. Bought furniture had supplanted the rough handiwork of our fashioning. The bear skin which had acted as a wind stop where the chinking had come loose was not in evidence. And certainly the soundly finished walls rendered it unnecessary. Tom was just a little sheepish about this luxury, and seeing this I dusted my pants before I sat down.

"We used to have to scrape our feet when we left the cabin so we wouldn't muss up the street," I marvelled, "and now you've got windows you've got to make a deal with before you can spit through 'em."

"All right, you Choctawland stump farmer," he said grimly. Rising, he took down from behind the curtain which formed his wardrobe a masterpiece of flamboyant haberdashery. It was bluer than the sky would dare to be and redder than a rose would want to be. There were frogs, spangles and epaulets, all of gold, and a horrible feathered hat.

"Your uniform?" I gasped.

"No," he laughed gleefully. "Yours. Nobody but the commanding officer deserves anything like this."

"My first official act will be to have you court-martialed." I gazed at the gaudy suit miserably. "Is this really the regular uniform of the Mississippi Militia?"

"There's no set uniform," he confessed. "I picked this out myself, so the prospective volunteers will be properly impressed."

He turned out to be perfectly right. However much of a jackass I felt when I presented myself in this regalia, the frontier saw nothing funny about it. The only thing most backwoodsmen knew about an officer was that he wore a fancy uniform, and as far as they were concerned the more gaily he was dressed the finer the soldier he must be. I saw at once that I commanded their respect and attention as I would not have if I had appeared in my normal garb.

Half of them knew who I was, and of these a fair percentage called me by my first name. But the uniform set me apart, and O'Rourke had plastered the forest with bills citing my military achievements in high-flown and truthless terms. The gathering of would-be volunteers looked at me uncertainly as I rode up and acknowledged their murmur of greeting by a salute with my preposterously long sabre.

At the outset I had decided that the common military exercises would be useless to the purposes of the Yazoo Invincibles. But I foresaw that the men would expect the only type of drill they'd ever heard of: the parade maneuvers of a foot soldier. They would have felt cheated without it and would have lost interest in joining up. So it was about this that I talked in my opening address. A duller subject never existed, but the technical terms with which I spiced my harangue made their mouths water for professional understanding.

That was a sort of humoring I could afford, for I was comfortably aware that most of them were highly skilled in the things I really wanted them to know. They could shoot, ride and trail an enemy ably. They lacked nothing but *esprit de corps,* of which the first element is complacence. I was willing to go to any lengths to give it to them.

I paid the price, for it was a drillmaster's nightmare which ensued. Not everybody had a gun, but everybody—once it had been explained to them that smoking in ranks wasn't feasible—had a quid of tobacco. No matter how skillfully the rear rank spat—once it had been explained to them that turning around while at attention wasn't soldierly—it was bound to make the front rank nervous. This diverted the rear rank and compensated in large measure for their inferior position.

While I was earnestly demonstrating a maneuver I was apt to hear: "Pull in your ears, Pete, I'm goin' to let fly."

Having once been a professional, it was hard for me to remember that I wasn't one now. Several times I barely held back words that would have lost me all my recruits at this first session. The hardest thing for me to bear was their cheerful verbosity, which soon won free of their awe. When I gave a command to a particular man, I invariably received a hearty: "Why sure, Daunt" or "Here goes, Colonel—and if I don't do it right the drinks are on me."

The session was epitomized for me by a sergeant instructed to make what corrections he could while the men were standing with individual interpretations of the position of port arms. Noticing that he was having quite a discussion with each soldier, I strolled within ear reach to see what was taking him so long. As I approached he'd just finished with one man and had stepped in front of another.

"Howdy, Bob," the sergeant began, "how's your folks?"

"Middlin', Steve," his subordinate replied. "That colt of yours foaled yet?"

"No, but if it don't pretty soon that damned old mare's goin' to bust. Looks worse'n my old woman the time she whelped a pair. Fixin' to have a big crop this year?"

"Well, we're clearin' a few more acres. Say, am I holdin' this shootin' iron the way the colonel's got it in mind?"

The sergeant, having thus earned and been given permission, now looked at the gun as if noticing it for the first time. There were a dozen things wrong with the way the man was carrying the piece, but my representative cocked his head admiringly.

"Why sure," he said, "the colonel'll be right pleased."

Notwithstanding the strain on my disposition, the drill was a practical success. All concerned were well satisfied with the afternoon and left with a favorable opinion of military life. Having assured ourselves of this by a tour of the taverns, we were ready for the next step.

"They'll come to the lick," Pace said confidently, "but we'll salt it just the same."

At drill the next morning Harry announced there would be quarter races for all comers during the afternoon, after which all who wished to put their names on the roster of the Yazoo Invincibles could do so. Then he went on to inform them there would be a parade, a barbecue and several barrels of whiskey accessible to enrolled volunteers only. This was like offering tabbies catnip—and mice, too.

Military life was turning out to be as delightful as everybody had hoped, and the candidates were much cheered. Seeing that I could now bear down a little, I began to be more critical, insinuating the knife of discipline into men who didn't quite know what was happening to them. One or two of them started to jib, but my uniform was too much for them. The cooperative instinct may often take grotesque forms, but there's no surer index of man's adaptability. It was of their own volition that these fellows had subjected themselves to orders only the day before, but already they were beginning to be saddled with the feeling that to obey was an inevitability.

Yet any annoyance they may have felt was more than compensated for by the quarter races in which everybody was free to ride his horse and back his judgment. I'd seen such meets in Virginia, but the backwoods was the scene of their flourishing. Not many frontiersmen have a horse that can really race for a mile. If they do possess one they haven't the time or facilities to train it. And if they do train it they can't find a course to accommodate it. But most saddle nags can manage to hustle for a couple of furlongs, and a straightaway of that length isn't too difficult to find.

Best of all, at that brief distance the speedier horse frequently loses. Much more than in the ordinary race the premium is on the rider, and woe be to the innocent. It was made to order for Mississippians, who would break their own necks or those of their horses with indiscriminate zest. Failing that they'd bet all their assets and any amount of imaginary credit on a steed they'd never previously set eyes on.

I didn't bet on but one race. Tim's rawboned gelding was not an animal to lure anybody's money, though I knew it to be better than it looked and signally responsive to its master's wishes. It was Tim himself that I was backing, partly out of faith in his resourcefulness but largely out of sentiment. As the other onlookers were going by their judgment of horse flesh or their knowledge of past performances I found many birds of prey around me. Finding myself viewed as a good thing, I defended my choice, inventing points of form to justify an opinion based on good will only. In the end I found myself wagering quite a lot more than I had intended to.

While the starter was counting and the remaining five horses were being nervously jockeyed close behind the scratch, Durham's mount stood stock still some yards back from the line. The rider looked as lifeless and uninterested as his nag; but just as the starter had his tongue on the word "go" Tim gave a full-throated imitation of a panther scream.

It was lifelike enough to make many a man there start, and I know it brought the gooseflesh out on me. The horses reacted to it with considerably less reserve. More even than the howl of the wolf pack do frontier horses dread the cry of the catamount. I have seen them go wild with fright while safe in their sheds when such a scream was heard from afar. The effect close at hand during this moment of tension was catastrophic. One man was promptly thrown. One horse reared up on its hind legs for a minute of unmanageability, and the remaining three bolted off the course away from the sound. Tim's mount, recognizing the source of the yell, was more influenced by the whip which was simultaneously applied to it. Although two of the other contestants recovered enough to try to catch up it wasn't a close race.

To say that my bets were paid graciously would be to exaggerate. Durham's methods strained even the go-as-you-please sportsmanship of Mississippi, though the losers could find no loophole. There is nothing in the broad canons governing quarter racing to prevent a man from shouting.

As for Tim, he utterly failed to understand what the controversy was about. "I was just encouragin' my hoss," he asserted mildly. "Speedy, ain't he?"

Some disgruntlement notwithstanding, it was an afternoon generally enjoyed. The good will thus earned, abetted by the promised barbecue, brought us fully as many recruits as we had hoped to get. Thereafter, the militiamen paraded execrably to their own joy and the admiration of the spectators. Later they feasted well and drank better, leaving the empty barrels with a morale the equal of any unit in any service.

McConnell, who walked off with his own generous share, was even more content with the roster he carried. "We've got more than enough names to impress the governor. The Yazoo Invincibles won't have any trouble in getting chartered with a showing of votes like this."

"You mean to say we ain't yet licensed?" Tim asked.

"Not a one of you until this roster has gone to Jackson for recording and returned approved." Tom chuckled. "The recording's the main thing, Tim. Having us on the muster rolls of the state is what's going to make it hard for anyone we have to get rough with to put us in the wrong."

"When are you going to have the next drill meeting?" Caradock asked.

Tom looked at him sidewise. "We're not going to advertise what we've got until we have to go into action. The only way any other community can beat us now is to start a home guard of their own."

CHAPTER XXXI

HAVING LEARNED that a steamboat was due to make one of the rare winter calls, I remained in Roseville a couple of days after the mustering of the Yazoo Invincibles. It had been a long time since I'd heard from Emily, and I hoped for some letters. In the course of time they would have found their way to me at Council Lodge; but to my state of mind a week or so made a lot of difference.

While standing with the rest of Roseville to see the passengers come ashore I heard McConnell say: "Just a minute, Daunt; a friend of mine."

Watching him idly, I felt my heart come up and wallop me in the throat. The hand he was bending over was Emily's. I believe I could have had a duel if I'd wanted one. It's a fact I pushed past some newcomer with less ceremony than I should have used, but in place of heeding his angry remonstrance I grunted an apology he could keep or throw away. I was in a hurry.

The number of ideas the mind can juggle simultaneously is amazing. My hurry was not all out of delight at seeing my betrothed. There was worry driving me, too, in as much as I hadn't heard from her in weeks. She might have changed her mind, might even have married somebody else. Then, not strong enough to hold me back, was the fear that she hadn't changed her mind. I hadn't expected her, wasn't ready. It'd be easier if nothing was required of me. Counterbalancing that craven qualm was a reckless amusement. I was in for it now, make or break, and so was she. Last and meanest was an annoyance with Tom for seeing her first. How did it happen that he had the quick eye for her that should have been mine?

By the time I reached her all the conflicting ideas seemed to have killed each other off, and I didn't have mind enough left for a decent greeting. "Hello, Emily," I said.

One look at her told me what I chiefly wanted to know, and my churning blood quieted. She had been looking for me. In place of being astonished to see me she had been worried that I wasn't there. Her word of salute wasn't much more eloquent than mine had been.

"I thought maybe you hadn't got my last letter. Have you been all right?"

"I didn't get any letters scarcely," I said, wondering where we could find some privacy, "and I am now that you're here."

McConnell was naturally feeling out of his depth. "I didn't know you two were acquainted."

I stared at him, wondering why he wasn't aware of anything so important. "Of course, we're acquainted," I declared. "We're getting married, you know."

"No, I didn't know," he said feebly. "When?"

The query spun the wheels of my mind. We intended to wed, we wanted privacy, and Emily had to have a residence. I looked at her and saw nothing in her face to discourage me. When I turned to Tom again I was cool, assured, brisk.

"Today if we can. Do you think we can find a Bible thumper who knows enough to read the service?"

McConnell was not the man to remain astonished for long. "Emily," he asked, "are you really prepared to be abducted?"

"Don't ask me questions," she said succinctly. "Answer his."

"So be it." Tom frowned thoughtfully while lighting his cigar. "Let's see, Daunt. There's only one preacher in town, and he must have ordained himself, though I can conceive of many laying hands on him. We might be able to round up another sin chaser or so, but they don't officiate at weddings, they haunt 'em. By the time one of them got through telling you what a miserable business true wedded bliss is you'd probably throw him out the window and choose unpenalized vice. Now Harry Pace is a magistrate if you don't object to a civil wedding."

I looked at Emily. "I'd prefer that, though it won't be very ceremonious."

"I married once with every flourish known to Christendom," she said quietly, "and it didn't seem to help. I'll chance it once without."

Suddenly I looked and felt blank. "Not expecting you, I didn't bring along what's left of my wardrobe. I haven't any sort of a suit here."

"Oh, yes you have, Colonel," Tom chortled. While I stood lock-jawed in contemplation of that stage-soldier's costume, he launched into an enthusiastic description, adding a sketch of how I'd come by it. "He owes it to his position," he concluded.

For a moment I had the fear that Emily would think I owed it to her, too. At such a time a man is defenseless to a degree, half cowed, serious beyond any hope of holding his own. Had she crowded me I probably would have become sullenly stubborn, but once again she spoke quietly. Touched by a wild look in my eye, she took my arm soothingly as she did so.

"When the time comes he can render unto the Yazoo Invincibles the things that are theirs. I'm marrying him in his civilian capacity, Tom. Just see that he gets his moccasins on the proper feet."

McConnell grinned and shrugged his acknowledgment of defeat. "While we're tending to arrangements you'll have to go some place. We'll take her to Mrs. Bennett. She used to be Mrs. Walters, you know, Daunt, but she went home and got married again last fall. She'll be just the one."

Remembering the indomitable woman whose baby I had once delivered, I brightened. She'd had a kindness for me ever since, and I knew she would do her best for Emily.

"Where's your luggage, honey; is your maid seeing about it?"

"There isn't any maid, Daunt." She was going to say more on the subject, but I wasn't interested then and went in search of her baggage.

When Tom bore her off, promising to see Pace as soon as she was given in charge, I hastened to his cabin. My buckskin hunting shirt had to be scrubbed right away if it was to dry in time for the ceremony that evening. When it was steaming by the fire, I started in to curry myself. By the time I was tubbed the first fruits of Tom's forethought arrived in the form of a darky skilled in barbering. Soon after he had parted me from my beard and two thirds of my hair a fellow named Billy Saunders arrived. I think the thick brush that crowned his burly frame was naturally dark, but it was a point open to debate. At any rate he was Roseville's first blacksmith and a friend of long standing.

"Hello, Billy," I brightened. My own company was both inadequate and a burden to me. "Come in and rest your feet."

"Can't, old hoss," he told me. "I left four mules stompin' and two men cussin' to come here, but I promised Tom McConnell I'd bring you this as quick as it was made."

He held out a charcoaled paw and opened it. Against the sooty background of his palm gleamed the brightest gold ring I'd ever seen. With a whoop I scooped it up. I'd vaguely thought of borrowing one for the ceremony, then sending south for a permanent replacement. To be able to avoid such an awkward arrangement was a boon of price. Delightedly examining the circlet, I saw that, although patently no jeweler's work, it was a neat job of hammering.

"Did you make this?" I asked admiringly.

"Sure," he grinned. "I used to make 'em out of nails for my brats, and it's no more of a trick to make one out of a gold piece. It's about the size of the one Tom brought around, but if it don't fit bring it over to the shop."

I clutched my prize tightly, lest something should somehow happen to it. "Coming to the wedding, Billy?"

His face grew suddenly expressionless. "I'll likely have to work late, but I shouldn't wonder if I turned up sooner or later."

When he'd gone and I'd put the ring away his words came back to me. After turning them over I was sure I knew what he meant, and I pounded my thigh with a clenched fist. For a while I was occupied with planning what I would do, but then I just waited, feeling signally forlorn.

My wedding preparations hadn't taken as much time as I'd counted on. I desperately wanted a drink but knowing I'd have to respond to numerous toasts later I rigorously refrained. I had one cigar to fend off eternity, and when it was gone there was no help for me at all. Betimes I sat until the effort of containing myself wore me out. Alternately I paced the cabin till my muscles were taut and cramped.

Why the deuce did there have to be a ceremony? It must have originated, I reasoned, as a devilish scheme of a celibate clergy to discourage matrimony. There was, and I could see it clearly, no other reason why such a nasty obstacle should be thrown gratuitously in the way of right-minded people. A public ceremony, forsooth, at a time when any criterion of delicacy called for the strictest privacy! A public exchange of vows of such a nature that the two concerned should only dare murmur them even when alone! Society wanted people to marry, and then countenanced this wanton obstructionism. I couldn't understand it.

When I had chewed that bone until it was stale I didn't even have the solace of indignation left. I merely endured because I did not cease to be. Yet all this while my watch was acting suspiciously. There were hours whose full-length acquaintance I had positively made that it simply failed to register.

Eventually Tom arrived. Glad as I was to see him or anybody, I was too far gone to show it. I just hunched by the fire in a state of undress and stared at him with the eyes of dull misery.

"Well," he said, and I begrudged him his cheerfulness, "you step off in just an hour."

"An hour!" I answered, looking at the watch I held clutched in one hand. Either he and the timepiece were in cahoots or I'd been wrong in my calculations after all. "You sure you're not slow?"

"No!" he snorted with brusque heartiness. I glowered. While I'd been holding a dry wake over infinity this fellow had been toasting me at The Merchants Meeting. "I've got to get cleaned up and change now," he chatted. "You all ready?"

"I guess so," I said.

He peered down at the depths I occupied from the heavens of good cheer where he sat enthroned. "Dry as a dromedary," he pronounced.

"I thought I'd better not get started," I muttered.

"You were quite right, but a wise moon only lets the tide ebb so far. Now it's time for the turning. I'll fix you up."

He did so. From somewhere he conjured up that Yazoo rarity, a lemon. With winter-cold well water he fixed me a whiskey sour. Halfway through the cigar he then put in my mouth he gave me another, and I was a whole man again.

"Now get dressed," he ordered.

My hunting shirt wasn't new, but, as such things do, it looked better weathered. I left it unlaced and the linen one of Tom's I wore underneath was displayed in contrasting purity. Discarding my original intention of wearing my linsey-woolsey trousers, I reached for those of my uniform. When worn with the matching coat they were unspeakable, but beneath the leather tails of my hunting shirt they supplied a needed richness of color. Next, searching around, I found a pair of leggings and moccasins I hadn't bothered to take with me when I'd left our joint roof. Indian work they were; I'd bought them from Yancey Shevlin in the months of my green enthusiasm. Tim's mirth at their gaudiness had discouraged me from wearing them much, but now they were just the thing. Tying one of Tom's stocks, I snugged my shirt with my knife belt and picked up my pistol.

It was while I was checking its load that McConnell, who'd been busy with his own preparations, turned to view me. "I wanted you to perk up but not necessarily quite that much. What are you expecting to do with that pistol?"

"Would you go without one tonight?"

"On reflection, no," he acquiesced. "But where are you going to carry it?"

Fumbling around to decide that question myself, I stuck it in my belt. All things considered, I felt good now that I was dressed and eager to get moving.

"You've got the ring?"

He showed it to me and fobbed it again. Then he gave a final touch to my stock.

"Now, for God's sake, don't step in any mud puddles."

But I was cool now that something was at last happening. I don't deny being self-conscious as we approached the court house, but it wasn't a feeling that dampened me. As long as I had to be paraded for everybody else's entertainment I meant to do the best

I could for them and to get as much fun as possible out of it myself. I walked as I dressed, like a woodsman, but with a touch of the soldier and a fillip of barbaric pride. I was taking a mate, which was an occasion for rejoicing, and I was willing to be sunny toward anyone who didn't get in my way.

Most of Roseville and a lot of strays must have been there. When someone cried: "Here's the colonel!" they all turned to appraise me.

"Hi, yi!" some exiled mountaineer sang out. "Give him a log, an' he'll drum like a partridge!"

I don't recall the interim before another shout told of Emily's arrival, so it couldn't have been protracted. The next thing I definitely knew Tom had taken me in tow, and I was watching her come toward me on the arm of Carruthers Blaine. I don't know whether she was beautiful; I never have known. Yet then more than ever her face was what it had always been for me, the one that most reflected all that I asked from salt to tenderness.

She was looking at me, but I could no more read her expression than guess the one I wore for her. She didn't look excited, palely composed rather. I wondered if she was thinking of the time she had kept a similar tryst, perhaps wih higher hopes, surely while she was at an age when good fortune was less suspect. Well, I told myself, maybe the less she expected the better off she'd be. But as my sails flapped in that doldrum she blew me out of it with a sudden smile. Recovered, I drew her arm through my own and turned to confront Harry Pace.

His eyes met mine, and that moment meant more than any of the rest of the ceremony. His face was expressionless, but I knew that for a perceptive instant our minds were of one impulse. Once when it had been to me as a foreign land he had spoken to me of Mississippi. Through urging me to seek out the man at my right he had started the train of circumstances that led deviously to this climax.

Yet there was more to it than that. Whatever else had happened to me or was likely to happen I had committed myself to the country. This wedding to a daughter of the state was only another manifestation of an already established union with the land. It showed a basic faith in the upper valley and in myself as a citizen of it that was something new. Many a man had been driven to the New Purchase by matrimony and the burden it put upon him that he was elsewhere unable to shoulder. Especially of late, some investors had brought their wives along with other evidences of prosperity. I, however, had come there with no responsibilities, and now I was founding a home. The health of the district lay in it.

Viewed thus, the rite was a matter of public interest after all. As far as Pace was concerned it was the only part that mattered.

"You all have come to hear these two tell you they aim to get married," he announced. "I'm listenin' on behalf of the state. I, then, have the authority to say they are married, and that's all I'm goin' to say. Accordin' to regulations I could read to 'em and jaw 'em, or ask 'em questions. But those are questions they've answered to each other—and won't know for a while whether they've told the truth or not. Speakin' for the State of Mississippi, as a citizen of this community, and as a friend, I hope they have."

He looked at me. "Talk up, Daunt. Give your whole name and tell us what you got in mind."

After it was over the cheering audience stood waiting to engulf us as we walked out. That, however, was a contingency to which I'd given thought, and I whisked Emily past Magistrate Pace on the dead run for one of the windows behind him. Before anybody had grasped what we were about we were safe outside and had skipped to haven in Harry's house, there to await refreshment and the company of chosen intimates. For a minute then we were alone to delight in each other.

Emily was as pleased about our evasion as I had been keen to accomplish it. She was still laughing excitedly when I released her, looking as she had done but one other time in my experience, that day on the raft.

"The last time I was married I didn't get thrown out the window. Maybe that was what was wrong."

"You did well for a novice," I chuckled. "If you always jump that quickly when I tell you to we'll get along fine."

"I won't," she promised, "but this time you took me by surprise. You'd been looking so nervous I didn't think you had any presence of mind left."

"Nervous?" This was my first intimation that I had looked anything but coolly self-contained. "Well, anyhow, I had my eye on that window the whole time Harry was talking. It's something you learn in the New Purchase."

The caution I'd learned along what old Artenay called the wild Yazoo promptly stood me in further good stead. Perceiving that it was the earnest intent of the men assembled to get me drunk, I was armed against them. Two factors abetted me. One was that most of them had a very handsome start on me. The other was the natural law that the man who doesn't want to succumb stays free of the influence far more than the one who is giving himself to the occasion. Perforce I drank a great deal, but courtesy does not bid a man to take a drink not of his own choosing. Fending off the loaded punches and cocktails with which they were anxious to trap me, I stuck to straight whiskey and branch water. In the end I was able to slip off with Emily, leaving a group that were enjoying themselves far too much to miss us.

McConnell, true to his role of best man, had stayed loyal to us throughout. Now he led us to a pair of waiting horses.

"You know where the Bennett house is, Daunt. Right out September, on the edge of town. They've already cleared out for you, and the door's on latch. And here's a handful of what you wanted."

The Bennett cabin was neat and cozy, but I was sure we weren't out of the woods yet. My head was singing, but while Emily gaily inspected the premises I tried to listen. In the meantime I was wandering around, too, but not to admire Mrs. Bennett's taste in *décor*. I'd remembered that Carruthers Blaine, who lived with them, owned a fowling piece, and I finally located it. My pistol would have served in a pinch, but this was much better.

Emily returned from her tour of the bedroom to find why I hadn't accompanied her. "What are you doing with sand in your pocket, and why are you pouring it in that gun?"

"It isn't sand, it's small shot." I wadded the gun and opened the door. My ears were still singing so I couldn't be sure. "Do you hear anything, honey?"

She thought I was whimsically drunk. "I hear horses," she said placatingly, "but never mind——"

The only effect of the liquor on my brain was that I was so intent on my own thoughts I could make no allowance for anybody else's. I thrust the weapon into her hands.

"Take this while I catch that bear rug up from the floor."

She accepted the weapon hastily, as if glad to get it away from me. By now she half believed I was worse than drunk. "Daunt," she sought to test this fear, "have you gone crazy?"

"It's a shivaree!" I said urgently. "They're coming to haze us!"

"Who is?"

"Anybody who feels like getting in on it. I've heard them tell about such frontier stunts, and we're the first couple to get married hereabouts. I was sure they wouldn't pass us up."

Relieved as to my state of mind, Emily looked self-possessed again. "I've heard of it myself, come to think of it; but it's all in fun, isn't it?"

"That's the idea—all the fun for them and none for us. But I'll teach 'em to let snapping turtles alone." I rolled up the bear rug, talking mostly to myself, more interested in effect than fact. "They ought to know better than to try snipe hunting with me. I killed meat along this river while those farmers were still following mules around a Carolina corn patch."

My bride watched me dump the bundle by the door, then lope into the other room to snuff the candle there. "Are we off on our honeymoon now?" she asked with a quietness that at last got to me.

Listening, I made sure I had a few seconds to spare for explanation. "I'm trying to see that our honeymoon doesn't get off to a sour start, darling. I know what I'm doing."

"It would help some if I did, Daunt. In the first place where are we going with those knickknacks you insist on?"

"Just to the edge of the woods, not forty yards away. You see, if we're not in when they arrive——"

"They won't get much fun out of it," she finished, "and will go away quickly, which is what we want. But why are you using the bar then?"

My eyes gleamed. "A flank attack is best carried out if the enemy is already frontally engaged," I quoted. "We're going out the back door," I went on, picking up the bear skin again. "I'll douse the light when you've got the door open."

Once we were outside our harriers seemed very near. I led the way swiftly and unrolled the skin in the deep shadow of the woods.

"Lie down and wrap your cape around you," I directed.

"I reckon I won't mind this kind of marriage once I get used to it," she said. However, she was feeling better when we were stretched out, snuggled together. As our unwanted visitors rode up she squeezed my hand excitedly and giggled under her breath.

Whoever they were, they wanted to be stealthy and had got past the stage of knowing how. They halted to dismount not ten yards from us, very much amused with themselves. We could hear them chuckling and talking in stage whispers, audible as a shout.

"They must just have hit the hay," one said. "Their lights went out while we was only a little ways back."

"Maybe they forgot to bar the door," one suggested. "Let's find out."

"Wouldn't they be surprised to see us?" a third queried.

The possibilities inherent in this contingency were searched out with gusto. I heard Emily gasp, and for a second I regretted the softness that had induced me to load with only small shot. Eventually somebody was delegated to make trial. I could just follow his shadowy figure to the doorway. My head was ceasing to buzz, and I could hear him stumble over something on the way back.

"It's barred, damn it!"

"Thought it would be," someone commented. "The colonel's too old a coon not to climb a tree. Well, let's give it to 'em."

I estimated at least twenty of them as they advanced to the attack, shuffling, stumbling and jostling one another.

"What are they going to do?" Emily whispered.

They answered for me. What seemed like every sound in the catalogue of raucousness hit our ears all at once. Pans were banged, cow bells clanged, a riverman's fog trumpet was blown, guns were fired. Symphonically the shouting began. Men imitated Indians, wildcats and wolves, or just yelled like the drunks on a spree they were. The enraptured lovers they imagined to be within might well have rushed to the window to see what was going on.

That such a startled investigation was expected was clear from the sudden silence that fell. When nothing happened a few self-appointed spokesmen began urging capitulation.

"Come on out, Colonel, and show us the bride."

"There ain't no use lyin' doggo. We ain't goin' away without seein' you."

"If you don't come out to us, we'll bust in to you."

"Let's give it to 'em again," one suggested, "then if they don't come out we'll knock the door down."

The repeat lasted longer than the original but wasn't punctuated by as many shots. I judged that their guns were all fired and that at night in their condition the odds were against any speedy reloading. At the conclusion of their racket they clustered around the door and started banging on it.

Freeing my hand from Emily's, I picked up Blaine's fowling piece. "The counterattack," I quoted didactically, "is best undertaken at the moment the foe is most confident of success."

"Don't miss," she besought me.

There was little chance of that. The virtue of a fowling piece being to scatter, and the target being large, darkness was small hindrance. I had charged the weapon heavily, and it sounded like a small cannon.

Had I shot at a covey of quail I wouldn't have caused any more alarm. The roar of the gun, so much louder than a rifle or a pistol, scattered them as if by its blast. And those nipped by the shot were thrice confounded. Some that were hit fell to the ground, and others dropped to avoid any follow-up fire. Most, however, were bent on finding cover. Being frontiersmen, they didn't say anything after the first affrighted squawks of pain and astonishment, so they wouldn't be singled out.

The lone exception overjoyed me. "Colonel!" he howled. "You've got to let me in! We're bein' bushwhacked!"

The rest of them I couldn't see now that they were hugging the ground or hiding behind trees, but I knew what they were doing. They were squeezing themselves flat and at the same time, drunkenly inept though they were, trying to reload without making a sound. I wasn't afraid of any random shooting. None of them knew where my shot had come from, and each would be afraid that his gun flash would draw counter fire.

It's a poor man that doesn't love his own joke. I nearly strangled holding my laughter back, and did not try to withhold the tears. When the fellow at the door, despairing of my charity, fled with an "Oh, God damn you, Colonel!" I nearly broke control. Emily was having a hard time, too. It was only by kissing her that I secured a respite for either.

"What'll happen now?" she asked at last.

"They'll figure it out in a little while, then they'll go away." I knew they would, too, once the play had been taken away from them.

It took about ten minutes, during which period I decided to pay them no heed. Then a voice was raised, which I recognized as that of the blacksmith who had made our wedding ring.

"Is that you, Daunt?"

I raised my head from its close engagement with Emily's and imitated a catbird derisively. The sound was so brief they couldn't tell just where it came from; at the same time, catbirds not being nocturnal, it told them all they needed to know.

There was a chorus of laughs, sheepish albeit relieved. Then there was an exchange of comments, profane and self-castigating, among themselves. Finally Saunders sang out: "All right, Daunt, you got us whipped. We're going for our hosses."

This time the catbird's note was acquiescent instead of defiant. While I watched they rose up out of the ground or materialized from the darkness beyond, moving toward their mounts. In general they were silent, but there were a few grunted comments.

"The colonel's been there before," one said with grudging admiration.

"Yep," his companion agreed, "we'd ought to've been more careful huntin' an old he-b'ar like that."

When they were almost out of hearing I helped Emily to her feet. In one minute we were inside once more, the back door barred behind us. In another I had turned from relighting the candle and was gazing at her triumphantly. I was mightily pleased with my-self, and she saw I was pleased with her, too, as I had every reason to be. Putting down the gun, she smiled at me indulgently until I held out my arms.

"Honey," I said, still too amused to feel the remorse I tried to put into my voice, "I hope it hasn't been too upsetting."

"No," she said thoughtfully, resting her head against my shoulder, "but I wish I was the kind that kept a diary."

Not being in condition to see what she was driving at then, I nodded cheerfully. "It'd make a dandy entry, but I don't think we'll have any trouble remembering. I know I'll never forget that man hammering on the door and begging me——"

But when I made this move to reawaken my mirth she pounded me on the chest until I stopped. "Now," she said when I was silent, "you seem to know everything in advance, he-b'ar. Is that all that's going to happen?"

"Yes," I declared confidently. Then I looked at her again. "No, I'm wrong, honey. That isn't all."

CHAPTER XXXII

As HECTIC AS THAT NIGHT had been it was half the honeymoon the frontier could spare us. The Bennetts had to have their cabin back, and I had to give Williams his already overdue relief. After our late breakfast I purchased a horse for Emily with the money I'd won on Tim's racing ability, and by early afternoon we were on our way to Council Lodge.

It wasn't till then, so engrossed had we been in the pleasanter side of life, that she reopened the subject of how she had fared at Natchez. "Charles left me absolutely everything, including more debts than the value of the estate. I left my maid behind, and we'll have to sell the rest of the slaves, too, Daunt."

That would be a bankrupting blow at this juncture. "We won't sell them," I said after a minute. "Anybody that's anxious about paying the debts can attend to that, and they'll have to come up here to get them, too."

I had reined in, and she halted her own mount. "I know it's bad, but there's so much legal business to unravel we'll have a little time. We'll get the crops planted anyhow."

"There's no use planting a crop we can't harvest." I stared ahead gloomily, trying to recover from the shock of the news enough to begin figuring out a cure.

"I've been working at it ever since the lawyer told me," she said. "There are people that rent slaves, Daunt."

"Yes, that's so." I welcomed the suggestion as offering a thin slit for hope, but I wasn't glad about it. Men who made a living by farming out slaves usually ran them into the ground by poor keeping and overwork. Still it might be possible to worry through the season with such sullen, dispirited labor—if we could find it.

Recalling that this was our season for carefree merriment, I succeeded in smiling at her. "Well, we'll do something about it. Just now I think you're right that the only thing for us to do is to get as much possible accomplished with the hands we have before they're taken away."

The night we spent in the forest was the other half of our honeymoon. After we'd eaten we leaned against a rest I'd fashioned of poles and a blanket and watched the flames, just happy to be together. In that hour of quiescent enchantment coming problems seemed easily surmounted, and past troubles had no claims against us. Reality as affecting us didn't extend beyond the aureole of the firelight—and at that we could probably see into the future as far and as clearly as anybody else. Then later under the trees we loved well and slept soundly. It was a fine night to have just behind us when we rose to face what we must.

It was then I told Emily something I had meant to the day before. However, her information about the slaves had seemed to be enough bad news for one day.

"I've turned your old cabin over to a couple of the hands," I began. "I took out everything that was in it and put it in your covered wagon."

"Good," she approved. "I didn't want to go back there any more than you wanted me to. Where did you build the new cabin—up on the little bluff?"

I grimaced. "I never got around to building one, honey. There was so much to do, and I didn't know you were coming so soon, you see."

She gulped, but hardship was no novelty to her, and she gave no other sign of disappointment. "Don't worry about it, Daunt; we'll get along all right."

We did after a fashion, but the heavy rain that started that morning didn't make it easy at the outset. The lean-to in which I had slept during the winter hadn't seemed an unpleasant place to bivouac, but it surely looked dismal that watery afternoon of our arrival. We were soaked, our paraphernalia was soaked, the woodpile was dripping, and there was a small puddle in the open fireplace before the shanty.

I looked the premises over carefully, seeing them as my bride must see them. If there was anything to be said in their favor I couldn't think of it. Finally I squished the water first in one moccasin then in another and looked at Emily appealingly.

"Well, we're home, honey."

A wet branch drifted down to alight on her shoulders, entangling itself in a lock of hair that had escaped from her wimple. No doubt it was cold and clammy. She disengaged herself from it as if defending herself from a giant insect.

"If you can decide what part's the threshhold, carry me across and give me a drink."

I hadn't known her to take anything except punch before, but she handled the stiff whiskey and water I gave her with mastery. She had need of it. By cutting into the heart of the logs I found dry wood. Yet the fire burned fitfully, supper was a soggy mess, our clothes dried insufficiently and the blankets far less. This night was not the luxurious campfire by which we had dreamed the night before; this night was the cold, endless darkness beyond it.

That whole tag end of winter and beginning of spring was rough. I drove my astonished darkies, not by any means beyond their capacities, but well beyond the limited opinion they held of their own capacities. I think they might have balked if they hadn't chosen to become superstitious about my sudden fury of energy. For above all I drove myself, working for hours after I'd released them to rest.

We moved into the covered wagon, although that was the full extent of our domestic progress. As far as that's concerned, even if she'd got a cabin Emily didn't have too much time to be in one. When not busy with her domestic chores she was out with the rifle or the fowling piece, acquiring a proficiency many frontier women already had. We had to have some alternative to corn meal, sweet potatoes and salt pork; and fresh meat, fowl and fish were the only things procurable. If Emily was a novice at stalking and found my guns heavy, she had the patience to wait fatefully by the water run or the artificial salt lick. She also attended to trotlines and snares. Except for bringing in and butchering the occasional deer I could afford to give her no help.

By spring we'd quintupled the cleared land and made more

available for planting by ringing trees. All the time I had been working, as it were, looking over my shoulder. Plant as I would it would be in vain if the darkies were taken from me now. I had to be able to chop and hoe the cotton a couple of times, so the crop wouldn't be smothered in its own luxuriance of growth or killed off by competing weeds. If I could get that far I would have a breathing spell that might give me time enough to find more field hands.

The first chopping was accomplished in good order, and the cotton grew swiftly from the spontaneous soil. Some days later two men rode up to where I was making an inspection of my fields. One was just a young lout, but the other belonged so obviously to officialdom that I groaned. His heavy red face was good looking enough; but not liking his errand I wasn't much taken with him and greeted him noncommittally.

"I'm Vincent Long, deputy from Adams County," he pompously announced. "I've got a writ of attachment for six niggers belongin' to Charles Philips."

Because he was so patently watching to see me wince I looked blank. "Why don't you see Charles Philips about it, then?"

That threw him off balance. "Why, he's deceased!"

"Well, arrest him then," I suggested. "Don't tell me your troubles, mister."

He put his hands on his hips. "Don't you know what deceased means? It means he's kicked the—" I must have overdone my look of polite interest because he broke off. "Oh, shucks—you knew that."

Now that he had come down from his throne I wanted to be on better terms with him. "Have a drink," I said by way of making a new beginning.

Instead of being mollified he stiffened his face. "I don't never drink, thank the Lord."

I didn't believe the Lord would give him a "you're welcome" for that thanks, but I didn't say so. Although considerably discouraged, I kept on trying.

"You've come for the darkies, eh? I can let you have them in a few days."

"I'm taking them now," he said flatly.

Without directly arguing I turned to show him my fields. "Those six are the only hands I've got now. If you're an Adams County man you know what cotton is. We'll have to chop again soon."

Cotton being an unfailing source of interest to Mississippians he examined my crop. "You'd ought to chop in two-three days," he admitted.

"Well, let me keep them just long enough to do that and then take them. You'll likely have to wait around for a boat when you get back to Roseville as it is."

"I will," he declared, "but I'd rather wait in Roseville."

"Well, I'll bring 'em to you down there," I said, growing desperate. "Or if you decide to wait around here I'll show you some prime hunting."

"I wouldn't trust you to bring 'em," he retorted. "Anyhow there's going to be a revival meetin' in Roseville, and I don't hunt nothin' but men."

Realizing that I had no more points of communication with him than I did with a Choctaw, I desisted. Smoldering, I watched him and his helper round up my frightened hands and, without giving them time to get such belongings as they possessed, herd them away. Just as they were leaving Long took it upon himself to give me a final prodding.

"Next time don't get funny when the law comes around. It don't go in these parts."

It was only when he'd ridden on that I bared my teeth in an angry grin. Need in straits had given me inspiration while he had been busy.

"Now," I muttered, to the trees if they cared to listen, "I'll show that teetotaling, revival-meeting slug from the slick side of civilization just what does go in the backwoods."

Leaving a note for Emily, who was off turkey hunting, I trotted down to the river and launched my pirogue. Going by canoe I wouldn't have to pass Long, and, riding with the current, I'd make better time than I would on a horse anyhow.

A few weeks earlier Tim had dropped by to consult me about farming. As he had then expressed his intention of spending most of the summer clearing his land I was reasonably sure he'd be there, and such was the case. He listened to what I had to say, then chuckled.

"If I know niggers they're not goin' to push 'em very fast on foot. They'll spend a couple of nights on the trace anyways. Now we can wait back of my place till they pass, or likely enough we can go north tonight and run smack into 'em."

Adopting the latter course, we reached the trace before dark and made sure that our quarry hadn't passed. Long, as we had suspected, didn't have sense enough to camp away from the path; and in an hour or so we stole to the edge of his campfire. Basking in the great blaze was the deputy himself, sound asleep, his assistant, drowsily on guard, and my six slumbering hands.

The guard was astonished to find Tim's hand closing on his throat. The deputy was no less amazed to find me kneeling on his back. We blindfolded them and tied their hands, though of course they'd be able to free each other in short order. In the meantime we and the darkies had vanished into the night.

It was the next day but one, while my hands were busy in the fields, that a group of men rode up to where Tim and I stood. Six of them were neighbors, which is to say they lived within twenty miles of me. With them were the deputy from Adams County and his assistant.

A planter called Marshall was spokesman for the party, a fact that pleased me. I had treated his son for the ague the year before, and as the boy happened to be one of my patients who lived Marshall thought highly of me and my abilities.

"Colonel," he said, when we'd exchanged amenities, "we've got a ticklish problem."

"I reckon we all have our troubles," I said piously, "but if there's anything I can do to help, let me know."

"This man here," Marshall said, pointing to Long, "claims he got some hands from you on a writ and that night they were stolen. And—well, what tracks we could find headed this way. Have you seen anything of 'em?"

The deputy meanwhile had been peering at my hands. "Them's the same niggers he's got right here!" he shouted. "He's the one that stole 'em! Help me arrest him!"

"You'd better be careful who you accuse around here," the planter told him sharply. Then he turned to me again, obviously embarrassed. "I'm sure it's all right, Colonel, but we'd like to hear your side of it. He's asked us as a law officer to help him, you know."

"Well," I said, "I can't say I like the way he talks, but if he's got a writ of attachment for any hands of mine, of course he can have 'em."

That touched off Long's fuse. "I had a writ, but you stole that, too, damn you!"

Marshall swung to face him. "One more speech like that and you can hunt your niggers yourself. Now have you got a writ?"

"No," the deputy admitted, "but——"

"Did you see Colonel Godolphin take it?"

"No, he sneaked up on me and——"

"How do you know it was he?" the planter demanded.

"It's bound to be him!" Long cried. "Why just two days ago me and my man was here, and there's two of our words to his one."

"What day did you say you was here?" Tim asked stolidly.

"The day before yesterday."

"Well, the day before yesterday," Durham said to Marshall, "Colonel Godolphin was on my plantation way down river from here."

We all looked at each other for a minute. It was the planter who came to a decision first.

"Whatever's going on I wish I'd never got in it. Colonel, I'm sorry to have bothered you. You and Mrs. Godolphin drop in on us some day right soon, do you hear?"

By the time his posse had taken itself off the deputy had come to a decision, too. "Colonel, can I speak to you aside for a minute?"

"I can't take those niggers without a writ," he admitted, when we stood alone, "but I didn't figure from the way you acted t'other day that you didn't aim to let me have 'em at all."

I didn't commit myself, and after a pause he went on talking. "I could go get me another writ at Natchez, but it'd take a long while, and I'd hate to have to admit I'd got beat out of that first one. Now suppose I waited around till you got your cotton chopped?"

"You go on to that revival," I suggested, "and by the time your soul's all nice and shiny again, which ought to take a few days, come on back and the darkies are yours."

By the time a less aggressive deputy from Adams County had slipped down stream—I'd stipulated that they go by raft so that the darkies could take their belongings—my cotton was a promising crop. I would never have believed before coming to the frontier that anything could grow so vigorously. It was sturdy with broad leaves which cut off the sun from the ground below. Therefore, it should win out in any competition with weeds for some time to come.

This was the breathing spell for which I had fought. If I could find some hands reasonably soon I'd save myself from bankruptcy. I hated to leave Emily there alone, but it couldn't be helped. At that she was no worse off than many another frontier woman, nor, indeed, than she herself had often been while married to Philips. And, of course, I left Talisman behind with her, the first time I had traveled without him since the day her uncle had given him to me.

Sometimes, as in the case of my loss of slaves, disaster crowns a logical sequence of events. At others it's just suddenly there like a hole in the pocket. The night of my arrival in Roseville I was discussing my problem with Harry Pace when Williams, the man who acted in my stead while the Yazoo Invincibles were being formed, burst in upon us. He was dishevelled, worn out and winded, but his message didn't take much breath.

"Tom McConnell's dead!"

As Harry's eyes met mine in a misery of recognition I knew that he also was thinking that he'd lost his best friend. Then we turned to Williams.

"What did he die of?" he demanded, and again I was sure his thoughts were my own. Neither of us considered a natural cause. Moaning, Williams slumped down into the chair I'd vacated.

"Bullets, but I don't know who fired 'em."

"Well, tell us what you do know," I said harshly.

"We was ridin' up the valley—Tom had had to see a couple of clients down near the Old Purchase border—and was goin' to spend the night on the Stebbins plantation, about ten miles down river

from here, you know. When we got near there we heard a lot of rough shoutin' that didn't sound right, and Tom rode on ahead to find out what the hell. Just as I got to the edge of the clearin' I heard shots and saw Tom fall. It was most dark then, but I could see maybe a couple of dozen men. They kept shootin' at Tom even after he'd dropped, so I was sure he was a goner. I knew I couldn't buck that crowd, and they hadn't seen me yet, so I hightailed."

"How long ago was that?" Pace asked.

"About two hours. I could've made it faster, but I done one thing on the way. There's a pretty good woodsman that belongs to the Invincibles down the line. I told him to get on the trail and find out where the polecats was headed for."

"Good work," I commended him. "Go around to all the taverns and pass the word that the regiment starts mustering at dawn. Have riders go around to the plantations, too."

When he had left us Harry groaned. "The way Williams said it happened, it sounds like somebody recognized him. Who the devil could have done it, Daunt?"

Whether I was right or wrong I hadn't had any doubts from the instant Williams began talking. I told Harry about Alexander Pope Cummins.

"Well, we always knew we'd have to tangle with that Turkey Run bunch; and Tom knew it better than any of us." Harry ran a hand through his hair. "But we can't go shootin' up a town just because we suspect some that live there, names and faces mostly unknown. All you know for sure about this Cummins even is that he had it in for Tom."

I was just remembering why I left Council Lodge and how important it was for me to hurry. "It's hard to see what we can do," I agreed, struggling with temptation. Tom was dead, and I couldn't help him; but Emily was alive and expected me to be on my way to find field hands. If I spent much time chasing marauders I might as well count that year's cotton lost. In the next few minutes, while Harry was deep in his own thoughts, I tried to hide out from my responsibility behind the argument that it would be useless to follow when the outlaws had so much of a start. When that failed

to give me sufficient cover I made a sweeping gesture, as if clearing the way for fate to take its course.

"Harry," I said, "I turned over my maps to you. Have you got them handy?"

I spent the next hour or so poring over my old sketches and notes, in an effort to call to mind the terrain between Roseville and Turkey Run. Thus I found I could piece together a fair representation of the valley on the south bank, where lay most of the settlements and plantations. Along the generally swampy northern bank I had fared but once. That was the time I lost Goober—and Cummins, I was sure, had been my chief opponent then also. As the sketches showed me nothing else suggesting a course of procedure I thought of that sorry adventure more and more. That had been over a year and a half ago, and because horsethieves had used the cabin and the trail leading to it then was no guarantee they did so still. Yet if they did, it was one definite point where they might with patience be isolated and identified.

I smoked cigars till my tongue was burnt trying to make up my mind whether it was worth while to order such a course. At a crisis when prompt action was so desirable, I hated to be responsible for surrounding a disused shanty on a long-forgotten path I might have the devil's own time finding.

While Pace and I were breakfasting the next morning the scout whom Williams had set on the track of the raiders came in to make his report. After returning his sheepish salute I did away with the military formalities that might have tied his tongue.

"Thompson, how are you? Get the dust out of your throat and let's hear what you found out." Looking relieved, he refreshed himself and sat down. "Were you able to follow them at all?" I prompted.

" 'T wasn't any trick, Colonel. I started for the Stebbins place when I heard shots from over at Brown's. That's the next plantation. By the time I got there Brown's cabin was burning, and the varmints who'd set fire to it was just ridin' off with all the slaves and hosses."

"What about Brown himself?" Pace asked.

Thompson shook his head. "I didn't see him or none of his folks. I reckon they was all in the cabin, dead. Anyhow 't wasn't any trick to tail after 'em, though I only done it for a ways like Williams told me to."

"You did just right." In my eagerness I leaned forward. "Were they headed for the river?"

"Nope, they was headed the other way." The woodsman got his bearings and demonstrated with a hand. "They was slantin' toward the high hills."

That was a disappointment, undermining as it did my only hypothesis, but I refused to surrender it. From the fact the outlaws struck right into the middle of our territory and weren't heard of below there, we had known that they cut into it from the hills or the river. But for them to go and come by way of the hills—at least all the way—didn't make sense.

"Harry," I said, "in the open woods up on those ridges a party like that would leave a trail like the Natchez Trace. You know damn well they aren't going to make a road for us that we can follow right into Turkey Run or wherever it is they hide the slaves until they can arrange to get 'em out of the country."

"Sellin' stolen niggers is a tricky, dangerous business," he agreed. "They sure ain't doin' it where anybody can look at 'em."

"Now the north bank—I know because I've been there—offers them everything this one doesn't. Along most of it there's no chance of them meeting any witnesses, even dogs couldn't track them, and they could hide till bears grow bushy tails." Unfolding a sketch of the valley I located the raided plantations and started running my finger obliquely to the Yazoo. "Suppose they hit for the ridges to keep clear of the valley settlements and followed a long slant like this to where there didn't happen to be any plantations to speak of." Bemused, I was mumbling to myself as I completed the imaginary course. "It's possible."

"Don't just say words," Harry said impatiently. "Talk."

Nudging a bit of ash that had fallen from my cigar, I left it at a roughly hazarded point on the map. "Do you remember when my horse, Goober, was stolen?"

"I remember somethin' about it, Daunt. Do you think that was the same gang?"

"Yes. Of course, that was a long time ago, but if it is the same crew they may be still using the cabin I mentioned. I got the impression that it was a regular stopping point on a regular route."

Pace, who'd been tilted back, let his chair legs hit the ground. Looking at my sketch, he indicated the cigar ash. "Is that the cabin?"

"Around there is all I can say. I didn't have my bearings and can only place it in a guess relation to where I came out. There's a hell of a swamp all around there, but they had a way through it. It might not be the same bunch of thieves at all. It might take weeks to locate the cabin, though I think I can do better."

"On the other hand it's the only place we know of where we have a chance of treeing some of these bastards." Harry leaned back again, spat in the fireplace and regarded me quizzically. "Well, what're you goin' to do, Colonel?"

Agreeing with him that further discussion was pointless, I belted in my hunting shirt and picked up my pistol. "We can't overlook the part of the route we know they took. Wait till the men start coming in from the plantations, take Thompson here, and follow them as far as you can. If you lose them, bring your command to the river opposite the cigar ash here and wait for me. If their trail leads to the river again wait for me where they crossed. I'm going to take some of the men already mustered, and head straight down the valley. With luck we'll find where they crossed; otherwise I'll try to find that cabin."

CHAPTER XXXIII

BECAUSE OF THE DEEP canebrake we had to traverse we left our horses at the river. But aside from the hard business of pushing through the cane and crossing the swamp beyond, we found the trail I was looking for without difficulty the next day. This was a pleasant surprise and the last of that nature for a while.

Not being sure whether the cabin was up or down valley from the point where we cut into the trail, I cast both ways before I located where it had stood. It was burnt to the ground. Preconception is such an insidious thing that for a moment I was baffled and hopeless. Having fixed my mind upon the cabin I felt that the trail unconnected with the cabin had no significance. It required a little time and an effort of will for me to realize that the burnt shanty was neither more nor less than that. On the other hand the trail was obviously still in use, and it was difficult to see that either business or pleasure would lead honest men to beat a path through such villainous country.

The sergeant in direct charge of my little command was Saunders, the blacksmith. "Billy," I said, as we held consultation apart, "we're probably too late to head off the gang we're gunning for, but if we run this trail out from end to end maybe we'll know how to stop 'em from hitting us again. It may take a few days, of course."

"Don't worry about that, Daunt," Saunders said. "The boys figure you know what you're doin'."

For this blind faith I believe I had my honeymoon to thank. Willing though they were to follow me on the parade ground I don't think these backwoodsmen would have been so amenable to my leadership in the forest if I hadn't once shown my mastery of their own brand of tactics.

I nodded acceptance of this vote of confidence. "We'll head up the valley, and it's just possible we'll run into 'em."

There were no fresh tracks on the path, and it was near sundown before we encountered any. The horses had been coming our way, but at this point they turned north up a branch trail. I turned to a man called Price, whom I had picked for his reputed ability as a tracker.

"Is this the bunch we're after?"

He coursed back and forth a little ways as a hound might do. "There ain't as many of 'em as you said there'd ought to be, Colonel; but them tracks ain't been made more'n two hours ago."

In a way it was discouraging. If the outlaws had a maze of trails through here it would complicate our problem immeasurably. But this was a live scent, and I couldn't pass it up.

For hours we got nothing out of it but exercise. The sun had already set as far as we among the trees were concerned when Price, from his forward position, signaled us to halt. "I heard hosses, Colonel," he reported when I joined him.

"Moving?"

"Nope. Just talkin' to each other the way the critters do come dusk."

"Find out if there's a watch on the trail," I ordered.

But when he returned to tell me that a guard was indeed posted I was silent for a while. I didn't know who were encamped just ahead of us; nor had I positive knowledge of their business. All I had to go on was their presence athwart a trail at one time used by murderers and thieves. I was a militiaman acting without specific authority. If I proved wrong the offense would be as little pardonable to myself as to the state.

At length I raised my head, and the gesture was a man's death warrant. "Get that guard out of the way, Price. You can have a helper if you want it."

"I don't need no help," he asserted and stole back down the heavily shadowed trail.

A slim, quiet Kentuckian, Price was older than the rest of us. I didn't know much about him except that he made a living of sorts by locating and rifling bee trees. His knowledge of this art, as well as his superior qualities as a woodsman, were said to stem from the fact that he had lived much with Indians in his youth. I was inclined to believe this when, a half hour later, he dropped something in front of me and squatted to cut himself a plug. When he didn't speak I stooped to examine the thing he'd brought with him. In the poor light I could just see it against the ground, but my fingers were more discerning. No doubt it was perfectly normal human hair, but it felt horrible.

"Good Christ!" I whispered, "what the hell did you scalp him for?"

"Take it easy, Colonel," he retorted equably. "You didn't hear him squeal, did you?"

"No," I snorted, "but——"

"Well, if a man don't sing out when you take his scalp he ain't goin' to holler at you just for walkin' by him. That's what you wanted, wasn't it?"

When you've ordered a man's death, as I had, it's silly to worry about what becomes of his hair. "Well, anyhow," I said, "that was good work, Price."

The path thus left free for our unchallenged passage was in effect a tenuous causeway between two large pools. Beyond these it penetrated a wall of cane. Winding through this for about fifty yards we peered out at a meadow where there was still enough light to permit close examination. On the foundations of this firmer ground there were no less than four cabins. Several horses were grazing; but there was no sign of cultivation, and I gave a sigh of satisfaction. Whether we had run down our own direct enemies or not here was somebody's hideaway. This swamp island was no fastness of innocence.

Smoke was coming out of two of the cabins but men were in evidence near only one. I counted eight of them, but as the twilight grew dim seven of them went inside. The one who remained was evidently a guard, and I exchanged glances with Billy Saunders.

"They must have niggers in that other shanty," he whispered.

Having observed that the windows of the outlaw's cabin were covered with oil paper I wondered why the men went indoors so early. Oil paper was a common makeshift in a region where not many people had glass, but on a sticky summer night like this the interior would be suffocating.

Very shortly I ceased to wonder. First there were only a few mosquitoes, then there were hordes of them, and they all liked us. Only the fatalistic acceptance of misery that the frontier makes a condition of survival enabled us to stay where we were. Worst of all we could not even slap at our torturers because of the nearness of the man on guard.

I also ceased to wonder why our foes thought it necessary to have a fire in their shack. The night that had been sticky soon became clammy, and by the time it was fully dark I was shivering.

"Billy," I growled, "tell Price to take that guard, so we can get inside before we're all eaten up and have the ague."

A camp shorn of its night security is relatively easy to seize. As they presumably took turns being mosquito bait I didn't think the cabin door would be barred, and Price had found out that I was right. Hearing no restless tossing, we simply crept in. Saunders built up the fire, and when we could see well we took over at gun point.

Having done so well, I thereupon acted the fool. We were all worn out, and I let rest be the order. I did, indeed, post a guard by the cabin which held our prisoners now as well as the slaves they had stolen, but as it seemed unreasonable that we would be attacked during the remainder of the short summer night I didn't put a man down past the canebrake. The probabilities were all in my favor; but I should have had my head taken off and almost did.

Knowing that everyone else needed his sleep as badly as I did, I took the early dawn watch myself. I didn't sleep on post, but such of my mind as the mosquitoes left free for thinking was on the future rather than the present. I thought of how I would question our prisoners after breakfast; I put the answers in their mouths; I went further than that and planned how I'd act on the information they gave. I was so engrossed that several of the grazing horses whickered before I paid any attention. Then I heard an answer from only a short distance down the trail.

Cursing the carelessness that might have trapped us, I hazed my groggy men out of the cabin and led the way to the shelter of the cane not far from the trail. When the enemy passed by us a couple of minutes later we closed in on the trail behind them. We now had a line of retreat, and I stopped sweating.

At that point I discovered that instinct boosted by folly had done for me all that genius could have done. In brief, we weren't only occupying a secure defensive position but an ambush. Perhaps the fact they had encountered no sentinel had made the newcomers wary. At any rate they were advancing cautiously. Had they not done so we might not have had time to get ready for them, belly down in the narrow intervals between clumps of giant cane.

Seeing no one and drawing no fire, they bunched together as if holding council. We could have picked some of them off as they loomed against the dim horizon, but I waited. Finally they dismounted and went forward, leaving the group of foot-weary darkies they'd been herding behind with the horses. Smoke still came from the chimney of the cabin we'd been using, and it was natural that they should go to that building for clues as to what was going on. I think most people would have reasoned so, though some commanders wouldn't have permitted a mass investigation. In the absence of any such prevention the consuming curiosity of the West drove them all to see for themselves.

In a minute they were clustered around the door, starting to filter through it. The light wasn't good enough for drawing a fine bead, but one wasn't necessary for such a target.

"Now!" I whispered.

Several outlaws dropped at our volley, but that was only a secondary result. The cabin offered the cover they wanted, and they took it in a rush, jamming through the door one behind the other. It was like scatting mice into a trap.

We could have had that shelter and had fled it in panic. The cabin would ward off bullets, true, but it was no blockhouse with loopholes for the guns of the defenders. After the usual design of such buildings there were only two windows, both in front, bunks and the fireplace occupying the other three walls. There'd be a heavy blood tax for leaving the door they'd entered so eagerly.

Of the five men we'd dropped one rallied enough to make for

the cabin. He didn't reach it. I thought there might be an answering volley from the windows, but the oiled paper remained in place. No doubt they saw that the advantage of such an exchange would be all with us, as a window is a far more specific target than a section of a canebrake.

I had them boxed but didn't yet have a scheme for putting the lid on, and for a little I couldn't get my mind down to it. It was much easier, for instance, to speculate as to the identity of the newcomers. In numbers they matched the party which had murdered Tom, although I had thought that group had left us well behind. Still the contrary was possible. Maybe they'd been delayed by the need to rest the slaves they were driving in this difficult country. Or perhaps, not finding themselves pressed, they had made more raids near the point where they'd crossed the river.

Annoyed at the way I was wasting time, I tried to pin my brain down to work again. Whoever they were, their leader presumably saw his dilemma by then and was launched in the race to outthink me. His greatest handicap was that he didn't know how many men were opposing him. On the other hand he might know of factors which were hidden from me.

He certainly held some advantages. Of these the most conspicuous pertained to physical comfort. His men were in a dry cabin while mine were wallowing in mud and water amongst the cane. In the early morning such an amphibious situation was chilly, while they were blessed with a fire. We'd abandoned our rations in our haste, and they couldn't be so deep in council that they wouldn't solace themselves with breakfast after an all-night journey. In fact, the heavy smoke now coming from the chimney indicated they'd stoked up the fire for just such a purpose.

Hungrily watching that smoke, I gave over trying to think of anything except how much I'd enjoy a hot breakfast. And in that moment of idling, the brain I'd been vainly squeezing yielded a thought as casually as a tree drops a nut. If someone were suddenly to cap that chimney, so my brain hypothesized and found the fancy pleasing, wouldn't the inmates find it unpleasant?

Wouldn't they though! And by that time I was really thinking. As most frontier fireplaces are made from clay and by amateurs most cabins are smoky. The one I was looking at was no exception. My eyes had smarted while in it the night before, although most of the smoke had been wafted up the passage designed for it. What if all of it was forced back into that ill-ventilated shanty?

"Billy," I said to my sergeant, to see how my idea struck him, "what do you reckon would happen if a hunting shirt was tied over that smoke hole?"

He looked at me as if I was crazy, then his eyes widened. As a blacksmith he thought constantly in terms of fires and was familiar with them in all their workings.

"With them windows papered over that way? Why, Daunt, before they could get it out they couldn't see free drinks in a Methodist hell. Do you want me to try it?"

"No," I lied. I wanted anybody to try it except myself. However, I'd thought of the idea and I couldn't convince myself that anybody else's neck was of less value to him than was mine to me. "I want you to stay here with most of the men, Billy, and cut 'em down if they try to make a break through that door. Send a few around to where they can watch the other sides of the cabin though so they can nail anybody who tries to dig out under the base logs. Then if I get that chimney blocked I don't have to tell you what to do."

I took but one man with me, an agile, broad-backed youngster named Boyd, who didn't seem to mind getting shot at. Our preparations consisted of getting into a favorable position by circling through the swamp and cane a few hundred yards to the eastern side of the clearing. Sunrise was imminent, and the low sun striking into the eyes of anyone peering out from chinks between the logs would be an invaluable ally. For nearly half an hour I fidgeted nervously, twisting the length of vine I'd cut myself until the first beam struck the base of the cabin. By the time I got my shirt off the sun was blanketing the whole eastern wall.

"Come on!" I said, starting to sprint.

Two shots were fired at us as we drew near, but a space between the logs isn't a port that permits sighting. At that we couldn't have been very alarming to them. We were without rifles nor did we carry anything that looked dangerous. We reached the nearest corner of the shanty with Boyd a stride in front. He had just time to bend and brace himself when I landed on his back. My eye found a niche while I was in the air, and my foot was in it by the time I'd gripped the overhang of the roof. Flinging the shirt ahead of me, I gave a spring, got a handhold higher up and wrenched myself aloft.

"Boyd, skedaddle!" I barked, as I scrambled toward the chimney.

Although uncertain of what I was up to, the inmates of the cabin weren't for it.

"That shirtless hoss is on the roof," I heard one announce.

"Well, he didn't have nothin' to start a fire with."

"Let's get him off there anyhow," a third urged.

I had my shirt over the chimney before the first bullet broke through the roof. It was the herald of a fusillade. A ball ploughed along my calf and another lodged in my shoulder, nearly knocking me off. To save myself I hugged the chimney, brushing the shirt partly out of position in the act, and got a taste of my own medicine. Blind and choking, I had to work the shirt into place again by touch.

"That must have got him!" an outlaw said.

"Maybe so," a voice I recognized as that of Cummins cried, "but the son of a bitch has done somethin' to the smoke hole! Load up and let him have it again!"

By that time I had my length of vine around the edges of the shirt, had pulled it taut and painfully tied some sort of knot. My eyes were still streaming. The strength was almost gone from my left arm. I tried to guide myself down the roof edge, but the shock from my wounds was catching up with me. One hand wasn't enough when my foot slipped on the blood running down from my leg. I rolled down to hit the ground joltingly and lay there in a state of semiconsciousness.

The curious thing about my condition was that it permitted me to realize what was happening without letting me feel that I was concerned. I definitely remember thinking that I had done my stint and that others—it wasn't clear to me who they were just then— should be able to finish up. Impersonally I heard the shouts of alarm from within and reviewed their problems. They wanted to open the door to let the smoke out, but they didn't want to open the door to let the bullets in. They wanted to tear the paper from the windows, but they didn't want to get shot while doing it. They were trying to squelch the fire only to find that a doused blaze smokes worse than ever at first. They were choking and blinded, knowing they had to leave and aware of their handicaps against uncertain odds.

Then I heard shots, death screams, and loud offers of surrender. Some of the haze left my mind at about that point. Remembering that I should be in charge, I opened my eyes and blinked them clear. The recurrence of pain told of receding numbness, and I found it possible to rise and sidle along the cabin.

I'd rounded the corner up which I'd climbed when a man dashed past me with Price in pursuit. Capable though the bee hunter still was in many respects his best running days were over. He was losing out in the race, and the knife he hastily threw passed the runner by. It wasn't until the fugitive looked back derisively at this moment of escape that I recognized him as Alexander Pope Cummins.

He was reaching the far end of pistol range, but I had always been accurate with that weapon. I had put my ball where I wanted to when I had tried not to kill Cartwright. Now, steadying myself against the cabin, I again put my bullet exactly where I wished. There was a hoarse scream, and the man I held responsible for Tom McConnell's murder and Goober's far more miserable death pitched over.

At almost the same time Saunders came hurrying toward me. His face told me that I looked even worse off than I was, which was bad enough. No doubt with my bare torso so smeared with blood I appeared to be wounded in a dozen places instead of only two.

"Sit down, Daunt," he said. "You ain't got any business bein' on your legs."

"I'm not too bad off yet, Billy," I told him. "Tie some Spanish moss over my hits and get me out of this swamp."

He patted my unharmed shoulder soothingly. "I'll snake you out of here right enough, but you got to rest up first and we got to find out if any of them balls stayed in you."

"One did, but we won't fuss with it this side of the river." I was feeling dizzy, but I held his eyes. "You keep us marching till we find Harry Pace, if the fever gets me. I know what I'm talking about, Billy."

The danger of infection was serious, but I was much more afraid of the ague, which in my weakened condition would be deadly. After shooting one outlaw who wouldn't tell us the quickest way to the river we easily found another who would. Only in swiftly reaching the healthy high ground beyond the south bank of the Yazoo did I see any hopes of pulling through.

That was a rough journey, although the route was an avenue compared with our way in. I was unconscious part of the time and delirious another part, but I remember we waded down a bayou to the river and swam it to the mouth of another stream on the other side. It was by this water route that the outlaws, coming down from the hills, had eluded our efforts to find their place of crossing the river.

If I don't remember much of the journey, luckily even much of the pain, I do remember the trouble in my mind. Whether my brain was lucid or delirious the same woeful thought throbbed through it. After what had happened to me I couldn't possibly go on to try to find any more field hands—I wouldn't be in shape to do so for weeks anyhow. I'd have to tell Emily we were bankrupt. I'd have to sit by and see what was left of my cotton go unpicked. I'd have to give up my plantation until I had somehow made enough money to start operations again.

I don't recall when we joined forces with Harry Pace, but at a certain point I waked to hear his voice. My fever hadn't broken, but my mind was fairly clear. I was lying in a lean-to in the cool of the morning. There was no taint of swamp in the breeze that blew deliciously over me. Turning my head, I saw Pace with his back to me, talking to a couple of the regiment's other officers.

"Like I said last night, we're headin' for Turkey Run to finish things up right after breakfast, but one of you two—you can flip for it—will have to take the Colonel and the niggers to Roseville. Take Godolphin to the Bennetts'."

"What about the niggers?" one of the pair asked.

Then it came to me. Those darkies were masterless until the law should find the heirs of the murdered owners. Meanwhile they had to be fed and housed somewhere. I pushed myself up with my sound arm, glaring with fever, excitement, and the force of the will I sought to impose.

"Those darkies!" I croaked. "Get Williams—Tom McConnell's man—to take them out to my plantation. I'll feed them! Harry, I've got to have them!"

CHAPTER XXXIV

FIRST I HAD TO GET THE FEVER out of my system, then the infection caused by my wound. After that I had to start getting back the blood lost when the bullets went in—and when the one in my shoulder was taken out. It all took time, during which my chief occupation was worrying about Emily, my cotton crop and the Yazoo Invincibles.

Tim brought me word of the Invincibles while I was still too weak to do more than sit up. "I was turned loose especial to tell you we done all right, Daunt. It was mostly a quiet day, too. Harry Pace just said the Mississippi State Militia is takin' over the town, and any cuss who didn't believe it would be hung, put case he wasn't already shot. Our boys was all together and unexpected. They wasn't all together, and a lot wasn't alive after you got through with 'em. There wasn't much fightin', and most of what there was the Invincibles did."

"Did you get 'em all?" I asked eagerly. "Did you get Jack Garland?"

"We got every bird on the roost—and him first of all. He was in his store and didn't quite get the idea we wasn't customers till Harry jerked him over the counter."

"Did you hang him?"

"Nope. I figured we would, but Harry wants 'em all tried in Jackson. He's lookin' over everybody in town and any that smells like outlaws he's sendin' to the capital under guard."

"Sending?" I echoed. "Isn't Harry going along?"

"Oh, he'll be there for the trials, but I reckon he hankers to stay in Turkey Run for a while."

"Well, he used to own a lot of land in the Old Purchase. Maybe he still does," I said. "He's probably got business to attend to."

Tim looked at me admiringly. "Daunt, you can always figure everythin' out; and here I was thinkin' all along that Harry was stayin' there on account of that female he's been spendin' his evenin's with."

"The devil you say! Who?"

"I don't know, but she fed Harry and some of the other officers when we first got to town, and he's been a mighty regular customer ever since. Of course, maybe he just goes for the grub, but if I ever met a she critter as pretty as that I wouldn't even care if she could plough, let alone cook."

Shortly afterwards Tim left for The Merchants Meeting where only my envious thoughts could follow him. I had expected to see him the next morning, but it wasn't until several days later that he again showed up. He had, I could see, something on his mind which he was finding it difficult to unload.

At last, after he'd given me a small drink and taken one in keeping with his robuster health, he blurted out, "I done sold my claim, Daunt. I'm leavin' hereabouts today."

I opened my mouth, then couldn't think of anything to say. Tim shifted restlessly.

"I was aimin' to try plantin', but I got to thinkin' while I was away at Turkey Run and I knowed I couldn't go back to it. It just ain't my style, and this ain't no country for me no more."

"Yes, I know," I said finally, staring at the rafters. "Where are you going?"

"Well," he said, perking up a little, "there ain't no country this side the Mississippi loose enough to hold me. I'll likely try Arkansas or Texas."

Sitting up in my bunk, I reached for my belt. From its sheath I drew my great-grandfather's knife, the ivory-handled weapon I knew Durham had always coveted.

"Here," I grunted.

He turned it over carefully, nodding to himself and whistling between his teeth. After he'd diffidently handed me his own we had one more drink, then he left me. Outside I heard a panther scream and lifted one hand in a little gesture of farewell.

Thrusting his knife into my scabbard, I leaned back, thinking of

the man and the part of my life that went with him. It was a country's loss not to be able, as he put it, to hold such a fellow; but it
couldn't be helped on either side. A region couldn't remain static to
accommodate him; and he could not adapt himself to a more settled
land without forfeit of genius.

It wasn't until I was almost strong enough to make the ride to
Council Lodge that Pace returned to Roseville. He came to see me
the next afternoon to report on the activities of the regiment, but
word that he was married had long preceded him. After we had
talked over the cleansing of Turkey Run I referred to this rumor.

"If it's true, Harry, I'd like the pleasure of meeting the bride."

"Anybody would," he said complacently. He consulted his watch.
"We figured on folks callin' today, so she's bein' extra careful of her
war paint; but she'd ought to be ready by the time we get there."

This was not the case, though it wasn't long after Pace had
bawled "Company, sugar!" that I heard the rustle of silk. I rose
and turned.

The woman I had known at Natchez-under-the-Hill, and one
other time, as a countess entered the room. She was not dressed and
made up as the ruthless amorist of those days, however. What Pace
had called her war paint was rather a gilding of the lily, so deft
that a man couldn't be sure where nature left off and art began.
Her walk had changed, too. It was not the voluptuous glide I remembered; it was merely the stepping of a graceful young woman
reasonably conscious of her charms. As for her eyes, they passed
over me indifferently to meet those of her husband. Once there they
smiled.

"Hon," Pace said, "this is the Colonel Godolphin I was tellin' you
about. He's the war chief of the Invincibles, you know."

A look of mild interest acknowledged my bow. "Aren't you also
the one that got married recently—the one for whom Harry performed the ceremony? You must bring your wife to see us."

She needn't have poked me with that reminder. I certainly wasn't
going to break the truce of silence. Recalling her claims to noblesse,
though, I noted that her voice lacked the foreign tang that had
always left me in doubt. Therefore I couldn't refrain from one
question.

"Are you a native Mississippian, ma'am?"

"Oh, no, Colonel, I come from Florida." Undoubtedly her accent was Southern, but whether it was genuine or not was once again something I couldn't decide. Mentally I smiled in acknowledgment of defeat as she went on. "But you see when Papa died last year, I thought land out West here would be the best investment for the money he left me. The funny thing is that when I bought my property I insisted on the Old Purchase because I thought I would have more desirable neighbors. Then I found the nearest town was just full of those awful old outlaws."

"Never mind," Harry comforted her. "You'll get your price, honey. You'll find you done some pretty good speculatin' when you bought that section."

Of course, she had done better speculating when she had invited the officers of the Yazoo Invincibles to dine; but then I wasn't sure that Pace hadn't got a good bargain, too. She was intelligent, well-mannered, likeable, and sightly; and she would perhaps prize a ménage better than a young girl who had never been without one. As for her singing and other former activities Pace had been away while she was at Underhill; and he might not care anyhow. He was a remarkable man and like the frontier itself valued things only in terms of the present. On the other hand I believed him capable of cutting her throat if she tried to make a fool out of him, and I took her to be clever enough to realize as much.

On the way back to the Bennetts' by way of The Merchants Meeting I had time for more general reflections on the subject. There wasn't, after all, much difference between her fortunes and those of most others who desperately sought success along the Yazoo. She had left a district where she could no longer live on desirable terms, made the effort, taken the risks. Now, married to one of the richest men in the valley, she was not undeservedly one of the certain winners. I chuckled. She might not be a countess, but the children she got by Harry Pace would be princes in the land, so reckoned by themselves and succeeding generations.

In order to be able to look as fit as possible I took an easy two days for the journey to Council Lodge. It was the first time since my parents died that I had returned to any place with the knowledge that somebody was waiting for me. The thought gave me an inexpressible feeling of having my own unassailable community. Yet when I arrived I couldn't forbear to visit the cotton fields before I greeted Emily. My plantation was what I had done with myself, and I wanted to see how I stood before I faced my wife.

Williams and the hands he directed had done my work well. The plants stood tall in clean rows; the bolls were grandly full, just short of bursting. I breathed deeply and ascended the hill.

Emily didn't run toward me, as I thought she might. She just put down the gun she'd caught up when Talisman started barking and stood waiting. I was a little uncertain of her until I saw her eyes.

"I wanted to come to you," she said when she had assured herself that I was all right and we were at peace after the passion of greeting, "but I found I couldn't. Daunt, I've got to have a cabin now."

"God knows you deserve one," I said remorsefully. "You'll get one right after the cotton's picked."

She pulled out of my arms to look at me. "I wasn't complaining. I know you haven't had the time before. But we're going to have a child."

"You mean now?" I asked dumbfoundedly, looking, I suppose, as if I expected her to produce it on the spot. I'd counted on children, of course, but that was on the docket for later, after the plantation was more developed and the house was built. Introducing them this early caught me unprepared for the idea.

She peered at me, her eyes growing worried. "We've never talked about it much—don't you want one?"

While recognizing that the sexes were mutually incomprehensible on many points, I also thought there was unclouded understanding as regards others. The preposterous nature of the question startled me out of my daze.

"Why, Hell, honey!" I blurted. "I'm a man, ain't I?"

Having cleared the atmosphere we started to talk. During the next hour we named the boy after Tom McConnell, gave him Harry Pace for a godfather, raised him and saw him through the University of Virginia. It wasn't until he had his degree that we at last settled down to the actualities of what had happened during our separation.

But the baby was on my mind, the exciting thought pulling me early awake the next morning. It was marvelous to consider that I would have children to whom this new land of my loving would be the natural state of things. Everything that had seemed so strange and so wonderful to me they would take for granted. All that had been wrought out of the wilderness they would accept as only children can accept what they see around them. They would be of the country as I could never quite be of it. They—and this was the most difficult point for me to realize—would not be transplanted Virginians but Mississippians, pure stock.

After awhile I could stand inactivity no longer. Sliding out from the covers carefully, so as not to disturb Emily, I pulled on my hunting shirt and slipped into my moccasins. There was just enough light for my purposes as I strode toward the site I'd long ago picked out for my house. Emily had asked for a cabin but I meant to have more than that before the child arrived. I couldn't pay for the brick mansion of my earlier fancies without ruining the plantation that was my source of income. Cotton was said to be reaching a fabulously new high, but most of the capital I expected was already earmarked for reinvestment. Nevertheless, there was a type of commodious dwelling within my means.

After the harvest, then, I built Council Lodge, the house, of the seasoned trunks from the past winter's tree felling. I was my own architect, and surely no professional would have sanctioned such a building. In the absence of stone, brick or mortar, the foundation was of piles. On this I crisscrossed the mighty hardwood boles with no more preparation than barking.

In form it was simple, as it had to be. On each side of the entry hall there was a great room. Flanking these were connecting wing cabins, divided in two. Putting a cookhouse on behind and running a frame for a porch all along the front I had it: a drawing room and two guest rooms on one side; a dining room, our own bedroom and a nursery on the other. I had seen far more elaborate dwellings— Spring Hill was such—but this would offer us what we wanted. Anybody who felt the need of more space could go outdoors.

Emily had gone south with the charter boat to visit her people for the first time since she was remarried and, more than incidentally, to order what we needed in the way of household furnishings. When I turned the hands I'd been using back to Williams, who was staying on as my overseer, I kept two of them with me. We also went down the Yazoo, but our conveyance was a raft of big timber, our destination not Natchez but Vicksburg. There I not only had enough sawed out of my raft to floor and wainscot my house but sold enough board feet to buy bricks, mortar, plaster, windows, lathes, shingles and their freight back. The only cash I spent in the building was to hire the craftsmen who returned with me to make the fireplaces and finish the interior.

Winter often forgets itself in Mississippi and one Sunday not long after the housewarming it was mild enough at Council Lodge to make sitting on the gallery pleasant. Although I had not quite reaccustomed myself to broadcloth and boots I was enjoying my relaxation. In the drawing room there were several shelves full of books I hadn't yet had time to read, but my great-grandfather's volume of John Smith was the one I had chosen to take outside with me. I had hardly more than opened my book and had my drink brought out to me, however, when a neighbor called.

I liked what I knew of him, but the hour was much too delightful to waste on conversation with mere acquaintances. Putting a glass in his hand and a cigar in his mouth to keep him occupied, I leaned back in my chair. Now that I listened I could hear Emily playing softly on the piano, but my thoughts soon went on to something else.

Putting my hands behind my head I puffed on my cigar, giving warm consideration to the whole creation, finished and unfinished, of Council Lodge. I was devoting my life to building for myself just about what I had forfeited when I was a youngster in Virginia; and although the intrinsic irony was very clear to me it left me undisturbed. If I had cherished Spring Hill it was only as one prizes a valuable gift. But Council Lodge was of my own great making.

I had forgotten my guest, when he recalled himself to me by speaking. "You certainly stole a march on everybody, Colonel, putting up this place while the rest of us are still living in cabins; but I reckon you'll want to build again in a few years."

Slowly I turned from examining a little white cloud through a smoke ring. "What for?" I demanded.

My raised eyebrows made him smile uncomfortably. "Oh, this is fine; I didn't mean to criticize. But it won't last like a brick or frame building, you know."

"It'll see us into the ground."

"Yes, of course, but——" He nodded deprecatingly in the direction of the music. Emily had greeted him upon his arrival and her advanced state of pregnancy was no secret to him or anyone else with eyes. "How about your son?"

I blew another smoke ring. Council Lodge would be a wonderful place for a boy, but Spring Hill had been a fine one, too.

"Let him build his own house," I said. "He will, anyhow."